a Death in the Family

OTHER BOOKS AND AUDIO BOOKS
BY MARLENE BATEMAN

Motive for Murder

Light on Fire Island

a Death in the Family

An Erica Coleman Mystery

MARLENE BATEMAN

Covenant Communications, Inc.

To Janet, my friend

Acknowledgements

I OWE A DEBT OF gratitude to fellow authors Rachael Anderson, Rebecca Talley, and Braden Bell, who read the manuscript and gave many helpful suggestions. I also want to thank Holly Horton for her editorial expertise and insightful comments. Thanks also to Kelly Sullivan, Stella Chase, and Annetta Cochran for their valuable assistance. A special thank-you goes to my talented editor, Stacey Owen. Finally, I owe a debt of gratitude to the great cooks that tested the recipes: Stella Chase, Lori Woodbury, Monica Miles, Chaleh Reed, Kimmi Abbott, Chelsea Jones, and Tiffany Jones.

Chapter One

"YOU WANT ME TO DO what?" Erica Coleman stepped off the side of the quiet road and stared at her husband's spunky, white-haired grandmother as the pale lemon sunlight of an Oregon morning splintered through the sycamore trees.

"You heard me. Investigate the company. Why should I hire a stranger when I've got a private eye that had the good sense to marry into the family?" Blanche Coleman continued striding along like a spry sixty-year-old instead of someone about to celebrate her eighty-first birthday.

Erica was nearly pulled off her feet by Bandit, her cousin's black lab who didn't like the idea of being left behind. Erica took a firmer grip on the leash and hurried to catch up. As they rounded a corner, the narrow silver line that marked the Pacific Ocean was just visible through the trees. An orange tabby appeared ahead, daintily picking its way across the road. Blanche glared at Bandit as he tugged at the leash, causing the cat to scurry off into the undergrowth.

"I hope you can hold onto that dog. Why did you have to bring him along, anyway?"

"Shaun thought he could use some exercise."

"I've never forgiven him for bringing that mutt home," Blanche grouched. "It was cute to start with, but it forgot to stop growing."

"At least it's not a Great Dane."

A grim look appeared on Blanche's face. "As much as I loved having Shaun come back and live with me after his divorce, but that would have been too much."

They were quiet for a moment. "Why do you need a private investigator?" Erica finally asked, knowing it had to be something serious.

Ever since Erica and her husband, David, along with their children, had arrived from Utah to celebrate Blanche's upcoming birthday, Blanche had been acting strangely, leading them to believe something was wrong. Usually Blanche was calm, in control, and untroubled, but now she seemed anxious, preoccupied, and jumpy. Once she'd made a cryptic remark about her will.

"Now that I've opened my big mouth, I wish I'd kept it shut." Blanche frowned. "It's just that I've been thinking about hiring a private investigator for quite some time, and asking you seemed the logical thing to do—as long as that's all right with that investigative agency you work for."

"Pinnacle. And I'm sure it will be fine. My boss is very flexible. I'm glad to help—you know that. What's going on?"

Blanche was silent—apparently debating whether to say anything more. It wouldn't do any good to press, Erica knew, although she was dying of curiosity. She'd learned *that* long ago when she'd first started dating David and fallen in love with his scrappy grandmother. Perhaps a change in topic would help.

"Do you walk every day?" Erica asked as Bandit continued tugging on the leash—apparently hoping to see another cat.

"Never miss a day. I've had to give up a lot of things over the years but not walking. My doctor says that's what keeps me so healthy. And walking releases tension."

"Chocolate ice cream does too. If the first pint doesn't relax me enough, the second one always does." Erica brushed back her long hair and peered at Blanche. "I hear you've been working too hard."

"Can't be helped. I've been running Sun Coast Sales and Rentals ever since Lawrence passed away, and I'm not going to stop now. I like to keep my eye on things, and lately there's an awful lot to keep an eye on." The last was said in a melancholy tone.

So that's what this was about—the family business. "I thought Sun Coast was doing well. Has the economy made it so people aren't renting beach equipment and ATVs?"

"Sales are down, but rentals are up. But that's not it. Something else is going on." Blanche's pale blue eyes were shining, as if some emotion was being held tightly in check. "We'll talk more about it later. I don't want to spoil the day, and besides, all you can do is just keep going, no matter how dark things look. That's what I always say."

And she had. At least a hundred times, Erica thought with an inward grin.

As the road turned toward the ocean, Florence's surf-fringed shore came fully into view. The September breeze was cool and invigorating, as it almost always was on the Oregon coastline. Bandit's tail wagged gently as they came into a patch of sunshine.

"Are you ready for your birthday party next week?" Erica asked.

"I'm looking forward to it. Kristen's planning it. I'm glad she's working for Sun Coast now."

Kristen, a distant relative and a frequent visitor for many years, had recently moved to Florence from England. "It was nice of you to let Kristen live with you until she finds a house," Erica commented.

"I've got plenty of room." Blanche was cavalier, but Erica knew the woman was delighted to have the bright, bubbly Kristen living with her.

They turned onto the last stretch. "You're not too tired, are you?" Erica asked.

Blanche made a dismissive noise. "If I was, I could take the leash and let that horse pull me the rest of the way."

They turned off the road and toward the house, starting up the long, cobbled driveway, which was bordered by groups of red geraniums, white petunias, and blue lobelia. "The flowers are gorgeous," Erica exclaimed, "except for that one spot." She pointed it out. "There are only three red geraniums in that group instead of four."

"I know your knack for noticing details is what makes you a successful PI, but sometimes it makes me want to smack you." Blanche's words were tempered by laughter spilling over in her voice. "Good thing I love you, else you'd drive me crazy." Then she gave Erica a sly look. "I'll tell the gardener—unless you'd like to fix it yourself."

"That'd be great!" Erica's face lit up with enthusiasm.

Blanche smiled. "If you like this, you ought to see Martha's garden. Last time I was there, she had the most amazing display of daffodils, hyacinths, and tulips in front of her house. It smelled heavenly! Nothing slow about her when it comes to gardening."

It was too bad, Erica thought, that Martha wouldn't be here for her mother's birthday party. But then, no one expected Blanche's only daughter to come—Martha never came to any family events.

As they rounded the curving driveway, the house came into view, its stone walls glowing like warm honey in the fall sunshine. A veranda ran the full width of the first story. Enormous white columns supported the second story with its endless windows, some of which were shaded by towering white oaks and red cedars.

A car pulled out of the attached garage and stopped near them. Kristen rolled down the driver's side window and smiled cheerily at them. Her chin-length, highlighted hair framed her heart-shaped face. Blanche's grandson Shaun, whom she'd formally adopted as her son when he was two, was in the passenger seat. His tall, lean frame was nearly folded in half and looked uncomfortable in the small sporty car.

"Hi! Just getting back from your walk?" Kristen's voice had a distinctive English accent. "I'm going to drop Shaun off at work, get some petrol, and then run a few errands. After that, I'm going to Eugene to do some shopping. I want to get you something special for your birthday, Grandma."

Although the family ties that bound Kristen and Blanche were remote, the two had grown close over the years, and like Erica, Kristen called Blanche "Grandma."

"Oh pooh," Blanche told Kristen. "I already told you—I don't need anything."

"Then I'll just have to get you something you don't need!"

Shaun leaned over and looked at his mother. "Since you're enjoying Bandit so much, I thought I'd get you a puppy of your own."

Blanche gave him a ferocious look. "Don't you dare! One mutt around the place is enough."

Shaun laughed and sat back.

"Do either of you want to go to Eugene?" Kristen asked.

"I do," Erica said. "But I need to get cleaned up first."

"I'd like to go into Florence, if you don't mind stopping at the beauty salon to pick up my wig," Blanche said. "I'll go with you right now unless I'm too aromatic after my walk—"

"Oh, Grandma, you're fine! Erica, I'll pick you up when I bring Grandma back."

Shaun hopped out and had his mother—who protested his gallantry—take his place in the front seat.

Blanche rolled down her window as Erica walked around the side of the car. "Say, Erica, would you do me a favor?"

"Anything."

"I was hoping you'd say that." Blanche's eyes twinkled mischievously. "Would you call Martha?"

Erica blinked. "Martha? But—but I've never talked with her before."

"Then this would be a really good opportunity, wouldn't it? Listen, I know she's perfectly happy staying in her own little world, but maybe if someone else invites her—she might come to my birthday party next week. It's a long shot but worth a try. Besides, even if she says no—which she will—it'll do her good to hear from someone in the family. You'll do it for me, won't you?" Blanche smiled winningly.

"You're not playing fair. You know I could never say no to you."

"I know," Blanche said, her eyes twinkling even more. "And I love you too!" Like a queen, she signaled to Kristen to go. As the car moved forward, Blanche waved her fingers in a grand gesture of farewell.

* * *

Going into the house, Erica stopped in the foyer with its creamy marble floors and unsnapped Bandit's leash. She went through the dining room and out the French doors to the patio, where David sat at a round glass table finishing his cereal. He looked up with the boyish smile that still melted her heart and which she'd fallen in love with when they met at the University of Utah, where they were both majoring in law enforcement. All the things that had made her heart stop were still there—his handsome features, firm mouth, and bright, slate-blue eyes.

Blue morning shadows lay over the lawn and flower beds as she kissed him and looked around. "Where are the kids?"

"They're in the game room, taking advantage of being on vacation and playing video games."

Erica explained her plans to go with Kristen. As suspected, David had no interest in shopping unless they were going to a Home Depot or Tools "R" Us.

"What if I take the kids to the sand dunes and you meet us there when you get back?"

"Sounds like a plan," Erica said. "I'll call you when we get back."

"Great." He gave her a hug and another kiss. "Don't be long."

* * *

Kristen wasn't back by the time Erica had showered and dressed, so she went to Blanche's small, sunny office. Sitting at the cherry wood desk, Erica found her grandmother's address book.

Best to get the call over with. Erica punched in the numbers.

"Hello, Martha?"

A friendly, childlike voice answered. "This is me."

"This is Erica. Erica Coleman."

"Erica Coleman?" The voice was unsure.

"David's wife."

"David?" The voice was bewildered now.

"David is Blanche's grandson—Pamela's son. I'm David's wife."

"Oh, yes. How are you?"

"I'm good, how are you?"

"I've been *sick*," Martha declared earnestly. "Sick as a *dog*. Thank goodness Gail was here to take care of me." Enthusiastically, she launched into a recital of her bout with diarrhea, including the number of times she'd run to the bathroom and how long she had spent there.

Waaaay too much information. Erica shifted uncomfortably in her chair.

When Martha began describing the color and level of liquidity, Erica began feeling queasy and broke in desperately. "Martha, I was calling to see if you were coming down for Grandma's birthday."

"Why, no." Martha's voice conveyed surprise that she would even be asked.

"Everyone would love to see you."

"No, they wouldn't." Martha's reply was honest and spoken without the slightest bit of ill will. "I don't know any of them—except Mom and Pamela. She's my sister-in-law."

And my mother-in-law, Erica thought, smiling to herself. "Yes I know. Well, we'd all love to meet you, including Kristen—she just moved here."

"Kristen?"

"Randy's niece—from England." This was met with such a deep silence that Erica felt compelled to add. "You know Randy—"

"He's my brother," Martha said proudly, "but he died four years ago."

At least Martha remembered Randy, even if she hadn't attended his funeral. "Well—I just wanted to let you know we'd love to have you come."

"That was nice of you, but this is a busy time of year for me."

As Martha didn't have a job, it was hard to know exactly why autumn was a busy time, but Erica had done her duty. "If you change your mind, please come."

"I won't, but tell Mom I sent her a birthday present."

"All right. I hope you feel better soon."

"I do too," Martha said plaintively. "I've read every single magazine in the bathroom."

There was a beep on Erica's cell phone. Some blessed person had come to her rescue. "Sorry, Aunt Martha, I have to go. I have another call."

* * *

That night, as the family began to arrive, Erica busily rearranged various bowls and platters which the caterers had placed on the buffet table. Pamela came over and put an arm around her daughter-in-law's shoulders.

"I'm afraid I have bad news."

"Uh oh." Erica looked up from the fruit salad. "Did one of the kids break something?"

"The caterers asked me to talk to you. Apparently, you won't stop rearranging the food."

"And that's a bad thing?"

"They'd prefer you let them handle it."

"What? I'm only arranging it so it's neat and organized!" Erica flung a hand toward the kitchen, where one of the hardier caterers peeked around the corner, gauging her reaction. "*They're* the ones that won't leave it alone. I arrange it nicely, and they come and move things around."

"Yes, well—they *are* the ones Blanche hired to cater the dinner." David's mother was always gentle. One corner of Pamela's mouth turned up. "Dear-heart, I know it's hard for you, but I have orders to keep you away from the table. Don't make me get your grandmother."

Erica gave in and went to find David.

When everyone was gathered, Blanche asked Shaun to offer a blessing on the food. Everyone began dishing up their plates and seating themselves at the formal dining room table, which was so long it looked like it went into the next state. Above, three crystal chandeliers marched the length of the ceiling.

When David and Erica's three children asked if they could eat out in the gazebo, Blanche gave in easily. Carrying their plates, the children zoomed outside as the evening sun spread its golden light on the lawn.

As David and his grandmother chatted about her upcoming birthday, Erica thought about the first time she had attended one of Blanche's birthday parties. She and David were dating and, along with other family members, watched as Blanche Coleman had made a grand entrance, descending the wide stairway in an elegant green dress. Although she was a small woman, Blanche managed to give an impression of height because of her regal manner. During a quiet moment that night, Blanche had welcomed Erica into the family. When Erica blushed and explained she and David were not engaged, Blanche chuckled.

"I have no doubt David plans to ask you to marry him—I've never seen a man so in love. And he'd be a fool not to—why just look at you!" She then clasped Erica in a warm hug. Erica and Blanche bonded quickly, and when Blanche discovered Erica had no living grandparents, she insisted on filling that role and then some.

Now, Erica eyed Blanche thoughtfully, wondering again what was disturbing her. It was clear David had the same thoughts, for when his grandmother went to the kitchen for more rolls, he asked Shaun and Kristen in a low voice, "What's wrong with Grandma?"

"I don't know, but she has been in a stroppy mood," Kristen said, using a British expression.

"Why do you ask?" Shaun sounded curious.

"She seems worried and lost in thought all the time," David said. "Sometimes I'll walk into the room and she'll be sitting there, staring at nothing."

"Grandma's been on edge ever since we got here," Erica went on. "She said something about changing her will, and then this morning Grandma asked if I would do some investigating for her."

"Investigate?" Shaun did a double take as Blanche came back with the rolls and took her place at the head of the table. She sat with her back straight, making no concession to old age. Yet she was undeniably quieter than normal—and watchful somehow—as the conversation flowed.

Erica threw a question at Kristen. "So, how do you like Oregon now that you've moved here?"

"I love it! It's one of the most beautiful places on earth." Her sincerity was obvious. "However, now that fall is here, I'm starting to worry about the winter."

"Oregon's not a good place to live if you're scared of snow," David teased.

"Take up skiing," Erica advised. "Then you'll love the snow and pray for more."

"I don't know how to ski," Kristen admitted.

"Shaun could teach you," Blanche said, a matchmaker gleam in her eye. "He's a great skier."

Kristen turned to him, her light gray eyes shining. "Would you? I'd love to learn."

Shaun's face lit up, making him look much younger than his forty years. "Sure. We have some great resorts around here." Then he hesitated. "I mean, if you really want to."

"Oh, I do. I do!" Kristen exclaimed in her charming English accent.

"I'm glad you came here to work for the company, Kristen," Blanche said. "I keep trying to talk David and Erica into moving and working for Sun Coast, but they won't budge."

Blanche had never made any secret that she wished more of the family worked at the company she and her husband, Lawrence, had started. Blanche's son, Randy had been responsible for Sun Coast's rapid growth and expansion. Of Randy's three children, only Trent had followed in his footsteps. Trent's brother had no interest in business and lived in Florida, while his sister lived in Strasbourg, France. Erica thought it a delightful coincidence that she had a cousin living in nearby Lausanne, Switzerland. She and David were both close to their cousins and had once flown to Europe to visit them. Besides Trent, only Shaun, and now Kristen, worked at Sun Coast.

"We love living in Utah," Erica explained to her grandmother yet again. "Besides, David loves his job."

Shaun turned to David. "Are you still with the police department in Farmington?"

"I am," David replied. "I'm one of the few lucky cops able to work in the same city where I live."

"At least Kristen had the good sense to come and work for Sun Coast," Blanche said in a voice that held a note of rebuke.

"That's because they finally expanded into Internet sales—my specialty," Kristen said brightly.

"Sun Coast was just waiting for you to get more experience there in England," Shaun said.

"No, you thought I was dodgy," she teased. "You're a big executive vice president—you could have hired me sooner. But Trent saw my sterling qualities and hired me, so I'm here at last."

After dessert, they moved to the spacious family room, and Erica went to the tall windows, pulling the dark green draperies closed. She'd always envisioned those velvety curtains as similar to what Scarlett O'Hara had cut up for her dress. Erica went to where David stood and inclined her head to where Kristen was talking to Shaun in her animated way.

"Look at that. Those two have been inseparable all evening. I think romance is in the air—I've never seen Shaun look so happy and content."

"I've noticed," David replied.

Kristen certainly had a way of lighting up the room with her liveliness and megawatt smile. Right now, Shaun was gazing at her as if the air Kristen breathed was made out of sugar and spice. Usually, Shaun hung back unless someone took the effort to talk to him, but tonight—with Kristen by his side—he stayed right in the middle of the conversation.

Noticing that her grandmother's wig was askew, Erica went to sit beside Blanche on the couch.

"I'm going to straighten your wig," she whispered and adjusted it before sitting back, satisfied. "All fixed. You can relax now."

"You mean *you* can relax," Blanche said. "It wasn't bothering *me.*" She patted her wig as David walked over. "Thin hair is the curse of the Coleman women. Thank goodness Martha and I look ravishing in wigs. I hope someone gives me one in Cleopatra-black for my birthday. That's something I've always wanted."

"We'll have to remember that for your next birthday, since David and I already bought you a dish drainer," Erica said with a straight face.

Kristen erupted in giggles. Then she and Shaun went to the elegant fireplace, looking at framed pictures of the Coleman family that were displayed on the delicately veined, white marble mantel.

Blanche turned to Erica. "I forgot to ask—did you call Martha?"

"I did. She's been sick. Diarrhea. And she gave me the full particulars."

Blanche laughed uproariously. "I can just imagine!"

"Number of trips, color, consistency—the works."

Blanche laughed harder, tears coming to her eyes. "I swear, Martha has the social awareness of a two-year-old." Then she patted Erica's hand. "I have another favor to ask you."

"I am *not* calling Martha again."

Her grandmother smiled. "You went above and beyond the call of duty on that one. But I don't think you'll mind this favor because it involves Shaun." She eyed Erica. "You and Shaun seem to get along pretty well, don't you?"

"Oh, yes. I really like Shaun."

"He's one in a million, isn't he?" Blanche's face softened. "But he needs to get out of his shell. I've been trying for years to get him to live up to his potential, but it's like pushing a wet rag uphill. We've had a considerable number of discussions about it."

Erica cringed. Having a dynamic Blanche forcefully lecture timid Shaun was like sandblasting a cracker. She tried to stand up for him. "It's just his personality. Shaun's a little reserved."

"I don't know where he got that from—not from his father and certainly not from me." Blanche sounded aggrieved. "I'd always hoped Shaun would show more of the leadership qualities his cousin has shown at Sun Coast."

Ah, yes, Erica knew how well the dynamic Trent was doing. "Isn't Shaun doing his job?"

"Yes, but it's imperative he step things up—and not one notch, but several." Blanche's tone was so forceful and urgent that Erica stared.

"Does this have something to do with what's going on at Sun Coast?"

A muscle twitched in Blanche's jaw as she stared stonily ahead. Then she sighed heavily and met Erica's eye. "I'll get into all of that another time. I don't want to talk about it now, else I'll be so upset I won't sleep a wink, and I get precious little sleep as it is."

More evidence that something serious was bothering Blanche, but again, Erica knew it was useless to try and force it out of her. Erica's thoughts returned to Shaun. "Ever since I've known him, Shaun has struggled with low self-esteem. It must have been hard on him to have his father die when he was so young, and then to have his mother abandon him—"

Blanche scoffed. "Don't go blaming past history for Shaun's behavior—that's sheer nonsense. *I'm* the one who raised Shaun, and he's capable of great things. He simply needs a little jump-start. Certain circumstances have convinced me to make some changes at Sun Coast. However, Shaun will need a little support. Kristen's been helpful, but would you talk to him too? Build him up a little? It's vital that Shaun starts doing more *now*." She looked around furtively and lowered her voice. "There's some people I don't trust, and I'm going to shake things up. That means Shaun will have to step up."

"Sure, I'll be glad to, but what's going on? What changes are you going to make?"

The shutters came down over Blanche's eyes. "I'll let you know about that later, when we make our plans. I've been digging but haven't been able to get to the bottom of it. That's where you come in. With your experience, you'll be able to find out what's really going on."

Shaun, Kristen, and David meandered over, and they chatted until it was time for bed. Everyone said their good-nights, and David and Erica rounded up their children then went upstairs with Blanche. The children hugged their great-grandma and scurried off to their rooms. Then Erica and David each gave Blanche a good-night hug.

"Now, don't stay up late," David teased.

"Don't be telling me what to do," Blanche replied saucily, wagging a finger. "At my age, I can do whatever I like."

* * *

An unusual sound penetrated Erica's consciousness. She blinked and rolled over. The red numbers on the clock said 7:13. Had a dream awakened her? David was still asleep, his face peaceful. Erica was about to close her eyes when the sound came again. It was a scream, high and thin—like a falcon. Erica slid out of bed and flung on a robe. With David close behind, she rushed to Blanche's bedroom.

The door was open.

Kristen was standing beside the four-poster bed, looking stricken. She looked at them then at the bed, and her face twisted in grief as she wailed, "She's dead!"

Chapter Two

ERICA RACED TO THE BIG mahogany bed where Blanche lay. Erica watched David put his fingers on his grandmother's neck to feel for a pulse. When he shook his head, Kristen began sobbing. Erica's hair covered her face like a veil as she bent over and gently trailed her fingers down Blanche's cheek. David moved close, and Erica burrowed her face fiercely into his chest to scourge away her stinging tears.

"No," Erica whispered. "Grandma *can't* be gone."

After a few minutes, David said quietly, "I need to let Shaun know." When he left, Kristen and Erica clung to each other.

In a minute, Shaun raced in, his face wild with shock. He dropped to his knees and took hold of his mother's hands, tears coursing down his face.

The blue brocade curtains had not been drawn, and the room was dim in the early morning light. Tears flowed as they tried to understand that although only last night Blanche Coleman had been happy and alive—today she was gone.

David returned and told Erica in hushed tones, "I called my mom. She wants me to come and pick her up." Although David's mother, Pamela, lived in nearby Mapleton, she didn't drive. A horseback riding accident in her teens had left Pamela with severe chronic back pain.

David held Erica close a moment. "I can be back in twenty minutes. Mom said she'd be waiting."

"Shouldn't I call the coroner?" Erica asked.

"Wait till I get back. But would you call Trent and Carrie? They'll want to come."

After he left, Erica called her husband's cousin Trent and his wife, Carrie, who lived in Florence. Erica knew Trent would take his grandmother's death hard. Of all the grandchildren, Trent had been the one most interested in working for Sun Coast. Randy, Blanche's son, had been a brilliant businessman and the successful, charismatic CEO of Sun Coast for many years, and his son Trent had followed in his footsteps. When Randy passed away of cancer, Blanche named her grandson Trent as acting CEO.

When Erica's children woke, she had them come in for a final good-bye. Seeing their pain magnified Erica's own. Then David returned with his mother holding onto his arm. Pamela was tall and thin, and her hair was cut short and fitted her like a brown satin cap. Her lined face had the gray, haggard look of one who had suffered much. And indeed she had. Seven years ago, she and her husband, Norman, had been in a serious automobile accident, which had killed David's father and exacerbated her back injuries. Now, Pamela couldn't ride in a car for longer than an hour.

Leaning heavily on her cane, Pamela went to Erica and hugged her tightly. "How are you, dear-heart?" Then Pamela stepped to the bed and rested a soft hand on Shaun's shoulder. Shaun clasped her hand, and the two of them stared glassy-eyed at Blanche.

Trent, a big, solidly built man with short black hair and blunt features, burst into the room, striding to his grandmother's bedside. His petite and pretty wife, Carrie, hung back, lips trembling, her long brown hair disheveled.

When Pamela shifted her feet and swayed precariously, David took her arm and led her to a chair by the window, where she covered her face. Her thin shoulders heaved as she wept. Erica called the coroner, and when she returned, the family gathered around Pamela, speaking in whispers.

"I knew Grandma was old, but she always seemed indestructible," Trent murmured.

"Yes, but she was old." Carrie stood next to Trent by the wall, well away from the bed. "Her heart must have given out."

"But last night Grandma didn't even seem tired," David interjected.

"I don't understand it—she was so healthy!" There was a quiver of emotion in Erica's voice.

Shaun choked out, "It's so unreal."

"I know," Kristen said, giving Shaun a comforting hug. "It's a shock."

A somber air permeated the room as the enormity of death touched them—the personal and timeless phenomenon of a loved one's spiritual transition from mortality to the spirit world.

With pain in her heart and tears on her face, Erica looked around. It was hard to believe that although Grandma's body was here in this room, her spirit was gone. Then again, perhaps her spirit *was* here—looking on. Everything spoke of her: the silky robe thrown over the easy chair, the perfumes on her dresser, and even the bedside table, which held papers and a saucer with a chocolate-covered strawberry and a few stems.

It wasn't long before the coroner, a soft-spoken, middle-aged man with dark eyes and a compassionate manner, arrived. He introduced himself as Dr. Luis Rodriguez then asked, "Who is the closest relative?"

"I'm her daughter-in-law," Pamela said then motioned to Shaun. "This is her son, Shaun Coleman."

"I'd like to talk to you both when you're ready, but for now, take all the time you need." Dr. Rodriguez stood off to the side as the family gathered around Blanche, talking softly and weeping. Then Shaun, Pamela, David, and Erica moved over to speak with the coroner.

"I don't understand," Pamela told Mr. Rodriguez while wiping her cheeks with a sodden tissue. "Blanche was healthy and well for her age. She had a checkup a month ago. The doctor said everything was fine—so good she could live to be ninety-five—like her mother."

"If you'd like, we can do an autopsy to determine the exact cause of death," Dr. Rodriguez said in his soft voice. "While most elderly people die of causes incidental to age, families often like to know the exact cause of death."

"I think I'd like to know exactly what happened," Pamela said.

Trent hurried over, his black eyes concerned. "You're not really thinking about having an autopsy, are you?"

Pamela looked abashed. "Well, yes, I was."

"Why?" Trent asked frankly. "Grandma was old, and her heart gave out. An autopsy isn't going to bring her back. I think you ought to leave her alone."

Pamela flinched as if struck, and Erica said, more sharply than she intended, "There's nothing wrong with finding out."

"But an autopsy isn't going to change anything," Trent argued in that forcible way of his. "What's the point of doing an autopsy on an eighty-one-year-old woman?"

"It's natural to have concerns about this," Dr. Rodriguez broke in, speaking in gentle tones. "Death is unnerving, even when it's anticipated and doubly so when it's unexpected—even if the deceased is elderly." He looked at Trent. "We often perform autopsies on older people if they're not in a nursing home, under hospice care, or in a hospital. It helps the family have closure and provides peace of mind. It won't take away your pain, but it often brings a measure of comfort."

Pamela had been listening intently. "I'd like to have it done. What do you think, Shaun?"

Hesitation was written all over Shaun's face. Finally, he said, "I guess it's all right. How long will it take?"

"A preliminary result will only take a few days. We'll take samples then release the body. The full report will take longer depending on the tests and if we have to consult other agencies."

As the family watched Blanche Coleman's body being taken out, a chill came over Erica. It was an eerie feeling—a certain foreboding she could not put her finger on.

"I wish I'd asked Grandma exactly what she wanted me to investigate," Erica choked out to David. "I knew she was worried, but now it's too late."

David held her close, his eyes shining with tears. "It's hard to believe she's not here."

"I know. Grandma was always there for me, even before we got married."

"She loved you," David said, his voice raw. "You two had a special bond."

They did. Their relationship was something Erica had always been grateful for. A thought came to mind. She and David had always shared quotes—ever since their college-dating days when they'd taken an English literature class together. Now, Erica recalled a quote that seemed to fit the occasion.

She recited softly: "'Between grief and nothing I will take grief.' William Faulkner."

David squeezed her shoulder. "At least we know that someday we'll see Grandma again."

"I know," Erica said, forlornly laying her head on his shoulder. "But what are we going to do until then?"

* * *

Shaun fell into a chair, looking as if he was in some kind of stupor. Pamela opened her purse and fished out her anxiety medication, and David brought her a glass of water.

Taking off her glasses, Pamela rubbed her eyes. "Where did Trent go?"

"He's going to call his mother. Carrie went home to get the children."

Erica knew that news of Blanche's death was going to be hard on Trent's mother, Nora. After her husband, Randy, passed away, Nora had returned to England to care for her aged mother. Trent had been the one who'd encouraged Nora's niece, Kristen, to move to Oregon and work for Sun Coast.

"I suppose I'd better call Martha," Pamela said, reaching for the cell phone in her purse.

David, Shaun, and Erica talked in whispers. Trent came in and sat beside Pamela until she was finished.

"How's Nora?" Pamela asked.

"Shocked. And sad," Trent said. "Mom said to give her love to everyone. She wishes she could come for the funeral, but she has to take care of her mother."

"Martha didn't seem sad at all," Pamela said, looking bemused. "In fact, Martha didn't even know if she'd come for the funeral."

"What?" Kristen was appalled.

"That's Martha," Shaun said, sounding tired. "She doesn't go anywhere—doesn't even drive."

"After Martha got married and moved to Lake Oswego, she stayed there," Pamela explained. "She didn't come back when my husband died or when Randy passed away. Imagine—not going to either one of your brothers' funerals. But then, Martha's never concerned herself with the family or even Sun Coast. She's only interested in garage sales, flea markets, and things like that."

"How does she go to garage sales if she doesn't drive?" Erica asked.

"Her stepdaughter, Gail, lives with her and drives her around," Pamela said. "Tomorrow, I'll call and ask her again to come, but I don't think she will. I've tried to stay in touch and call her once in a while, but Blanche was the only one who went to see Martha regularly. You know, I haven't seen her since she left Florence."

When Kristen once again looked surprised, Shaun explained wryly. "Some extended families are close, but the Colemans were never joined at the hip."

* * *

David and Erica gathered their children in their bedroom, and after a prayer, they talked, listened, and wiped tears away.

Later, David called Blanche's bishop. He wanted to come immediately, but David said afternoon would be better. When Bishop Kreiberg arrived, Erica showed him into the sitting room then went to get her children while David invited the others to join them.

Trent hesitated, glancing at Carrie, who looked uncertain. "I don't know—I've never been too active, and what about the children?"

David clapped his arm around his cousin's shoulder. "This is only about trying to get a little comfort. Our children are already in there, if your two kids would like to come."

The large double doors of the sitting room were open, showcasing a beige carpet with a red rectangle in the middle. Erica had always loved this room, with a shiny grand piano in one corner and three display cases in the others where Blanche displayed her crystal and Armani collections. The doors were locked at night because of those expensive collections. Erica smiled, remembering how, when Blanche was redecorating, she had sent Erica samples of wallpaper—asking her opinion. In the end, she had chosen Erica's favorite, buff wallpaper with narrow red stripes.

Everything was a blur as Bishop Kreiberg talked about Blanche. Erica and David clutched each other's hands as everyone reminisced. Laughter bubbled up one moment, giving way to tears the next. Kristen patted Shaun's back when he became emotional and scrubbed at his eyes. Pamela sat pale and quiet in one of the brown leather recliners, and Trent kept his arm around Carrie's shoulders.

The children clustered on the floor, except for Aby, Erica and David's sixteen-year-old, who sat next to her grandmother. The children seemed to take comfort in Bandit, who let them stroke his fur and wrap their arms around his neck. The box of tissues went around the room, and although many tears were shed, they were healing tears. From the warm feeling in the room, Erica had no doubt that Blanche was present, doing her best to comfort her loved ones.

Then, unexpectedly, Erica remembered her grandmother's words, and it was almost as if she could hear Blanche speaking: "You just keep going, no matter how dark things look. That's all you can do." Erica's lips curved upward at the memory.

Shortly after Bishop Kreiberg left, the doorbell rang. David and Erica went to the foyer and opened the door to a tall man in his late sixties with a lean body.

"Walter!" Erica cried, greeting the man in a neat dark blue suit with a hug.

"Trent called, and I asked if it would all right to come by," Walter said, his long face looking drawn and a bit anxious. "I hope I'm not intruding."

"Never," Erica assured him. Walter Hancock was a close family friend and had been the attorney for Sun Coast Sales and Rentals ever since Lawrence and Blanche first started the business.

"It's good to see you, Erica." There was a light in Walter's eyes. "You're as lovely as ever."

"Always the charmer," she said with a smile and led him into the sitting room.

When they went in, Pamela rose awkwardly to give Walter a hug. His eyes were red rimmed as he shook hands formally with everyone—including the children—offering condolences. Trent gave him a long hug. Pamela seemed to take comfort in his gentle tones as he spoke fondly of Blanche. But his tone turned bewildered as he admitted, "Blanche's death was so unexpected. She was always so vigorous and energetic."

Erica thought the same and reached out to hold David's hand. "It was a shock."

"If there's anything I can do, please don't hesitate to ask," Walter told them earnestly.

Trent spoke up. "Would you happen to have a record of the awards Blanche and Lawrence won over the years? I know they were honored for a lot of different accomplishments. It would be helpful to have that when writing her obituary."

"Certainly. I'll get that to you tomorrow."

Walter stayed for some time then finally rose. "I won't intrude any longer, but I did want to pay my condolences."

"We appreciate you coming," David said as he and Trent walked Walter to the door.

"Grandma considered you part of the family, as we do," Trent told him in a husky voice.

Pausing at the door, Walter spoke, his faded blue eyes swimming with tears. "It was a privilege to know her. Blanche Coleman was a great lady."

* * *

The next morning, Erica woke to a sense of being under a dark cloud. When she recalled the events of yesterday, her eyes filled with tears. It was still hard to believe. She and David talked for some time, making plans for the day. There would be much to do helping the family begin making arrangements for the funeral.

When they trailed downstairs, Kristen and Pamela were eating at a small table that was adjacent to the kitchen. Dark circles beneath Pamela's eyes showed she hadn't gotten much sleep.

"The children already ate," she explained. "They're outside."

"Hi, you two," Kristen greeted them. Although her eyes were red, she seemed determined to be cheerful. And that's probably the way Blanche would have wanted it, Erica thought.

Kristen nodded toward a covered dish on the table. "I made eggs and bangers."

"Bangers? This I have to see," David said, lifting the cover off the plate. "Oh, it's only eggs and link sausages." Then, feigning fear, he held the lid in front of him for protection. "They're not going to explode, are they?"

"Making fun of me and my English words, are you?" Kristen smiled good-naturedly. "I thought I'd be fairly knackered this morning since I couldn't sleep, but I woke up early and decided to make breakfast for everyone."

David dished up massive amounts for him and Erica. "It was nice of you to make a nice breakfast, Kristen. Nothing more relaxing than having someone else cook." He looked at Erica, who was looking on in horror at the plates that were heaped high. "Let's see, wasn't it John Gunther who said, 'All happiness depends on a leisurely breakfast'?"

"He said *leisurely* not *gigantic*," Erica said, sliding some of her sausages back into the bowl.

* * *

Several days passed in a haze of gray skies, rain, and mourning. More than once, Erica found herself looking into a room, expecting to see Grandma. She missed her grandmother's sparkling eyes and dry wit, which had always been as salty and bracing as an ocean breeze.

After some cajoling, Martha decided to come to the funeral after all. Since her stepdaughter, Gail, was out of town, Shaun drove to Lake

Oswego and brought her to Florence the day before the viewing. Vicki, who came in three half-days a week to cook and clean for Blanche, prepared a room for Martha. The night of Martha's arrival, Pamela arranged for a family dinner at a nearby restaurant, and when she invited Walter, she asked if he wanted to come that afternoon to see Martha. He arrived dressed immaculately in a dark suit and tie.

"Hello, Walter," Erica said, ushering him into the foyer. "Goodness, you're formal."

"I came directly from a meeting," he explained. "Martha hasn't arrived, has she?"

"Not yet, but she should be here soon."

"I haven't seen Martha since she got married. I wonder if she'll recognize me," Walter remarked as they went into the family room. He greeted Pamela then asked, "Where's David?"

"He went to Sun Coast to visit with Trent."

Thirty minutes later, the front door opened. The three of them went to the white-floored foyer, where Martha, wearing a shapeless blue sweater, stood looking up at the huge crystal chandelier. She was a plump, amiable-looking woman in her midfifties, and her eager round face looked around with unabated interest. Shaun carried Martha's battered suitcase and a well-used duffle bag.

"I'll take these upstairs," he said. "Then I have to go to work, even if it's only for a few hours."

"Do you remember me, Martha?" Walter asked, extending his hand.

Martha blinked and tilted her head with its dark brown, untidy hair. "You're Walter," she said, peering at him from behind large eyeglasses. Then she frowned in disapproval. "You got old."

"I'm afraid so," Walter said with a smile. Erica thought how kind Walter was not to mention that he wasn't the only one who had aged.

As Pamela limped forward to give her sister-in-law a hug, Erica whispered to Walter, "Sorry about that."

"It's quite all right," Walter said. "Martha never was one to sugarcoat the truth, no matter how unpleasant."

Martha waved a tissue. "I hope none of you catch my cold. It's been dreadful—settled in my throat and makes me sound like a bullfrog."

The distinctive smell of Mentholatum wafted from Martha as Erica introduced herself. "We spoke on the phone last week."

Martha smiled broadly. "Nice to meet you. Do you mind if I walk through the house? It's been so long since I've been here."

"Of course not," Pamela said. "Your mother did a lot of remodeling over the years. I can show you around the main level, but I don't do stairs, so I'll let Walter and Erica take you up."

They went from room to room, and in the game room, Erica interrupted the children's movie to introduce Martha to Aby, twelve-year-old Ryan, and ten-year-old Kenzie.

"I'm happy to meet you," Martha repeated three times, shaking each hand with great energy.

They went up the thickly carpeted stairs, and it was fun to watch Martha, whose eyes were bright and beady as she expressed amazement at this and that. She occasionally held a tissue to her nose while regaling them with select childhood memories. Erica giggled at many of the anecdotes.

Back on the main level, they went to the sitting room, where Pamela waited in one of the recliners.

"It's too bad your back hurts all the time," Martha said in a commiserating tone. "The doctor says I've got a lot of things wrong with me, but my back's okay." She looked around wistfully. "Mom wanted me to come back and live here. But now she's gone."

Then she ran a foot over the multihued brown carpet. "This is a great color. You could spill fudge ripple ice cream, and no one would ever know!" Erica laughed at that. Martha opened her large purse, pulled out a tissue, and holding her used one aloft, looked around. "Where's the garbage can?"

"I'll get it." Erica pulled out a pair of disposable gloves from her pocket, put them on, and retrieved a wastebasket from beside the bookshelf. She took it to Martha, who looked at her curiously.

"The gloves are just a precaution," Erica explained, without mentioning her aversion to garbage cans.

Martha tossed the tissue in, basketball style. "Two points," she said, smiling as it floated in.

* * *

Pamela had reserved a room at Morgan's Country Kitchen. After the hostess ushered them in, Carrie went with Erica to the restroom. Erica took two bars of Lava soap from her purse and offered one to Carrie. She looked trim and attractive in a white top, jeans, and strappy four-inch heels that about doubled her height.

"I should be used to your mania by now," Carrie said dryly as she took the soap, "but I'm not sure I'll ever feel comfortable with it."

"Hey, Lava is the only way to go. It's pumice powered *and* has moisturizers," Erica said. Some people just didn't appreciate quality.

"Okay, you convinced me," Carrie said. "You can stop the commercial now."

Back in the dining room, Carrie sat next to Trent, who had taken his place at the head of the table—the spot where Blanche used to sit. He took charge of introducing Martha to everyone.

Martha seemed intrigued by Kristen and asked, "Why do you talk funny?"

"Do you mean my accent?" Kristen grinned. "It's because I grew up in England."

Understanding washed over Martha's amiable face. "Oh! You're a foreigner."

During dinner, Martha talked incessantly and made a number of frank observations. Once she blithely announced, "Look, Shaun spilled soup on the tablecloth." Carrie gave a little silvery laugh at that from behind her napkin. Another time, Martha observed, "That girl didn't eat her broccoli." Heads turned toward Erica's daughter Aby, whose cheeks flushed.

Despite Martha's chatter, a slight but discernible gloom permeated the atmosphere. Everyone seemed to feel the absence of the Coleman matriarch. Kristen tried to draw Shaun out, but he remained subdued, spending most of his time pushing food around his plate. Trent talked to Walter and Kristen about Sun Coast, and the children talked among themselves until conversation turned to the person who was uppermost in their minds—Blanche Coleman.

"I still can't believe she's gone," Erica said. "At times I find myself remembering something I want to tell her before I realize she's not here anymore." There seemed to be a small empty place in her heart, and Erica wondered if the pain would ever go away.

"When I moved here a month ago, I thought I'd have years with her," Kristen said dolefully. "Grandma was always so active—I thought she'd keep going for years."

"And all the time, her heart was getting weaker," Trent said glumly.

Walter commented, "The last time I saw her, Blanche said she'd been to the doctor, who told her she had the constitution of a mule."

There were a few smiles at this, but Martha's brow furrowed. "But Mom's death didn't have anything to do with how healthy she was."

"What are you talking about?" Trent asked, his voice billowing out and filling the small room.

Martha squirmed but fluttered on, "Well, after what Mom said when she came out, you know—about what was going on with the company—I thought something might happen."

The room went very still. It was as if everyone was holding their breath. The children knew something was up and watched the adults in silent confusion.

Martha's eyes went from one to another. "I didn't mean—oh, I shouldn't have said anything," she stammered. Her voice was pure distress. "It's just that . . . well, we're all family here, so it's okay, isn't it? I mean, no one else knows."

"No one else knows *what*?" Carrie said brusquely.

Visibly flustered, Martha's hands twisted in her lap. "And . . . and Mother *was* very old and—and the police haven't even come, have they?"

Erica wondered what Martha could be getting at. Everyone darted quizzical looks at each other, trying to make sense out of Martha's confused chirruping.

After meeting blank looks all around, Martha blurted, "I mean, that's good . . . isn't it? For the family?"

The room remained deadly silent. Erica tried to think what Martha could mean as the woman's cheeks flamed red.

"Why would the police come?" Walter asked in a deep, sepulcher tone.

"Why, to arrest someone." Martha sounded surprised—as if he had asked something self-evident. She stared at Walter, as if he could straighten everything out. "Isn't that why they're doing an autopsy? I mean, don't they always do an autopsy when someone has been murdered?"

Chapter Three

MURDERED.

The word hung in the air, striking a response in each of them as it reverberated around the room like a clap of thunder. Erica's first instinct was to reject it, yet the investigator in her saw Carrie's face harden and how Trent set his glass on the table so hard that soda splashed up and over the rim. Pamela's face went still and blank as the swell of offense and scandal rose.

"What did you say?" David words sounded as if they were choking him—as if they were almost too big to get past his throat.

There was a rumble as Walter cleared his throat. "We think your mother had a stroke or a heart attack." He spoke to Martha gently, as though he were explaining something to a child.

"We're pretty sure that's what it was, although Shaun and I asked for an autopsy because we wanted to know the exact cause of death," Pamela added in a strained voice.

"You *asked* for an autopsy?" Martha was incredulous. "Was that a good idea? I mean, shouldn't you think of the family?"

Erica's voice was stiff as she asked, "What do you mean by that?"

"Are you implying that someone in the family was responsible for Grandma's death?" There was a warning note in Trent's voice.

"How could you even *think* such a thing?" A tide of bright color rose on Kristen's cheeks.

"I—I guess I shouldn't have said anything." Martha sounded alarmed. "I just assumed from what Mom told me, and with her dying so suddenly—"

"What did Mom tell you?" Shaun asked sharply.

Every eye was on Martha, who blinked uncomprehendingly. "Well now, it—it was something to do with the company. Mom said some bad things that were going on. She was upset and said she was going to change the will."

"That's drivel." There was a lash in Trent's tone.

Pamela spoke up in an unnaturally high voice. "You can't actually think someone in the family had a hand in her death."

As Trent and others leaned toward her, Martha's eyes darted from one angry face to another, her gaze piteous and bewildered. Martha's mild, amiable face showed such alarm it reminded Erica of a sheep shrinking back from predatory wolves.

Abashed, Martha dabbed at her eyes. "I'm always saying the wrong thing." She turned to David. "Can we go back to Mom's house now?"

By unspoken mutual consent, they all began to rise, collect their things, and file silently outside. The air smelled of rain, and thunder muttered dully in the distance. The wind had shifted direction, and the clouds were sharkskin gray. On the way home, David and Erica tried to make small talk, but while Martha joined in, Pamela was oddly silent.

Back at the house, Erica asked her children to get ready for bed, then she and David went to the kitchen, where Kristen and Shaun had just come in through the side door from the garage. Pamela and Martha were there. Usually, Erica's mother-in-law had the calm, serene features of a Madonna, but now her expression was strained, and she looked every bit of her fifty-nine years as she said goodnight. Leaning heavily on her cane, Pamela headed for the bedroom on the main level, which her mother-in-law had always kept ready for her.

"Trent and Carrie are coming over," Shaun announced. "Walter too."

"I think I'll go to bed," Martha said and beat a hasty retreat.

David said to Erica, "I'm going to check on Mom."

In a little while, Trent, Carrie, and Walter arrived. Trent's eyes swept the foyer.

"We dropped the children off at home," he said. "Where's Martha?"

"She went to bed," Erica replied.

"Figures." They went into the sitting room. Trent and Carrie sat on one couch, while Erica, Kristen, and Shaun took the other. There was a mild uproar as everyone talked at once.

"Off her rocker."

"Always knew Martha was certifiable."

"I'd always heard she was different, but Martha's flat-out crazy."

"Our dear Aunt Martha needs to be committed."

"I didn't know she was daft." This was from Kristen.

When David came in, Carrie asked, "How's Pamela?"

"She's pretty rattled," David said. "Mom took her medicine, but she's having a hard time."

Feeling sorry for her mother-in-law, Erica racked her brain for some way to help. "Maybe I ought to stay with Pamela after the funeral for a few days," she told David. "You and the kids could drive home since you have to work and they have school, and I'll fly home later."

Carrie overheard. "That's nice of you, Erica, but Pamela wouldn't be having such a hard time if it wasn't for Aunt Martha. I'd like to strangle her." She stopped and looked at David, who had a strange expression on his face. "What is it?"

"It's just something Mom said." When the others looked at him expectantly, David went on. "She said that while Martha tends to blurt things out, she always tells the truth."

"Oh, come on," Kristen said disparagingly. "You can't actually mean—"

Trent scoffed. "Martha's an overgrown child who never learned to think before she speaks. Dad told me that once, when he and Martha were little, Grandma took them shopping and Martha asked an old lady, 'Why doesn't your skin fit your face?'"

Everyone laughed, then David said, "My dad told me this story. When he, Martha, and Randy were little, Grandma and Grandpa used to take them to an all-you-can-eat buffet. One night, they were having dessert when a waitress stopped and asked if they needed anything. Martha asked the waitress for a bag so that Randy wouldn't have to put his extra cookies in his pants pocket like he usually did. Dad said Randy was furious!"

Walter cleared his throat with his distinctive rumble. "I've known Martha since she was a little girl, and she's always blurted out whatever was on her mind. Once when Martha was in high school, she told me my breath smelled like a rotten egg." Walter smiled. "I'm sure it did; I had garlicky fettuccine for lunch that day. Hearing unwelcome truths blurted out can be shocking."

"But there isn't any truth to what Martha said," David said with a frown. "It's all nonsense."

Walter's face was grave and absorbed. "I agree. But in the past, there has always been a kernel of truth at the center of Martha's unfortunate pronouncements."

"Grandma said Martha was slow," said Kristen, "but she sounds nuts to me. Pamela told me Martha's health isn't good. Maybe it's affecting her mind."

"That must be it," Carrie shuddered. "Imagine, thinking someone actually killed Grandma."

Trent was dismissive. "Martha's seen too many TV shows."

Disturbed and uneasy, Erica listened to the swirling conversation without joining in. What Martha said couldn't possibly be true, and yet Blanche had voiced the same concerns to Martha that she had mentioned to Erica. All of this seemed too terrible and impossible—yet left questions in Erica's mind.

When Walter stood and said good night, Erica walked him to the door. "I feel bad we talked about Martha like that," she said.

"And yet I can understand everyone's feelings." Walter reflected a moment as he stood by the door. "They're trying to deal with the shock of her accusation."

Accusation? "You're not taking what Martha said seriously, are you?"

Walter remained silent, a faraway look in his eyes. "Did you notice that each of the stories about Martha had one thing in common? No matter how embarrassing or tactless Martha was, her comments have always been based on truth."

* * *

There seemed to be a cloud over Erica when she woke. It took a few moments to recall the events of the previous night, but in the light of a new day, it was easy to dismiss Martha's ramblings and wonder why anyone had taken them seriously enough to be disturbed. The shower was running, and after a few minutes, David came out toweling his dark hair. He bent over to kiss her.

"Good morning, beautiful. Feeling any better?"

"Yeah. I let Aunt Martha get to me too much last night."

"Everyone did." David sat beside her on the bed. "It's too bad that on her first visit in a hundred years she had to say something crazy."

"It sure got everyone upset, didn't it?"

"I didn't take kindly to Aunt Martha suggesting that one of us committed murder."

"Aunt Martha may be a little different, but she's harmless."

"Just like you." David moved close and started to nuzzle her neck.

"What's that supposed to mean?"

"You know—a little strange but essentially harmless."

Erica sat up so straight her spine could have lined up with a brick wall. Careful to keep her voice normal, Erica asked, "In what way, exactly?" David didn't see the glint in Erica's emerald eyes nor her hand that snaked out to grab a pillow.

"Oh, like having everything lined up, wiping down car seats, and don't get me started on the Lava soap—"

"Is there something funny about being organized and clean?"

Realizing he'd stepped into a minefield, David attempted a retreat. "Now sweetheart, you know it's perfectly all right with me if you always keep six rolls of toilet paper under the sink and line up your perfumes from largest to smallest."

"That's a load off my mind." With a quick swing, Erica whacked him with the pillow.

"Hey!" David twisted and grabbed a pillow, but not before she got him twice more.

"Still think I'm harmless?" Laughing, Erica jumped up to dodge David's attack and hit him again. "You got something against being neat and having clean cars?"

Whap, whap, whap.

David landed several blows, rolled across the bed, and struck again. "No, but you're a neat freak. Why do you have to rearrange Mom's kitchen every time we visit?"

"She *likes* me to straighten things." Erica applied an evasive maneuver, shook her head to get her long hair out of her eyes, and struck another blow.

"There *is* such a thing as going overboard. I mean, who polishes the inside of kitchen cabinets?" David lunged across the bed, feinted, and landed two quick blows.

"'That which seems the height of absurdity in one generation often becomes the height of wisdom in another.' Adlai Stevenson," Erica quoted. She dodged and landed a couple of strikes. "Besides, I don't do that—you're confusing me with my mother. Even though Mom taught me to be neat and tidy, I have to admit she does go a little overboard."

"A little?" David chuckled grimly. "Her house reeks of ammonia. And I hate taking off my shoes and putting on those stupid little booties."

It was with a great deal of satisfaction that Erica got in a particularly telling shot to the head. A bit breathless, she asked, "Is there anything else you'd like to mention, buster?"

"There is." David rolled to avoid his wife's frontal assault, went too far, and fell off the bed with a great thump. Erica began laughing hysterically.

"How can you laugh when I'm lying on the floor, mortally wounded?" David called from the floor. "And to answer your question, I'd like to mention your fanatical need to provide a home for every cat, dog, and groundhog you come across."

"Better with me than an animal shelter!" Erica held a pillow in readiness, expecting a sneak attack, but waiting to see the whites of his eyes before striking.

Suddenly, David popped up, holding a pillow in one hand to deflect her attack and using another to whack Erica before dropping out of sight again.

Losing all sense of caution, Erica threw as many pillows as she could over the side of the bed. "So I'm organized and I like animals. You got a problem with being surrounded by adoring pets and always being able to find *what* you need *when* you need it?"

David's hands came up from across the bed in surrender, and he rose slowly. "Okay, okay. Truce. I'm glad I have an organized wife."

"That's better."

"Someone who loves to pick up pillows from the bedroom floor."

Erica picked up the closest pillow and, holding it out, asked sweetly. "Like this?"

He nodded.

Whap. Whap. Whap.

* * *

Erica slipped her casserole in the oven, took off her gloves, and was putting dishes in the dishwasher when Pamela came in. "Good morning, Erica. Something smells good."

"It's my world-famous breakfast casserole."

"Oh, I love that." Pamela opened a cupboard, closed it, and opened another. She frowned and turned to Erica. "You've rearranged the kitchen, haven't you?"

Erica was pleased. "You noticed."

"Of course I noticed, dear-heart. I can't find anything."

"I organized everything so you can find anything in a jiffy."

"I'd like to jiffy you. Where are the baking dishes?"

Erica opened the cupboard to the left of the stove. "Ta-da! Handy, right?"

Pamela peered inside. "Where are the 9 x 13 ones?

"I put those in storage."

"Why would you do that?"

"They're so—odd. The square ones are much nicer."

"And why is that?"

"Because they're square. Each side is even. Why would they even make a pan that's nine inches on one side and thirteen on another? That's just bizarre." Erica shook her head and began wiping the counter.

When Martha came down later—brilliant in orange pants and a flowered blouse—she sauntered to the counter and sniffed at the steaming dish appreciatively. "That smells really good. What is it?"

"It's called Tiffany's Breakfast Casserole,[1]" Erica said. "Hope you have a good appetite."

"Never had a problem with it yet," Martha said complacently.

A hint of a smile played around Pamela's mouth as she said to Erica, "I see you put the casserole on a rectangular cooling rack."

"It's the only one Grandma had." Erica gave a slight shrug. "We live in an imperfect world."

When Shaun came in, straightening his tie, Erica told him, "Breakfast is all ready. My kids prefer cereal, so they've already eaten." She called David in from the backyard, where he'd been bouncing with the children on the trampoline.

Everyone was at the table next to the kitchen when Kristen came in dressed for work in a cream-colored suit. "Sorry to be late. Smells like you've made something wonderful for brekkie."

"I take it brekkie is English for breakfast?" Erica asked.

When Kristen nodded, Pamela said, "I'm learning a whole new language."

David had to tease. "So is it lunchie for lunch and dinkie for dinner?"

"No, but we could always start a new trend," Kristen replied.

---

1   See the appendix for this recipe.

After a blessing on the food, they dug in. As Martha dished up a second helping, she remarked, "Too bad Mom isn't here; she would have liked this."

A feeling of sadness washed over Erica, and she gently set down her juice. David reached for her hand under the table as Martha went on blithely, unaware of how Shaun pushed his plate away.

Ever observant, Kristen noticed and spoke up in her lively way. "Isn't the weather beautiful today? It's supposed to be in the mid seventies."

Martha had just taken a bite of toast. "That's the way I like it," she said, spraying crumbs.

Turning to Shaun, Kristen asked, "Did you call your mom and let her know about the funeral?"

Shaun jerked in surprise. "My mother just passed away."

"I meant your biological mother."

"Tammy?" He stared. "Why would I do that? I don't even know where she is."

"Haven't you ever tried to contact her?"

"Why should I?" Shaun looked incredulous. "She's the one who abandoned me after my father died. Tammy didn't want anything to do with me."

"You don't know that for sure," Kristen said.

"I'm as sure as anyone can be after thirty-seven years of silence." His mouth had a straight, grim look.

"There could be a lot of reasons she hasn't contacted you," Kristen spoke up spiritedly.

"Right now, not caring tops the list, so let's drop it."

When Pamela took her dishes to the sink, she glanced at the clock. "You two better scoot. You know how Trent is when someone is late."

"You're right," Kristen said, rising. "Shaun, would you give me a ride in?"

A look of delight came over Shaun's face. "Sure."

* * *

On the morning of the funeral, Erica stood in front of the mirror as David zipped the back of the black dress she'd borrowed from Carrie. Erica stood there for a while, fingering the pendant—two sterling silver hearts that had a diamond embedded in the spot where the two hearts were linked.

David wrapped comforting arms around her. "I remember when Grandma gave that to you—when you graduated from the University of Utah."

"I was so happy she came." There was a crack in Erica's voice. "Grandma told me that when she saw this necklace in a store's window display, she had to buy it because she felt like her heart and mine were forever linked."

"And you cried when she gave it to you—just like you're crying now."

Feeling like her heart was coming loose, Erica laid her head on David's shoulder and wept.

* * *

The funeral went by in a blur. At the viewing, there were murmurs of sympathy, the sweet fragrance of flowers, and hugs and handclasps from a wide circle of Blanche Coleman's friends and acquaintances, as well as numerous employees from Sun Coast Sales and Rentals. Pamela grew shaky after a while, and a chair was brought for her. Martha was bright and happy, chatting brightly with everyone. Carrie's beauty was sharp and a little brittle, as usual, while Trent moved about the room, clapping people on the back. His tailored suit fit him well, and his expensive watch and ring gleamed as he moved around, seeming to know everyone. Trent's charm and ease talking with people contrasted sharply with his cousin Shaun's. Shaun visibly struggled, falling into awkward silence at times with those he did not know well. Although Kristen's eyes were glimmering and swollen, she remained by his side, filling in the gaps when Shaun had difficulty finding words.

During the service, Erica and David clung to each other as words of comfort were spoken regarding the plan of salvation and the assurance that one day they would be reunited. When the grandchildren sang a Primary song, Aby and Trent's oldest child, Courtney, choked up and could not finish.

Brown and golden leaves shivered in the chill of the gray autumn day as the mourners made their way to the Florence National Cemetery. The grassy plots sloped slightly with ponderosa pines, weeping willows, and honey-locust trees lining the edges. Headstones marched down the slope in neat rows that had a look of age about them. A few had crumbled around the edges.

Shaun dedicated the grave, and afterward, the pallbearers laid their boutonnieres tenderly on the casket. Then the great-grandchildren came forward. They pulled a flower or two from various floral arrangements and put them on the casket. How she would miss Blanche! Erica's knees felt weak as she went and laid a single white rose on top of the casket. David put his arm around her as she fought the urge to break down and sob. Once again, the words her grandmother had said on that Saturday morning walk echoed in her mind. *All you can do is just keep going, no matter how dark things look.* Erica laid her hands on the smooth casket.

I'll try, Grandma. I'll try.

* * *

Most of the family went back to the gravesite after lunch to see the final resting place of Blanche Coleman. Erica picked up a few stray flowers and added them to the mound covering the filled-in site. The family stood in small groups, talking in subdued tones.

Shaun took several roses from a bouquet and walked a few plots away to put them on his father's grave. There was a light, warm breeze as Erica went to stand by him. Silently, they studied the headstone. Wayne Coleman—beloved husband and son. Died while serving his country in Vietnam, January 17, 1975.

"Grandma told me your mom and dad got married a few months before he shipped out."

"It was right near the end of the war," Shaun said. "I had just turned one." The soft moist smell of autumn was in the air, and the golden leaves, tinged with red and brown, shone in the late afternoon sun. Shaun went on, his voice low in remembering.

"Sometimes I still wonder why Tammy abandoned me. When I was a kid, I figured it was my fault—I hadn't been loveable or good enough. For a long time, I tried to be perfect—to get all A's, to excel at sports . . . I thought that if I could be good enough, my mom would come back."

Shaun had never talked about this before. Tears stung Erica's eyes, and she ached for him as she thought of his heartache.

"Your mother didn't leave because you weren't good enough, and it certainly wasn't because you weren't loveable. She left because of *her* not you."

Shaun dug a toe into the grass. "I guess, but even now, I feel like I'm not good enough—not smart enough. Just not 'enough.'"

It had always been apparent Shaun lacked self-confidence, but Erica had never known why. She felt a surge of sympathy. "You *are* good enough," Erica told him. "Those feelings are coming from your past—they don't reflect reality. You need to root them out and change them."

"And how do I do that?" Shaun asked skeptically.

"I'm not sure, but I think a good first step is to realize they *are* wrong. Then tell yourself the truth—that you're a good, worthwhile person."

"That's nice of you to say—"

"I'm not saying it to be nice. I'm saying it because it's true."

Kristen meandered over. When she saw the name on the headstone, Kristen patted Shaun's shoulder in sympathy. Erica walked back to Blanche's gravesite and eyed the flower arrangements. One arrangement had an assortment of flowers including three gerberas in the middle. Three! Honestly, it was getting so you couldn't even trust floral shops. Erica pulled one out and, when she straightened, saw that Walter had come up on her unaware.

"It's better now that there's an even number," Erica explained. "Grandma would have wanted it that way."

One corner of the old lawyer's mouth turned up. "She might, at that." Then he said, "Did you know how proud Blanche was of you? First when you graduated from the police academy and later when you became a private investigator." He looked at the grave. "Blanche always said she could depend on you."

Erica fingered her necklace, her throat tight with unshed tears. What a blessing Blanche had been in her life—she had always been there for Erica, and now Erica had the chance to do something for Blanche. "I wanted to ask you something," she said. "Grandma wanted to hire me—said something was going on at Sun Coast and that she was going to make some sort of change. I think it had something to do with Shaun. Do you know what it was?"

There was reserve in the old lawyer's manner as he sidestepped her question. "Blanche always had lots of plans and ideas."

Walter knew something he wasn't telling. Erica was sure of it. A new uneasiness stirred. "I know how loyal you are to Grandma. She trusted you. And she trusted me too or else she wouldn't have wanted to hire me. Grandma said something about her will—did she make any recent changes?"

Walter stood silently for some time. "Yes, she did. Two weeks ago."

* * *

The next morning, Erica, David, Pamela, and Martha drove to Walter Hancock's office, which was just off Highway 101, on 12th Street. It was a solid, square building made of red bricks.

The conference room was furnished sparingly with a long table and a dozen upholstered chairs. Looking and acting like a courtly old gentleman, Walter shook their hands then went to stand at the head of the table.

Pamela sat next to David and Erica while Martha beamed at them from across the table next to Trent, who wore his suit with a tightly knotted tie, and Carrie, who wore a black dress. When Walter opened his prodigious briefcase, silence fell. Every eye was on the lawyer as he pulled out his files.

As he looked over the papers, Martha could stand it no longer. "What did she leave me?"

"Martha!" Pamela protested.

Blinking like a surprised owl, Martha whined, "I just wanted to know."

"And you will, Martha." Walter was gentle. Besides an educated shrewdness, the most overt qualities of Walter's personality were benevolence and kindness. He cleared his throat. "I want all of you to know I've always had the deepest admiration and respect for Blanche Coleman. She was a close friend, whom I will dearly miss." Walter's voice vibrated with emotion, and he paused to collect himself.

Finally he was able to continue. "Ever since she and Lawrence first started Sun Coast Sales and Rentals, Blanche showed herself to be an astute businesswoman. She and her husband turned one store into five. After Lawrence passed away, Blanche acquired Aspen Clothing and Manufacturing and Panda Motor Sports, and Sun Coast became a stock corporation. Blanche and Lawrence asked me to act as executor of their wills. Lawrence left nearly everything in his will to his wife, and Blanche's will has, for the most part, remained the same—until a few weeks ago.

Trent and Carrie exchanged looks. Martha wiggled in her seat, and when Walter paused to take a sip of water, it dawned on Erica that Walter, that staunch bastion of tranquility, was nervous.

Walter shook his papers. "Blanche made a codicil to her will a few weeks ago."

"What's a codicil?" Carrie asked, nervously winding a piece of hair around her finger.

Pamela replied, "An amendment." David looked at his mother in surprise.

"That's right." Walter rattled the papers in his hand. "Blanche and Lawrence's will was rather lengthy, so rather than rewrite it, we made two codicils. I'll get to them in a minute."

The tension, which had already been high, increased, and Carrie said to Trent, "See, I told you something was up." Her eyes on Walter, Carrie had the look of a tigress watching an elusive rabbit.

Are all will-readings fraught with this much hostility and friction? Erica wondered. She could tell that Carrie and Trent were primed to make a scene, and Erica only hoped this meeting ended before that happened.

"Blanche's share of stock in Sun Coast Sales and Rentals will be divided among family members, with her children, Martha and Shaun; her son Norman's widow, Pamela; and Randy's widow, Nora, receiving a combined total of 70 percent. The remaining 30 percent will be divided between the grandchildren. Of her liquid assets, Blanche left significant amounts to a number of charities. The will directs that I continue acting as the administrator for Martha's share of the estate." He turned to Martha, who looked puzzled. "That means I will continue to send your monthly check."

Once again, the lawyer faced the family. "Blanche arranged for all of her children, their spouses, and her grandchildren to receive a one-time check upon her death."

When Walter named the amount, Martha put a hand to her mouth in excitement. "Now I can buy a nice display case so I can show off the pretty things I've bought. And I can get some more chickens. And a new stove—"

"I'm sure you have great plans for the money, Aunt Martha, but let Walter finish," Pamela admonished testily, her hands flat on the table.

It was unlike Pamela to get so worked up, yet the tension in the room was a tangible thing, and like her mother-in-law, Erica wished Walter would hurry on and finish.

"Blanche wanted each member of the family—as well as Gail and Vicki—to receive one piece from her Armani and Lalique collections. I'll take care of that disbursement later. There are a number of bequests for her housekeeper, Vicki, and other employees. I can go over them if you'd like."

"No need for that," Trent replied vigorously. "I want to know about the changes Grandma made in the codicils. And tell us in plain English. No lawyerese."

"I'll do my best." Walter seemed unperturbed, but he tapped the papers together on the table, as if to give himself a few moments. "One of the changes has to do with management positions at Sun Coast Sales and Rentals. Blanche named her son, Shaun Coleman, to succeed her as chairman of the board."

"What?" Trent sounded both incredulous and angry.

Walter went on as if Trent hadn't spoken. "She also named Shaun CEO."

Trent's wide face flushed red as he jumped to his feet. "That's impossible!" His words exploded like bombs. "Shaun can't be CEO *and* chairman of the board!"

"If you will take your seat, I'll go over the second change." Walter's voice was chill.

"Sit down, Trent," David admonished. "Let's hear the rest of it."

Breathing heavily, Trent finally sat.

"The second change is regarding Blanche Coleman's personal estate. After taking out the funds for charities, bequests, and the one-time checks, the residue will be divided in two parts. The first half will be divided between Martha, Pamela, Nora, and Blanche's grandchildren and great-grandchildren.

"The second half will go to her son, Shaun Coleman."

Chapter Four

EVERYONE WAS SURPRISED, BUT TRENT Coleman looked shocked—absolutely shocked. His dark eyes were bulging out of his head when he jumped to his feet again and shouted, "Grandma never would have done something as crazy as this!"

His wife joined him in full cry. "Grandma said Trent was going to replace her at Sun Coast and become chairman of the board." There was a whiny, complaining tone in Carrie's voice, and not for the first time, Erica felt it was about the most annoying sound a human voice could contain.

Trent's face was dark and furious. Looking like he might explode, he questioned, "How can Shaun jump from executive vice president to chairman? And to make him CEO as well is insane."

"I realize this change comes as a shock," Walter said gently, "but I assure you this is what Blanche wanted."

"This is impossible!" Trent vehemently slammed a hand on the table. "Shaun can't handle both positions. It gives him too much power—the board wouldn't be able to supervise him. Besides, having one person in both positions is just not done."

"The board is set up to fully oversee and control the chairman, and while this hierarchy is unusual, it is not unheard of for one person to be the senior representative of the shareholders and also the senior decision maker for a company." Walter paused. "I assume you've heard of Bill Gates?"

"You can't compare how Bill Gates organized things years ago to this situation." Trent flung out his arms in an appeal to the family. "Can any of you see Shaun as chairman *and* CEO?"

Spoken with derision, the words were like an unexpected slap. Blood rose in Erica's cheeks as though the blow had been a physical one directed at her.

Walter gave Trent a clear unflinching look. "If you want other examples of people who have been both CEO and chairman of the board of directors, you can look right here at Sun Coast. After Blanche took over Aspen Clothing and Panda Sports, she kept her position as CEO while remaining a chairperson." There was force behind the lawyer's pedantic manner. "Blanche asked me to help Shaun with the chairman position and knew others at Sun Coast would assist him in his duties as CEO. Trent, you'll become the new chief marketing officer."

"But I've been CEO for the last two years."

"You've been *acting* CEO," David said dryly. "There's a difference. Maybe Grandma didn't like the way you've been running things."

Trent stared at him balefully. "If Grandma had had any complaints, she would have told me."

Shaun had been watching the duel of words, and at times he'd opened his mouth as if to speak. But no words had come out—until now. In an uncertain voice, he said, "Mom never mentioned any of this to me."

Without giving Walter time to answer, Pamela broke in. "What I don't understand is why Grandma would give half of the estate to Shaun while the other half is divided between all of us." Her eyes were narrow as she stared at Walter. "That doesn't sound like Blanche—she's never played favorites before."

Martha's face showed the naive perplexity of a child. "Why is Shaun going to get half while the rest of us have to split the other half?" She gave Shaun a baleful glare. "That's different from what Mom told me she was going to do. Did you talk Mom into changing her will?"

"No, I didn't," Shaun replied, looking wretched.

"You must have done something to talk Grandma into this," Carrie sputtered.

"Changing the will was Blanche's idea," Walter said, sounding weary. "Let me explain the division a bit further. I've already gone over the stock for Sun Coast. Half of Blanche Coleman's personal estate will be divided between Martha and the widows of her two sons: Pamela and Nora. Smaller portions will go to the four grandchildren: Nora's three children, Trent, Brian, and Michelle, and Pamela's son, David. A smaller amount will be set up in a trust account for the great-grandchildren. There is also a stipend for Kristen. Included in Shaun's half of the estate is the house and its contents."

Trent began to speak, but Walter held up a hand. "That means the price of the home and its contents will be subtracted from Shaun's half of the estate."

"And you think that makes it fair?" Trent was incredulous.

"It doesn't matter what I think," Walter told him in his dry, exact voice. "Blanche made her will according to her personal desires."

Agitated, Carrie shifted in her chair. "But why would Blanche change her will and give most of the money to Shaun?"

"Blanche knew questions would arise over the division and asked me to explain two things. First, she left the house to Shaun because she wanted him to have the home he grew up in, especially since, at her request, he had come back to live with her after his divorce. Second, Blanche asked me to remind the family that the money is hers to do with as she pleases and anyone who grumbles ought to be glad they're getting anything at all."

"That's it?" Trent was disbelieving. "That's the explanation of why Shaun gets half?"

Martha's lower lip was trembling. "It's not fair."

Walter cleared his throat with a rumble. "Why Blanche changed the will doesn't matter as much as the fact that it represents her desires. Since you all loved her, I'm sure you'll respect her wishes. Blanche Coleman never acted without putting a great deal of thought into what she did."

The meeting was over. Erica felt limp from the roiling emotions. The change to management at Sun Coast was a huge surprise. Erica thought Trent had been doing well. As for the unequal division of the assets, Erica didn't personally care about the money but worried that the unequal distribution might cause hard feelings between Shaun and the others. Even Pamela and Martha were upset by it.

Looking dazed, Trent shook his head. "I don't get it. Grandma always intended on me taking over as chairman. And she gives half of everything to Shaun? I don't understand the sudden change."

"It wasn't sudden," Martha said. "Mom told me she was going to change her will when she came to see me." All eyes went to her, and under the spotlight, Martha began to flutter. "She shouldn't have told other people, though."

"What makes you think she told someone else?" Pamela's voice was sharp.

Martha's eyebrows lifted in surprise at the question. As if it was the most obvious thing in the world, Martha said, "Because whoever she told killed her. He didn't want Mom changing the will. He didn't know she already had." She looked troubled. "Wait a minute. Maybe I'm remembering it wrong. Maybe Mom *had* changed it and was going to change it back. I forget which way it was." Martha looked at everyone in confusion. "I can't think with all of you looking at me, but I'll try to remember what Mom said. But either way, she was killed because of her will."

Martha's words had a chilling effect, not only on Erica but on the whole family, who looked at each other with new suspicion in their eyes. It was awful to think Martha could be right. But it was even worse to think that the person who stood to gain the most was Blanche's own son, Shaun Coleman.

* * *

That afternoon, David and Erica spent time with the children enjoying the warm fall weather and playing in the backyard. After a rousing game of badminton, Erica left them jumping on the trampoline and came inside to get a drink of water. When she heard the sound of a vacuum cleaner, Erica stopped, thinking about what Martha had said. Then she raced up the stairs. The sound was coming from Kristen's bedroom.

When Erica burst into the room, Vicki, a small woman in her early fifties, jumped. Holding a hand over her heart, she turned off the vacuum, looking alarmed.

"Have you cleaned Grandma's bedroom?"

Vicki's eyes were wide. "I washed the bedding and was going to clean the rest of the room today."

"Just leave everything as it is." Erica was almost sure that preserving the scene wasn't necessary, but one of the mottos she lived by was "Better safe than sorry."

Vicki nodded, her round face solemn. "It's true what they say? That Mrs. Coleman was murdered?"

So, rumors were already spreading. Erica had no answer and, with a little shiver, wondered, *What if the rumors are true?*

* * *

On Saturday, Pamela joined David, Erica, and the children to visit Trent and Carrie. Then they took a picnic lunch to Woahink Lake. Afterward, they drove to historic Florence and stopped at BJ's 48 Flavors in Old Town for ice cream. They sat at tables outside the shop, licking their cones in the golden light of a fall afternoon and watching people stroll by.

Sunday morning, Shaun invited Kristen and Martha to go to church. Martha declined, but Kristen said she'd be happy to go. Erica felt a deep homesickness for her grandmother as Shaun drove along Munsel Lake Road and parked next to the familiar white-steepled building, which was surrounded on three sides by pine trees.

Bright-faced missionaries stood by the door as ushers, and after shaking hands, Erica and her family took their seats in the small chapel. A number of members of the Florence Ward came over to offer their condolences. During the services, Erica recalled the many times she and David had sat with Blanche in those blue upholstered pews. She knew David was having similar thoughts as, more than once, he lifted a hand to wipe away moisture from his eyes during sacrament meeting.

At the beginning of Sunday School, Pamela sneezed as the teacher—wearing a lime-green tie—set his briefcase on the floor by his daughter's Tinkerbell lunchbox. Pamela sneezed several more times during Relief Society, which was in a strangely configured corner room that had two doors. Erica passed her mother-in-law a tissue as the Relief Society president stood behind a table in the corner and gave announcements. Behind her on the wall hung a quilt with squares in a star design. The chorister, an older lady with short curly gray hair and a dimple in her cheek, wore dangling seashell earrings that bounced as she energetically led the song. During the lesson, Erica kept stealing glances at a painting on the north wall that showed a bent, elderly woman passing through the veil and coming out on the other side, strong and upright, reaching out to Jesus Christ, who waited with an outstretched hand. Erica's heart warmed to think this might have been Blanche's experience.

Driving home, she and David held hands, and it seemed the world was tilting a little less.

* * *

When they walked into the house, the refrigerator was open, and two feet wearing thick black shoes showed under the door. Martha straightened up, looking comical with her large eyeglasses peeking over the top of the door.

"I was looking for something to eat," she explained.

"Did you remember we're having a family dinner?" Erica asked. Surely Martha could smell the savory, spicy scent wafting through the kitchen. "I put the chicken on to cook this morning for Chicken Enchiladas.[2] Since Shaun's taking you home tomorrow and I'll be leaving in a few days, I thought it might be nice to have the family together."

"It smells wonderful, but I'm hungry now."

David chuckled then turned to hide his smile.

"How about some tinned soup to tide you over?" Kristen suggested.

"What's tinned soup?" Martha asked, her nose wrinkling.

"Soup in a can. Come on, let's look in the larder."

"What can I do to help?" Pamela asked then turned her head to sneeze.

"You can go right to bed," Erica said as David went to check on the children. "There's not a lot to do anyway." She escorted Pamela to her bedroom.

As Pamela changed, she asked Erica to get her a decongestant from the bathroom.

"Will this do?" Erica asked, showing her a box of cold capsules she'd found. Pamela nodded. Erica took out a foil packet, bent the corner, and attempted to peel the foil off. No go. When that didn't work, Erica ran her fingernail between the foil and the plastic. She tried poking it and, in one last desperate attempt, gnawed on one end.

"One thing on my bucket list," Erica growled, "is to meet the guy who decided to encase pills in these plastic and foil sheets and punch him in the nose. Several times."

Reaching into a drawer, Pamela plucked out a pair of scissors. "It's the only way."

Erica snipped away. "Too bad you caught a cold."

"I only hope it doesn't settle in my throat like Martha's did."

"Me too." Erica handed her the tablets and a glass of water. "Need anything else?"

---

2   See the appendix for this recipe.

"I'm fine, thanks."

On the way out, Erica noticed the picture by the door was tilted. She straightened it then glanced back at Pamela. "That's better, isn't it? You'll be able to rest easier now."

"Thanks. I wouldn't have gotten a wink of sleep."

Aby was busily texting at the table as Ryan and Kenzie begged their father to go outside and play with them. After Erica assured him she had sufficient help with Shaun and Kristen, David allowed the children to pull him outside.

"I'm glad to help," Shaun said, "as long as you're not afraid of salmonella, botulism, or E. coli."

"Maybe you ought to stick to setting the table," Kristen said with a giggle.

"You wound me," Shaun said, putting a hand over his heart as if in pain. "No one has ever died from my cooking. Of course it was touch and go that one time as to whether we'd get George to the hospital in time—"

Erica laughed. When Shaun was lighthearted like this, his face became boyish and even more attractive than usual. "First, let's wash up." Erica went to the sink and grabbed one of the bars of Lava.

"Why are there two bars of soap?" Kristen asked.

"The one on the right is hers," Shaun explained. "The one on the left is for us heathens and unwashed masses."

A light dawned in Kristen's eyes. "That explains why there were two bars in the loo off the kitchen."

The French doors opened and in came Martha carrying her empty bowl from the patio. She beamed at everyone. "Are you starting dinner then?"

"Yes, we are." Erica brought out her blue recipe file.

"You brought your own file?" Kristen was astonished.

"I never leave home without it." Erica pulled out a card. "I thought cheesecake would be good for dessert. I bought two crumb crusts yesterday. Do you want to start on that, Kristen?"

"Sure."

Martha clasped her hands together. Her cheeks were pink, and her eyes bright with pleasurable excitement. "This is fun! What can I do?"

"Why don't you help Kristen?" Erica pulled a bowl from the cupboard. "After you wash your hands, you can break the eggs in this.

And Shaun, you can chop the tomatoes, slice the olives, and mash the avocado."

"Grunt work, eh? And I thought I was going to be the sous-chef."

"Oh dear," Kristen exclaimed as she peered into her bowl. "I poured in a little too much vanilla. But I guess that won't hurt."

Erica tried to hide her distress. "It's important to be precise in cooking," she explained kindly. "That's the beauty of it, you see. You follow the recipe exactly, and everything turns out fine."

"For you, maybe." Kristen sounded doubtful.

While the cheesecake was baking, Kristen and Shaun shredded the chicken. Erica set the table in the formal dining room, placing the plates exactly two inches from the edge and eight inches from each other. David came in and filled pitchers with ice water.

Shortly after Trent, Carrie, and their children arrived, Pamela appeared, looking rested. When Walter arrived, he came into the kitchen and asked what he could do to help.

Erica looked at him and shook her head. "In that suit? Never."

"It may surprise you to know this, but suit coats are removable."

She smiled. "Everything's done anyway. Let's get everyone seated and we can eat."

It was fun to have the family together, but Erica missed her grandmother's invigorating presence. Blanche would have added her sparkling opinion to every conversation. Erica had worried about residual tension, but Trent and Carrie were polite to Shaun—although a bit cool. Erica had been a part of the family long enough to know that while Trent had quite a temper, he never stayed mad for long.

Taking a second helping, Kristen enthused, "These enchiladas are delicious! They're almost better than steak and kidney pie."

"Just about anything would be," David said dryly.

Pamela changed the subject. "Kristen, I was surprised this morning during Sunday School when you answered a couple of the teacher's questions. How did you learn so much about the Church?"

"One of my best friends in England was LDS. I went to church with her once in a while."

Talk turned to other things, then Carrie asked Erica, "Did you guys go to Heceta Head Lighthouse Saturday?"

"No, I wish we could have, but we ended up going to Woahink Lake. It was beautiful there."

"I know how much you like Heceta, Erica. Maybe we can all go one evening while you're here," Trent offered.

"That would be great," Erica exclaimed. "Maybe we could have a cookout on the beach."

"Yay! That would be fun," Kristen said enthusiastically.

"Too bad you can't come, Martha, but Shaun's taking you home tomorrow, isn't he?" Carrie spoke in a deceptively innocent voice. "He'll have to miss a lot of work."

Trent frowned at Shaun. "Why didn't you take Martha home today? Then you wouldn't have to miss work tomorrow."

"I wanted to spend Sunday here, especially since Erica planned a family dinner."

"I'll be glad to get home," Martha said. "Then I can go walking again. I go for a walk every afternoon in Bryant Woods. It's a beautiful place right behind my house. In fact, I ought to go for a walk now. It helps the digestion."

"Is that so," Carrie said, uninterest in her voice as they began to clear the table.

"Shaun and I will go with you," Kristen spoke up brightly.

"I will too," Erica declared, wanting to show her support.

Martha eyed Trent's solid figure as he carried a load of plates into the kitchen. "You ought to come too, Trent. A walk would help that paunch of yours." Carrie gasped, and Erica and David grinned.

Affronted, Trent replied, "It doesn't seem to have worked on yours."

Martha remained complacent as she patted her belly. "That's because I feed it too well."

* * *

"I wish you were coming home with us, but I'm glad you're staying a few more days with Mom." David leaned against the car, looking regretfully at Erica. On the front porch, Pamela hugged Aby, Ryan, and Kenzie while Bandit looked on, his black tail swishing gently.

"She's having a really hard time. And so is Shaun."

David shook his head. "The poor guy walks around like he's been shell-shocked. The idea of taking over as CEO and chairman has overwhelmed him. But then, he's never had much self-confidence."

"And Trent's outburst sure didn't help."

"He'll cool down. Trent said Grandma planned to make him chairman of the board, but I'm not so sure," David said. "In most companies, that's an elected position."

He gathered Erica in his arms and spoke into her hair. "I'm going to miss you. They say 'home is where the heart is,' so I guess I won't really be going home since my heart will be staying here with you."

Actions were better than words. Erica pulled back slightly and kissed him.

There was a groan, and they pulled apart to see Ryan holding his stomach. "Ugh."

"Just get in the car," David said, tousling his son's hair.

Erica hugged her children. "I'm going to miss you, but I'll call every day, so save up news for me. And we'll Skype."

After everyone was buckled in, David rolled down the window, and Erica leaned over to kiss him again. "Call me when you get to Boise tonight, okay?"

"Sure. And I'll call every day, depending on how my shifts run."

Erica joined Pamela on the porch, and the two of them waved until the car was out of sight.

* * *

An hour later, Martha called loudly to Erica, "He's here!" She'd been watching out the window for Shaun ever since he called to say he was on his way home from Sun Coast. She flung the door open as Shaun strode up the front porch steps.

"Looks like someone's eager to get home."

"Oh, I am!" Martha assured him, clutching her black purse to her chest as they stepped into the foyer. "I even brought down my suitcase and duffle bag so you wouldn't have to." Shaun looked over to where they were stacked against the table by the wall.

"And look at this." Martha plucked two white sacks off the table. "Erica and I made sandwiches. We made two for you. Bandit wanted to eat them, but I wouldn't let him. And there's potato chips and Twinkies for dessert!"

Shaun chuckled. "You'd think we were going to Timbuktu."

"Timbuktu?" Martha's eyes became worried. "I thought you were taking me home."

"Just joking, Aunt Martha." Shaun picked up her suitcase, and Erica brought the duffle bag. On the porch, Erica shut the door, opened it, then shut it again.

"Do you always do that?" Shaun asked.

"Do what?"

"You know." He inclined his head toward the door.

"Of course. It's always good to make sure the door is shut."

Shaun smiled as they walked to the car. "So David's going to be Mr. Mom while you're gone?"

"Yeah. He'll take shifts that let him be home when the kids get out of school. And my mom helps out a lot—she lives two houses away. And I have two married brothers who live down the street." Not for the first time, Erica thought how wonderful it was to have family to rely on.

"Close family." He swung Martha's ancient suitcase into the trunk.

Martha buckled her seat belt. "Thank you for driving me. Gail had to work today, or she could have come and got me."

"Glad some people find me useful." When Erica gave him a curious look, Shaun explained. "Trent has never felt I was capable of doing anything right at Sun Coast."

"Well, don't mind him." Erica tried to be consoling. "Besides, isn't it against corporate policy for bosses to think employees do anything well?"

She was rewarded by Shaun's booming laughter. He was still smiling as they pulled away.

* * *

Later that morning, Erica went to the garage and unlocked the tan Camry that Shaun said she could use during her stay. She vacuumed it, cleaned the windows, and wiped the steering wheel and seats before storing a box of moist towelettes in the glove compartment for future use.

It was such a nice warm day that at lunchtime, she and Pamela took their sandwiches to the patio. It was a beautiful spot, with hanging baskets of pink and white petunias lining the patio roof. As they ate, cedar waxwings pecked at a bird feeder hanging from a sycamore.

"Dear-heart, I've been thinking," Pamela said, breaking into Erica's thoughts. "Is it okay if we stay here for another day or two? I don't feel like going home yet."

Erica reached out and patted her mother-in-law's hand. "Sure."

The phone rang, and Pamela went in to answer it as Erica gathered up their dishes. "Yes, this is Pamela Coleman. Oh, Dr. Rodriguez." She gripped the receiver, listening hard. "Hold on a minute." Holding the phone to her chest, she whispered to Erica. "It's the coroner. He has the results of the autopsy and wants to meet with me and Shaun this afternoon." Pamela's face was pale. "When will Shaun be back?"

"Between two and three. See if you can meet him at four."

"Would you come with us?" When Erica nodded, Pamela told Dr. Rodriguez, "We can meet you at four o'clock. My daughter-in-law, Erica, will be with us." When Pamela hung up, there was a frightened look in her eyes. "Why didn't he tell me the results over the phone?"

"It might be their policy to give the results in person." It was a lame guess, meant to calm her mother-in-law, but inside, Erica felt a sinking feeling. Something was wrong—very wrong. Why else would Dr. Rodriguez make them drive fifty miles to his office in Eugene?

As Pamela looked at her, Erica knew they were both thinking the same thing. What kind of news was so bad the coroner would only tell them in person?

Chapter Five

A FEW MINUTES BEFORE FOUR o'clock, Shaun, Pamela, and Erica were sitting stiffly in Luis Rodriguez's cramped office. Erica shivered a little as she watched him. How could a man's face be so blank and yet so foreboding?

"I can see you're all anxious," Dr. Rodriguez said, "so I'll get right to it." He opened the file that was front and center on his desk. "I'm sorry it took longer than normal to get the results, but we had to send tissue samples to other laboratories. I'd give you a full toxicology report, but much of it is clinical and hard to understand, so I'll stick to the basics."

"That's fine," Erica said, darting a sideways look at Shaun, who was gripping his chair so hard his knuckles were white.

"Blanche Coleman's heart was essentially in good condition—there were a few deposits in the arteries, but that's to be expected in a woman of her age."

"So it wasn't a heart attack?" Pamela asked in a shaky voice.

"That's correct. Also, there was no indication of a stroke."

"No stroke," Shaun repeated tonelessly.

"Blanche Coleman died from internal bleeding, which was caused by excessive levels of Amitriptyline in her body."

Confused, Pamela glanced at Erica then at Mr. Rodriquez. "What is Amitrip— Amitroplin—oh I can't pronounce it. I don't recall her taking anything that sounded like that."

"The common name is Elavil. It's a prescription drug, but no doctor would have prescribed it for her because, according to the list you gave me, Blanche was taking Coumadin. Elavil significantly increases the effects of blood-thinners like Coumadin, and taking them together often results in either a stroke or in excessive internal bleeding."

The room seemed devoid of air, leaving Erica feeling choked.

Pamela leaned forward. "I don't understand. You say Elavil is a prescription but that her doctor wouldn't have prescribed it. How did Blanche get it then?" Her voice was high and thin.

Dr. Rodriguez's face was full of sympathy as he looked at Erica then Shaun. Erica knew what that glance meant. He was giving them a choice. One of them could explain it to Pamela or he would. Erica glanced at Shaun, who seemed stunned into silence.

With tears flooding her eyes, Erica took her mother-in-law's hand—a simple gesture of consolation when no words would have worked. "It means Grandma was poisoned."

* * *

At home, Erica called David and, in a broken voice, gave him the news. There was a long silence as Erica sat cross-legged on the green spread on her bed. With all her heart, Erica wished she could have been with her husband to hold and console him. And she could have used some comforting herself.

When David finally spoke, he stammered, "I . . . I can't believe it."

"I know. It seems unreal." Erica still felt numb. The coroner's words had been such a shock.

"Martha suspected this, but I didn't really think she could be right."

"I didn't either," Erica admitted. "I wonder if this has anything to do with what was going on at Sun Coast. Oh I wish Grandma had told me exactly what was bothering her." Her voice broke, and fresh tears began falling. The numbness was starting to wear off, letting in sharp pain.

"How is Mom taking it?"

"She cried all the way home—couldn't even talk."

"How do you feel?"

"Like throwing up." Erica sighed. "I don't know what to feel. One moment it feels like I'm in a dream and the next the reality hits me and I'm crying. Then, I'm angry and want to start hitting somebody or something. And then I start thinking about how I can go about finding out who killed Grandma—and believe me, I'm going to find out." Erica's voice was determined.

"Look, I'll call Chief Brown first thing in the morning. I'm sure he'll give me time off. I can be in Florence by tomorrow afternoon."

As much as she wanted David there, Erica had to be realistic. "I've thought about that, but really, what could you do? You've already taken extra time off work, and the kids need to stay in school. Besides, I don't want them in the middle of this."

"But what about your job? I know your boss has been okay with you working part-time and allowing you flexible hours because of the kids, but this is going to require a big block of time."

"I already called Doug. He said to take all the time I need—that things are slow. The other investigators can pick up any new cases. I asked him if I could use Pinnacle's databases to do background checks and anything else I need, and he said that was fine."

"Good. Is there anything I can do? It's so frustrating not to be there."

"I know. Say, would you call Aunt Martha and let her know?"

"Sure. Anything else?"

"Calling Aunt Martha qualifies you for sainthood, but there is one other thing. Could you call poison control and find out more about Amitriptyline? Since you're a police officer, they'll tell you everything you need to know." She spelled it for him.

Suddenly, emotion exploded inside Erica's head in a soundless burst that was so real, she felt the reverberations in her chest. Icy anger settled into an all-sustaining flame. "I'm not going to let whoever did this get away with it." Erica's voice was steely. "I'm going to find out who killed her."

"That means investigating the family." Erica could tell by the warning in David's voice that he was unhappy. "This is going to be tough on you. And the family."

"I know."

"Check for any disgruntled business associates. Walter or Trent might know if Grandma had any enemies."

"I'll ask. But there's one thing I'm worried about. I'm not a homicide detective."

"Don't underestimate yourself, Erica. You found out who killed that man in Florida last year. You've got an amazing memory and the ability to see details that others overlook. Plus, you're a top-notch private eye. Not many investigators can say they've solved every single case they've taken. Besides, a private investigator is in the business of searching for the truth, and that's what we both want. Stay strong. You can do this."

* * *

When Erica called Carrie to give her the news, Carrie broke in with a question before Erica could say anything. "Did Shaun get back from taking Martha home?"

"He did, but it sounded like a harrowing trip. Shaun told me Martha chattered the entire way and complained nonstop about his driving—telling him a hundred times that her stepdaughter Gail never drives as fast as he did. She even asked Shaun how many accidents he'd caused." Carrie laughed and Erica went on. "Anyway, he dropped her off in town."

That seemed odd. "Why didn't he take her home?"

"Martha said she wanted to meet Gail at the floral shop where she works and would go home with her." Then Erica told her about the autopsy. Again, she felt the cold wind of loss and emptiness that had been part of her life since her grandmother died.

Carrie was shocked. "I can't believe that old bat Martha was right."

"Will you let Trent know?" Erica asked. "I called, but he was in a meeting."

"Shoot. How am I supposed to tell him that his grandmother was murdered?"

* * *

Erica had to hurry.

Dr. Rodriguez had said he'd already notified the police, which meant they could arrive at any time to examine the house. While the police might be willing to share information, Erica couldn't count on it. She might not get someone as understanding as Patrick Lund, the detective she'd worked with in Kissimmee, Florida. It would be best to examine the house herself.

Now.

Any clues she found might help her uncover the killer. Erica remembered the chocolate-covered strawberry on her grandmother's nightstand. Perhaps it had been injected with Amitriptyline. Ingestion was the most common method of poisoning, although it was by no means the only way. Later, David would be able to tell her what forms Elavil came in so she could determine if the poison had been inhaled, ingested, absorbed, or injected. Erica went through the main level of the house, including Blanche's office. In the refrigerator was a container that held the last of the strawberries. The police would surely want to test them.

Putting on long, heavy-duty rubber gloves and protective outer clothing, Erica forced herself to dig through the garbage, looking for clues. Erica wished she could have done it sooner, but who knew that Blanche had been poisoned? Besides Martha, anyway. Erica was thorough but failed to find the box the strawberries came in.

After a quick shower and armed with a pencil, notepad, and box of plastic bags, Erica went to Blanche's bedroom. Being a former police officer, she knew what precautions to take to avoid contaminating the crime scene any more than it already had been. Before entering, she pulled on a pair of the disposable gloves she always kept in her pocket. Other than the bedding, the bedroom hadn't been disturbed—as far as she knew.

As she surveyed the room, tears welled up in Erica's eyes. It still seemed impossible that her grandmother was gone. How many times had they sat in that pair of blue chairs by the window and talked? It took a few moments for Erica to blink away the tears. Then her heart fluttered, and Erica had a sudden, inexplicable feeling that someone was in the room, listening, watching, waiting.

She's here. Grandma is here, now!

The feeling was so strong, Erica's mouth opened in wonder, and she looked around. She clasped the pendant on her necklace. Was it possible Grandma knew she was here to find the killer? A peculiar sense of urgency washed over Erica, and she felt that feisty Blanche Coleman *did* know—and that she wanted the person responsible for her death to be held accountable. Erica felt a surge of determination. She *would* find out who had killed her grandmother.

"I love you, Grandma," Erica said softly, and a warm feeling glowed in her chest. With new resolution, Erica began going over the room, inch by inch. First, she examined the floor on hands and knees. Vicki had put the bedspread on slightly crooked—one side was almost an inch longer than the other, so Erica straightened it. Next, she pushed aside the heavy blue drapes to see if the windows were locked and if any dust had been recently disturbed. It didn't look like it had, but then, Vicki was a meticulous housekeeper.

In the walk-in closet, Erica inspected everything—from the clothes hanging on rods to the shelves with their rows of shoes, purses, and wigs. While going through the drawers in the mahogany dresser, Erica had to stop a few times and blink to clear her vision, which blurred when she recognized a familiar necklace, bracelet, or pair of earrings her grandmother had worn.

In the bathroom, which was papered with sprigs of green ferns, was a cluster of bottles: prescriptions, vitamins, and assorted supplements. One bottle held fish oil capsules. A hypodermic needle could have been used to withdraw the oil and replace it with poison. It would also have been a simple matter to introduce Elavil into the bottle of powdered fiber. But who could have done such a thing? Only the family and Vicki had regular access to the house.

Determinedly, Erica pushed those thoughts away and wrote down the name of each bottle. Taking great care not to smudge existing fingerprints, Erica opened each one to count the number of pills left. Then, Erica took one pill or a sample of powder from each container, put them in separate baggies, and labeled them. She'd send them to David and have his police chief run them through the lab if the Florence police detectives proved cantankerous and refused to share information.

Last, Erica examined the nightstands. One held books and several magazines. On the other was a pile of papers topped with a saucer with several green stems and a chocolate-covered strawberry that had shriveled. There was no way Erica could take a sample of the berry. A fresh cut would be readily noticeable and could lead to unwanted animosity between her and the local police. Above all, Erica wanted a smooth, working relationship. That was the best way to unmask the killer.

Gingerly, Erica pulled out the papers under the saucer and skimmed the pages. It was a business plan for Orion Parasailing. It seemed odd that there was no name, address, or phone number attached, but whoever had written it had been very thorough. It included a marketing plan, analyses of economic trends and local competition, projected labor and advertising costs, and projected sales and revenue. It must have come from someone Grandma knew well. Briefly, Erica wondered if the business plan could have anything to do with Blanche's murder.

* * *

Early that evening, when Erica felt a tightening of sadness in her chest, she slipped outside. Bandit was excited to have company and pranced about like a carousel horse as they crossed the silken lawn to the back of the yard. Erica went to a stone bench nestled under a dogwood tree that grew near a narrow creek. Nearby, a late-flowering rosebush laden with pink roses smelled like heaven. Erica pulled on a pair of gloves and patted Bandit. Grief overwhelmed her, and impulsively, she wrapped her arms around the dog, her hot tears falling on his black fur. When Bandit pulled free, Erica looked up to see him galloping across the lawn to Shaun, who came to sit beside her.

She wiped her face as Bandit playfully pushed at Shaun's hand with his snout.

"Why are people afraid to show emotion?" Shaun asked—a gentle comment that told Erica he had noticed her removing traces of her tears.

She had no answer.

As Shaun scratched Bandit behind the ears, Erica said, with a slight unsteadiness in her voice, "Dogs can be very comforting. Research shows petting dogs can actually lower your blood pressure."

"I've heard that. I tried to tell Mom, but she didn't buy it. I think she was afraid Bandit would worm his way into her heart if she softened at all." Shaun wore a slight smile. "Did you notice Mom wouldn't ever call Bandit by his name? It was always, 'that dog,'—'Get *that dog* away from me,' or 'The gardener told me *that dog* was digging in the garden.'"

Erica laughed. "Say, next time you come to Utah, bring Bandit. David and I have an acre lot."

"Didn't you tell me your parents gave you and your brothers each an acre from their farm?" When she nodded, Shaun added, "So David married you for your land, eh?"

Erica smiled. "That and my menagerie."

"What's the latest count?"

"Let's see—currently we have two dogs, two cats, a rat, tropical fish, and two hamsters. Oh, and a parakeet, which is currently on loan to Ryan's classroom. I'm trying to talk David into getting a parrot, but he says we have enough pets." She put on a look of incredulity. "Can you believe it?"

"There's no pleasing some people. By the way, how's that strange little dachshund of yours?"

"Snickers? She's as neurotic as ever."

He laughed. "I remember you telling me about her anxiety disorder when you were in Florida, working on that murder case. Is she still sneaking around and stealing your shoes at night?"

"Yep. Even now, when I'm home, she'll go into my closet after I've gone to bed, snatch a shoe or two, and put it in her bed. Snickers ends up with a huge pile and burrows under them at night to sleep."

A plane droned overhead, and Erica looked up to see the silver glint in the blue sky. "Do you think Grandma is looking down on us?"

"If she is, I bet she's plenty mad and shaking her fist at whoever poisoned her." Shaun shook his head. "I still can't get my head around the idea that someone killed her."

"I can't either. Did you know Grandma wanted to hire me to investigate Sun Coast?"

Shaun's head whipped around. "You're kidding."

"Even though Grandma's gone, I'd still like to find out what was going on. And I'm also going to find out who poisoned her." Shaun leaned forward, resting his forearms on his thighs. Erica went on. "I bet Grandma had an awesome reunion with Grandpa Lawrence and your dad."

"I wish I'd known my dad." Shaun's voice was matter-of-fact but subdued.

Erica picked up a twig and began breaking it in pieces and tossing the bits into the slow-moving water. "Someday, you'll be with him and Grandma and Grandpa."

"I know, but I miss them now." They sat companionably, listening to the calming sound of rippling water. "It's amazing that Martha seemed to know Grandma had been murdered."

"And nobody listened." Erica threw the last of her twig in the water. "By the way, how are things going at Sun Coast?"

"Don't ask," Shaun groaned. "Trent is still furious that I've taken over his position. It's like working with a wounded bear." Shaun threw a stick for Bandit to chase. "I don't know what Mom was thinking. I'll never be half the leader Trent is."

"Sure you will. Grandma had great expectations for you."

"Which she never let me forget. Mom was always trying to force me to become someone I'm not. Being chairman is bad enough, but how am I supposed to be CEO as well?" His face was drawn and haggard, showing the strain he was under. "It would be different if Sun Coast was a single store, but there are five of them, plus the Internet division and two other companies. I feel a lot of pressure when I think about all the employees who'll be out of work if I foul up."

"You're not going to mess up. Grandma knew you'd do a good job."

"Mom didn't see me for who I am. She was always after me to change—to be more aggressive, more forceful."

"I think Grandma just wanted you to live up to your potential. It doesn't matter if you're quiet and reserved, as long as you have confidence in yourself."

"Says my beautiful, outgoing cousin who has tons of self-confidence."

"I used to be shy," Erica admitted. "Then in junior high, a friend told me that how I looked and how I acted were two totally different things. I didn't know what she meant. Then she told me that I needed to act as confident and beautiful on the inside as I looked on the outside." Erica blushed. "I don't know about the outside part, but I started working on the *inside* part. I prayed a lot, took classes on self-esteem, read books and articles in the *New Era* and *Ensign*. Eventually I began feeling better about myself—more confident. If I can do it, you can. I'll give you titles of some good books to read."

"Thanks." He looked at her. "I think it helped that you had parents who loved you."

"I've been blessed that way," Erica agreed. "But your parents loved you too."

Shaun shot her a sidelong glance. "I know Blanche and Lawrence did, although it was weird growing up, knowing Mom and Dad were actually my grandparents."

"I've always wondered why they adopted you when they had already been named as your guardians."

"Mom said she didn't want to be hassled by people thinking she was 'just' my grandma and that she didn't have the final say in important decisions—whether it was at school or the doctor's office, or whatever."

Erica went back and said, "I know you were too little to know your father, but did you ever find out why your mother left?"

Shaun looked as vulnerable as a boy with his crestfallen face. "All I know is that Tammy was hooked on drugs." He shrugged as if it didn't matter. "But it's all right. I've got enough problems right now without thinking about my past."

"I'm sure things will work out at Sun Coast."

Shaun scoffed. "And how do you know that?"

"Because I've been praying for you."

* * *

Early the next morning, Erica went to Walter Hancock's office. She wanted to tell him about the autopsy results in person. In the garage, she wiped down the Camry's steering wheel and seats with moist towelettes and sealed them in a ziplock bag, which she put in her purse to discard later. Then she drove to the lawyer's office.

When Erica opened the door, Walter turned from the bookshelf, and on impulse, she threw her arms around his spare frame. Walter patted her back gently, and then Erica took a seat beside his desk. Everything was neatly sorted into various holders. No need for her to straighten anything here.

"I believe I know why you came," Walter intoned solemnly, sitting behind his desk. "I talked with Trent this morning, but please give me the details." When she was done, Walter asked a bit wistfully, "Is there any chance the poisoning could have been an accident?"

"I'm afraid not."

He grimaced. "It's difficult to take it all in. And it turns out that Martha was right—as usual."

"We all misjudged her." Erica sighed then switched gears. "The morning before she died, Grandma asked me to investigate Sun Coast. She was worried about something but didn't give me any details. Do you know what was bothering her?"

"I wish I did. I knew Blanche had been troubled about the company for quite some time, and although she usually confided in me, she didn't this time. I regret now that I didn't pursue it."

"Well, I'm going to pursue it. David and I both know Grandma would want us to find her murderer."

"I have no doubts about that." Walter picked up a folder but hardly seemed aware of doing so. "Blanche was never vindictive but did think people ought to be held accountable. She would definitely want her murderer brought to justice. Do you really think her murder is connected to Sun Coast?"

"It's a good possibility." Erica crossed her legs. "But Martha thought Grandma was killed because of the changes she'd made in her will. Did anyone else know about them before the reading of the will?"

"As far as I know—I was the only one."

"All right. Like most of the family, I was a little surprised at the lopsided will. Pamela said it seemed out of character, and I agree. The only thing I can figure is that there was some special reason behind it. Was there?"

Walter set the folder down, laced his bony fingers together, and put his elbows on the desk. "I'm not at liberty to reveal Blanche's thought processes."

"Even if it might help me find out who murdered her?"

A closed look dropped over the lawyer's face. Erica knew his unwavering loyalty to Blanche made him reluctant to share information. "I don't believe that's the case here," he said finally. "Blanche did change her will after she came across a particular piece of information, but since that's not relevant to her murder, it isn't something I can discuss."

"Trent was acting CEO. Why did Grandma drop him and put Shaun in his place?"

There was a flash of uneasiness in Walter's eyes. "Blanche had her own ideas and kept her own counsel." The doors had closed, and Walter Hancock was again the reticent lawyer.

"Grandma was going to tell me more about what was going on at Sun Coast but died before she could," Erica reminded him. "If she trusted me that much, I think you can."

Walter's bushy eyebrows came together as he gave her a judicious, appraising look. "You're right. If Blanche was going to hire you, then there's no reason not to tell you what I know in regards to the company. Unfortunately, that's precious little. Blanche wanted to have someone replace Trent as CEO. For a time, she considered Carlos Morales, who has always done an excellent job. However, Blanche always thought of Sun Coast as a family business and tried to place family members in leadership positions. Then she decided to have Shaun take over." Walter hesitated, as if debating on how much to confide. "I had the feeling Blanche suspected something was going on at Sun Coast, but she wouldn't tell me what it was or who was doing it."

"Something illegal?"

"I don't know."

Erica sighed. "Do you know of anyone who might have a grudge against Grandma?"

"I've given it some thought but can't think of anyone. Now, if it was Lawrence, it would be a different story. He had a number of enemies, but Blanche was more diplomatic and not as harsh."

"All right." Erica pulled out her notepad. "I need to know more about the hierarchy at Sun Coast. Can you explain that to me?"

Walter shifted in his chair, apparently settling in for a long explanation. "The structure changed when Sun Coast acquired Aspen

Clothing and Manufacturing and Panda Motor Sports. After those two buy-outs, I filed IPO papers with the Securities and Exchange Commission so stock could be sold on Wall Street. Four months later, Sun Coast went public, becoming a stock-based corporation with a general voting membership."

"I understand."

"The board used to consist solely of family members until Sun Coast became a stock corporation. After the acquisition of Aspen and Panda, the owners of those two companies became board members, along with other selected executives. That's when Blanche became a true chairman of the board. Since she owned the company and the majority of the stock, Blanche negotiated a deal so every family member working for Sun Coast automatically became a member of the board."

"Such as Shaun and Trent?"

"And now Kristen. I'm also a member, as is Carlos Morales."

"I see. Were you surprised when Grandma told you she was naming Shaun as the new chairman?"

"I was." Walter's long face was grim.

"You don't approve."

"I tried to talk Blanche out of it."

"You don't think he can do the job?"

"I like Shaun, but I don't believe he has the leadership qualities needed to run a company as large as Sun Coast. Currently, there are three stores in Oregon, from Newport down to Coos Bay, and they've expanded into California at Bolsa Chica State Beach and Santa Monica. The acquisition of Aspen and Panda Motors has been highly advantageous but has added layers of complexity to the company." Walter rested his elbows on the desk. "Shaun has been an executive vice president, but he's not ready to be CEO. He's too timid, for one thing. The CEO needs to be forceful and dynamic—someone with leadership skills to keep the company moving forward."

"Someone like Trent?"

"Exactly. Trent is a natural leader. He's energetic, efficient, and dedicated. He's the most dedicated employee Sun Coast has. Trent is also skilled at monitoring and capitalizing on new trends."

"He sounds perfect for the job."

Walter hesitated. "In many ways he is. Trent's taken after his father, who was the most extraordinarily successful businessman I've ever known. But Trent does have a few weak spots. He can be a little too forceful and heavy-handed."

"Grandma picked Shaun for a reason. Maybe all Shaun needs is a little more experience and a good dose of confidence. He's certainly smart enough."

"Agreed, but it doesn't make sense to put Sun Coast at risk while Shaun takes time to learn more about the company and develop confidence." Walter looked disapproving. "Besides, there's no guarantee that he *will* develop those qualities. Oh, I agree that Shaun is intelligent and somewhat capable, but too often I've seen him hang back during meetings when he should have been speaking up. That's simply not acceptable for a CEO. Of course, Trent does tend to shoot down other's opinions, but I have doubts about Shaun's ability to come out of his shell enough to handle his new responsibilities."

It was depressing to know Walter had such misgivings. Erica had hoped that he would fully support Shaun, but apparently, Walter had much more confidence in Trent. When Erica's cell phone rang, she glanced at it.

"It's Kristen. Do you mind if I take it?"

"Go ahead."

After listening, Erica replied briskly. "It's all right, Kristen. I knew they'd come sometime. I can be there in ten minutes." She stood. "I need to get home. The police called and are on their way to the house."

Chapter Six

When Erica came in through the garage, Kristen hurried over. "I called you at the barrister's office because the guards, ah, the police"—Kristen shot a sidelong glance at the uniformed officers standing in the foyer—"wanted to speak to everyone who was here the night Grandma died." Kristen was flustered—unlike her usual confident self. She added, "I called Shaun, and he's on his way."

They walked over to a detective who was in his early fifties and had a neatly trimmed goatee. "Erica," Kristen said, "this is Detective Vince McGuire."

Detective McGuire took off his hat to reveal short brown hair mixed with gray. Erica liked his firm handshake and intelligent brown eyes.

"Thanks for coming," he said then nodded toward three men who were standing by the dining room table. "If it's all right with you, they'll go over the house while I take statements. Is there someone who could show them around?"

Vicki stood in the doorway to the dining room, her round face pink with nervous excitement. When Erica beckoned, the small woman bustled over.

"Vicki, would you show these men around the house?"

"Sure." Vicki nodded her head in a determined fashion.

"If you don't mind," the detective said, "we'd also like to take fingerprints while we're here."

Vicki's eyes went wide. "I thought you only did that if you were arresting someone."

"That's correct, ma'am." He shrugged his shoulders lightly in his dark blue uniform. "However, we're hoping it might speed up the investigation. If anyone objects to being fingerprinted, that's no problem."

Erica pointed toward the small table next to the kitchen. "They can use that table."

After Vicki led the men away, Pamela came in and handed Detective McGuire a paper. She explained to Erica, "He asked for a list of family members and their addresses and phone numbers."

When Shaun came through the front door, introductions were made. Then Detective McGuire told him, "If you don't mind, I'll take your statement first." They went to Blanche's office, and when Shaun came out, Pamela went in. Then it was Erica's turn.

Detective McGuire sat in a chair by a small round table. As Erica took the chair across from him, he said, "I'm sorry for your loss. It must have been a great shock." Unexpected tears stung her eyes.

Would the pain ever lessen?

"Did your grandmother receive any threatening phone calls?" The detective began. When Erica shook her head, he asked, "Have there been any recent quarrels or bad feelings between Mrs. Coleman and anyone in the family?"

"Not that I know of."

"I understand one family member thought Blanche had been murdered." He consulted his notepad. "Martha Bessinger, Blanche's youngest daughter." His dark eyes watched Erica intently.

"No one took her seriously—it seemed so unbelievable. Part of that is because of the way Martha is—she's a little . . . different. Childlike. She blurts out the first thing that comes to her mind."

"Why did Martha think her mother had been murdered?"

"Because of the autopsy. Martha thought the only time an autopsy was done was when someone was murdered. Also, Grandma told Martha that something was going on at Sun Coast and that she was going to change her will." Erica shrugged lightly. "So Martha jumped to the conclusion that someone killed her."

"I see. Did anything unusual happen the day before Blanche died?"

"Grandma said she was worried about something at Sun Coast and that she wanted to hire me to investigate."

"I understand you're a private detective. Did Blanche say what she was worried about?"

"We didn't have a chance to talk much, but Grandma did say she was going to make a change at Sun Coast and asked me to support Shaun. She also said something about her will."

Now was probably as good a time as any to tell Detective McGuire. He seemed like a good guy, and Erica hoped for the best. "Even though Grandma didn't tell exactly what she wanted me to investigate, I'm going to look into things at Sun Coast and investigate her murder."

The detective's lips tightened. "I understand your concern, but rest assured we'll do everything we can to find the person responsible for your grandmother's death."

"I'd like to help in any way I can with your investigation."

"I'd appreciate that," Detective McGuire said evenly, giving her a measured look. "And I'd be grateful for any help you can give us. However, we handle most investigations ourselves. There can be problems if we involve civilians, and you don't want that, I'm sure."

"Of course not. And I should have explained that I was a police officer for several years, so I know enough not to interfere with your investigation. In addition to my police training, I've had eleven years of experience as a private investigator." Erica kept her tone pleasant and matter-of-fact. "Since my grandmother wanted me to investigate, I plan to do that. I hope we can work together."

Detective McGuire was an astute officer and picked up on the slight challenge in her words. "And if not, you're going to proceed on your own."

Erica nodded slightly, keeping her expression agreeable but firm.

"You're not going to have an easy time—it'll be hard for you to investigate family members."

When Erica agreed this was so, the detective rubbed his goatee and studied her—as if taking measure. Finally, he said levelly, "We'll see how it goes, but I think we'll be able to work together."

* * *

After Detective McGuire left, Erica figured it was time to let Pamela and Kristen know that Blanche had wanted to hire her to investigate.

They were in the family room, and the green draperies were pulled aside, letting in the fall sunshine. With her voice full of suspicion, Pamela asked, "Investigate what?"

"Sun Coast. Grandma said something was wrong, although she didn't know exactly what."

"What does that matter now that she's gone?" Pamela wore a look of incomprehension.

"It matters to me," Erica said softly. "Grandma asked me to do this for her, and I'd like to follow through. I'm also going to investigate her death."

There was a stunned silence. Then Kristen asked, "Won't the guards do that?"

"They will, but I'm also going to look into it."

"Does David know about this?" Pamela's voice was unusually shrill.

Erica looked at her curiously. "Yes, and he's been very supportive." She looked around at the others. "Shaun and Kristen, did either of you talk to Grandma after she went to bed that night?"

"I did," Shaun spoke up. "She was sitting in bed, reading."

"Okay." Erica turned to Kristen, whose room was next to Blanche's. "Did you hear anything from Grandma's room that night?" Was that a flicker of something that played across Kristen's face?

It was hard to tell, because Kristen didn't look Erica in the eye before saying, "No."

Then Erica asked her, "What were you doing in Grandma's bedroom the next morning?"

A dull flush dusted Kristen's cheeks. "I take the newspaper up to her every morning." As anger flared, her English accent became more pronounced than usual. "I can't believe you're asking us these questions. Do you really think one of us killed Grandma?"

As much as Erica prayed that was not the case, it was a possibility she could not rule out.

* * *

Trent called the next morning. "Are we were still going to Haceta Beach tonight? My kids have been asking."

"Sure," Erica said. "Pamela, Kristen, and Shaun are coming too."

This was met with no great shouts of approval, but then, things had been chilly between Trent and Shaun since the reading of the will. Trent said, "All right, we'll meet you there at five."

Late that afternoon, Shaun shook his head as Erica wiped down the seats of his Ford Expedition before getting in. "Let me guess, in a previous life you were a car detailer."

"How did you guess?" Erica said with a smile.

Ten minutes later they rounded a curve, and the Haceta Head Lighthouse came into view—a dazzling white tower against a backdrop of Sitka spruce and shore pines. Although banks of dark clouds hung low in the west, the sky above the lighthouse was blue and clear.

When they pulled into the small parking lot, Trent and Carrie were just getting out of their Cadillac Escalade. Their two children—twelve-year-old Courtney and nine-year-old Chad—gathered their gear and headed off. Twenty yards away, a six-foot-wide strip of fist-sized gray rocks marked the beginning of the sandy beach. Over Pamela's objections, Shaun swept her up and carried her across.

"I could have made it," Pamela tried to sound gruff. "I *have* a cane. Now you'll have a hernia."

"And you *won't* have a sprained ankle." Shaun laughed, his brown hair shining in the late afternoon sun.

Laden with sling chairs and coolers, Kristen and Carrie picked their way across the rocks. With his usual take-charge attitude, Trent directed others on how and where to set up the shade tent and portable grill. The children flitted to and fro like giddy butterflies, and with a huge smile, Kristen grabbed Shaun's hand. "Come on—let's get the kids!"

Chad and Courtney shrieked in delight as Kristen and Shaun bounded after them. As they raced along the waterline, plovers and sandpipers scattered in a great gray, brown, and white cloud, screeching their disapproval of the human interlopers. When Shaun tackled Chad, Courtney leaped on top of Shaun's back, clinging like a monkey. Kristen's clear laughter rang like chimes over the beach. Erica was tempted to run after them and join in the fun, but right now, she felt positively lazy—and reveled in the feeling.

Trent opened a cooler and handed out drinks. The sun was hot, but the breeze from the ocean was cool and refreshing. To their right, the slender lighthouse stood like a white stony pillar on its rocky cliff overhanging the sea. Dark clouds hung low in the western horizon.

Pointing them out, Erica asked, "Do you think we're going to get rained on later?"

"Nah, we'll be fine." Trent was always sure.

It had taken some persuasion to convince Pamela to come, but Erica was glad she had persevered when she noticed her mother-in-law gazing so contently at the brilliant blue ocean rolling toward them with a gentle swell. Kristen and Shaun continued to frolic on the beach with the children.

"Since Erica is going to stay in Florence for a while," Pamela said to Carrie and Trent, "I thought I would too."

"I heard Erica's sticking around so she can try and pin Grandma's murder on one of us," Carrie said, a venomous tone in her voice.

It was an outrageous statement, even for Carrie, and Pamela gasped. Seeing her mother-in-law's face suddenly turn anxious, Erica fought the urge to strangle Carrie. Too bad she hadn't brought duct tape or she would have used it to tape Carrie's mouth shut.

"Carrie!" Trent's voice was as thunderous as his face.

"What? Don't tell me that either of you are thrilled to know Erica thinks you're capable of killing someone." Carrie spoke to Erica. "It just seems odd you'd suspect one of us when Grandma was poisoned by some crackpot—someone who worked at Sun Coast or somebody that hated her."

Erica pressed her lips together. She'd promised Pamela a peaceful evening, and now drama-queen Carrie was doing her best to ruin it. "I have to conduct a *full* investigation," Erica said, hoping that would end it. But *noooooo*—Carrie wasn't about to give up.

"I don't know why you think you can do better than the entire Florence police department," Carrie said scornfully. "They came to our house and asked a lot of questions, including how much we benefitted from Blanche's death. But then, all of us benefited, including you," Carrie added cattily. "But the person who gained the most is Shaun."

That was true and something Erica knew she should never lose sight of, but she hated hearing the way it rolled off Carrie's sharp tongue. Erica looked off to where Shaun, Kristen, Courtney, and Chad knelt with a few other children, examining a collection of flotsam thrown up by the ocean. Farther out, the sun reflected off the ruffled water in quicksilver flashes. So much for a relaxing evening. Since the damage had already been done, Erica decided to ask a few questions.

"Grandma said there were a lot of things she needed to keep an eye on at Sun Coast. Do either of you know why?"

Startled, Trent shot back, "Sun Coast is a big company. There's always a lot going on."

"Grandma wasn't exactly the strong, silent type," Carrie said. "If there had really been a problem, you can bet she'd let you know about it."

That was true. Erica studied Carrie, remembering how Blanche had once confessed to Erica that she sometimes thought of Trent's petite wife as Carrie the Cat—all pretty and fluffy on the outside but dangerous with sharp teeth and nails. It occurred to Erica that Carrie was the type of person who showed only what she wanted you to see. There was a squawk, and a pair of great, gawky cormorants rose from the hillside into the air and lumbered away into the sun.

"I wish you wouldn't get involved in this, Erica," Pamela said, looking upset. "Let the police handle it. I have nightmares about you being a private investigator. Look at Columbo. He always has people shooting at him."

Everyone laughed, breaking the tension.

"Don't tell me you watch *Columbo* reruns," Trent said with a grin.

"I enjoy them, yes." Pamela sounded a little huffy.

Smiling, Trent stood and stretched. "Hey, if anyone wants to take a tour of the lighthouse, you'd better do it now before it closes. The kids told me they didn't want to go, and I'm going to pass too. I'll cook the chicken while you guys are gone."

Pamela looked at Chad and Courtney, who were splashing along the shoreline. "I'd never make it up that trail, but I can help keep an eye on the kids if the rest of you want to go."

With a shrug of her slender shoulders, Carrie said, "The lighthouse is boring, but I guess I could use the exercise hiking up the trail."

After Shaun and Kristen toweled off, the group started up the gravel-packed path. Erica breathed deeply, enjoying the scent of pine needles mixed with the briny tang of the glittering blue ocean on their left. Partway up was a large house painted a brilliant white that had once served as the light keeper's house and which was now a bed and breakfast. A gull perched on the shining red roof, its head tucked under its wing. A veranda ran the full length of the house, and the green expanse of lawn was bordered by a white picket fence.

Just before the lighthouse were two white storage buildings with red roofs. The door to one was open, and the visitors stepped inside, where it smelled of salt air, sawdust, and oil. On the walls was a collection of pictures that told the story of the lighthouse.

Going on, they reached the red-roofed lighthouse. Attached to its base was a small room with four boarded-over windows. A number of people milled about, waiting for the next tour. Carrie and Kristen wandered over to the railing to look out over the ocean and cove below. A pair of puffins flew by, and Erica delightedly pointed them out as she and Shaun sat on one of the cement benches.

"How are things going with your new position at Sun Coast?"

"Not good." Shaun hung his head.

"Has Trent been helping you?"

"Are you kidding?" Raising his head, Shaun gave a bitter smile. "All my dear cousin does is stalk the halls in his suit, waiting for me to fall on my face. And he won't have long to wait. The whole thing is a joke." He shook his head. "I don't understand why Mom did this. She knew I was no good at upper management. Trent's the one who should have been named the chairman or CEO."

"Grandma wouldn't have named you chairman if she didn't think you could do the job."

"What if she made a big mistake?" Shaun's voice was low.

How could he think that? If only Shaun could see the many top-notch qualities he had. And Blanche was nobody's fool—she knew how to hire talent and how to get the best she could out of people.

"Grandma's not the sentimental kind. She wanted the best person for the job, and she picked you." Erica punched Shaun playfully on the shoulder. "You've got to believe in yourself a little more. This new position will take some getting used to, but you can do it."

"I'm not even sure what I'm supposed to be doing. Everyone I work with is proficient and knowledgeable—they know how to run programs, extract data, and a million things I don't."

"Oh, Shaun." Erica's voice was full of sympathy.

Shaun seemed to shake himself. "Enough of that." A smile flashed across his face—one that was so charming, Erica could see why Kristen was attracted to him. "I didn't mean to be so gloomy. I am trying. I talked to some of the other executives, and they've agreed to take on extra responsibilities until I can get my feet under me. I've told them they'll be compensated. I've also asked Carlos for help, and he's set up all kinds of training sessions."

"I know you're staying up late every night, reading and studying."

"Yeah, Carlos has given me a lot of stuff to study, and I've also been reading some of those books on self-esteem you told me about."

Before Erica could comment, the guide, a thin, gray-haired woman with glasses, announced the last tour of the day was starting and herded them into the base of the lighthouse. The interior was cool and pleasant and smelled of wax, soap, and paint—a mixture of clean odors that told of ceaseless attention and care.

The guide pushed back the glasses on her nose and began her rehearsed spiel. "Construction on Haceta Head Lighthouse began in 1892. Laborers were paid two dollars a day and worked ten-hour shifts. The lighthouse remained isolated until Route 101, the Pacific Coast Highway, was built. Anyone want to guess how tall the lighthouse is?" No one did, so she went on. "The lighthouse is fifty-six feet tall. Electricity was hooked up in 1934, and the light was automated in 1963."

They climbed the iron steps of the spiral staircase past the service room where the lighthouse keeper stored his supplies and on to where the great light was housed. Erica pulled out a wipe from her pocket and, while cleaning her hands, stared in awe at the lantern—a huge polished machine—as the prisms and lens slowly revolved.

"Haceta Head Lighthouse has a first-order Fresnel lens and flashes white once every ten seconds," the guide said. "It's the strongest light on the Oregon Coast and can be seen twenty-one miles away." A couple of brown pelicans flew by the windows, causing some of the tourists to chatter excitedly. The guide went over to the windows. "We get a lot of birds up here. Also, sometimes you can catch a glimpse of a migrating gray whale. They come quite close to shore in spring."

The guide went back to the light as the tourists watched the lens circle round with a brilliance brighter than sunlight. "Years ago, the lens rotated by a weight lowered on a cable, similar to a grandfather clock. The lighthouse keeper would periodically rewind the weight, but a motor was installed once electricity was hooked up."

Their footsteps echoed on the metal stairs as the tour group filed downstairs, winding past the curving red brick walls. Erica offered her wipes to Shaun, Carrie, and Kristen.

"What's up with the wipes?" Carrie asked. "You already used one when we were in the lighthouse."

"But we used the handrails coming down," Erica explained. "And they have a lot of germs."

They returned to the beach, where Trent had the chicken ready. From the ice chest, Kristen pulled out the Carrot Raisin Salad[3] that Erica had made. Pamela set out the scalloped potatoes and baked beans that had been kept hot in a second chest. Meanwhile, Erica made sure the paper plates were two inches from the edge of the table.

---

3   See the appendix for this recipe.

Everyone was ravenous and ate quickly. Kristen gave Erica an engaging smile as she took a bite of the carrot salad. "This salad of yours is terrific."

"Thanks. It's my mom's recipe. I've always loved it."

Chad and Courtney finished first, and Pamela gave them a bag of bread to take to the beach for the birds. They were met by a screaming committee of seagulls that wheeled and dove at the crumbs like bombers. Later, Erica and Trent tossed a beach ball with the children until Chad and Courtney lost interest and went after Kristen and Shaun, who were walking along the beach. At times, the four of them would crouch to investigate shells partially buried in the sand.

Pamela joined Erica and Trent, surprising them by how well she managed with her cane while slogging through the loose sand.

"I do have some good days, dear-heart," Pamela said when she noticed Erica watching her. After a while, Pamela returned to sit with Carrie. Most everyone else on the beach had left, alarmed perhaps by the dark clouds that hovered at the horizon and were now ablaze with orange from the setting sun. Trent removed his shoes and socks and turned up his pant legs so he could walk in the shallow water. Erica slipped off her sandals and carried them.

It was peaceful there in the sun-washed air when Trent said, "It's too bad life can't be all like this." He threw out a hand to indicate the sandy beach, ocean waves, and children playing. A pair of seagulls coasted by, hoping for a handout. "Tonight's been a nice break, but I'm worried about Sun Coast." When Erica threw him a questioning look, Trent went on. "Shaun has never been a standout at his position as executive vice president, and now he's supposed to be CEO *and* chairman?" Trent's eyes were like dark, hard marbles. "Shaun can't handle one position, let alone two."

"I don't know much about his duties, but I bet if you give him a little time, Shaun will learn what he needs to do. Walter's going to help him, and Carlos is doing a lot. Shaun also said some of the executives are going to take on more responsibility until he gets the hang of things."

"They won't do that for nothing."

"Shaun said he was going to compensate them."

"Oh, that's just great." Trent threw up his hands in disgust, frightening a pair of low-flying seagulls who were wheeling over the water. Their wings flashed white in the sun as they veered away. "This is exactly what

I'm talking about. Sun Coast can't afford Shaun handing out money left and right. And it wouldn't have been necessary if I'd been appointed CEO." A wave rushed up and splashed their legs as Trent went on, looking worried.

"We're going to lose tons of business because of Shaun. Just this afternoon I was on the phone with a rep from one of our biggest suppliers. I've been working on a deal with them for months, but when he found out I was no longer CEO, he didn't want to talk with me anymore. Months of work—gone—just like that." Suddenly, Trent kicked the remnants of a sandcastle, sending sand flying.

"I'm sorry," Erica said sincerely. It was obvious Trent cared deeply about Sun Coast and was frustrated to think the business was going to suffer.

If only he would give Shaun some slack—let him learn and grow into his position.

The tide was coming in, and as they strolled along, waves curled and rolled onto the shore, one after the other.

"I've got a list a mile long of all the improvements I've made at Sun Coast. We've exceeded our sales goals every year since I took over as acting CEO, and despite the stagnant economy, business is up 6 percent. At the very least I should have been made chief operating officer, but Carlos got that position." Trent's voice was low and furious.

Erica sympathized with him. "I can see where you'd be upset, being put in a lower position."

"Shaun did a number on Grandma, but I'm not going to let him ruin the family business—I've worked too hard building it up." He slammed a fist into the palm of his hand. "I've started working on a report that shows how Sun Coast has grown because of my leadership. Once it's done, I'll meet with each and every member of the board to go over it. Then I'll call for a vote. Shaun will be out as chairman, and I'll be in."

Shocked, Erica asked, "Can the board really overrule Grandma's decision?"

His answer was firm and decisive. "They will when I'm done with them."

Chapter Seven

As she returned from a walk the next morning, Erica noticed clouds thickening in the sky. The gray light gave the day a brooding quality. She unsnapped Bandit's leash, and he trotted off. In the kitchen, the tile floor glistened where Vicki had mopped it.

Vicki looked up from where she stood by the pantry. "Did you have a nice walk?"

"It wasn't just nice, it was stupendous." Erica got a drink of water. "Autumn is my favorite time of year, and the trees here are so beautiful."

"Oh, Pamela wanted me to tell you that she went to Sun Coast. A friend drove her over, and Kristen's bringing her home at lunchtime." Vicki leaned on her mop. "Could I talk to you?"

"Of course. Let's sit down."

Vicki's cheeks were pink as they sat at the nearby table. "You said if I remembered anything about Mrs. Coleman that I ought to let you know, but I'm not sure if this is important or not."

"Anything you can tell me is helpful."

The housekeeper nodded, but her eyebrows were still drawn together with worry. "Well, I remembered one day that Mrs. Coleman got a phone call. It was a couple of weeks before you and your husband came. I don't know who Mrs. Coleman was talking to, but she was really upset."

"Do you know what the call was about?"

"I was putting groceries away—not really paying attention—but Mrs. Coleman said something like, 'I can't do that. Not when it involves my own grandson.' Then Mrs. Coleman said she'd look into it and told the person not to say anything to anyone."

"Anything else?"

Vicki shook her head. "Not about that, but there was one other thing. Mrs. Coleman had a big argument the day before she died."

"Who was she arguing with?"

"Shaun." Vicki's cheeks were a deeper pink now. "I feel like a traitor. Shaun has always been so good to me—"

"You're doing the right thing by telling me. What were they arguing about?"

"I don't know. I couldn't make out any words—they were in Mrs. Coleman's office. But both of them sounded really angry."

"Thank you, Vicki. If you remember anything else, please let me know."

* * *

Wielding her rolling pin, Erica deftly rolled out the dough, enjoying the pliant feel of the dough. Cooking always helped her relax and stimulated her thinking. She was replaying her conversation with Vicki in her mind when Pamela and Kristen walked in.

"What a coincidence—I was just telling Kristen what a wonderful cook you are." Pamela reached over and lifted the lid. "Hmmm, that soup smells heavenly."

Kristen came over and watched Erica slice the dough into triangles for crescent rolls. "You're making cobs?"

"I beg your pardon—"

"In England, we call those cobs." Kristen shook her head and muttered, "You Americans—"

Erica placed the last of the crescents on a cookie sheet. "The rolls are for dinner tonight, but the soup is for lunch. I was waiting to eat until you got here."

"Great." Kristen dished up three bowls, and they sat at the table. "Say, do either of you know anything about Shaun's mother?"

Erica lifted an eyebrow. "You mean his *biological* mother?"

"Good grief, you're as sensitive as he is," Kristen said, blowing on a spoonful to cool the soup. "Okay, *Tammy*. Do you know where she is now? I'd like to try and find her."

"*You'd* like to find her? Why?" Pamela was disapprovingly blunt as she stirred her soup.

"Shaun believes that she abandoned him, but maybe there were circumstances—"

Pamela broke in tartly, "Circumstances that are none of your business." Erica looked at her in surprise. It was seldom that Pamela sounded anything but good-natured. Erica could see both sides and so decided to remain silent and concentrate on eating.

"Shaun's been hurt his whole life because his mother left. It might help if he talked with her."

"You don't know that," Pamela said. "Besides, if Shaun wanted to find Tammy, he could have. It's not your place."

Kristen's gray eyes flashed. "Shaun thinks that if his own mother couldn't love him, there must be something wrong with him. He's hurting inside, but he doesn't have to. It could all get cleared up if Shaun could meet her and—"

"Shaun's old enough to know his own mind," Pamela's voice was sharp. "You shouldn't be meddling in something that's none of your concern."

"I just wondered if I could find her. There's no harm in that."

"There is, because you wouldn't stop there," Pamela said stiffly. "Look, don't try to force Shaun to open doors that aren't meant to be opened."

* * *

"Erica, this is a surprise!" Walter smiled as he came around his large cherry desk.

"I called your secretary and she said one of your appointments canceled, so I came right over."

Erica took a step toward a black leather chair, but her attention was captured by the three windows—or more precisely—the blinds. Each one slanted at various angles. She went over.

"Do you mind if I straighten these?" The lawyer gave her a look of acquiescence, and with a few twists of the wand, Erica adjusted the blinds so each set was open to the same degree. She looked at them in satisfaction as she took a seat. "They look so much better now, don't they?"

"Has Trent calmed down yet?" Walter asked. "I know the change in the will was a shock."

"He's still upset—thinks Shaun is going to run Sun Coast into the ground," Erica admitted. "In fact, last night Trent told me he's going to try and get the board to vote Shaun out as chairman. That's part of why

I came to see you. Can the board do that? Go against what Grandma stipulated?"

Walter looked astonished. "I had no idea Trent would try that. It's not uncommon for companies to vote and change leadership—all that's needed is a majority of votes. However, Blanche and Lawrence set up Sun Coast a little differently. Blanche has been the chairman ever since Lawrence passed away. I'll have to review the board directives to see if this is permissible."

Rats, that didn't sound good.

The lawyer frowned. "It's very possible Trent could convince the other board members to vote against Shaun. Trent can be persuasive and has ways and means of applying pressure."

Something in the way he spoke made Erica ask, "What do you mean by that?"

Walter brushed her question off. "I'll look into the regulations and get back with you."

A cloud must have crossed the sun, for a shadow fell across the room. "I wanted to ask a favor," Erica said. "I'm going to talk to employees at Sun Coast, but it occurred to me that you might be able to get more information because you're an insider."

There was a glint in the old lawyer's eye. "Ah, you want me to be a mole. Is that it?"

"Exactly." She gave him a sly smile. "See if you can find out anything."

"You might be better to ask Trent and Shaun—they're the ones at Sun Coast on a daily basis."

"I am going to ask Shaun."

"Not Trent?"

How could she explain the vague sense of uneasiness she felt regarding Trent—an anxiety that had started with Blanche's own words? Erica decided not to even try. "I don't think so. But you'd be perfect for the job. Your loyalty to the company is well-known. Everyone at Sun Coast respects you."

"All right. I'll do what I can, but I ought to tell you that I've already been keeping close tabs on the company—to see how Shaun is doing."

"Is that so?" Erica recalled how Walter had been less than thrilled about Shaun as chairman.

"Stop looking so worried," Walter said dryly. "I only wanted to see how Shaun was handling things. I still think Trent would have been a much better choice as CEO, but I've been hearing some good things about Shaun." Leaning back, Walter crossed his long legs.

"Really?" Erica was delighted.

"Carlos tells me Shaun's being proactive and reaching out to others for help."

"That's great." She wanted to hear more but, after glancing at the clock, decided she needed to move on. "I know you're busy, but I have one other question. I found a business plan for a parasailing business in Grandma's bedroom. Do you know anything about that?"

"Parasailing?" The lines on Walter's face deepened. "Blanche never mentioned it. What exactly *is* parasailing?"

"It's where a person is towed behind a boat while attached to a parachute. Grandma invested in other businesses from time to time, didn't she?"

"Occasionally, but she always consulted with me before making any decisions." Walter looked concerned. "Do you mind if I take a look at the plan?"

"Not at all. I made a copy because I thought the police would want it."

"I'll stop by tonight."

* * *

That evening when Walter arrived, he and Erica went to the family room. He looked over the business plan and handed it back to Erica. "It seems strange that there isn't an address or a phone number. Makes me wonder if it's legitimate."

Shaun and Kristen started to walk in then stopped when they saw Walter. "Oh, hello," Kristen said to Erica. "We didn't know you were in here with the barrister."

"Come on in," Erica invited. She looked at the pile of books and papers Shaun was carrying. "Homework?"

"You got it." Shaun stacked them on the corner table. "I've got a lot to learn; that's why I've got Mt. Everest here."

Reaching over, Walter picked out a book. "*How to Win Friends and Influence People.* That one's been around a while, but it's still very good. Oh, I see you have Stephen Covey's *The Seven Habits of Highly Effective People.* I was going to recommend that one."

Shaun eyed the books. "I've got enough reading material to last me until the next millennium. Unfortunately, reading is one thing; implementing is another."

"True, but you have to *know* before you can *implement*," Walter said. "One step at a time."

"I still don't know why Mom did this," Shaun grumbled.

"Because she was a sharp lady and a great judge of character," Kristen said, her voice bright. "She hired me, didn't she?"

"She wouldn't have put you in as CEO if she didn't believe in you," Erica reminded Shaun.

His eyes were still anxious. "But she knew I was no good at managing people. How many fights did we have about that?" He ran his hand distractedly through his hair. "There are so many others at Sun Coast who know more than I do."

Reaching over, Kristen took his hand. "Don't mind those toffs. You're just as good as they are." She made a face. "I wish Trent would support you like he did me when I started my first job. I called him all the time for advice. If it wasn't for Trent, I never would have made it."

"I'm glad he helped you. Most everyone at Sun Coast has been great." He gave a short laugh. "Yesterday Trent told me that I wasn't going to last long."

"Then prove him wrong," Walter declared. "From what I hear, you're on the right path—getting help from experienced, knowledgeable people. If you follow their advice, you'll do fine."

Looking encouraged, Shaun took a deep breath. "Actually, I've decided to act on something I read about. I'm hiring an auditing firm to go over the books."

Walter's expressive eyebrows shot up an inch. "You're going to do what?"

Shaun almost visibly wilted under the sharpness in the lawyer's voice, but he went doggedly on. "I thought it would be good to have a baseline established—a current, accurate picture of Sun Coast's current financial condition to track future changes. I've checked various accounting firms, and today I decided on one. Carlos told me how to prepare a statement of work, and once the accounting firm approves that, they'll sign a nondisclosure agreement. Then I'll have you review the documents, and we can set a date to begin."

Walter looked approving. "I'm impressed. Do you know how many times I've asked Blanche to do that and she never would?"

"See, Shaun?" Kristen smiled broadly. "You're taking charge already."

"The trouble is that I'm used to working in the background." Shaun squirmed a bit. "That's where I feel comfortable."

"Yeah, ruts are usually *very* comfortable," Kristen said. "But someone once told me the only difference between a rut and a grave are the dimensions."

Shaun laughed out loud.

Then Walter stood. "I'd better be going." When Shaun jumped up and shook his hand, Walter said kindly, "Work hard and you'll do fine."

The grateful look Shaun gave the lawyer had something endearing in it, and when Shaun spoke, there was new determination in his voice. "Thank you, sir. I'm going to give it all I've got."

* * *

Although the evening sky was slate gray, it had not yet started to rain. Erica was about to take an after-dinner stroll when the phone rang. She answered it, and a hysterical woman asked for Pamela.

"I'm sorry, Pamela isn't here. Can I take a message? My name is Erica Coleman; I'm Pamela's daughter-in-law." Erica's brow furrowed as she tried to make out the words, but the woman was sobbing and incoherent. "I'm sorry, but I'm having a hard time understanding you. Who am I speaking with? Gail? Gail Oakeson? Oh, yes—now I remember. You're Martha's stepdaughter."

The crying intensified, and Erica could hear a man's voice in the background. It sounded like he was trying to wrest the phone from Gail. After a few more seconds, he was successful.

"Pamela Coleman?" The man sounded fairly young.

"This is her daughter-in-law, Erica Coleman. Who is this?"

"Detective Simon Pocharski. I'm with the Lake Oswego police department. I understand Pamela Coleman is Martha Bessinger's sister-in-law?"

"That's right. Why? Has something happened?"

"A police officer is en route to your home and should be there shortly. I'm sorry Mrs. Oakeson called before the officer arrived."

"Why? What's going on?" Erica clung to the phone, a sick feeling of dread constricting her chest.

"It might be better to wait for the police officer. He should been there soon."

"Please, just tell me." If he didn't answer this instant, Erica would personally track him down and strangle him.

"A body was discovered in the woods. Gail Oakeson identified it as her stepmother, Martha Bessinger."

Chapter Eight

"I NEVER SHOULD HAVE LEFT." David's voice was husky and laden with regret. "How's Mom taking it?"

"Not the best. She had to take her anxiety medication, and Kristen's sitting with her now." Despite the warmth of her sweater, Erica shivered sitting in the front porch swing, where she had gone to talk to David. Solar lights lined the driveway, and as she talked, rain fell, collecting in puddles that reflected the black sky. News of Martha's murder had shaken her world, which hadn't had time to completely settle since Blanche's death. Many times Erica fell silent and wiped away her tears. Other times her voice broke, showing her deep distress. At length, their police training took over, and she and David mapped out a course of action.

"I'm glad you've got your revolver with you," David said.

"Me too. I learned my lesson when I didn't take it with me to Florida when I went to visit Wendy. It was frustrating when I needed a gun and I couldn't buy one because I was a nonresident. I've got it in a locked box in my room."

"I called Vince McGuire," Erica said. "He's the detective in Florence who's handling Grandma's case. He doesn't think Martha's murder was random—said it was too much of a coincidence for Martha to be killed shortly after saying Grandma had been murdered."

"Martha's murder does send up a lot of red flags, but let's hope they can find the murderer in Lake Oswego quickly." It was clear David hoped the murders were not connected.

Remembering how the detective had said Martha had been bludgeoned to death, Erica pulled her sweater closer and shivered. "I hope Martha's murder and Grandma's aren't related, but if they are, we're dealing with someone either very frightened or very ruthless."

By David's silence, Erica knew he agreed. "Detective McGuire also told me that Martha's house had been burglarized. The Lake Oswego police thought she might have been killed by a burglar."

"But her body was found in the woods." David sounded bemused.

"Yeah, kinda weird. Tomorrow I'm going to drive to Lake Oswego, meet Detective Pocharski, and see Gail. The poor woman was a wreck when she called."

"From what I've heard, she's always been close to Martha. I think Gail was only eight or nine when her father married Martha. She considered her a friend, so Gail always just called her Martha."

Erica then filled David in on what Vicki had told her.

"Well, that's the opposite of good. The police are going to be all over Shaun."

"I hated to tell Detective McGuire, but I can't hide anything during a murder investigation. I'm not sure Shaun is going to understand that I can't give anyone a free pass," she muttered, "which means that everyone in the family is going to hate me."

"I know it's hard, but don't forget that quote from Charles Dickens—the one you repeat so much—'Always suspect everybody.'"

* * *

By seven thirty in the morning, Erica was in the garage, wiping down the Camry's seats. It was necessary to have an early start since she'd be driving to Lake Oswego—after her appointment at Sun Coast.

The office for Sun Coast Sales and Rentals occupied the first and second floors of a modern-looking cream stucco office building on South Jetty Road, just off the Oregon Coast Highway. Last night's heavy rain had given way to light showers, and droplets fell from Erica's umbrella as she walked to the front desk.

The receptionist, Marge, was a middle-aged woman with frizzy hair who had been with the company for years. "Hello, Erica. I'm so sorry about your grandmother."

Erica tried to smile, but it came out lopsided. "Thank you. Is Carlos in? I have an appointment." After Marge checked, Erica went down the hall to find Carlos at his computer.

He jumped up, teeth flashing white against his dark skin as he clasped her hand. "It's good to see you again, Erica," Carlos said warmly. He grimaced slightly and shook his head, which had black hair touched with gray. "It was a terrible shock when Blanche passed away. She was the backbone of the company."

Erica looked around the office, her thoughts going back. "Grandma loved Sun Coast. She really threw herself into the business after Grandpa passed away."

Carlos nodded, his dark brown eyes wistful. "I thought a lot of your grandfather. Lawrence could be tough, but he was a great businessman. I learned a lot from him and Blanche."

Erica looked at Carlos fondly. Her grandmother had thought highly of this kind man. Other than Shaun, Carlos was the highest-level executive at Sun Coast. She took a seat across from him and asked, "Did you know Grandma was planning to make you the chief operating officer?"

"I had no idea." Apparently, Carlos still hadn't gotten used to the idea—surprise was evident on his face. "Blanche always liked to have family members in high positions."

It was time to fish for information. "Trent felt a little awkward taking your old position of chief marketing officer." Erica sat back and waited to see how he would respond.

A slow tide of color suffused Carlos bronze skin. "It's a high position, but since Trent was CEO, it's been rough. He feels—and rightly so—that any other position is a demotion."

Erica handed him the business plan she'd brought. "Do you know anything about this?"

He thumbed through it before handing it back. "It looks like a good plan."

"It was in Grandma's bedroom. I figured someone wanted her to invest in it. Any idea where she might have gotten it?"

Carlos hesitated, though Erica felt he was not the sort of man who hesitated often. He rubbed his chin as a motorcycle thundered by outside. "Have you asked Carrie or Trent about it?"

"Should I?"

"Trent may have mentioned something about a business his wife was interested in starting."

Erica gave a faint nod. Carlos Morales was the epitome of discretion and had given her direction without gossiping or conjecture. She would talk with Trent or Carrie the first chance she had.

"So, how are things going around here?" Carlos was sharp enough that Erica didn't have to add, "Since Shaun took over."

"So far, so good." His words were noncommittal. Carlos was a fair man but careful. When she tilted her head, he smiled, knowing Erica wanted more. "Actually, I've been pleasantly surprised. Shaun's determined to learn how things are run from the inside out, and he's talking to everyone from executives—the same ones he used to shy away from—to dock workers." Carlos's smile had more than a touch of satisfaction. "I know Shaun feels discouraged at times, but I told him that being aware of your weaknesses means you're halfway to overcoming them."

"So he's not acting like a hotshot and throwing his weight around, eh?"

Carlos laughed heartily. "There's a few around here that do, but not Shaun."

Erica couldn't help wondering if Trent was one of the few. "I'm glad you're working with him. I think if Shaun is given a little time and a few shots of confidence, he'll do a great job."

"I think so too," Carlos responded. "Shaun has always gotten along well with people, and once he learns a little more, he ought to do well." Carlos's chair creaked as he leaned back. "He has some excellent ideas about streamlining purchasing processes, but he's also cautious, which is good. I've told him it's best to move carefully and take certain precautions."

"Precautions? What kind of precautions?"

Carlos gave a wonderful imitation of a turtle retreating into its shell. "Oh, just about general business matters. It's wise to check things out and go slowly when making changes."

"Does this have anything to do with Shaun hiring an auditing firm?"

"Oh, so you know about that." Carlos Morales smiled. "Shaun read about that in one of the business magazines I gave him. I felt it was an excellent suggestion. It's a good idea for Shaun, in taking over a large company like this, to have a certified financial 'bill of health.'"

Something in Carlos's demeanor made Erica ask, "And how is Sun Coast's bill of health right now? Are there any internal problems?"

Carlos gave a little cough. "Sun Coast is in good shape, but it's always wise to have a verifiable measuring stick—a benchmark for future growth. It was a prudent move on Shaun's part."

He had neatly avoided answering her second question, so she tried again. "The reason I ask is because Grandma indicated there were problems at Sun Coast. Do you know what they could be?"

Once again, Carlos hesitated, and Erica suspected it was the hesitation of an honest man who didn't want to be dishonest. "I'm not sure what she had in mind."

Erica thanked him for his time and left. But she wondered. Was Carlos reluctant to speak because—like Blanche—he knew something was wrong but wasn't sure where the problem lay? Or did Carlos know about the problem and was trying to cover it up?

* * *

After leaving Carlos's office, Erica pushed her auburn hair behind her shoulders and went to track down Shaun. It was hard to be objective when investigating family members. On one level, Erica trusted all of them, yet as David had said, her motto had always been to trust no one. Even though she planned to ask Shaun to provide her with inside information, Erica intended to double-check everything he told her.

She found Shaun out back watching a new shipment of ATVs being unloaded. The rain had stopped, but water dripped from the roof's edge and everything shone wet—trucks, trees, and asphalt.

"I thought I'd find you in a cushy office," Erica said, "not out here on the loading dock."

Shaun's sleeves were rolled up, and he looked tanned and handsome. "I want to learn about the different departments and figured hands-on was better than someone just telling me what goes on."

"I'm sure it is. I wanted to ask you a couple of things."

Shaun led her away from the noisy dock as a forklift sped by. "Go ahead."

"I want you to do a little digging for me here at Sun Coast. I've asked Walter to find out what he can, and I'd like you to do the same."

"Do I get any cool spy devices like James Bond?"

It was good to see Shaun smile. "I'll see what I can scrape up." She glanced over at the men working nearby and lowered her voice. "Since you're going to various departments, this works out perfectly. You'll be right in the middle of things—be able to find out things I can't. Pay attention to anything that doesn't seem quite right. Will you do that?"

Shaun squared his shoulders. "Yeah, sure. If I find out anything, I'll let you know."

"One other thing. You had an argument with Grandma the day before she died. What was that about?"

"What?" Shaun looked puzzled. "I didn't argue with Mom. Who told you that?"

"Uh, I can't really tell you that."

"It was probably Trent." Shaun's voice turned cold. "You can't trust anything he says."

* * *

It was a perfect autumn day. The air was crisp and clean from the previous rain, the sky a tender blue as Erica took the scenic route north along the rugged Oregon coast. After the Haceta Head Lighthouse, Highway 101 was lined with beaches, artist communities, and temperate rain forests. An occasional fog blew in from the ocean, and mists snaked through the folds of the mountains, but fortunately the fog was thin and didn't hinder Erica's driving.

Leaving the highway at Tillamook, Erica turned inland and found a spot to eat the lunch she'd packed in a small cooler. She'd also brought soup and rolls for Gail. It was hard to eat as thoughts of Martha kept intruding.

Had a psychopath happened upon Martha in the woods? It seemed more likely that someone in the family had killed Martha. Although Erica hated the thought, Martha's death was a little too coincidental to be a random murder—especially after volunteering that she walked in the woods every afternoon. Convenient information if the killer was someone in the family.

Erica hated suspecting anyone in the family. She wouldn't have thought Shaun capable of murder, yet she knew that occasionally, shy introverts were capable of great violence when provoked. Kristen appeared friendly and outgoing, but was there something brutal and twisted beneath her sunny exterior?

Pamela was above suspicion, yet dismissing someone automatically went against Erica's training. Could Erica be sure Pamela was innocent, simply because she was her mother-in-law and unable to drive or even ride for long distances? And what of those times when Pamela *did* seem to get around—almost as if she didn't need her cane at all? There had been a few times when Pamela had seemed uneasy talking about Blanche. Did that come simply from the horror of knowing Blanche had been murdered or from something else?

Erica also did not want to suspect Walter, yet in the high stakes of business, finance, and legal matters, she was aware that illicit actions took place, possibly something Walter preferred to keep hidden. And what of Trent and Carrie the Cat? Erica was less sure of them. Even though she knew them fairly well, each one could have a hidden, dark side. Everyone knew Trent had a temper, but would he go so far as to commit murder? Carrie was a first-class whiner and loved to stir up drama, but again, it was hard to picture her as a murderer.

Unable to finish her lunch, Erica packed up and drove on. Near Lake Oswego, the clouds thickened, and the wind prowled high in the trees lining city hall's back parking lot, where the police station was located.

Inside, she was directed to the office of Captain Duane Stanbridge. The captain, a stocky man of medium height, made no effort to rise. Instead, he looked Erica up and down like a new car.

She stared back out of cool green eyes until he said gruffly, "Have a seat." Captain Stanbridge reached a hand across a desk that had an impressive number of files and papers scattered across its surface.

"Thanks for meeting with me." As she shook his hand, Erica found it hard to keep her eyes off the desk. Although it was apparently made of wood, nothing was visible except the back and side panels. The top could be leather, glass, or chrome, and no one would ever know. She wondered if the captain even remembered what the top of his desk looked like. Her hands itched to reach out and organize the debris, but she forced herself to look at the detective as he talked.

"Like I said on the phone, I don't feel I can help you. We're investigating the burglary and the murder of your aunt, and we'll let you know when we catch the killer." The captain's voice was polite, yet there was a sense of marble—cool and quiet.

She went straight to the heart of the matter. "Captain Stanbridge, you and I want the same thing—to find out who killed Martha Bessinger. I'd like to help with the investigation."

Captain Stanbridge looked at her impassively—an expression many police officers developed over time. "I'm not sure why you think you can accomplish more than trained detectives." His voice held a pinch of hostility.

"I'm not saying I can, but the more people you have working on a case, the better. I'm assisting Detective McGuire, and we're able to share information."

"If you do come up with tips or information, we'd appreciate it if you'd keep us informed."

So much for sharing. "Have you got any leads on the case?"

"It's early days yet."

"Before coming here I drove around the area where Martha lived," Erica said. "There are a lot of very nice houses a few miles away—homes where a burglar could expect a nice haul. But Martha's subdivision is fairly modest. I have to wonder why someone would target it."

With more than a touch of condescension, Detective Stanbridge replied, "Opportunity is the most common reason. Burglars cruise around looking for easy targets."

"I understand you think the burglar killed Martha. Why is that?"

"Because, Mrs. Coleman, the house was ransacked, and Martha Bessinger was found dead shortly after." Captain Stanbridge spoke as if Erica was a particularly slow learner.

"I was just wondering if you had any evidence."

"I'm not at liberty to reveal that."

In other words, there *was* no evidence.

The captain went on. "It's possible Martha was killed by someone other than the burglar."

"The person who burglarized the house has to be the same person that killed her," Erica blurted out, unable to help herself. "It would be too much of a coincidence otherwise. I mean, what are the odds of someone being randomly attacked the same afternoon her home is burglarized? The odds are astronomical."

Oops—Erica could tell she'd gone too far by the way Captain Stanbridge's face darkened. She was saved from the retort hovering on his thin lips when a man in his late twenties sprang into the room.

Choking back his response, Captain Stanbridge waved a hand toward the eager-faced man with short, fair hair. "This is Detective Simon Pocharski. I assigned him your aunt's case. Simon, this is Erica Coleman, Martha Bessinger's niece."

Simon wrung her hand enthusiastically. "I'm sorry about your aunt," he said with real sympathy. "It must be hard, coming so soon after the death of your grandmother."

Unexpected tears came to her eyes. Great. This was the last thing Erica needed—an emotional display in front of two police officers. She blinked rapidly. "Sorry about that. I never know when it's going to hit me."

Simon was understanding. "Don't worry about it. I often make people cry—usually when I'm booking them." He handed a file to Captain

Stanbridge. "Here's that information you wanted. Nice to meet you, Erica." He headed for the door.

The phone buzzed, and Captain Stanbridge set the folder on top of his garbage dump to answer it. Sitting idle, Erica could help herself no longer. Taking the closest pile of papers, she tapped them into a neat pile. Captain Stanbridge's narrowed eyes followed her every move.

"Tell him I'll call him back," he shouted into the phone and set it down with a thump. Glaring at Erica, he ground out, "What do you think you're doing?"

"Straightening a few papers. This pile could use organizing too—" Erica pointed, but Captain Stanbridge slammed one of his hands on top. His mouth had a straight, grim look.

"*Leave—my—papers—alone.*" Each word was heavily accentuated. The captain sat back and took a moment to collect himself. "Look, I know you want to help with the investigation, but we've tried collaborating with civilians before, and it doesn't work. Now, if you don't mind," he waved a hand toward the wreckage on his desk, "I have a lot of work to do."

She may have been dismissed, but Erica wasn't giving up. She'd come determined to do what she could to work with him since she believed Martha's death was tied in to her grandmother's. Erica already knew most officers didn't like working with people outside the police force, but she had to try. It was her best chance to get information that wouldn't be available any other way.

"I've been a private investigator for eleven years, so I have a lot of experience. I'm good at my job."

"I'm sure you're magnificent." Sarcasm oozed from his voice. "But you're still a civilian, and I don't want civilians involved in police business."

She took a deep cleansing breath. "I understand your reluctance. When I was a police officer, there were times when civilians interfered with investigations, but I assure you that—"

Detective Stanbridge scoffed. "Your assurances mean nothing. You're a civilian, and I don't want you involved."

Argggggghhhh.

How could she get past the prickly guard he'd put up against her? "I know enough about police work to stay out of your way, and I won't do anything to hinder your investigation. I believe I could be an asset. Working together can be a win-win situation for both of us."

"Having you stay out of this would be a win-win situation for me," he said dourly.

Erica had to struggle to keep her voice businesslike. "I'm already investigating my grandmother's murder, and it's possible her death and Martha's are connected. Surely you'd be interested in any information I might be able to provide."

"We have excellent detectives. They'll be able to uncover anything you manage to come across." The captain's voice oozed superiority. "Besides, you have a fatal bias—you're related to both victims."

Game over. It was time to stop hitting her head against the wall of the captain's mind. She stood. "If you change your mind, Captain Stanbridge, I'd be glad to work with you."

"I'll keep that in mind." Captain Stanbridge gave her a cold look. There was marble again—hard, unyielding, implacable. The good-bye in his tone was clear.

It was tempting to take the door off the hinges as she left, but the dozen uniforms scattered around were an excellent deterrent. As Erica went down the walkway between desks, she reached for her necklace and held it. She would solve this case, whether Captain Duane Stanbridge was willing to work with her or not.

Simon Pocharski's head turned as Erica approached and stopped by his desk. His face was warm and friendly. "I'm glad we had a chance to meet, Detective, since I'm going to be investigating Martha's murder as well as my grandmother's." Simon's bright eyes looked at her approvingly—salve to her soul after her experience with Captain Stanbridge—and she added, "I'm not sure if the captain told you, but I used to be a police officer. I'm a private investigator now."

"Awesome," he said, clearly impressed.

After her experience with the captain, Erica glowed at having someone react to her in a positive manner. She wondered if Simon might be able to help her. "I'm working with Detective Vince McGuire in Florence."

"I've talked with him about the case," Detective Pocharski said eagerly. "He thought there might be a connection between the two murders."

"Detective McGuire's been very cooperative about me helping with the investigation since I can provide inside information from the family. You understand that, I'm sure."

"Of course. And you'll help us here too, with your aunt's case, won't you? I mean, that's why you talked to Captain Stanbridge, wasn't it?" Simon glanced toward the captain's office.

What could she say? "Um, yes, I did talk to him about that. And the captain wants the case solved as quickly as possible." Erica put on a bright, winning smile. "I'm going over to Martha's house to talk with her stepdaughter, Gail. Would you be able to meet me there sometime today?"

She held her breath as Simon checked his calendar. He looked up with an enthusiastic grin. "I could meet you at two."

"Terrific. See you then."

Chapter Nine

TIRES CRUNCHED ON THE GRAVEL driveway as Erica pulled in beside Martha's house, which had ginger-colored bricks and paned windows lavishly covered in ivy. A gossamer curtain of fog hung in the air as Erica opened the car door, startling a cat that shot across the driveway and raced toward a shed in the back. A moment later, a woman in her midforties came out of the same shed, pushing her shoulder-length, brown hair behind her ears.

The woman brushed at her jeans and looked at Erica with friendly brown eyes. "You must be Erica Coleman."

"And you're Gail." Erica looked toward the shed. "I think I scared your cat."

Gail smiled. "It's Martha's cat, actually. She already had two house-cats, Cocoa and Nutmeg, then sort of adopted this one. It used to be wild, but Martha tamed it down—a bit too much if you ask me, because it decided to have its kittens in the shed."

"Oh! You have kittens? Can I see them?"

Three tiny bundles of orange and white fur slept in a towel-lined box in the corner. "The momma had them behind some boxes," Gail explained, "but Martha cleared everything up and moved the kittens into this box one day when the mother was gone."

"Would it be all right if I held them?"

"Sure."

Erica pulled on a pair of latex gloves and gently stroked the mother, who appeared anxious but not enough to move away. When Erica picked up a kitten, it hissed. "You don't have to be afraid," Erica cooed, holding it close. After petting it, Erica put it back and picked up another, speaking softly. "They look like they're about four weeks old."

"Around that."

Gently, Erica put the kittens back, and they curled up next to one another. The air felt wet and sharp as she and Gail went out into the drizzling rain. There was a fenced enclosure north of the shed. "You have chickens too?" Erica asked, going to the wire-fenced enclosure.

"Martha liked fresh eggs. She used to sell them too."

"Not many people have Barred Plymouth Rocks," Erica said. "I love their black and white feathers—they're the zebras of the poultry world."

"They were her favorite. Martha had names for each one, but I can't tell them apart."

"Oh, I almost forgot. I brought you some Beef Chowder[4] and rolls."

When Erica got the containers out of the cooler and handed them over, Gail's eyes grew misty. "That was very thoughtful. I haven't thought much about food lately."

"Then this soup will do you good—it's hearty and delicious."

They went into the small, cozy kitchen. Pots of African violets lined the windowsill, and a set of triangular shelves in the corner held an amazing assortment of ceramic figurines. There were more collectibles on top of the microwave. Erica peeled off her gloves and dropped them in the garbage, then Gail showed Erica into the front room, which overflowed with baskets, pots, scattered books, statues, and more figurines. Tired-looking silk flowers sagged in every conceivable type of container. Apparently, neither Martha nor Gail saw any need to torment themselves with tidiness. A calico cat was curled up in a corner on the flowered chintz couch.

"That's Nutmeg," Gail announced. Pulling on another pair of gloves, Erica sat next to the cat, gently stroking her while Gail settled into a chair.

"How are you doing, Gail?"

"Terrible." Dark circles under Gail's eyes testified to the truth of her flat statement. "I keep expecting Martha to walk in the door and tell me how the chickens enjoyed the potato peelings or to ask me to buy more fertilizer for the flowers."

"I'm sure this is very hard on you."

Gail wrung her hands together as if they were rags. "I know you came to talk about what happened to Martha, but it's too awful. I can't."

---

4   See the appendix for this recipe.

"I understand. I hope you don't mind, but I've arranged to meet Detective Pocharski here a little later." Looking haggard, Gail nodded in forlorn acquiescence as Erica searched for an undemanding subject. "I understand you work at a floral shop?"

"I'm a floral designer at Chaleh's Blossoms." Gail's face brightened a bit, and there was pride in her voice. "When I first moved here, I applied for a job although I didn't have any training, and Chaleh—that's the owner—took me on. I love working with flowers. Every day it's something new."

As they talked, the tension on Gail's face faded, and she positively glowed as she talked about her job. It was obvious she loved it. Then worry creased Gail's face as she confided that the owner, Chaleh, wanted to retire and might close the shop if she couldn't sell it. They continued talking, and as Erica expected, once Gail warmed up, she started talking about her stepmother.

"Martha had a lot of health problems, and I knew she didn't have a lot of years left, but I didn't expect her to be gone so soon and in such a terrible way." Gail shuddered.

"How long have you lived with Martha?"

"About six years. After my divorce, I needed a place to stay, and Martha took me in. We got along so well that Martha asked me to stay." Gail flushed slightly. "I know Blanche bought the house for Martha, and I hope no one in the family thinks I'm a freeloader."

"I don't think anyone has given it a second thought."

"I worked it out with Blanche—about paying rent, you see." Gail drew herself up in a dignified manner. "I've always taken care of myself and never want it said I don't pull my own weight. When I found out Blanche hired people to do the yard work for Martha, I offered to do it if she'd take a bit off the rent." Erica nodded as Gail went on. "I took Martha to her doctor's appointments, picked up her prescriptions, and did things like that." Gail looked so competent and good-tempered that Erica imagined Blanche was overjoyed to have her live with and watch over Martha.

"It seems to have worked out really well for both of you." Erica looked around. The furniture was comfortable but somewhat worn. The only thing that looked new was a large, flat screen TV.

Gail noticed her glances. "You've never been here, have you?" Then, she added, "What am I saying? No one has been here except Blanche . . .

and Randy before he passed away. Every time Blanche visited, she offered to buy new furniture, but Martha was content with what she had. She did love to watch TV though, so Blanche got her a really nice one. Martha loved watching old movies."

"Really? So do I." Erica felt a surge of connection toward Martha. "*Casablanca, Rear Window, Mr. Smith Goes to Washington, National Velvet*—"

"Oh, we've watched all of those."

Erica eyed the TV. "I'm not surprised the burglar didn't take the TV—it's so big—but why didn't he take the Blu-ray player? That could have brought in a few bucks at a pawn shop."

"I wish he would have taken it and left Martha alone," Gail said vehemently.

"Detective McGuire told me the house had been ransacked. Did the burglar take anything?"

"The only thing missing was the money Martha kept in her sock drawer—around three hundred dollars."

"So nothing else was taken? Did Blanche ever give Martha anything valuable, like jewelry, paintings, electronics—anything like that?"

"No, other than the TV and the fancy DVD player, Martha had pretty simple tastes."

Erica picked up a ceramic duck from the coffee table. "Martha liked knickknacks, didn't she?"

"Oh, yes!" Gail wore a sad little smile. "There are boxes of them in her closet—we haven't got room to display them all." She crossed her arms as if chilled. "You said you were going to stop at the police station before you came here. I don't suppose they caught the person that did it?"

"No, but they're working on it."

Gail glanced at her watch. "Oh dear, what time were you going to meet that detective?"

"At two."

"I should have said something earlier, but we got busy talking. I asked my boss if I could come in to work this afternoon." Gail's eyes were bright and anxious. "I'm sorry. I know I said I'd be here all day, but it's so hard without Martha being here. I thought it would be better to stay busy."

"When did you need to go?"

"Chaleh said I could come in whenever I wanted, but actually, I'd like to go before that policeman comes. Seeing him would just stir up horrible memories. If you don't mind, I'll give you a house key, and when you're done, you can lock up and leave the key with the neighbor."

"That'll work." Erica felt for the poor woman. "I hope my coming hasn't been too stressful."

"It's fine, really. Would you like to look at Martha's room?"

"I would." They went upstairs, and Erica swallowed hard as they went into Martha's room, which was painted cotton-candy pink. The room looked very much like Erica imagined it would—with innumerable knickknacks covering the dresser and chest of drawers. In the closet, shelves were crammed. Jostling for space with boxes, bags, and blankets, were two foam heads, one of which held a wig. On the floor were half a dozen containers that looked like tackle boxes.

"Do you mind if I look at these?" When Gail assented, Erica brought out the first box and put it on the bed. It was filled to the brim with bracelets, rings, and necklaces. "Wow, a treasure chest!"

"That's exactly how Martha thought of them." Gail sat on the bed as Erica fingered the rings, bracelets, and necklaces. "Martha bought a lot of jewelry at garage sales and liked to store it in tackle boxes because of all the dividers."

"Going to garage sales was one of Martha's passions, wasn't it?"

"Right next to gardening, cats, and chickens. I guess I'm responsible for getting her hooked on them. I started going to garage sales after my divorce. When I moved here, Martha went with me, at least until I started working on weekends. But Martha got a friend to drive her around."

"Leslie Flynn, wasn't it?" Erica asked, putting the box back. "I met her at the funeral. Could you get me her phone number?"

They went downstairs, and Gail wrote the number down. "There you go," she said, handing it over. Erica tucked the paper into her pocket then looked around.

"Detective McGuire said that when you came home from work, the door was unlocked."

"That's right. But Martha was really bad about locking up. She often left it open."

An invitation few burglars could resist, Erica thought. "I suppose the neighbors knew Martha liked to walk in the woods." Gail nodded, and Erica asked, "Did she ever talk about meeting someone during her walks?"

"Once in a while she'd tell me about someone she saw or talked with."

"Was there anyone she met there regularly?"

"No. Martha would have told me if there had been."

"All right. Detective Pocharski should be able to fill me in on the rest, but if you think of anything that might be helpful, let me know."

"I sure will." Gail put on a sweater and fished a key out of her bag for Erica. "If you have any other questions, call me. Oh dear, I almost forgot, will you let me know what the family decides about the funeral?"

"Of course. Pamela said she'd call you to discuss the services since you lived with Martha for so long. She'd like to have the funeral in Florence since Martha will be buried in the family plot. Shaun asked me to invite you to stay with us that night—we know it's a long drive."

Gail's look of gratitude was touching. "That's very kind. Yes, I'd appreciate that." She gave a little cough then said delicately, "Martha told me the change Mrs. Coleman made in her will disturbed some of the family."

Wryly, Erica thought back to the emotions unleashed during the reading of the will. "It did."

"She said Trent was especially upset." When Erica did not respond, Gail went on. "Martha said that when she said someone in the family had killed Blanche, nobody believed her."

"They do now."

* * *

When the black-and-white police car pulled up, Erica went outside on the front porch. Detective Simon Pocharski bounded out of the cruiser and over the lawn, a big smile of greeting on his face. With his lean, thin body, Simon reminded her of an eager greyhound.

As they walked inside, she asked, "So you came out when Gail called and said the house had been burglarized?"

"Yep, I was the first one here," Detective Pocharski said with a proud lift of his chin. "After I got here, Gail said she couldn't find Martha. When she told us Martha liked to walk in the woods, a search team went out and discovered the body." He lifted an eyebrow. "Now the newspapers are saying a homicidal maniac is running loose in Lake Oswego."

"They've got to say something sensational so they can sell their papers, don't they? Now, tell me what you found that day."

Simon buzzed into the front room like a happy bee, talking rapidly. "When I got here, drawers were pulled out and dumped, books were swept off the shelves, and there were papers all over the floor—like the burglar was looking for something specific."

"Yet the only thing missing was money from a single drawer?"

"He was in a hurry. Burglars like to work quick—get in, grab what they can, and get out."

"Or maybe the killer messed up the place deliberately—to make it look like a burglary." Erica spread her hands out to encompass the modest furnishings. "Look around. There's little of real value here. And why would a burglar leave a nearly new Blu-ray player behind?"

"I thought that was strange," the detective admitted. He stepped over to the window. "The burglar entered there, prying the window open. We found muddy footprints on the carpet."

"Were you able to determine a size?"

"Men's size eleven."

Erica frowned. "But the front door was unlocked. Why would a burglar force a window if the door wasn't locked?"

"He must have assumed it was. Didn't bother to check. Or else he exited that way." Simon spoke in short, energetic bursts.

"I'd like to look at the window from the outside."

Simon hurried outside with his same bee-like effect. Erica looked over the window then the lawn, tilting her head. "There were muddy footprints on the carpet?" she asked.

"That's right."

"But the lawn comes right up to the house. How did the burglar get dirt on his boots when the closest flower bed is five feet away?"

Simon's eyebrows went up as he looked at the flower bed filled with leggy purple petunias.

Bending closer to study the window, Erica ran her finger over the sill. "Look. There are lots of marks, but most are superficial. None of them are deep enough to get under the window frame."

Simon's body stiffened like a terrier catching an interesting scent. He moved in for a better look. "I see what you mean. The window couldn't have been pried open."

"It was merely shut, and the sill was splintered from outside to give the appearance of forcing."

As Simon examined the latch and sill, he swore under his breath. "You're right. Boy, I don't know how they missed that," he said scornfully. Then he looked at Erica. "But why would the burglar do that?"

"For the same reason he emptied the drawers and knocked books off the shelves—to make it look as if it was a burglary. He wanted to sidetrack us." Erica used the word "us" deliberately to put herself on the same team with Simon.

Simon nodded companionably. "He was trying to divert our attention from the murder."

"I don't think so," Erica said. "After all, Martha's body was going to be found sooner or later."

Erica looked around at the neighboring houses. The rain had stopped, and patches of blue sky showed through the clouds. "Did you get anything from talking to the neighbors?"

"Nobody saw or heard anything."

"I think I'll knock on a few doors before I go." They went around the side of the house, and Erica looked off into the woods. "And the murder weapon was never found?"

"Nope," Detective Pocharski replied cheerily.

"So the killer either hid it amazingly well or took it with him. If it was the latter, that could mean the weapon could probably be traced back to the killer."

"The weapon could have been a bat or tire iron—Martha was beaten pretty badly."

Erica winced at the thought. But she was still perplexed. "Why would a burglar break into the house, take practically nothing, then take the time to track down Martha in the woods and kill her?"

"Maybe he killed Martha first then came to the house," Simon offered.

"And force the window on a house he already knew was empty? Besides, if that was the case, the murderer would have to know Martha and where she lived." Erica thought for a moment. "I'm having a hard time connecting the burglary and the murder. Burglars rarely attack homeowners—unless surprised or threatened—and Martha wasn't even home."

A light dawned in Simon's eyes. "That's the same thing I've been asking myself."

"And why did the killer bludgeon Martha? Attacks like that are usually crimes of passion."

"There are a lot of things that don't really make sense," Simon agreed, "but we'll find out."

It was refreshing to work with a police officer who was willing to treat her as an equal and share ideas and information. They went to the backyard, which was not fenced. A well-worn path, cushioned with pine needles and leaves, led into the woods.

Erica asked, "What was the time of death?"

"Between 17:30 and 18:30. Gail arrived home at 18:20."

"Would you show me the spot in the woods where she was killed?"

Simon looked regretful. "I haven't got time today, sorry. But next time you're in town, give me a call." His eager look came back. "Maybe the captain would come with us."

Like that was going to happen. "Detective McGuire thinks the same person who killed Martha also poisoned Blanche Coleman," Erica said as they went to the front yard.

"Yeah, he thought Martha might have been killed to keep her quiet—that someone didn't want her telling people her mother had been murdered. Either that, or Martha knew something else the killer didn't want her talking about."

After Simon drove off, Erica began knocking on doors, starting with the houses that bordered on Bryant Woods. In her work at Pinnacle Investigations, one of her fortes had always been neighborhood investigations. She got little information today though. At her last stop, Mrs. Blevins, a voluble woman in her thirties, answered the door with a baby on her hip. Erica went through all of her questions then asked if Mrs. Blevins knew Martha.

"I knew her pretty well," Mrs. Blevins said, shifting the baby to the other hip as she stood in the doorway. "Martha was a sweet person but a little unusual. But then, since she was your aunt, you know what I mean. Martha had a tendency to exaggerate about everything, especially about the amazing things she bought at garage sales."

"Oh, so you knew Martha went to garage sales?"

"Everyone that lived within ten miles knew." Mrs. Blevins smiled wryly. "Martha was always finding necklaces with precious jewels or sets of books worth hundreds of dollars or solid-gold picture frames. Well, everyone knew the jewels were rhinestones, that you could get the same books on Amazon for ten bucks, and that her gold frames were brass."

"Did she ever show you stuff she bought?"

"All the time," Mrs. Blevins said somewhat wearily. "I feel terrible about it now, but sometimes I wouldn't answer the door when Martha came over. She liked to talk and talk, and I didn't always have time to see a bunch of dime-store necklaces." She sighed. "Now I wish I had."

* * *

The late September sun took the chill from the morning and shone on the baskets of pink petunias hanging on the patio, where Pamela and Erica ate a leisurely Saturday breakfast. After, Pamela took in the dishes, and Erica went over her notes. Bandit sprawled nearby on the grass.

Vicki came out holding the phone pressed against her ample bosom. "It's Detective Vince McGuire," she whispered then handed over the phone with an air of a person having done her duty.

"How did your visit go yesterday with Detective Stanbridge?"

"Thanks for warning me about the good captain." Erica's voice dripped with sarcasm.

Detective McGuire chuckled. "Well, I don't know him very well, and I didn't want to scare you by telling you what I did know."

"He acted like I was a splinter in his thumb," Erica remarked, "and one of his theories is that Martha was murdered by a burglar, but you know how likely that is." She swatted at a pesky fly. "Another theory is that Martha was killed by a murderer who just happened to be in the neighborhood while her home was being burglarized by someone else."

"Were you able to look over the crime scene?"

"Detective Simon Pocharski went over it with me." Erica explained about the window, footprints, and Blu-ray player. "Afterward, I talked to some of the neighbors. One lady said Martha liked to talk about stuff she bought at garage sales and that she exaggerated the value quite a bit."

Detective McGuire considered. "Maybe someone didn't know Martha was exaggerating and thought she had a lot of valuable stuff." He paused, "Have you asked your family about their whereabouts the afternoon Martha was killed?"

"Carrie said she took the children to a birthday party—dinner and a movie. Trent was at the Sun Coast store in Coos Bay. I called the store and confirmed he was there, but he was gone a long time. Trent says he stopped at other stores in the area—to check out the competition."

"Aha. So neither one has an iron clad alibi."

"Have you gotten the results back yet on the fingerprints?"

"There's been a holdup since they're doing an extended search. But I got the lab results from the samples we took from the house. The Portland lab rushed them."

"And?"

"Before I get to that, I wanted to ask if you were present when the decision was made to have an autopsy done." When Erica said she was, Detective McGuire asked, "Who decided to have the autopsy, and how did the rest of the family react?"

"Pamela wanted it done and asked Shaun about it. He was a hesitant at first but agreed. The rest of us didn't really care one way or another. Wait a minute. Trent was against it. Why do you ask?"

"Because traces of poison were found in two places. There was Amitriptyline in the chocolate-covered strawberries in the refrigerator and also in the strawberry in Blanche Coleman's bedroom. It stands to reason that the person who poisoned the strawberries would not want an autopsy done."

Chapter Ten

AFTER TALKING WITH DETECTIVE MCGUIRE, Erica left the patio and went inside the house. Hearing the tinkling of the piano, she went to the sitting room, where Kristen sat at the grand piano. Shaun stood behind Kristen, peering over her shoulder at the sheet music.

"I didn't know you played the piano," Erica said.

Kristen looked up and giggled. "I don't. Shaun was showing me some of the basics, like where middle C is. I'd like to take lessons someday." She ran her hands over the ivory keys. "This is such a beautiful piano, but then, everything in this house is beautiful." She rose and went over to one of the display cases as Pamela walked in.

"I love these," Kristen said in delight, peering at the figurines. "They're Armani, right?"

"That's right," Pamela said, settling in a recliner. "Blanche loved collecting them."

Kristen went to the opposite corner to look at another display case. Shaun trailed after her, saying, "Mom also collected Lalique Amber Crystal."

Kristen pointed at a vase. "I love this one—with the figures all around it."

"You've got a good eye," Shaun said. "That one is worth about $6,000, and the plate next to it with the serpentine design is around $3,500."

"Holy cow," Kristen exclaimed.

"That's why Mom had extra-strong doors installed, so she could double-lock this room," Shaun said. "She kept her collection here because it's the only room in the house without windows."

It was regrettable to throw a sour note in the peaceful atmosphere, but Erica had to speak up. "Detective McGuire called a few minutes ago."

Kristen stopped prowling the room. "Does he have anything new?"

"The lab results came back and showed that the poison was in the chocolate-covered strawberries. There was a strawberry and some stems on a saucer by Grandma's bed. But I don't remember Grandma carrying them up. Did either of you take some upstairs to Grandma?"

Frowning deeply, Kristen said, "I didn't. Do you really think I'm a chancer?"

Although Kristen's English accent was charming, Erica didn't always understand her words. "A what?"

"An opportunist. You really *do* think one of us killed her, don't you?"

Inwardly, Erica winced. It was so difficult investigating family. The usual hard questions took on a thorny and complex twist when it was family members she had to ask. "I'm only trying to find out how the strawberries got upstairs." Erica then asked Shaun. "What about you?"

"You don't really think I'd poison Mom, do you?" He sounded insulted and angry.

Erica sighed. It was such a struggle to balance her need to ask questions with the feelings of the family. "Do either of you know who bought the strawberries?"

"I didn't buy them," Shaun said coldly.

"Neither did I," Kristen replied. Then she shivered. "Imagine someone poisoning the strawberries." She wandered to the coffee table and idly picked up a statue of a boy and a puppy. "I bet Grandma took the berries up herself. She often takes a snack upstairs at night."

Erica decided to try another question. "Shaun, where were you the night Martha was killed?"

Was that a disturbed look flickering over his face? If so, it came and went quickly. Shaun gave a sharp exasperated sigh. "I was working late. I've been putting in a lot of hours lately." His face hardened. "And no, I have no witnesses. Everyone else had left."

Erica looked at Kristen, who was still by the coffee table. "Where were you Thursday night?"

The hand that held the statue was not completely steady. "I was at a movie."

"With friends?"

"I went by myself." Kristen turned and took a step, but her toe caught the table leg. As she stumbled, the statue fell. There was a resounding crash as it hit the corner of the table and shattered. Kristen gasped. She knelt as Shaun hurried over. Using her cane, Pamela awkwardly got to her feet and limped over.

"Do you think I could glue it back together?" Kristen's voice was tremulous as she picked up a couple of the larger pieces then searched Shaun's face anxiously.

"We can try." It was a magnanimous offer since the figurine appeared shattered beyond repair.

Kristen's eyes filled with tears. "I'm so sorry!"

"Dear-heart, it was an accident." Pamela tried to comfort her.

After the mess was cleaned up, Pamela left to go shopping with friends while Erica, Shaun, and Kristen remained in the sitting room.

"I feel terrible, breaking something of Grandma's." Kristen was still crestfallen.

Shaun put an arm around Kristen's shoulder and gave her a comforting squeeze. "Don't worry. I happen to know Mom didn't like that statue. In fact, she offered me money several times to break it."

Kristen raised limpid eyes to his and gave Shaun a luminous smile.

After sitting quietly for a few moments, Erica said, "I keep expecting Grandma to walk in the door any moment."

"Me too," Shaun admitted. "Every time I come home, it's a jolt to remember she's not here."

"It's a hard thing to lose your mother." Kristen rose and, going to the mantle, picked up a picture and came back. It was a picture of a boy holding the hand of a much younger Blanche. "Uncle Randy told me how Blanche adopted you. How old were you in this picture?"

"Three or four, I guess." Shaun studied the picture of Blanche, who was smiling down at Shaun. "Mom was a lot older than my friend's mothers, but she did everything they did—and more. She helped me make a volcano for my science project, bandaged my skinned knees, and taught me to ride a bike. Mom came to every one of my soccer games. You should have heard her cheer! She also kicked my butt when she caught me sneaking out in the middle of the night." Shaun's smile was lopsided, and his eyes were bright.

If he said any more, Erica knew she would cry.

"And you never heard anything from your biological mother?" Kristen asked.

"Tammy was a drug addict. All she cared about was her next high. At least that's what my adopted dad told me."

"Lawrence told you that?" Kristen sounded scandalized. "But maybe she stopped using. People do, you know. I'm still surprised you haven't tried to find her."

Shaun scoffed, "Why should I? If Tammy wanted to be part of my life, she knew where to find me."

"Maybe Tammy was afraid you'd reject her."

"And she'd be right." Shaun's voice grew rough. "What kind of a mother would leave her child and never call, never write? You don't know how many times I checked the mailbox when I was a kid, hoping she'd write—how many birthdays I sat by the phone, hoping she'd call. Well, she never did." His mouth was a hard, white line. "If you had been in my shoes, you'd feel the same way."

"I have been in your shoes." Kristen looked at him levelly. "I was adopted."

"I didn't know that," Erica said in surprise.

"I wanted to contact my biological parents for a long time but didn't because I thought it would be disloyal to my adoptive parents." Kristen's voice became emotional—and her English accent more pronounced. "But when my dad died, I told my mum what I wanted to do. By then, Randy had married my Aunt Nora, and Trent and I got to be buddies. Trent's the one who helped me find my biological parents." Her gray eyes glowed in gratitude. "He's the best—always there when I need him."

"What happened when you found them?" Shaun asked softly.

"I was too late. My dad had died years and years before, and my mum died when I was eighteen. Now if I want to visit them, I have to go to a cemetery in England." Kristen squeezed her eyes shut, as if holding back tears. When she opened them and looked at Shaun, her bottom lip trembled. "That's why I feel strongly about this and why I envy you, Shaun. Your biological mother might still be alive. You have a chance to get to know her. I'd give *anything* to be in your shoes. If I'd started sooner, I might have found my mum before she passed away. But I waited too long—and I've regretted it ever since. I don't want you to make the same mistake."

* * *

The afternoon sun shone down, burnishing Erica's auburn hair as she stood on the front porch with Bandit, watching Walter climb out of his car.

"Thanks for coming over. Sorry for bothering you on a Saturday."

"It's no bother." Walter wore a neat sport shirt and pressed slacks. As he came up the steps, he eyed the leash dangling from her hand. "You must have been out for a walk."

"Bandit and I go every afternoon about this time. Shaun's so busy lately that I've taken over dog-walking duties." She unsnapped the dog's leash, and the Labrador lumbered over to Walter, earning a pat on the head. "I think I enjoy our walks almost as much as Bandit does."

Going inside, Walter watched as Erica closed, opened, then closed the door before showing him into the family room. Tactful as always, he made no comment, just gave her an amused look as she sat on the couch.

Walter took a straight wingback chair in front of the green drapes, which were open, revealing a view of the manicured lawns. "What did you want to talk to me about?"

"A couple of things. First, the police have the results of the lab work. The Elavil that killed Grandma was in the chocolate-covered strawberries."

Walter raised an age-spotted hand and covered his eyes, as if in pain. "They were her favorite," he whispered. Then he lowered his hand. "Where did they come from?"

"I don't know. The original box was thrown away. Vicki put them in a plastic container in the fridge, but she doesn't remember what store they came from. No one admits buying them."

"I didn't send them," Walter said quietly.

"All right. I also wanted to ask you about Martha. I talked with her stepdaughter, Gail, but she was still frazzled and I didn't want to upset her further by asking a lot of questions. What can you tell me about Martha and her ex-husband?"

"For the record, Phillip Bessinger was a scoundrel. He was fifteen years older than Martha and had been married before, with one daughter, Gail. When Phillip and Martha began dating, Blanche and I both felt he was after Martha's money. When Blanche looked into his background, she found Phillip had a criminal record. When Martha told Blanche she wanted to marry Phillip, they had a huge fight. Phillip talked Martha into eloping. It only took a couple of years before Phillip realized Martha was not the golden goose he'd hoped for and deserted her."

"Why didn't Martha move back home?"

"Blanche asked her, but as you know, one of Martha's most blatant idiosyncrasies is that once she's settled, she stays put. After Martha moved to Lake Oswego, she stayed there like she was planted. I'm surprised, actually, that Martha came for Blanche's funeral. She didn't come for her brothers' funerals or her father's."

"I can't understand that."

"It's strange, but Martha has always been very self-absorbed. Other people never entered very deeply into her consciousness." Walter's long face was somber. "Martha never called anyone either—another one of her peculiarities. Pamela and Blanche were the only two that called her."

"Since Grandma bought the house for Martha, I assume she paid all of her expenses."

"Correct. Blanche asked me to handle all of Martha's finances." Then he asked, "Do you still think Blanche's murder is tied to whatever Blanche was worried about at Sun Coast?"

"That's the biggest lead I have right now, but I need to do more digging. Right now, I'm coming up with more questions than answers, but at some point, the answers will come. Speaking of digging, were you able to find out if the board could vote Shaun out as chairman?"

"I wish I had good news, but after Sun Coast was incorporated, the bylaws were changed. Now the board is allowed to vote on whomever they want as chairman."

"Great." Erica frowned morosely.

"To depose Shaun, Trent would need a two-thirds majority. Besides Pamela, Trent, Shaun, and Kristen, there are six nonfamily members on the board—Carlos, myself, and two executives each from Aspen and from Panda Motors."

"Which means Trent might be able to get a majority." Erica didn't like this at all.

"How is the family taking your investigating?" It was said gently—as if Walter knew how difficult it was investigating family.

Looking into Walter's faded blue eyes, Erica felt like she could trust this man to the ends of the earth. "Everyone is pretty unhappy with me for asking so many questions."

"That's to be expected. No one likes to think of themselves as a suspect."

Erica moaned. "But if I'm going to do my job, I can't cross anyone off the list, except maybe Pamela. All of them are upset with me for asking questions."

Walter laughed, a short, dry bark. "Don't let them get to you, Erica. Just keep doing your job, and when things are over, the dust will settle. It's natural for people to consider themselves beyond reproach. But deep down, everyone understands you're simply trying to find the truth."

Erica doubted it but didn't say so. "I've been asking everyone where they were the night Martha was killed."

Walter looked at her with shrewd eyes. "And you want to know where I was. I went to visit my daughter that afternoon. Sandy lives in Corvallis, and it takes a little over an hour to get there.

Feeling like a scoundrel, Erica asked, "So she can vouch for you?"

"As it turns out, she can't. Sandy wasn't feeling well, so we didn't go out to eat as we'd planned. I drove back and spent a solitary evening at home."

* * *

Sunday morning dawned wet and gloomy. They took umbrellas to church, but since those would have been useless in the blustery wind, Shaun dropped Pamela, Kristen, and Erica off near the door before going to park.

In the chapel, Erica was looking up the opening hymn when she came to a torn page. Rummaging in her purse, she pulled out a tape dispenser and began repairing the page.

Kristen gave her a strange look and, leaning close, whispered, "You carry tape in your purse?"

"Of course."

"Is this a Mormon thing?"

"It's an Erica thing."

After the block of meetings, the wind had died down, but it was still sprinkling. On the way home, they talked about the Sunday School lesson, which had been about trusting in the Lord.

"I never thought about how important trust is, but the teacher explained it very well." Kristen sounded impressed. "I liked the part where he said we need to trust ourselves, as well as the Lord." She gave Shaun a significant look.

"What?" Shaun asked.

"One of your problems is that you don't trust yourself," Kristen stated frankly. "You keep wondering why Grandma put you in as chairman, don't you?"

"Well, yes." There was a disconsolate note in Shaun's voice that tugged at Erica's heart.

"Grandma did that because she trusted you," Kristen said. "Now you have to trust that the Lord will bless and help you."

Pamela spoke up. "It's like that scripture we read in Proverbs: 'Trust in the Lord with all thine heart; and lean not unto thine own understanding.'"

"I love the one in Philippians," Erica said. "'I can do all things through Christ which strengtheneth me.'"

"There you go," Kristen said, giving Shaun a bright smile. "You don't have to get through this by yourself. God will help you." She looked at him confidently. "You believe that, don't you?"

A sheepish smile lit Shaun's face. "Actually, I do—though I suppose I haven't been acting like it. But that's going to change."

* * *

Martha's funeral was eerily similar to Blanche Coleman's, which had been held a little over a week ago. A few of Martha's friends from Lake Oswego attended, including Leslie Flynn, who shared Martha's passion for garage sales. Pamela's back was hurting, and after a luncheon at the church, Trent and Carrie took her, Gail, and Erica home. Trent helped Pamela up the front porch steps and into the house. He and Erica paused in the foyer as Gail and Pamela went to their rooms.

"Thanks for bringing us home," Erica said.

"No problem." Trent glanced around. "I sure miss Grandma. The house isn't the same without her." He shook his head. "I hate to admit it, but attending Martha's funeral was like going to a funeral for a stranger. I didn't really know her at all." He spread his hands. "Don't get me wrong, I feel terrible that someone killed Martha, but I just never had a connection with her, you know?"

"I understand." Erica also wished she had known Martha better.

Trent heaved a sigh. "Life has certainly been hectic lately. Carrie and I have been meaning to have you and Pamela out to the house for dinner one night, but we haven't gotten around to it."

"Well, let's plan a night that would work for you."

"Let me check my schedule," Trent said, pulling out his phone. He grimaced. "Busy week. The only night I have open for a while is tomorrow."

Erica laughed. "And here I thought you'd be scheduled a month out. Tuesday it is. But let me bring the main dish."

"Hey, you're not going to get any argument from me—I've tasted your cooking, remember?"

After checking on Pamela, who said she wanted to take a nap, Erica went to the family room, where Gail sat by the fireplace, looking forlorn.

Sitting beside her, Erica said, "You must miss Martha very much."

"I do," Gail replied simply. "It's turned my life upside down—I hardly know what to do." She rubbed her forehead worriedly. "I suppose the family will want to put the house up for sale soon. Do you think they might sell it to me?" There was a touching appeal in her tone. "I'd like to buy it, depending on the price. I've been putting money aside, but now it looks like I'm going to lose my job, so I have to be very careful. Plus, a couple of years ago, I let a friend borrow quite a lot of money. He said he'd repay me with interest, but he took off and I never got a dime of it back." Gail shook her head sadly. "I never thought he'd do that to me."

"How awful! I'll talk with Pamela and Shaun. Maybe they would reduce the price for you. After all, you took good care of Martha and the house for a lot of years."

Gail clasped her hands hopefully. "That would be wonderful."

"I wanted to ask you something," Erica began. "Martha said that during her mother's last visit, Grandma said she was going to change the will and that she'd also said something about Sun Coast. Did you happen to be there when Grandma talked about those things?"

"I wasn't, but Martha told me about it later."

"Can you remember what she said?"

Gail's eyes went distant as she tried to remember. "Let me think. When Blanche got here, I was just leaving to go to work. I put on my coat, and Blanche told me to button up since it was cold outside. But then, January is always cold. She complimented me on my coat. It was plum colored—a lovely shade."

Erica smiled to herself. Obviously, the only way Gail could remember was to go through a play-by-play account.

"When I got back that evening, dinner was ready. I suspect Blanche had a lot to do with that, as Martha usually didn't cook. We had a nice evening, and after Blanche went to bed, Martha told me her mother was worried about Sun Coast and about someone who worked there."

"Did she say who?"

Gail screwed up her face in another monumental effort to remember. "She might have, but now I can't think of who it was. Oh, wait, there was one other thing. Martha said she told her mother that this person—I wish I could remember the name—was a good person and that Blanche shouldn't fire him."

That sounded like Blanche meant to take action. "When I called Martha, she said she'd sent a birthday present. Do you know if she sent chocolate-covered strawberries?"

"Not unless she found them at a garage sale." Gail smiled then shook her head. "Actually, I think Martha sent kitchen towels. I thought about telling her that towels weren't the best present for a rich woman who never did dishes, but I didn't want to hurt her feelings."

It was nice of Gail to be so tactful. "One other thing. Did Martha have a will?"

"She didn't. Blanche asked her about it once, but Martha didn't think she needed one since she didn't own anything valuable."

"Do you mind if I ask some questions about your father?"

"Not at all."

"Are you two close?"

Gail scoffed. "Hardly. We talk a few times a year, but that's it."

"Do you know if the divorce between your father and Martha is final?"

"Of course it is." Gail's eyes widened. "My father remarried, so they had to have been divorced. Why do you ask?"

"I'm trying to find out who had a motive for killing Martha."

"And you think my father . . ." Gail's voice trailed off.

"If the divorce was never finalized, Phillip might have assumed Martha would inherit a sizeable amount of money after her mother died. If you'll write down your father's full name, marriage date, and the county where they were married, I'll check public records."

* * *

Later that afternoon, Pamela felt better, so she and Gail went to the cemetery. Erica wandered into the backyard and meandered over to the white gazebo, where she had sat so often with her grandmother. Blanche had planted climbing pink rose bushes nearby, and their heavenly scent caused an aching inside as Erica sat on the blue-flowered cushions. She'd been with her grandmother when Blanche had bought those very cushions. Erica looked around the white latticed enclosure, thinking about the many times they had sat here talking. It was the little things Erica remembered that meant the most—Blanche's bright eyes, bubbling laughter, dry wit, and penchant for floral blouses. When her eyes began to sting, Erica dug her cell phone out of her pocket and called David.

"Hi, sweetheart," he answered. "I wish I could have been there with you today." David had tried to work things out and come, but in the end, he'd decided to stay since Aby had an ACT test and Ryan had an important concert.

Just hearing her husband's voice steadied her. "Me too, but it went all right, although it was sad. Closed casket, of course."

"I bet the chapel was packed."

"How did you know? I didn't think there would be very many people there."

"Everybody turns out for the funeral of a murder victim." Then David asked, "Who spoke?"

"Martha's bishop gave a good talk. He reminisced a bit about Martha—made everyone laugh. Shaun spoke. Last night, Shaun said he was nervous, but it didn't show. He did a great job talking about the plan of salvation. At lunch, Kristen asked him some questions."

"That's awesome." David sounded impressed. "How was Mom?"

"Awful. Gail had a hard time too. She's staying with us tonight and driving home tomorrow. Oh, and guess what? I talked to Walter, and he told me that Carrie met with him yesterday."

"What did Carrie the Cat want?"

Erica giggled. It had definitely been a mistake to tell David what Grandma had called Carrie. "She wanted to know if she and Trent had any reasonable chance of contesting the will and winning."

"Are they out of their minds?" David was appalled. "Why are they asking Walter? He's the one who *wrote* the will."

"Carrie's so impulsive, it probably didn't enter her mind that it was totally inappropriate. Walter told them he didn't think any judge would overturn the will."

"I guess that put her back in her place."

"You'd think so, but remember this is Carrie we're talking about. Oh boy—I can't count the number of times I've offended her. That's why I was a little surprised that Trent asked me and Pamela to dinner. I think Carrie would prefer I stayed ten miles away, but Trent's been fine."

"Maybe it'll give you a chance to find out a little more."

"My thoughts exactly."

* * *

That evening in Blanche's office, Erica stared at the phone after replacing it in its cradle. She was really starting to hate the telephone. Lately, there had been nothing but bad news, and this call from Detective McGuire had been more of the same. Sitting at her grandmother's desk, Erica felt so tired. She leaned forward and laid her head down.

Where to go from here? Why had she ever decided to pursue a murder investigation when it involved family members?

A slight sound made her lift her head. Kristen stood at the door. "Sorry. Were you asleep?" When Erica shook her head, Kristen came closer. "Is something wrong?"

"I'll say. Detective McGuire just called. Remember I told you there was a delay in checking out the fingerprints the police took from the house?"

Kristen nodded, her eyes anxious.

"They got the results today. There were two sets of fingerprints on the saucer in Grandma's bedroom. One was Grandma's, and the other was Shaun's."

"But Shaun said he didn't take up the strawberries." Kristen's voice was a whisper.

"Exactly."

Chapter Eleven

SINCE SHE WANTED AN EARLY start the next morning, Gail declined breakfast, saying she'd stop along the way to break up the drive to Lake Oswego. Erica walked out to see her off. Gail's face looked so haggard that Erica worried about her. Erica shook her head as she returned to the kitchen. It was hard enough to lose your stepmother, but to also face the imminent loss of your job and home made everything so much worse. It must be awful for Gail to have such turmoil in her life.

A few minutes later, Erica heard the front door open and the tickity-tack sound of dog nails on the marble floor. She returned to the foyer as Shaun unsnapped Bandit's leash. The lab lolloped over to Erica, leaning against her expectantly. Erica obliged by putting on her gloves and scratching Bandit about the ears.

"Have a good run?"

"Nothing like it to clear your mind," Shaun said exuberantly, a sheen of sweat on his face.

"I was talking to Bandit." Erica giggled. "Say, could I talk with you?"

"Right now, or can I shower first?"

"Now, if you don't mind. It'll only take a couple of minutes. Let's go out to the patio."

Shaun filled and carried out a tall glass of water. "So what's up?"

"Detective McGuire got back the results of the fingerprint dusting. Do you remember the saucer that was in Grandma's bedroom? The one that had the strawberry on it?"

"Let me guess." Shaun took another swallow of water. "They found my prints on it."

Erica looked at him levelly. "I asked if you took the strawberries up, and you said you didn't."

"I didn't, but I did touch the saucer that night while I was talking with Mom."

"Something you never mentioned. Until now."

Shaun looked out over the green lawn as if trying to compose himself. "You asked if I'd taken the plate up, and I told you I hadn't. I didn't think about fingerprints until later. When I was talking with Mom that night, I noticed the saucer was close to the edge of the table, and I moved it back so it didn't fall. I suppose that makes me suspect number one?" His tone was bitter.

"Of course not, Shaun, but I have to look at everyone and consider everything."

Shaun folded his arms. "And you're looking a little closer at me because I'm the one who gains the most financially, right?"

It was true—Shaun *did* gain the most. And yet, Erica wasn't as suspicious of Shaun as others in the family. That had to stop, Erica told herself. No matter how difficult, she had to put aside personal feelings and investigate everyone equally. She couldn't allow herself to be blinded by personal likes and dislikes.

Going on, Shaun said, "Someone at Sun Coast told me you were asking if anyone had seen me the afternoon Martha was killed. So you didn't believe me when I told you I was working in my office."

"I always double-check." Then she asked, "Have you had a chance to ask around at Sun Coast?"

"I've talked with a few people—didn't get anything. I also talked with Carlos. We've gotten closer since we've been working together so much, and I asked if he knew what Mom was worried about. He admitted knowing something was bothering her, but she never told him what it was." Shaun took another drink. "I'll keep checking around. Unless of course, the police drag me off to jail first."

* * *

Later that morning, Erica drove to Walter's office. He welcomed her in, and she noted with satisfaction that the blinds were all tilted at precisely the same angle. He noticed Erica looking at them and in a teasing voice said, "I had a word with the cleaning crew."

"Sometimes you have to be firm," Erica said with a smile. She pulled her chair closer to the desk. "I wondered if you'd found out anything at Sun Coast."

"I've talked with a number of people, but most didn't know Blanche was worried. Those that did were quite guarded in their comments. I got the feeling they knew more than they were saying. I'll keep trying." Walter glanced toward the door, and Erica turned to see Trent standing in the doorway, his face flushed.

"Seems to be my day for drop-in visitors," Walter said genially. "Come in, Trent."

Trent stayed where he was, his black eyes on Erica. "I need to talk to you, but I can come back later." Tension rolled from him in tangible waves.

"It's all right. I can go." Erica started to rise.

Trent seemed to change his mind. "Actually, you can stay if you want. I won't be long." He shut the door and strode over. "I found out this afternoon that Shaun hired an auditing firm to go over the company's finances. Quite a few people at Sun Coast knew about it. I felt like a fool when I had to admit I didn't know a thing." Trent's voice was full of scalding bitterness.

"Personally, I thought hiring an auditing firm was a good move," Walter said.

Trent stared at Walter then Erica. "So you know about it too—both of you!" He took a deep breath. "Hiring auditors is expensive. Sun Coast can't afford to throw money down the drain like that. The economy is shaky, business is uncertain, and Shaun's throwing money away without a care in the world." Trent went on, his lips thin and his face flushed. "I knew the power would go to his head. I've said all along that Shaun's not ready for this position and this proves it."

Erica made a small noise, which Trent took for the dissent it was. He pointed a finger at her. "If I don't stop Shaun, he's going to ruin Sun Coast!"

She was not a child to be scolded. Erica spoke up. "Getting a clear, measurable account of Sun Coast's financial standing sounds like a good idea to me."

"Carlos believes hiring auditors is a smart move, and I don't need to tell you what an astute businessman he is," Walter said.

Trent stared. "It's bad enough Grandma was taken in by Shaun's manipulations, but now he's got both of you hoodwinked." Trent shook his head in disgust. "The only reason Shaun is chairman is because he coerced Grandma into giving him my position. Fortunately, wills can be changed."

"I've already told Carrie the will can't be broken." Walter's tone was frosty.

"I'm going to give it a good try," Trent promised, his voice tough and determined. "This harebrained decision of Shaun's to hire an auditing firm has made me decide to contest the entire will—not just the part about him being chairman and CEO. It was bad enough Shaun got Grandma to give him the lion's share of her estate. I had decided to let that go but not anymore."

This time, Trent pointed a finger at Walter. "I should have been named chairman and CEO—I'm the one who's been leading Sun Coast for years. I've worked too many years building up the company to stand around while Shaun runs it into the ground."

Apprehension settled like a stone in Erica's stomach as Trent ground out, "This company was mine before Shaun weaseled his way in, and believe me, it's going to stay mine."

* * *

That evening, as Erica put the food in the trunk of the car, she thought about how she'd originally wished Kristen and Shaun had been invited to dinner tonight. But now that things were heating up between Shaun and Trent, Erica was guiltily grateful Shaun was not coming.

While Pamela waited for Erica to wipe the seats and steering wheel, she tapped her cane impatiently. "Someday I hope you'll overcome this odd compulsion."

"You *want* me to be a slob?" Erica said, enclosing the used wipe in a plastic baggie.

"I can't see you ever being that, but a little more relaxed would be nice."

They arrived at Trent and Carrie's luxurious home, and Trent came out to help carry in the food. He set two covered cookie sheets on the counter, saying, "You really didn't have to do all this."

"Oh, but I did. You see, I'd like to go to the sand dunes, but it's more fun to go with other people, so I'm hoping you'll go with me this Friday." Erica put her pie in the fridge. "Dinner for dune buggies. Seems like a fair trade." Because of the tension created by her investigating, it was getting harder to socialize with Trent and Carrie—but Erica knew she needed to as much as possible. You never knew when some chance comment might prove to be a piece to solving the puzzle.

"Actually, Chad and Courtney have been asking about going to the Sea Lion Caves."

"We can do both," Erica said. "But I'll have to make dinner again."

"You don't have to do that," Trent assured her. He lifted the foil off a corner of one of the cookie sheets. "So what are these?"

"Easy Chicken Rolls.[5] They're simple to make and super yummy."

"The children will love them," Pamela said.

Carrie walked in wearing slim jeans, her long hair in a pony tail. "I already preheated the oven, so go ahead and put them in to bake. I'll finish the green salad."

"Perfect. Want me to set the table?" Erica asked.

"Not when you've made dinner," Carrie said. "I'll have Chad and Courtney do it."

"Take my advice, let Erica set it." Pamela's brown eyes twinkled.

Carrie stopped. "That's right. I'd forgotten about Erica's mania." She handed a stack of plates to Erica. "Knock yourself out."

"Having things straight makes a more enjoyable meal for everyone," Erica said complacently as she placed the plates two inches from the edge of the table. Trent left to check on the children, who were supposed to be doing homework.

"So, Erica, have you found out anything about Grandma's death or Sun Coast?" That nasal voice of Carrie's made the question sound like a complaint.

Erica opened the oven door a few inches to check on the rolls. "Nothing major."

"I still don't understand why you're investigating. Surely the police can find out more than you can," Carrie said, tossing the salad as she discounted Erica's usefulness.

Ouch. If she ever got a swelled head, Erica thought wryly, all she needed to do was talk to Carrie to return it to a normal size.

From her position at the table, Pamela defended her daughter-in-law. "Erica's an excellent investigator."

Patiently, Erica added, "The police have limited resources and a heavy workload, while I can focus solely on finding out who killed Grandma."

Still skeptical, Carrie tapped a manicured finger against her cheek. "Are you going to try and get Walter to pay you with money from the estate?"

---

5   See the appendix for this recipe.

Pamela's eyes widened in shock, and Erica had to fight the impulse to slap Carrie. "I won't even dignify that with a response," she replied frostily then turned her attention to folding the paper napkins, running her thumb along the edge with a little more force than necessary. She glanced up at Carrie, who was filling glasses with ice. Wouldn't it be great if Carrie turned out to be the killer? Then Erica shook herself, reminding herself she had to stay objective. Also, she couldn't afford to lose her temper. She needed to stay on Carrie's good side so she could find out more from her and Trent. Unfortunately, Carrie the Cat wasn't done.

"I can see you trying to find out who poisoned Blanche—and Martha, I guess—but why are you investigating Sun Coast?" Carrie's baby blue eyes were hard with suspicion. "The company has nothing to do with what happened to Grandma."

"I'm not so sure," Erica responded evenly. "Grandma was worried about something there, and whatever it was could easily provide a motive for her murder."

Trent returned in time to hear Erica's comments. "I don't think you have to go far to look for a motive," Trent said, taking a seat beside Pamela. "I know Shaun's prints were on the saucer in Grandma's bedroom." There was a great deal of malicious pleasure wrapped in his words.

Carrie's head whipped around in surprise. "Really, Trent?" Then she looked at Erica. "You didn't mention that little tidbit when I asked how things were going."

"Shaun was in her room that night and moved the saucer," Erica said. "It doesn't mean he bought the strawberries."

"I never *said* he bought them—Kristen did." Carrie's sandals tapped a staccato beat on the tile as she brought over the green salad and put it on the table.

Erica's mouth fell open. "Kristen bought the strawberries?"

"Well, yeah." Carrie sat by her husband, looking almost as surprised as Erica felt. "You didn't know that?"

"No, I didn't. Did Kristen tell you she bought them?"

"She didn't have to. I was at the house when two boys delivered them. Kristen's name was on the card."

"Why didn't you tell me this before?"

"You never asked." Carrie's words had a brittle quality.

"Yes, I did, I called and talked to—ah, Trent."

Rats, Erica thought. She *hadn't* talked to Carrie.

Trent broke in. "Erica, when you called and asked if we'd bought the strawberries, Carrie was in the shower. When I asked her if she'd bought the strawberries, she said no."

She had messed up, Erica knew, by not talking with Carrie personally. The timer buzzed, and Erica went out to switch pans then came back to sit by Pamela. In a milder tone, Erica asked Carrie, "What did the card say?" When Carrie hesitated, Erica added, "You must have read it to know the strawberries were from Kristen."

A slight flush colored Carrie's face. "Well, so what?" She went on in a defensive tone. "It was just a regular birthday card. There wasn't any personal note, just Kristen's name at the bottom."

That didn't sound like Kristen. She was never brief and to the point.

"You never told me about that," Trent said, his voice stern and disapproving.

"I didn't think it was important." That annoying whine was back in her voice again.

Erica got down to basics. "Tell me about the two boys that delivered them. What did they look like?"

"I don't remember." Carrie tossed her head, and her long hair rippled over her shoulders. "They were just boys. I guess they were about twelve or thirteen. One stayed in the driveway on his bicycle. The taller one had long brown hair."

"Can you remember anything else about them?"

Carrie thought hard. "Oh yeah, the boy at the door wore a ball cap for the Oregon Ducks."

That was a useful bit of information. As Erica filed it away in her head, Pamela looked around to make sure the children weren't around then asked Trent, "I hear you're going to try and get the board to vote Shaun out as chairman. Is that true?"

Before her husband could answer, Carrie jumped in. "Why shouldn't he? It's not right for Shaun to steal Trent's job. Everyone knew Trent was going to take Grandma's place—everyone!" Carrie's sharp face looked mutinous. "And Shaun also talked Blanche into giving him half of the estate—when he's already been living in that huge house for years and not paying any rent. That isn't right."

That was it. Erica's face flushed as she replied tightly, "Shaun moved back because Grandma begged him to—she hated being alone. And for your information, Grandma told me Shaun took care of all the maintenance for the house, cars, and grounds. If he can't do it himself, he hires people to do it, saving Grandma a lot of hassle. Shaun does more than enough to pay for his room and board."

Neither Trent nor Carrie looked impressed. The oven timer went off, and Trent said, "I think we ought to leave this alone tonight. Carrie, if you'll pull that out of the oven, I'll get the children."

During the meal, everyone unwound and relaxed. It turned out to be a more enjoyable dinner than Erica had thought possible. After finishing their pie, the children raced off while the adults went to the front room. Erica was loathe to go back into investigative mode, but it had to be done. She looked across to where Carrie and Trent were sitting close to each other on a black leather couch.

"There was a business plan for Orion Parasailing in Grandma's bedroom. Do you know anything about that?"

A flash of alarm showed in Carrie's blue eyes. "What's that to you?"

"I'm investigating, remember?"

"That's Carrie's plan," Trent said mildly.

Pamela had propped her feet on the hassock and asked, "I didn't know you were trying to start a business, Carrie. What kind of a business?"

"Parasailing."

"Oh my," Pamela responded in amazement. "I've heard of that. But isn't it dangerous?"

"Not at all." Carrie gave a silvery laugh. "It's a blast—I love it. You can't believe how much fun it is, sailing up in the air. I've always loved adventure sports, and parasailing is a real rush."

Erica was curious. "Would this be an offshoot of Sun Coast or your own business?"

"My own business—Orion Parasailing." Carrie directed a look at Trent. "I tried to talk Grandma and Trent into having Sun Coast offer parasailing—the coast here is perfect for it. I even said I'd run the department, but Grandma thought parasailing was insane and Trent wasn't sure people would be interested. So I decided to do it on my own." When she thrust out her chin like that, Carrie could look very determined.

"And you asked Grandma to invest in your business?"

"Yes, I did. She invests in other businesses; why not this? She turned me down flat the first time, but Trent helped me do more market research and write up a more complete plan."

"Since then, I've done a lot of reading on parasailing," Trent said. "It's exploding in popularity. Carrie and I both talked to Grandma, and she promised to look over the plan."

"I read it," Erica said. "It sounds like it could be really successful."

Carrie seemed to blossom. "I *know* it can be a success," she gushed. "The only problem is I need capital. Parasailing equipment is expensive—a good winch boat can cost up to $50,000. But the rest of the equipment—helmets, wind meters, quick releases, windsocks, harness, canopies, and towlines—aren't that expensive. And the profits are terrific. At peak times, I can charge $30 for ten minutes. And it wouldn't take a whole lot of people to run the business. I'd run one boat myself and do the bookwork—at first anyway. I want to get started right away before other people pick up on it and I have a lot of competition."

Trent took his wife's hand and clasped it firmly. "We're going to use our inheritance money to get Carrie's business off the ground."

"Well, good for you, dear-heart," Pamela said sincerely. "I'm sure you'll do well. It sounds like you've been working really hard on this."

"I sure have." Carrie's voice was intense.

Erica had been watching Carrie. "This business really means a lot to you, doesn't it?"

"I just want to do something on my own, you know?" Her blue eyes were soft. "Trent's so busy with Sun Coast and works such long hours—I'd like a project of my own." Carrie's voice was earnest. "I'd like to show people that Trent's not the only capable one in the family."

There was such passion in her voice that Erica was taken back. This was not just a whim. Carrie had put her heart and soul into this. Erica had underestimated Carrie—thinking that all Carrie cared about was designer clothes, a big house, and a fancy car, but Erica had been wrong. Apparently, Carrie felt a deep need to prove herself—just as her husband had proven himself. Still, Carrie needed money to get it off the ground. But just how far was she willing to go to fulfill her dream?

Chapter Twelve

As Shaun chowed down on his cereal at the patio table, Erica set her own bowl down then went to straighten the flower pots so they were in a straight line along the edge of the patio.

"Harmony is restored. Now we can relax," Shaun teased gently when Erica came back. "You must be into feng shui."

"No, but I *am* into neatness and order. Nathan does a great job keeping up the yard but forgets to line things up after mowing the lawn." Erica took a bite of cereal and looked around at the sunshine-dappled trees with their brown and golden leaves. "It's so nice to be able to eat outside—I love how warm it's been lately." Lately, they'd been enjoying a stretch of Indian summer.

Then she said, "I'm going to meet with Walter tomorrow morning at Sun Coast. When we're done, would you be able to come in and talk with us for a few minutes?"

"Sure, just give me a call when you're ready for me."

Erica dabbed at her mouth with a napkin. "Have you been able to find out anything?"

"I have, but I need to check on something before I can tell you about it." There was a grim set to Shaun's jaw. "I'll fill you in as soon as I can."

That sounded intriguing—too bad Shaun wouldn't tell her about it now; then she could fill in Detective McGuire when she went to meet with him that morning.

Shaun picked up his bowl and drank the last of the milk. "I've been wondering. What happens if you never find out who killed Mom? There's always going to be some doubt in your mind that I'm the one that did it, isn't there?"

Such a thought had never occurred to her. But Erica wouldn't let doubts enter her mind now. It would tear the family apart if the killer was never found. All the suspicions people harbored toward each other would grow and fester. She just *had* to uncover the murderer.

"I'll find out." Erica put as much confidence in her voice as possible.

"You still think I'm the one that argued with Mom the day before she died." When Erica didn't deny it, he went on. "Can't say I blame you—we did argue a lot, mostly because Mom wanted me to be more outgoing and more aggressive. But I've never been what Mom wanted me to be—Trent's clone." Perhaps sensing Shaun's distress, Bandit thrust his nose into his owner's hand. Shaun responded by absently stroking the dog's head.

Erica finished the last of her cereal. "Did Grandma always push you like that?"

"No, it was only this past year." His chair scraped on the cement as Shaun slid back.

"Why was that?" Erica was curious. "You'd already been at Sun Coast a couple of years. Did anything specific happen?"

He thought about that—his eyes distant. "Not that I recall. I've tried doing what Mom wanted, but I never was quite the person she wanted."

"I don't think that's true," Erica said thoughtfully. "Grandma was very proud of you. The day before she died, she told me you were one in a million. She *meant* that. Grandma loved you so much."

Shaun came back from that faraway place, and his eyes met Erica's. "I know she did. And I know she wanted me to believe in myself. Mom saw things in me that no one else did. After she died, I started praying, asking Heavenly Father to help me be a better person so I could be the kind of person Mom thought I was."

Pushing her bowl to the side, Erica leaned over and squeezed Shaun's hand. "Grandma knew the kind of person you are. She saw so much good in you—all of your wonderful qualities." She released his hand and sat back. "The other day I was thinking about a wonderful quote. It's by Johann von Goethe, as I recall. 'Treat people as if they were what they ought to be and you help them to become what they are capable of being.' That's what Grandma was doing for you. She wasn't seeking to change you as much as trying to bring some of your wonderful qualities to the foreground. I know Grandma had a tendency to come on too strong," Erica paused to smile, "but she loved you and wanted you to live up to your potential. I think Grandma knew you better than you know yourself."

Shaun looked at her sardonically. "If I have so many good qualities, then why did my biological mother abandon me?" His voice was flat and bitter.

Erica couldn't help but stare. Shaun had never spoken of this until at the cemetery, yet lately, it seemed to loom over him. Perhaps it was only natural to examine your life and your place in the world after losing a loved one. Erica knew she was much more introspective now than before Blanche had passed away. Kristen felt Shaun's battle with low self-esteem had its roots in Tammy's leaving. Perhaps Kristen had something there. It was an idea Erica had considered possible, but now it seemed probable. Certainly a child whose mother had left him would wonder why. And children have such a tendency to blame themselves—even for things they have no control over.

"You've been fighting dragons all your life, haven't you?" Erica said quietly.

Shaun seemed to shake himself and leave speculation behind. "It's only the present that matters—this moment. I can't change the past, but I can shape the future."

"Wow. That was profound. Is that from one of those self-esteem books?"

"My secret is out." Shaun grinned. "I can quote entire passages from memory. I can also leap tall buildings in a single bound."

How handsome Shaun was when he smiled! "I know you've been working hard. Carlos and Walter are both impressed with how well you're doing at Sun Coast."

"They are?" Shaun's face lit up with pleasure. "That's nice to hear because sometimes I feel overwhelmed thinking about how much I have to learn. I'm still not sure I can do this."

A slight breeze ruffled Erica's hair. "Don't give in to negative thoughts. Kick them out by thinking positive ones. You *can* do it; just give yourself time. Keep reading those books and praying. God will help you. Ask and ye shall receive, you know."

"I haven't felt good about asking God to help me at Sun Coast. It seems so . . . mercenary."

"That's Satan again, trying to stop you from getting the help you need. Heavenly Father wants to help us with *every* part of our lives."

The French doors opened, and Kristen stepped out, carrying a slice of Zucchini Bread[6], which had been spread thickly with cream cheese. "You had a lot of little loaves in there," she said to Erica. "Hope at least one of them was for us because it looked too good to resist."

"I made plenty," Erica assured her. "I got up early and made enough so I can take some over to Sun Coast later today. I heard you talking on the phone in Grandma's office for quite a while. Is everything okay?"

"Yeah, I was just talking with my mum. Neither one of us knows when to shut up." Kristen grinned and looked around at the maples, which had turned scarlet from their tops to their lowest branches. "Isn't it a beautiful morning?" She pulled out a chair and sat at the table.

Erica smiled, thinking Kristen would have said that if icy sleet was coming down in vertical sheets. Yet it *was* beautiful. Late fall was a lovely time in Oregon, especially in the evening when windows were lit and wood smoke drifted out of chimneys.

"How did your dinner with Trent and Carrie go last night?" Kristen asked.

"It was nice. But I was a little surprised when Carrie told me she was here at the house when the strawberries were delivered and that there was a card with them. A card from you."

"From me? But I didn't send them." Kristen's cheeks reddened, and she set down her bread.

Shaun's face darkened as he looked at Erica. "Are you accusing Kristen?"

"I'm only telling you what Carrie said," Erica explained. "This morning I looked around but didn't see the card. Perhaps it got thrown away."

Kristen looked hurt. "Erica, you don't actually believe Carrie, do you? I'd hardly send a box of poisoned strawberries to Grandma and put my name on the card, would I? I'm not daft."

With Shaun glowering at her, now was not the time to explain there was such a thing as a double bluff—when someone put their own name on an incriminating bit of evidence in order to feign innocence and make people think someone else had done it.

Shaun spoke up. "Maybe the card was thrown away by whoever signed Kristen's name—so we couldn't compare the handwriting with Kristen's."

---

6   See the appendix for this recipe.

Calming down, Kristen picked up her bread. "I don't know why Carrie would say such a thing. I get the feeling she doesn't like me."

"And yet you and Trent are so close," Erica said.

"Yeah, he's awesome. Trent's always been so good to me." She gave a little sigh of contentment then looked at Shaun. "Anyway, talking with my mum made me think about *your* biological mother."

"Oh, brother—not again," Shaun said tiredly.

Kristen was certainly persistent, Erica thought. Once Kristen got an idea in her head, she pursued it to the bitter end.

"I bet your mother hasn't contacted you because she's ashamed."

Shaun flushed angrily. "Don't call her my mother. And I couldn't care less what Tammy feels or thinks. One of the few things Dad told me about Tammy is that she cared more about drugs than her own son."

Ouch. What a damaging thing to tell a boy.

"It's not always that simple," Kristen argued. "Tammy might have really loved you, but when you're addicted to drugs, your life isn't your own."

"Kristen has a point," Erica broke in. "When people get hooked on drugs, their priorities get turned around. I know—I worked with a lot of drug addicts when I was a cop."

"I've had friends who were hooked, and I saw how drugs blunted their sense of morals," Kristen said, her voice charged with emotion. "People start doing things they never would have dreamed of doing before they got addicted."

"Spare me," Shaun said in a biting tone. "Everyone is free to make their own choices."

"Your mo—Tammy could have loved you, but if she was caught up in drugs, she may been unable to help herself," Erica explained. "Drugs take over a person's mind and body."

"Tammy got what she really wanted—drugs—and left behind what she didn't want—me." Shaun's face was like flint.

"She was an addict," Kristen cried, white-faced. "You don't know what it's like to be under the influence of something that turns you into something you're not. And it takes more than willpower to quit. Why are you being so judgmental? I thought your church was all about being charitable and forgiving."

Shaun's face was stony. "There are some things you can't forgive."

"Excuse me? Did I hear you right?" When Shaun remained silent, Kristen went on. "I was waiting for a good time to tell you, but apparently, there's not going to be one, so here goes; I've been looking on the Internet and think I've found Tammy."

Shaun's body jerked as though he'd been hit by a jolt of electricity. "How could you do that? This is none of your business!"

Kristen slowly rose to her feet, her body rigid. "You've got a lot of unresolved feelings, and you're never going to get over them unless you face her. You know what? I'd give anything to meet my biological mother, *anything*. I wouldn't care what she'd done, but you—you have a chance to find your mother and you want to drop it?" Kristen eyes sparked fire. "You know what? Tammy isn't the only addict in your family. You are too because—because you're addicted to being *stupid*!" Kristen stomped into the house, slamming the door so hard it was a wonder the glass didn't break.

* * *

Since she and Pamela planned to go shopping, Erica decided to go for her walk right after breakfast. It was a struggle for Erica to snap a leash on Bandit as he kept prancing about, eager to leave. Going down the front steps, Bandit pulled her toward the gardener, who was weeding around the three-tiered fountain in the flowerbed.

"Nathan! How are you today?"

The old man with the weather-beaten face straightened, clutching a handful of quackgrass in one hand and a trowel in the other. "I'm grand. And you?"

"Perfect."

"You must like to walk; I see you all the time. But don't you usually go in the afternoon?"

"Yep, but I have a lot of things going on today, so I decided to go now." She patted Bandit. "Thanks for adding another geranium to that group at the top of the driveway. It looks much better now—nice and even." Erica noticed Nathan's bare hands. "Why aren't you wearing gloves?"

"Sometimes I like to feel the soil. Even when my hands get black like Bandit." He held up his dirt-streaked hands and wiggled his fingers.

"What kind of soap do you use?" Erica blurted out without thinking then blushed.

Nathan took no offense. "Whatever my wife buys. Soap is soap."

"Au contraire, Lava is the best soap you can buy. Did you know it has pumice in it, a by-product of volcanic activity that can be used to clean even the dirtiest of hands?"

A glimmer of understanding showed in Nathan's eyes. "Oh, I understand. Your husband, he sells Lava?"

"Um, no, but he uses it and loves it." Bandit, bored by inaction, pulled at his leash, and Erica took an involuntary step toward the driveway. "You were working here the day before my grandmother died, weren't you?" When Nathan nodded, she asked, "Did you happen to see a couple of boys on bikes come to the house?"

"Yes, I think I did."

"Did you get a good look at them?"

The gardener shook his head. "I was carrying some bags of leaves out back when I saw them in the driveway. They were gone when I got back."

"Did you see anything unusual or different the day Grandma died or perhaps the day before?"

Nathan hesitated then brushed at his knees. "Nothing important."

"Anything you can remember, even if it was small, could help me."

Still he hesitated. "But it's such a small thing."

"Just tell me, please."

"It was when Shaun left. Usually, he drives very slow and careful, but this time, he backed out of the garage so fast the tires squealed. I was working alongside the driveway and, for a second, thought he might hit me. I figured he must have been late for a meeting."

* * *

Erica turned off Highway 101 onto Greenwood, parking beside a line of navy-blue police cars. She went inside the modern-looking, cream stucco building, and as she went to the front counter, she saw Detective Vince McGuire in the hallway. He waved her back, and they went to his office.

"Thanks for coming in," he said, sitting behind his desk. I've been thinking about this case and wanted to ask you a few questions, starting with Pamela and Blanche. Was there any animosity between them? As Blanche's daughter-in-law, Pamela stood to gain quite a bit from Blanche's death."

Erica didn't like him considering her mother-in-law—not when Pamela had gone through so much, with her back injury and losing her husband. Erica loved Pamela and had great respect for her. "You can take Pamela off your list of suspects. She'd never poison anyone. And she got along great with Grandma."

"I know she's your mother-in-law, but Pamela might have motives you don't know about. I also wondered about her disabilities. You've been around her a lot. Have you seen any signs they're not quite as serious as Pamela makes them out to be?"

"She's not taking pain medication for kicks."

Detective McGuire eyed her. "Shaun told me that he came home early one day and Pamela was upstairs. You told me she wasn't able to climb the stairs."

"I said it's very difficult for her."

"And yet she seemed to manage just fine when Blanche died. You said Pamela was there in the bedroom when they discussed having an autopsy done."

"David helped her up the stairs." Just because Pamela made it once didn't mean it was something she could do easily. There had been a great deal of emotion that day.

The detective shifted in his chair. "As a private investigator, haven't you done a lot of work for insurance agencies and found people who claim to be disabled but aren't?"

"Well, yes." It was true. At Pinnacle, Erica had done a lot of surveillance work on people who falsely claimed to be injured and filed for worker's compensation. Many times, Erica had tailed people who hobbled into the doctor's office, and later that day, shot videos of them roughhousing with their children in the backyard. But she couldn't imagine Pamela faking it.

She paraphrased what her mother-in-law had told her. "Pamela has good days and bad days."

Detective McGuire looked at her searchingly then picked up a paper. "I've been talking to people at Sun Coast. What do you think of Carlos Morales? He seems like a nice guy and my gut tells me he's clean, but I wondered if he resented not being named chairman or CEO. Could he have killed Blanche for revenge, after finding out he wasn't going to replace her?"

It wasn't a new thought, but Erica had her doubts. "Carlos has always known Blanche considered Sun Coast a family dynasty and that nepotism reigns supreme. Besides, he did get promoted to chief operating officer."

The detective had a few more questions, and after talking about Carrie, Erica informed him about the parasailing business. His eyes widened a bit. "It sounds like Carrie chafed a bit about being in the shadow of her successful husband and wanted to prove a few things."

"She certainly sounded excited about it."

Detective McGuire stroked his goatee thoughtfully. "And Blanche Coleman turned her down, eh? This opens a whole new line of motives for Carrie. The only thing standing in the way of Carrie starting her new business was getting the capital. But Blanche Coleman's death solved everything." He sounded pleased.

"And there's more." Erica told him that according to Carrie, Kristen had sent the strawberries.

"I'll talk with Kristen again," Detective McGuire said in his matter-of-fact way. "As I recall, Kristen told me she didn't buy the strawberries. It could be that someone else is trying to put the blame on her."

Just then, a bell went off in Erica's head. She sat very still as thoughts whirled furiously.

"What are you thinking?" Detective McGuire asked. "You have a strange look on your face."

"I just remembered something. When I told Walter that no one admitted buying the strawberries, he said he hadn't sent them." She looked up at the detective, perplexed. "But I hadn't told him the strawberries had been delivered. How did he know they were sent?"

Chapter Thirteen

"OH, LOOK! THERE'S A PLACE to park!" Pamela pointed out a spot in front of the two-storied Old Time Photo Studio. The narrow streets of historic Florence were crowded with small, eclectic businesses built side-by-side. Many of them boasted flower boxes and seating along the street, and Erica and Pamela enjoyed meandering in and out of the quaint shops. Each had her favorites. Pamela liked Leather Works and Newport Bay Candle Company, while Erica had to be torn away from Dog Style Boutique and Kitchen Klutter, a store that sold everything from shish kebab sticks to silicone mitts.

It was one thirty when Pamela said, "I'm starved. We need to get some lunch."

"Sounds good. Do you mind if we go to Charl's? It's right next door to Callie's Candies—that store that sells chocolate-covered strawberries. I've stopped a few times, hoping to see the boys Carrie said delivered the berries."

"Isn't that kind of a long shot?"

"The boys were on bicycles, so they have to live nearby."

Charl's Restaurant, an unpretentious building on Highway 101, had white siding with a large banner—"Support Our Troops"—tacked to the side. A string of clear lights lined the eaves. Just inside was a large display of gifts, which Pamela and Erica passed as the hostess led them to a rust-colored vinyl booth by a window. A waitress with brassy red hair and a black-and-white striped apron took their orders.

"Tonight is Relief Society," Pamela reminded her daughter-in-law. "We're going to tie some quilts and donate them to the Peace Harbor Hospital."

Keeping one eye trained on the sidewalk in front of the restaurant, Erica straightened the sugar packets, which had been stacked haphazardly in a wooden holder that had a white picket fence and a birdhouse on top. "Is Kristen going?"

"She thought it sounded like fun." Pamela took a drink of water. "I'm tickled that Kristen's going to church with us."

"She knows so much that sometimes I forget she's not a member."

"I've been talking with Kristen, and she'd like to meet with the missionaries once this mess is over."

The waitress came, sliding white plates with steaming halibut and fries in front of them. The kernel corn was in its own small white bowl.

"Mmmm—these are the best fries," Erica said, dipping one in ketchup. "So what does Shaun think about Kristen seeing the missionaries?"

"Kristen hasn't told him—wants to keep it low-key, she said. If you ask me, Kristen doesn't want Shaun to think that the only reason she's interested in the Church is because of him."

"I guess I can understand that."

"Then explain it to me." Pamela smiled as she dipped a bite of halibut in tartar sauce. "It's no secret Kristen and Shaun really like each other. They go out for lunch together every day and a date every Friday and Saturday night."

"And still they act like no one else knows." Erica laughed. "Did Kristen see much of Shaun when she came to visit Randy and Nora?"

"I think Kristen spent most of her time with her aunt and uncle, but she also spent some time with Blanche, so I imagine she and Shaun saw each other occasionally. I don't think things started to take off until she moved here."

"I'm surprised Kristen hasn't been married."

"Oh, she has," Pamela said. "I thought you knew. It was about five years ago, but they were only married a year. She didn't have any children—same as Shaun."

Erica checked out the window. "Did Kristen tell you that she thinks she found Tammy?"

"No," Pamela said, sounding dismayed. "Kristen is a darling girl, so cheerful and lively, but she has a little too much chutzpah if you ask me. And Shaun told me that she's always asking him questions about Sun Coast—what are his plans for the company, how he gets along with others—a lot of things he doesn't feel comfortable talking about."

Erica had heard the same thing, only from Kristen; who told her she'd been trying to get Shaun to talk about his problems at work but that he refused to open up to her. Women like Kristen believed in sharing the load, but Shaun was old-school enough to downplay problems and keep mum while trying to handle them on his own. Talk turned to Trent's plans to get Shaun voted out as chairman.

"That scamp!" Pamela shook her head with its shining cap of brown hair. "I love him, but Trent can say and do outrageous things when he's angry. But, he never stays mad for long."

Taking another look outside, Erica saw two boys ride past on their bicycles. She leaned closer so that her nose was practically touching the window. The boys were the right age, and one was slightly bigger than the other. They stopped at the light, waiting for it to change.

"I think those are the boys!" Erica jumped up and ran outside. *Bingo!* One of the boys wore an Oregon Duck cap.

They eyed Erica warily, and she curbed her enthusiasm. "Could I ask you a question? I wondered if you happened to deliver some strawberries to Blanche Coleman about two weeks ago? Her house is about half a mile away, on North Rhododendron Drive. The strawberries came from Callie's Candies." Erica pointed at the store.

The boys glanced at each other uneasily, and Erica gave them her most winning smile to allay the apprehension plastered on their faces. "Blanche Coleman is my grandmother. I was inside having lunch with my mother-in-law when I saw you go by." She inclined her head toward Pamela, who had come out and was standing by the door. Pamela gave them a friendly little wave, which seemed to relax the older boy a bit.

"Yeah, we delivered them. They were okay, weren't they?"

Obviously he didn't know about the poisoning, and Erica wasn't about to spook him by mentioning it. "Umm, they were fine. I just wanted to know who sent them."

"There was a card with the box," the boy said, suspicion creeping back in his eyes.

"Yes, but it got lost. Do you happen to remember who asked you to deliver them?"

"He didn't give me his name."

A man. Now Erica was getting someplace. "What did he look like?"

The boys exchanged uncertain looks, and the younger boy said, "I don't know. He was old."

"Can you describe him?"

"He had a hat. And he was wearing a jacket." He looked at the taller boy for confirmation. When the older boy nodded, Erica felt a bit bewildered. Who wore a hat nowadays? It had to be a disguise.

Then the older boy added, "He had an accent."

Accent? "Was it an English accent?"

"I dunno. He said he thought the store delivered, but they didn't. So he asked us if we could deliver the strawberries for him."

The shorter boy spoke up. "The man said it was for a birthday present but that he was sick and couldn't deliver himself."

"Then he handed me twenty bucks," said the boy with the cap. "So I was like, 'Sure!'"

"Thank you so much, boys. You've been very helpful."

* * *

That afternoon, Erica slipped her loaves of zucchini bread—or "goodwill-in-a-loaf," as she liked to call it—into a wicker basket and drove to Sun Coast.

Marge was typing briskly at her computer when Erica walked into the Sun Coast showroom. Off to the side, a young male employee was helping a couple decide on an ATV rental.

"Hi, Marge. Is Trent in?"

"I think he's in his office."

Erica handed Marge two small loaves of bread. "Fresh baked this morning."

"Why, thank you!"

Erica looked around discreetly. No one else was around except the employee and couple, and they were heavily engaged in conversation. "How are things going here?"

"Great." Then Marge raised an eyebrow. "Or is this something more than small talk?"

Perhaps it was best to be specific. "Grandma told me she was worried about something at Sun Coast. Do you have any idea what?"

Marge's round face looked startled. "No. I thought everything was going great."

"How is Shaun doing? I figure if anyone knows, you would."

Marge smiled—in fact, she almost purred. Erica knew there wasn't much around Sun Coast she didn't know. Marge glanced to her right and left. Then she leaned forward.

"From what I hear, Shaun's surprised a lot of people—well, pretty much everyone." Marge's smile was of pure delight. "Shaun's always been so quiet, but now he's taking charge. He's running everything past Carlos first, but that's probably a smart thing to do for now."

A call came in, so Erica nodded and started down the hallway, stopping at a few offices to chat with employees and pass out more of her goodwill bread. When she came to Trent's sunny office, Erica found him behind his mahogany desk, working on his computer. He wore a tailored suit and looked every bit the successful businessman he was. The minute Erica stepped into the office, she could feel Trent's power and magnetism.

"I come bearing gifts." She held out the basket filled with small fragrant loaves. It was an old cliché that the way to a man's heart was through his stomach, but Erica had always felt there was a good deal of truth to it.

"Thanks," he said, taking a loaf. "What kind is it?"

"Zucchini bread."

Trent examined the loaf—perhaps searching for signs of green. "Is zucchini bread some sort of weird Utah thing, like green Jell-O?"

"This bread is so delicious it would be loved anywhere in the country, believe me."

"That good, eh? I'd better make sure."

"Be my guest. I already sliced it."

While Trent unwrapped the bread, Erica noticed a few books on the bookshelf were sticking out, so she pushed them in. A few were in too far, so Erica aligned those as well.

"Want a job?" Trent asked, amusement in his voice.

She turned around, laughing. "You can't afford me."

Trent turned his attention back to the bread. "The slices are nice and thick."

"And there are an even number." When he looked at her questioningly, she added, "It tastes better that way."

Trent laughed. A big laugh for a big man. "You're cute, Erica. Kind of quirky but cute." He held out the bread. "You want some?"

"Can't turn down my own cooking." She took a piece and sat down. "So are we still on for going to the sand dunes the day after tomorrow?"

Trent sank into his own chair. "Carrie and I are both looking forward to it. We'll have to go in the morning because I have meetings that afternoon. I also talked with Carrie about going to the Sea Lion Caves. We could go next Monday if you're up for it. The kids have the day off—teacher prep day, and I guess I can take half a day off since Shaun's running the show."

She ignored the jab about Shaun. "That would be great. Erica swallowed a bite and crossed her legs. "Carrie sounds pretty excited about opening her own business."

"She sure is." His smile was a proud one.

"Now that you have the money."

The smile dropped from Trent's face. "What do you mean by that?"

"Nothing. But it is lucky that you and Carrie have the money to invest in her business. Now."

"If you think Carrie or I had anything to do with Grandma's death, you're crazy." Trent's black eyes narrowed.

Erica thought of her checklist for the day—offend at least one family member. Check. She murmured the same platitudes she'd given Shaun and soothed Trent's ruffled feathers.

Then he looked at her with observant eyes. "I heard you've been here a while. Dig up any dirt?"

Hmmm. Erica wondered which one of Trent's loyal minions had squealed. "People aren't too eager to talk."

"Gee, they're nuts. If I had a beautiful private investigator—who wasn't related to me—asking me questions, I'd spill my guts." When Erica laughed, Trent flashed a grin and went on. "I suppose you heard about the disagreement I had with Shaun about some of the things he's doing. We weren't exactly whispering. Or did Shaun complain to you about it?"

"He hasn't said a word." Erica didn't feel any need to explain that others had.

There was an upward quirk of an eyebrow. "Well, it doesn't matter. Shaun is in charge and can do what he likes—for now." Trent rubbed his forehead as if it hurt. "I swear, it's like having Homer Simpson take over the company. But it won't be for long."

"So you're still going to try and get the board to vote Shaun out?"

Trent looked astonished. "Did you think I was joking? Being chairman is an elected position now that Grandma is gone, and I'm going to call for a vote as soon as possible. I'm going to talk with every one of the board members and let them know exactly what's at stake."

"A number of family members are on the board, including Kristen. I'm not sure you'll be able to convince her to vote against Shaun."

A dark look came over Trent's face. "I hate to think Shaun is manipulating Kristen just like he did Grandma. I'd feel responsible, you see, since I'm the one who got Kristen hired on here. I'm sure Shaun will try to sway her, but I'll make sure she has all the facts." His charm and cordiality hid the cold calculation Trent Coleman would bring to any business matter.

"What facts?" Erica countered.

"The fact that Shaun twisted things and managed to brainwash Grandma."

"Shaun said he had no idea Grandma was going to make him CEO and chairman."

Trent scoffed. "And you believed him? I know you like to believe the best of everyone, but Grandma told me and my father that I was going to take her place. And now, after I've been acting CEO for years, Shaun thinks he can come along and kick me out?"

Erica was taken aback by the vehemence in his voice. A warning shiver sped along Erica's nerves as Trent went on. "Living with her gave Shaun lots of opportunities to suck up to Grandma and turn her against me."

"Oh, Trent," Erica said reproachfully. "I don't think that's what happened. Shaun told me that he doesn't understand why Grandma put him as CEO instead of you. He feels very inadequate."

"If there's one thing Shaun's good at, it's acting. Shaun may look like a choirboy, but he's not." Thrusting his chair away from the desk, Trent stood and strode to the window, apparently to get his emotions under control. When Trent turned back, his arms were folded tightly against his chest. "I notice that you're always sticking up for Shaun—it makes me wonder how objective you are in your investigation."

"I'm doing my best to keep an open mind and look at each clue—no matter where it leads."

"Then here's one thing you may not have thought about—what if he persuaded Grandma to change the will then she had second thoughts about it and told Shaun she was going to change it back? It could be Shaun made sure Grandma didn't have that chance."

The suggestion that Shaun could be the murderer didn't shock Erica. Despite Trent's claim that she had a blind spot with Shaun, Erica had never written Shaun off her list of suspects. Sure, it was easier to suspect someone like Carrie, but Erica had too many years of experience behind her to discount anyone. She'd met too many charming murderers. She listened as Trent went on.

"Don't the police usually focus on who stands to profit the most? And in this case, we all know who that is—Shaun. Since you're investigating, I'll give you some advice; take a long, hard look at Mr. Shaun Coleman."

* * *

That evening, Erica and Kristen sat reading in the sitting room. Kristen was curled up on the couch next to the grand piano, holding a bag of potato chips and munching away.

She held out the bag to Erica, who sat next to her in a chair. "Want a crisp?"

"No thanks."

Shaun came in and walked carefully across the beige carpet—as if the floor was loaded with unseen land mines. Bandit followed him.

"You certainly worked late tonight," Erica said. "I left a plate for you in the microwave."

"Thanks. I'll heat it up in a little while."

Shaun's face was tense. "Um, Kristen, could I talk to you?"

Kristen kept her finger on the page of her novel as she looked up. "Sure." When Erica started to rise to leave them alone, Kristen told her, "You stay there. If Shaun wants to talk about the little barney we had in front of you, he can do it with you here." She ran her fingers through her light blond hair, pushing it away from her face, then looked at him expectantly.

After sending Shaun an apologetic look, Erica settled back and set about trying to make herself as invisible as possible. Shaun sat next to Kristen, and Bandit moved over to curl up next to his master's black dress shoes.

"I've been thinking about what you said," Shaun began. "And you're right, I don't know what it's like to be an addict." He threw an anguished glance at Erica and plowed determinedly on. "Erica and I talked about it later, and she told me a little more about drug addiction. I still don't understand completely, but I'm trying. It's hard for me to accept that a person can't control their actions, even if they're hooked on drugs." His voice dropped a notch. "I guess part of what makes it tough is because

I grew up thinking my mother could have been with me if only she'd wanted to."

Kristen set her book aside. "I think Tammy wanted to be with you, but she was just overwhelmed. Pamela told me that Tammy took it very hard when her husband was killed in the war—that's when she started taking drugs. I guess they took over her life."

"All my life, I've either been hurt or angry about her leaving. So many times I wondered what Tammy was doing, wondered if she ever thought about me—" It tore at Erica's heart to hear the pain in Shaun's voice. A child would naturally wonder about his mother.

"That must have been terrible," Kristen murmured sympathetically. She took his hand. "I didn't mean to upset you by finding Tammy. I just think it would help you heal from the shadow of your past if you were able to talk with her. And in time, you might even develop a relationship with her—if you wanted." Kristen gave him an encouraging look. "You're not alone in this, you know. We'll work it out. You may not like what you find, but isn't knowing better than not knowing?" She peered into his face with a searching intensity.

"Maybe you're right." Shaun looked at Kristen. "I also thought about what you said about forgiving, and you're right—I'm not following what I've been taught. So I want to apologize. Our Church teaches us to be charitable and forgiving, but I've got a long way to go. Please don't judge the Church because of me. We're taught good principles—I'm just not the best at following them."

Tears gathered in Erica's eyes as Shaun went on. "I guess what I'm trying to say is that the Church is perfect, but I'm not." He grimaced. "I don't know if anything I've said makes sense. Maybe you're right, and I *am* addicted to being stupid."

Kristen blushed. "I'm sorry I said that. It was mean. I really don't think you're a prat. Sometimes I lose my temper. Will you forgive me?" A palpable current ran between the two as Shaun put a hand beneath Kristen's chin and raised her face to his.

"Is it okay if I go *now*?" Erica murmured plaintively.

Without taking her eyes off Shaun, Kristen nodded.

Chapter Fourteen

WALKING INTO SUN COAST, ERICA waved at Marge, who had a paisley scarf tied around her frizzy hair today. She was on the phone but smiled back as Erica went back to the conference room. Walter was already there, wearing an impeccable navy suit. They shook hands and sat at one end of the long conference table.

"Thanks for coming, Walter. I wanted to ask you something before we talk about Sun Coast. When you read the will, you said you would get the family together and give out the Lalique Crystal and Armani figures." When Walter nodded, Erica asked, "Could you hold off a few more days, possibly a week?"

"I'd like to get it taken care of, but if it's important, I'll wait."

"I'd appreciate that." How nice it was not to have to explain. Erica told him that Carrie had written the business plan and went over her visit with Carlos, saying, "I didn't learn much. I hope you had better luck."

Walter's comments were prefaced by a rumbling as he cleared his throat. "I talked with a number of employees. None of them knew of anything that would have made Blanche anxious. A few were complimentary of Shaun's growth. Apparently, he and Trent have clashed on a few issues, such as shipping, market research, and hiring an auditing firm, but Shaun has stood firm."

"Did you meet with Carlos?"

"I did. Carlos was vague, probably intentionally so, and admitted that someone in the company had done something questionable. Carlos said he'd called Blanche at home to discuss the matter and suggest the person be disciplined or fired. They argued, and Blanche told Carlos she couldn't do that to her own grandson."

That sounded familiar. Suddenly, Erica remembered. "Vicki told me she'd overheard an argument Grandma had on the phone with someone; it must have been Carlos. Vicki said Grandma had said she couldn't do that to her own grandson."

There was concern in Walter's faded blue eyes. "The only *grandson* working here is Trent, since she always referred to Shaun as her *son*."

"Did Carlos say what had been going on? It had to be serious if Carlos thought Grandma ought to fire him."

"Carlos wouldn't go into specifics. He said he was going to talk to Shaun about it, since the issue hadn't been resolved and he felt the CEO ought to know. Carlos admitted he held off telling Shaun because he wasn't too sure about him in the beginning and also because he'd hoped the person would make things right."

Erica's cell phone rang. "Hello, Shaun, hold on a minute." She looked at Walter.

"I've covered everything I had. Have him come in."

In a few minutes, Shaun entered, looking every bit the young, successful professional in a neat suit with a blue striped tie. "Hello, Erica, Walter." He shook their hands and sat across from Erica.

Standing, Erica put her hands flat on the table and, looking at the two men, said in a dramatic voice, "The reason I've called you here today is to tell you the butler did it."

Walter's gaunt face relaxed into a smile, while Shaun laughed outright. Shaun needed to laugh more often, Erica decided; he looked very attractive when he did.

Erica turned to Shaun. "Walter said Carlos was going to talk with you about some problem. Did he?"

"I'm not sure what problem you mean, but he did set up a meeting for tomorrow." Shaun looked puzzled. "I thought that was kind of weird since we talk every day, but he said it was important."

"I believe he's going to tell you about some problems here at Sun Coast," Walter said.

Shaun raised his eyebrows. "Is he? Well, isn't that interesting. He might be telling me something I already know."

"What do you mean?" Erica asked.

"I've found—if you'll forgive the cliché—a snake in the grass, and his name is Trent Coleman."

Erica caught her breath. "What's going on?"

"I can't give you a lot of details—you know how it is when you're investigating," he said, winking at Erica. "But I've been talking to a friend of mine, Marty Gleason. He works at the Sun Coast store in Coos Bay. We've been friends a long time, and when I called a week ago to check on the store, Marty had a few things to tell me, since he knew I was the new CEO. Marty had been afraid to say anything before."

"Afraid of reprisals, you mean?" Walter guessed.

"That's it. I reassured Marty that he could tell me anything, but he wanted to talk with his wife first before he said anything more."

"Has Trent been doing something illegal?" Erica asked.

"I'm not sure." Shaun shot a swift sideways look at Walter. "I'd like your advice on that once I talk with Marty."

Looking at Shaun, Erica tried to think what it was that made him look different today. Was it the steady eye contact or his assured manner of speaking? Whatever it was, Shaun no longer looked like a bewildered, hesitant boy, but a self-assured man.

Erica spoke up. "Although Grandma didn't know exactly what was going on, she made a couple of comments that made me wonder if Trent was involved. But he seems so devoted to Sun Coast that I couldn't imagine Trent being involved in any wrongdoing."

"I'll need to talk with Trent, and you can bet that conversation isn't going to be pretty."

Walter rubbed his chin. "When you meet with Trent, I'd like to be present, if you don't mind. As the legal representative of Sun Coast, I feel obligated to know what is going on."

"I'd like to be there too," Erica said.

Shaun's brown eyes, set beneath straight, dark brows, looked at her and Walter. "In other words, neither of you think I can handle it."

"There you go again," Erica chided, "letting your insecurities pop out. I'm going to speak for myself and Walter when I say that, yes, we think you can handle it, but we each have a special interest in this—Walter as a lawyer and myself as an investigator. So humor us." She smiled. "Besides, having two other bodies there might help diffuse what is sure to be an awkward situation."

Shaun considered. "All right. I'll let you know after I talk to Carlos and Marty."

Walter stood, and as Shaun made to rise, Erica asked, "Shaun, do you mind if I talk with you?"

Instantly, Walter understood her desire for privacy. He shook hands with them and left.

"I know you're busy, so I'll get right to the point. I happened to be talking with Nathan, and he mentioned that on the day before Grandma died, you zoomed out of the driveway so fast that Nathan wondered if you were going to hit him."

"So naturally, that proves I'm guilty."

"Oh, Shaun." Erica let the irritation she felt into her voice. She didn't mean to offend people—she just wanted to get to the truth. "I just wanted to ask why you were tearing out of the driveway. Surely there's a reason—Nathan says you're usually a very careful driver."

He grimaced. "I honestly can't remember pulling out of the driveway fast. But I can tell you that it wasn't because I'd just argued with Mom." With that, Shaun stood and left.

* * *

"Was Detective McGuire happy when you told him you'd found the boys who'd delivered the berries?" Erica had told David all about it the night before. Now it was the following afternoon.

There was a cool crispness in the air, so Erica pulled on a jacket as she went to sit in the gazebo. "Very. He had the same thoughts as you— that the accent, hat, and coat sounded like a disguise. But he wondered a bit because of the English accent."

"Did you ever find out anything on Phillip Bessinger? Grandma always felt he was a crook."

"I checked their divorce and it was final, so he wouldn't gain anything by killing Martha."

"That's too bad, but at least it's one suspect off your list."

"I thought the same thing."

"How are things between Shaun and Trent?" David asked.

"Civil but very cool. The tension is so thick when the two of them are together, it's like walking through molasses. I know Trent feels like Shaun cut the legs out from under him. Maybe that's why he's suggesting Shaun had something to do with Grandma's death."

David was quiet a moment. "You know, I've always felt sorry for Shaun. When we were growing up, his biggest problem was a lack of self-confidence. I don't think he ever got over being abandoned by his mother."

"How much do you know about Tammy?" Erica asked. "Is it true she was a drug addict?"

"That's what Grandpa told me. After Uncle Wayne died in Vietnam, Tammy started using drugs and was arrested a few times. Grandpa bailed her out and put her in a rehabilitation center, but when Tammy got out, she started using again. Even before she left, Grandma and Grandpa were the ones taking care of Shaun."

"That's so sad."

"I think that's why, in junior high and high school, Shaun started hanging out with some bad dudes."

"He must have been looking for people who would accept him."

"I tried to get Shaun to hang out with me and my friends, but he thought they looked down on him. Then, Shaun and his friends were spraying graffiti on a warehouse when the cops caught them. The other boys said Shaun was the ring leader. It was a stupid lie, but Shaun wouldn't rat on the others. He got off light since it was his first offense, but that made him see his so-called friends for what they were, and Shaun stopped hanging out with them."

"Good for him."

"After that, Mom ordered me to be Shaun's friend. She also talked to the bishop and the Young Men leaders, and they kept after Shaun until he was attending regularly. Everyone liked Shaun once they got to know him. He's a good guy."

"I'm glad he had you to lean on."

"Shaun and I have always been good buddies. I'm glad to hear he's doing good at Sun Coast. I'll have to give him a call." Then David asked, "How are you doing on the case?"

"Finding those boys was a big break, but I've still got a ways to go. I feel like I'm still stumbling in the dark. There must be something I haven't uncovered yet."

"I know what you need. Chocolate."

Erica smiled. David always bought her chocolate when she was on a tough case. He went on. "I'll send you some. It'll clear your head and help you think."

"Better send a case, then."

* * *

After talking with David and her children, Erica took a short nap. When she woke up, she went downstairs into the kitchen, where Bandit lay sprawled by the French doors. Pamela sat at the table, snipping out large circles out of blue fabric.

"What smells so good?"

"I hate to tell you," Pamela said, "but you were busy, so I bought a frozen lasagna. It's in the oven."

"Not a *frozen* lasagna!" Erica wailed. "Think of all the preservatives."

"You'll live."

"I have my doubts." With a heavy sigh, Erica walked over to the table. "What are you doing?"

"Getting a head start on next week's Cub Scout den meeting." Carrie was the den leader for the Bears, and Pamela was her assistant. Pamela held up one of the finished bean bags, which had a brightly colored feather secured to it by an elastic band. "I felt guilty about missing the last few weeks, so I volunteered to make the bags."

Erica eyed the portable sewing machine. "Need any help?"

"I'm good, but could you run over to Carrie's house? I'm going to stuff them with beans, and she picked up a bag for me."

"Sure. I'll go right after I make some Crab Dip.[7] I like to let it set so the flavors can mingle." They'd planned to watch a movie that night, and Erica thought crab dip and crackers would make a tasty snack.

Erica had her latex gloves on and was dicing the celery when Shaun and Kristen walked in carrying their scriptures. Shaun's face was happy and relaxed, as it usually was when he was with Kristen, which was as often as they could manage. They were a picture of a young couple falling in love.

"We were going outside to read," Kristen said, stopping to peer into the bowl by Erica, "but we can help if you need us."

"Read away. I'm nearly done."

Pamela looked at the quad Kristen held. "Is that new?"

"Shaun gave it to me," Kristen said proudly, holding the scriptures up. She then kissed Shaun on the cheek. "Isn't he a luv?" Shaun colored but wore a smile as they went out.

A moment later, Erica groaned. "Rats. We're don't have enough mayonnaise."

---

7   See the appendix for this recipe.

Pamela looked up from her sewing. "How much do you need?"

"A teaspoon."

"Dear-heart, a teaspoon isn't going to make any difference."

"Au contraire! Cooking is a precise activity. You need to follow instructions exactly." Erica threw the empty jar away. "You can depend on recipes to turn out fine as long as you follow instructions. No guessing. No wondering. No anxiety."

"I can't agree with you there," Pamela shook her head. "Sometimes my cooking doesn't turn out no matter how closely I follow the recipe. But that does explain why you like cooking so much—it matches your personality. You're a very precise person, not just in cooking but also in investigating and, well, just about everything you do."

"Thank you," Erica replied, pleased with the nice compliment. Too many people took her precision the wrong way—as if it was odd or wrong. Then she thought of a solution to her dilemma. "I know, I'll just borrow some mayonnaise from Carrie when I go over and get the beans for you."

* * *

When Carrie escorted Erica into the kitchen, Trent was there, munching on a cookie. "Hi ya, Erica. Want a cookie?"

"No thanks."

Carrie got the mayonnaise out and set the jar on the counter by Trent. She looked at him archly then asked Erica. "Now, tell me again; how much mayonnaise did you need?"

"A teaspoon."

Carrie held out a hand, palm up to her husband. "Pay up," she trilled. As Trent grumbled and pulled out his wallet, Carrie explained, "Trent didn't believe me when I told him that you wanted one teaspoon, so I bet him."

"I should have known better than to bet against your idiosyncrasies," Trent told Erica, placing a twenty in his wife's hand. He stuffed his wallet back in his pocket. "I need to help Chad with a science project, but I'll see you Sunday for dinner."

"Looking forward to it," Erica said as he left.

Carrie spooned a dab of mayonnaise into a container. "I know you're quite the cook, but I can't understand fussing over one teaspoon of mayonnaise."

"I like to be accurate. When you're precise, cooking is a very calming activity."

Carrie's big blue eyes opened wide. "How do you figure?"

"Because if you follow the steps correctly, you don't have to worry—you're practically assured a successful outcome."

Carrie gave one of her tinkling laughs that was so annoying. "I've been thinking about how you put me and Trent under a microscope, but not Shaun. If you ask me, you've got a blind spot with Shaun." She put a hand on a slim hip. "And what about you? You were there the night Grandma died. Who's investigating the investigator?"

Erica felt her face redden. *Count to ten*, she told herself. Then she replied, "The police are investigating everyone. I was fingerprinted and interviewed along with everyone else." Then she said, "Trent said you guys are going to contest the will. Is that something you really want to do?"

"We've already retained a lawyer." Carrie's face, usually pretty, suddenly took on the look of a pinched weasel. "First of all, Grandma told Trent that he would succeed her as chairman, and second, Grandma wouldn't have given half of everything to Shaun if he hadn't coerced her."

"What about Trent's not-so-subtle accusation that Shaun poisoned his own mother?"

"I see you're worried about that. If he didn't do it, then you'll need to catch the real murderer, won't you?" Carrie's eyes held a challenge.

"Don't worry. I'm going to find out who killed Grandma—whoever it is."

Chapter Fifteen

THE SUN WAS JUST PEEKING over the mountains, sending out early morning streaks of light, when Erica left for Lake Oswego. It had rained briefly during the night, making the air extra clear—like crystal—and Erica enjoyed the drive. Leslie Flynn, Martha's friend, had provided excellent directions, and Erica found the modest, white frame house easily.

The smile on Leslie's pleasant, round face was somewhat tremulous as she opened the door.

"Come in, come in." Leslie dabbed at her reddened eyes with a tissue. "You'll have to forgive me. I've been thinking about Martha." Leslie led the way into a front room that was nearly as crowded with knickknacks as Martha's. She sat in a chair opposite Erica and regarded her guest with an appraising yet friendly look.

"Thank you for meeting with me," Erica began. "I understand you recently got back from Hawaii. That would explain the great tan you have."

Leslie's face dimpled. "My sister and I went together, just the two of us. We'd talked about it for years and finally went. It was wonderful."

"You must have spent a lot of time on the beach."

"We did." Leslie patted her face self-consciously. "I should have used more sun block, I suppose, but I'm old fashioned enough that I like a bit of a tan."

"I do too," Erica said. "When I was growing up, I was jealous of people with great tans."

"I imagine they were probably envious of you—as pretty as you are. Actually, I think my tan made Gail a little jealous, because she got a spray-on tan right after I got back." Leslie gave a little giggle. "Then again, it could have been for the part she's playing at the local theatre.

It's a shame they made her pluck her eyebrows, though. I've never liked penciled-in brows."

It was time to get down to business. "Gail said you and Martha liked to go to garage sales."

"Laws, yes." Leslie smiled hugely. "It was our favorite thing to do. Gail would go with us if she wasn't working on Saturdays. We liked going to estate sales and auctions too. Do you go to garage sales?" She seemed eager to find a compadre.

"I don't go as often as I used to. It's amazing the things you can find. I used to buy a lot of clothes for my children, but now they'd die before wearing something I bought at a garage sale."

"You can get some great bargains," Leslie said. "A few weeks ago, I got a twenty-five-pound sack of kitty litter for a dollar. The sack had been opened, but hardly any had been taken out." Leslie looked introspective. "I meant to ask them what happened to their cat, but I forgot."

It was going to be a full-time job to keep Leslie on track. "Did Martha have any enemies?"

"Heavens no!" Leslie looked shocked. "Martha didn't have a mean bone in her body. Everyone loved her." The tears came back, and Leslie pulled a tissue from a pink box on the end table. "I still can't believe she's gone. If only Martha hadn't gone on a walk that day. Who would have ever thought a madman would be lurking in Bryant Woods?" Leslie's voice quavered as she looked at Erica. "You're working with the police, aren't you? Do they have any suspects?"

"They're still investigating. I'm meeting with Detective Pocharski later to go over the crime scene."

"I wouldn't go in those woods—too many crazy people around." Leslie shuddered.

Looking around, Erica remarked, "You and Martha like to collect things, don't you?"

"We couldn't help ourselves. When you can get cute things so cheap, it's hard to turn them down." Leslie's giggle sounded like a young girl's.

"Did you get those in Hawaii?" Erica's eyes were on three bronze tiki figures of varying height, arranged in a triangle.

"Why, yes, I did." Leslie had a proud smile.

"How long have you had them arranged like that?"

Leslie blinked. "Like what?"

Erica picked up the tallest figure and put it on one end and the shortest on the other so they were in a straight line. She sat back with a sigh of satisfaction. "They look much better now, don't you think?" Then, realizing she had gotten off track, Erica said, "Gail showed me some jewelry Martha had bought."

"Martha loved jewelry, but most of what she bought was junk." Leslie made a face. "You know, costume jewelry—bracelets that turn your wrist green once the finish rubs off."

"Oh, the kind of jewelry I buy." Erica smiled.

"Most of the jewelry people sell at garage sales is worthless. Estate sales can have better quality items. Gail likes them better too. She really knows her stuff. Gail's real good at planning too, and when she came with us, she would always organize our trips." Leslie leaned forward and rearranged the tiki figures back to their original triangle. "Sometimes you can find really good stuff at estate sales, and that's what Martha was always hoping to find. Auctions are trickier. You have to know your stuff. Martha's problem was she liked anything shiny, and usually the shinier something is, the cheaper it is. Gail tried to tell her what to look for, but Martha never could remember—even though her ex-husband used to be a jeweler."

"I didn't know that." Erica moved the tiki figures back in a line. *Ah, much nicer.* "Did she ever find any good pieces of jewelry?"

Leslie looked bewildered as she eyed the Hawaiian pieces. "In July, Martha bought a nice ring, but she lost it." When Erica looked sympathetic, Leslie went on. "I remember that because it was the weekend before the fourth of July. Martha asked me to come over for a picnic, and we were going to see fireworks later. Then she misplaced the ring. But a few months before that, Martha found a necklace she was able to sell for over two hundred dollars. And she only paid ten dollars for it!" Leslie seemed as excited as if she had found it herself.

"Wow, that's great. Did she take it to a pawn shop?"

"Martha has a friend who's a jeweler. He bought it. After that, Martha became really serious about looking for jewelry. She was so proud of herself—you know Martha. She acted like she had her own business. Martha kept records on everything she bought, writing it all down, whether it was a package of clothespins or an end table. Martha would then copy over all of her jewelry purchases on a separate paper that she called her 'weekly report' and mail it to her jeweler friend."

Leslie arranged the tiki figures back in a triangular cluster, setting the last piece in place firmly. Checkmate.

"Did he take her seriously?"

"I think so. At first, Martha used to send him everything she bought, but he told her to just send a description and a picture, and if he was interested, he'd ask her to send the actual item."

"I don't imagine that happened too often."

"No, it didn't," Leslie admitted. "And sometimes when it did, I wondered if it was just to make Martha feel good. He seemed like a very nice man. Martha found some nice things a few months ago at an estate sale, and he asked to see a pretty bracelet she'd bought. It was lovely—had a crisscross design with rhinestones. Of course, Martha was convinced they were diamonds even though Gail told her they weren't. But Martha liked it so well, she decided to keep it." Leslie paused. "Are you going to see Gail today?"

"I am. She doesn't have to go to work until later." Erica picked up the tallest tiki figure. Acting as if she'd never seen it before, she commented, "This really is lovely." When she set it down, she put it on one end and quick as a flash lined up the other figure. "Do you have the name of the jeweler?"

Leslie wrinkled up her forehead. "I've been trying to think of it. Good heavens, Martha told me enough times that I ought to remember. What was it? Oh yes, his first name was Bradley, same as my nephew. Last name was Quinn. Don't ask me how I remember *that*."

"It doesn't sound like Martha was very successful. Did she ever get discouraged?"

"Laws no. Martha never got down about anything, bless her heart. Even with her poor health and her mother badgering her to move back to Florence. And did you know Martha was starting to seriously consider moving back home? But as for finding stuff at garage sales, that necklace was enough to keep Martha going for years. Just like Pavlov's dogs, you know." Leslie's good-natured face beamed. "Besides, Martha just plain liked garage sales, and there were always plenty of bargains to keep her happy. Martha liked to watch that TV show *Cash in the Attic* and it kept her hopes up." She leaned over and pushed the tiki figures back into a triangle.

Erica contemplated them silently. Then she brightened. "I've got an idea. Why don't you put one of those tiki figurines in your bedroom and leave the other two here? Two is such a nice, even number."

"I like them here. Together."

That's what Erica was afraid of. Erica realized she was making a pest of herself; it was just so hard not to try and make things straight when they were crooked, or—she thought with a shudder—in triangles. Perhaps David was right, her OCD *did* make her behave oddly. It was not something she liked to dwell on. She preferred to think of it as making the world a better—and straighter—place. There was an awkward pause; then Erica asked, "Could I get a glass of water?"

"Sure. I'll be right back."

When Leslie returned, she handed Erica the glass then stopped. The tiki figures were lined up in a row. Leslie sighed. "I can certainly tell that you and Martha are related."

"Actually, Martha was my husband's aunt. I'm not related to her by blood."

"Could've fooled me."

* * *

Yellow poplars shone brilliantly alongside the road as Erica drove to the Lake Oswego police station. She loved the fall, when trees were dressed in gorgeous colors and there was a delightful crispness in the air. Pulling off the freeway, she paid attention to evidence of the changing seasons. Here and there, random trees were dressed in russet and deep ruby with an occasional brilliant burst of maple flame. Erica parked in the back next to the two rows that were reserved for Lake Oswego's black-and-white police cars. Carrying a sack, Erica hurried up the stairs to the cream-colored building. When she entered the corner office, Captain Stanbridge leaned back in his chair and eyed her speculatively as she sat in a wooden chair.

"I had an interesting phone call the other day—from Ken Brown," the captain informed her.

"*Chief* Ken Brown?" Why would her husband's police chief be calling?

"He had a few things to say about you."

"All full of praise, I hope?"

"You could say that. At first, I wondered if you'd asked him to call." When Erica began to sputter, the captain held up a hand and continued. "Chief Brown assured me you didn't. He said he's known you for years and that you've always done excellent work. Also, Detective McGuire has nothing but good things to say, as does Detective Pocharski, who told me all about meeting you at your aunt's house when you were here."

Captain Stanbridge's eyes narrowed. "I found it interesting that even though I made it clear we planned on handling this case without you, you persuaded Detective Pocharski to go over the case with you. It sounded like you practically had Simon jumping through hoops for you, but then a pretty woman can do that to a young, inexperienced officer."

Erica started sputtering, but again, Captain Stanbridge headed her off. "Now look here, Mrs. Coleman, you're a shrewd woman, I can tell, and a person who usually exercises good judgment."

Erica did her best to assume an expression of superhuman intelligence.

"And I suppose it's only natural—as a private investigator—that you would do anything to get information about the case. However, I'm willing to overlook your giving Detective Pocharski the false impression that we were working with you."

How magnanimous, Erica thought snarkily. Good thing the good captain didn't know she had arranged to meet with Simon again that afternoon.

Even so, Erica knew she was on a slippery slope—one she needed to get off as soon as possible. Her best bet was to direct his attention elsewhere. "I'm sure Detective Pocharski told you what we came up with at Martha's house."

"Yes—if you're talking about the forced windowsill and the footprints. I have to admit some of your deductions were sound. Your mind works like mine."

Surely the highest compliment Captain Stanbridge could bestow.

The captain rubbed his prominent chin. "I talked with Detective McGuire again today. Since you have an inside track with the family, his preference is that you proceed with your investigation."

And what about you, oh captain, my captain?

"I told Detective McGuire I would let you continue investigating here."

Was she supposed to kiss his feet? Erica tried to shake off her crabby thoughts by thinking on the bright side—such as how nice it was to have the captain's permission to continue something she was going to do anyway.

Detective Stanbridge looked at her strangely. For a moment, Erica worried he could read her thoughts. Thank goodness thoughts were not visible entities that hung in the air. "Well," he said with a touch of impatience, "do you have any new information?"

So that's what lay behind his look. He wanted details. Erica knew she had to pull a rabbit out of her hat in order to win his continuing approbation. The trouble was, she only had a very small rabbit. Erica explained only two stores in Florence sold chocolate-covered strawberries.

"I'd been keeping an eye on the one closest to my grandmother's house, Callie's Candies, and the other day, I found the two boys who delivered the strawberries. They gave me a description of the man who asked them to deliver the strawberries." She held up her white sack. "Since I was right by the candy store, I gave into temptation."

"What's that?"

Was he serious? What else could be in a sack from a candy store? Opening the sack, Erica offered Captain Stanbridge a sample. He pulled out a turtle. One of Erica's favorites.

"Chocolate might not be able to cure all ills," Erica said, "but it certainly is a step in the right direction." Taking the last turtle, Erica took a satisfying bite.

With a rough attempt at jocularity, Captain Stanbridge said, "I hope you're not trying to bribe an officer."

Perhaps he was human after all. "No, sir," she said with a smile. "But I thought I ought to share so I didn't eat them all myself."

"You don't look like you need to worry about eating too much chocolate."

An actual compliment! Would miracles never cease? "I believe in a balanced diet—a piece of chocolate in both hands."

Instead of chuckling, he looked puzzled.

Make that part human. And with that, Erica gave up.

Chapter Sixteen

When Erica pulled up at Martha's house, she glanced at her watch. She was early. Grabbing the sack of bread crumbs and cut-up apples, she went to the chicken pen, where the Plymouth Rocks were scratching contentedly in the dust. When they saw Erica, they clucked with excitement and waddled over as fast as their chubby bodies would allow. Smiling, Erica threw in her scraps, and the chickens scrabbled and jousted with each other to snap up bread crusts and bits of fruit.

While the kittens huddled in the corner watching her with bright green eyes, Erica filled the automatic waterer and feeder she'd bought. She couldn't believe how much the kittens had grown. After slipping on her gloves, Erica reached inside. Two of the kittens hissed—tiny wisps of sound. Erica scooped them up one at a time, stroking them until they quieted then setting them beside the feeder to nibble at the fish-shaped food.

Holding the last one, Erica murmured, "You don't have to be afraid of me. I'm not going to hurt you." Then she sensed a presence. Without turning, Erica said, "The kittens are getting tamer, aren't they?"

"How did you know I was here?" Gail said, coming closer.

"Just felt something and assumed it was you. You'll need to find good homes for the kittens."

"How am I supposed to do that?"

"Ask around, see if anyone you know wants a kitten. Or put an ad in the paper."

"I haven't got time for that. I'll just take them to the animal shelter."

"Don't do that!" Erica cried. It was unbearable to think they might be euthanized. They were just helpless little kittens looking for love and companionship. "I'll help you find homes for them."

When she and Gail went to the house, Erica stripped off her gloves, and Gail remarked, "I'm surprised you wear gloves when you like animals so much."

"I love them, but they do have germs."

Gail asked, "Would you like some coffee or a soda pop?" The older woman had a pleasant way about her and was always friendly and eager to please.

"A drink of water would be great."

Gail poured herself a glass of iced tea, and the women moved into the front room. It was a marvel how knickknacks covered every inch of available space. There was a solid blanket of ceramic bells, ducks, cats, and bears on the end tables. In the middle of one table was a large statue of a young girl petting a kitten. It looked familiar.

Gail noticed her looking at it. "Martha's mother gave her that since she loved animals so much. It's a twin to the one Mrs. Coleman has in her sitting room."

Erica rearranged a trio of dancing mice so they were in a straight line. "How does that look?"

"Fine." Gail seemed a little unsure what Erica meant.

"You are a woman of taste," Erica pronounced. Then she confided, "Some people arrange things—like tiki figures—in *triangles*." Her voice was disapproving. "Some people have no regard for symmetry." Erica stopped, suddenly aware she was letting her bias show. Not everyone felt an inward pang when things were not lined up.

Gail smiled hesitantly. "How was your visit with Leslie?"

"Very nice. She said Martha kept records on everything she bought at garage and estate sales and at auctions. Could I see them?"

Gail waved a hand at the bookshelf. "There they are."

"Wow." Rising, Erica went over to look at the rows of spiral-bound notebooks that filled the shelves. "Martha really *did* like to keep records."

"Not all of them are garage sales. Martha kept records on everything. These two shelves have the garage-sale binders." Gail began moving the baskets, glass bells, and snow globes at the front of the shelves then pulled out a notebook and handed it to Erica. On June 18, Martha bought two rings, writing that the first had clear stones that were "probably diamonds" and the other ring had a large green stone, which was "probably an emerald." She also listed her other buys—a metal watering can, two strings of icicle lights, a red floral skirt, a step stool, and a bent trowel. Everything was written in large, loopy handwriting.

"Looks like Martha was an optimist," Erica remarked. While not exactly realistic, what a wonderful way to be—always looking on the bright side.

There was a gentle smile on Gail's face. "She enjoyed writing down everything she bought and was as content as a child playing office. It kept her busy and happy. Martha used those notes to write up her 'reports,' as she called them, which she sent to Mr. Quinn."

"Leslie said Martha found a valuable necklace once."

Gail's face lit up. "Can you believe that? She sold it to Mr. Quinn for two hundred dollars, I think it was, but you'd have thought it was worth a million the way Martha acted."

Erica pulled out another notebook and looked at the dates. "Looks like she went to garage sales every week."

"It would have taken a disaster of biblical proportions to prevent Martha from going. She always took a sack lunch, and when she got hungry, she'd sit in the shade on someone's lawn and eat." Gail laughed at Erica's look. "That was Martha. She didn't mind, and it never occurred to her that someone else might."

That sounded just like Aunt Martha, Erica thought fondly. As they talked, Erica pushed back a few notebooks that were protruding. "Just thought I'd even them up," she explained. "Leslie also said Martha found a pretty bracelet that she really liked. It had a crisscross design and little rhinestones in it. Could I see it?"

Gail frowned, trying to remember. "Martha had so many, but I think I remember the one you mean. She kept the ones she liked in her jewelry box in her room. I'll see if I can find it." She hurried off.

Erica went to the bottom of the stairs and watched as Gail went up the stairs and into her bedroom. In a short time, Gail returned and handed her a bracelet.

Erica examined it closely. "It's pretty, but it doesn't look expensive."

"It's not. Martha was convinced those chips were diamonds, but I'm sure they're rhinestones." Gail took back the bracelet. "Have you or the police found out anything more about Mrs. Coleman?"

"Not much. I've spent a lot of time looking into things at the family business."

"How is that nice young man, the one who took over at Sun Coast?"

"Shaun is doing great. He's surprising a lot of people, I'm glad to report."

"That's good." Gail smiled. "When I was there, Trent seemed quite upset that Shaun had taken his place. I can understand his feelings though, since Blanche told Trent he would be CEO. Blanche could be cavalier and high-handed at times." Gail stole a look at her watch.

"Do you need to be going?"

"I do, but I was wondering if you would like to come and see where I work?" Gail's face was hopeful and eager.

"How far away is it? Simon was going to meet me here so we could go to the woods."

"About five to eight minutes."

"Oh, that'd be fine. I'd love to see the floral shop."

Erica drove, following Gail, and they parked in back. As they crossed the parking lot, Gail said, "When I came to Florence, I had no college degree and no skills, but Chaleh gave me a chance and trained me."

"That was a break." Not many people got that chance, Erica thought.

"It was, but now Chaleh wants to retire. With the bad economy, she's having trouble selling the shop and might have to close it. I'm worried sick about finding another job because we get calls every day asking if we're hiring. A lot of floral designers are looking for work."

The heavenly scent of fresh flowers met them as they walked inside. Shelves in the back held cases of floral foam, boxes of cellophane and foil, and row after row of vases, compotes, and baskets. An older woman with short gray hair, wearing a long flowing skirt and sandals turned from where she was arranging pixie carnations and white daisies in a vase.

"Well, here's our star!" she cried, grinning at Gail.

Gail looked confused. "What do you mean?"

"Don't tell me you didn't see the poster on the door when you came in—"

"I guess I missed it, but let me introduce you to Erica Coleman. She's Martha's niece. Erica, this is Chaleh Henderson, my boss."

Chaleh went to Erica with both hands extended and grasped hers. "I'm so sorry about your aunt. What a horrible thing to have happen."

"Thank you."

"What's this about a poster?" Gail asked.

"Come and see! I can't believe you didn't see it." Chaleh glided past the helium tank and bins of brightly colored balloons. "The people from the theatre brought it over."

They stepped outside to view the poster taped to the door. Chaleh explained to Erica, "Gail's in a play at Lake Oswego Theater House—*The Secret Garden*. She's playing Dr. Craven."

"Leslie mentioned you were in a theater group. I'm impressed."

Gail smiled shyly. "It's only a small theater, but I enjoy it. I loved being in plays in high school and decided to try out when I moved here."

"She's marvelous," Chaleh exclaimed. "So talented. She'll be on Broadway next. But then, Gail does an outstanding job in anything she does."

"Oh posh." Gail's face pinked up with pleasure.

They went back inside, and when Gail saw that some customers had walked in the front, she went to help them. Erica watched Chaleh slip support tubes onto the stems of gerbera daisies. "What a wonderful job to have—working with flowers all day."

"I've always enjoyed it. I'm really going to miss it."

"Gail said you were going to retire. Should I offer congratulations or condolences?"

"Perhaps a little of both. I'll miss the work, but having more free time will be great."

"And you haven't been able to sell the shop?"

"No takers yet." Chaleh put the gerberas in the floral cooler and brought out a bucket of roses. "My husband wants me to liquidate everything. He retired two years ago and has been waiting for the shop to sell so we can travel. I keep hoping someone will buy it, but I can't keep waiting."

As Chaleh peeled outer petals off the roses, she glanced out front, where Gail was helping a customer choose a planter. "Gail's a very talented designer, but it's going to be tough for her to find such a specialized job in a slow economy. I'd hoped she could buy the shop herself, but getting a loan today is almost impossible."

Another customer came, and when Chaleh went to help them, Erica went to admire the buckets of daisies, alstroemeria, tulips, and roses in the floral cooler. There was a smudge on the glass door, and she wiped it so she could see the tulips better. As she did, something stirred in her consciousness. What was it? She lost the thought when Chaleh came back to get some baby's breath.

Erica went out front to tell Gail she was leaving, then came back and told Chaleh, "It was nice to meet you."

"Same here," Chaleh said brightly. "And if you know anyone who wants to buy a floral shop, tell them to give me a call."

* * *

Erica left the door to the shed open and was playing with the kittens when she heard Detective Pocharski's Crown Victoria pull up. She threw her gloves in the garbage can, and when he climbed out of his vehicle, she thanked the young detective for coming.

"Glad to come." Simon grinned boyishly. "I'm sorry Captain Stanbridge couldn't make it."

What a surprise, Erica thought as they crossed the backyard and started into Bryant Woods.

"Guess what the latest news is?" With the barest of pauses, Detective Pocharski went on. "You'll never guess, so I'll tell you." Then, afraid that sounded rude, Simon added, "You probably would have made some good guesses." Erica stifled an urge to giggle.

Simon went on. "Rumors are going around that Bryant Woods is haunted. A boy that lives nearby says he saw Martha walking in the woods after she died. "

"That's kinda creepy," Erica said, making a face.

"I talked with the kid—his name is Travis—and he admitted he saw Martha *before* she died. But the rumor was already going around that he saw Martha *after* she died. And here's another creepy thing: I double-checked the date he saw Martha, and it was the day she was in Florence for Blanche's funeral. So she wasn't anywhere near Bryant Woods."

They started down the fern-lined trail, and wearing an eager expression, Simon said, "With this rumor floating around and Halloween coming up, word is that the woods are going to be packed with people on Halloween night." Simon was full of enthusiasm.

"With everybody trying to scare each other." Erica could see it now.

Simon's grin practically split his face. "Ought to be a blast. Can't wait."

"You mean you're going?"

He blinked. "Well, I, ah—I'll have to be there to keep the crowd under control."

"I see." Erica hid her smile as Simon led the way through thick woods of ash, birch, and an occasional stand of white cedar. At the first fork, he turned left, then right, and after a few minutes stopped near a tree that was dressed in ivy.

Simon pointed into a thicket of chokecherry and Russian olives. "That's where her body was."

They stepped off the trail, avoiding the sharp thorns from the Russian olives. Meticulously, Simon explained the crime scene. It was hard to listen impassively, knowing that this was the spot where Martha had been killed. It took all of Erica's police training to force back the emotions that churned inside. When all of Erica's questions had been answered, they headed back. They were nearly to Martha's backyard when Simon's radio blared. The crackling voice of the dispatcher asked Simon to respond to a 1042.

Simon responded then turned to Erica. "Gotta go. Car accident."

"Thanks for going over things with me. And, ah, have fun on Halloween."

"Will do!" Simon grinned at her then galloped off.

On an impulse, Erica turned and went back into the woods. The air smelled thick and damp, like wet leaves. What had Martha been thinking that day as she'd walked here? Did she have an altercation with someone she'd met in the woods? Or had Martha met someone she knew?

Determinedly, Erica pushed aside her gloomy thoughts. It was a beautiful fall afternoon, and she wanted to enjoy a few minutes before the drive back to Florence. As she strolled along, Erica filled her lungs with the heady woodsy air, savoring the restfulness of the quiet atmosphere. There were a number of forks, and Erica marked each with a stick so she could find her way back. It was very still except for an occasional burst of birdsong from a black-capped chickadee or a robin.

A small smile crossed her face as she strolled idly past willows and white oak. This visit to Lake Oswego had given Erica a fresh and unexpected line of inquiry, opening a whole new line of questions. Lost in thought, she continued deeper into the forest, which was filled with the warm odor of earth and pine needles. If she hadn't known a murder had occurred here, Erica would have thought it the most quiet and peaceful place on earth.

As Douglas firs whispered in the light breeze, Erica mulled over her visit to the floral shop. What was it that had nudged her while she was there? Something shifted in her mind, and she remembered something her grandmother had said.

She was still trying to make the connection when a rustle sounded in the woods behind her. Erica turned but saw nothing. With the long shadows of late afternoon slanting over the woods, she could understand a little better how the neighbor boy could have let his imaginings run away with him. For some reason, she felt suddenly uneasy but put it down to knowing the violence that had occurred here recently.

Patches of slanting sunlight crossed her path, and she turned left at another fork. As she thrust her stick in the ground, Erica glanced behind her, where the woods were thick and dark with firs and ponderosa pines struggling for light. Inwardly she shuddered, fighting against an involuntary shrinking that always came when she was faced with darkness. It was a weakness Erica fought from time to time, yet it was not an irrational one. It stemmed from a childhood incident when a teenage cousin had locked six-year-old Erica in a dark basement closet for five hours. It had taken years for the nightmares to decrease in frequency, and sometimes even now, they invaded her sleep.

Yet it wasn't just the coming darkness that made Erica fearful. Something didn't feel right. A short distance away there was a crackling sound. Erica looked into the brush where she thought the noise originated and saw nothing. Probably a rabbit. Still, her arms had goose bumps. Walking through the woods by herself no longer seemed a good idea.

Erica turned around and started back. At the first fork, a yellow warbler with bright feathers hopped across the trail, and Erica stopped in dismay. The stick she had pushed in the ground was lying in the middle of the path. Her breath caught in her throat when she saw it had been broken in two and lay a foot from where she had planted it at the edge of the path.

A cold wash of fear coursed through her, and Erica became acutely aware of the loneliness of the shadows around her. There were no faint voices of other hikers. Still, that didn't mean there weren't other people around, she reminded herself. Their voices could be muted by the thick woods. And it was possible a child had seen the stick and pulled it up and broken it.

And yet, it could have been broken by someone not so innocent.

Which was the way back to Martha's house? Erica looked around and on impulse went right, hurrying through a darkened copse of red cedar and noble fir. Erica watched the thick bushes on either side of her. In a nearby tree, a squirrel chattered, and the normalness of the sound helped her relax.

Another fork. Erica looked for her stick. At least this one was still in the ground, but it had been broken in half and the top was left dangling by a bit of connecting bark. Someone had done this. At least one other person was in the woods with her. But was the person dangerous?

For a moment, Erica considered calling out but decided against it. She started off again, glancing uneasily over her shoulder. The trees seemed to close in around her. How eerie the woods seemed now—and how deserted. Birdsong that had been coming from a thicket ahead of her stopped suddenly, and there was a burst of wings, as if the birds had been suddenly disturbed by something.

Erica felt a presence and thought she heard something move. Hurrying on, she came to another fork and another broken stick lying in the pathway.

She went left this time and, after a breathless few minutes, heard voices. Another minute and she overtook a middle-aged couple. It was such a relief to see people that she hurried over to them. They gave her a strange look, concerned perhaps, by how heavily she was breathing and the tenseness of her expression.

"Hello," Erica began, willing her voice to be calm so she didn't make the couple nervous. "I've been trying to find my way out, but I took a wrong turn."

"That's easy to do," said the curly headed woman. "We used to get lost all the time when we first started coming here."

Her husband nodded. "Some of the trails go for a long way."

"Have you seen anyone else?" Her words came out a little too strong.

The woman looked surprised. "Did you lose the person you were with?"

Erica didn't want to explain her fears that she thought she was being followed, so she settled for a simple, "Ah, yes."

The woman said, "We caught a glimpse of someone, but he went another way—was almost running."

"It was a man?"

The couple looked at each other. "Actually, I'm not sure," the woman responded. "I didn't get a real good look."

"Do you come here often?" Erica asked.

"We used to, but we haven't been in a while," the man replied. "I don't know if you heard about it, but a woman was killed here recently. I think that's kept a lot of people away."

"I did hear about that," Erica replied faintly then asked, "Do you know which way the subdivision is?"

The woman explained, and as Erica hurried off, the trees began groaning as the wind picked up. By the time she reached Martha's house, the sun had touched the horizon. Erica went to the shed and slipped on her gloves with hands that trembled just a little. Nothing like petting an animal to calm one's nerves.

Picking up a kitten, she stroked it gently, whispering, "You'll never guess what just happened."

Chapter Seventeen

THAT EVENING, PAMELA CAME INTO the game room, where Erica, Shaun, and Kristen were discussing which DVD to watch. Coming to stand in front of Erica, Pamela said accusingly, "I just got off the phone with David. What's this about someone following you in the woods when you were in Lake Oswego?"

Kristen's gray eyes widened as she turned to Erica. "What?"

"Nothing, really. I went to the woods with Detective Pocharski. He left, and I walked around a little more." Erica explained the broken sticks.

At first, Kristen had looked worried, but she relaxed. "It sounds like something kids would do."

"Or it could have been some maniac—the same maniac that killed Martha." Pamela's eyebrows drew together as she sat down heavily. "Erica, I *wish* you would just let the police handle things."

Shaun set the DVDs aside. "Who knew you were going to be in the woods yesterday?"

"I don't remember. Lots of people. But enough of that—I want to watch a movie."

"You're changing the subject, dear-heart," Pamela said.

"I sure am. Kristen, you and Pamela pick a DVD and get it into place while Shaun and I go to the kitchen and make some popcorn."

While Shaun put ice in four glasses, Erica poured in the kernels and turned on the popcorn popper. Raising her voice above the noise from the popper, she asked, "Did you get a chance to talk with Carlos?"

"I did. What I told him about my friend Marty went right along with what Carlos suspected."

"Have you talked with Marty again?"

"Yep. His wife is good with it, so I'm going to meet with Marty tomorrow, and he'll give me all the specifics. I've also been collecting other information so I'll be prepared to talk with Trent."

"Well?" Erica poured melted butter on the popcorn. "Now that it's a done deal, are you going to tell me what Marty said, or do I have to punch you in the nose?"

Shaun laughed as he poured apple juice in the glasses. "You'll find out when I talk with Trent. I've already asked him to come over tomorrow night. Be sure and bring your striped shirt so you can referee. I guarantee he's not going to like what I have to say." Shaun put the bottle of juice in the fridge. "I also found out Trent tried to talk Carlos into voting me out as chairman of the board. Trent even hinted that if Carlos didn't vote against me, he wouldn't have much of a future at Sun Coast."

"Oh no!"

"I assured Carlos that isn't going to happen. I know Trent is still pretty ticked at me, but what he doesn't realize is that I'm not the pushover I used to be. If Trent pushes me, I might just shove back."

* * *

Beginning one mile south of Florence, the Oregon Sand Dunes were an impressive natural wonder. The endless shifting sand hugged the coast, stretching for forty miles from Florence to Coos Bay. The morning sunshine was bright when Erica met Carrie and Trent in the parking lot. The children stood by the ATVs, which were already unloaded.

Trent came over, holding his helmet by the straps. "The kids were pretty excited about your idea of coming to the sand dunes." He looked toward Courtney and Chad. "Is there something you want to say to Aunt Erica?"

Courtney and Chad came over and threw their arms around Erica. "Thank you, Aunt Erica!" Then they scrambled for their ATVs. Courtney rode with Trent, while Chad hopped on with Carrie. Erica felt a heady excitement as she adjusted her helmet. They set off in a group, staying close at first, but after a while, they went off on their own, occasionally passing each other.

There was a unique exhilaration in riding over the golden sand, their nine-foot-tall orange flags waving in the breeze as they went up the hills and roared down the valleys. Erica enjoyed the warm, salt-laden air as she drove over the barren landscape, which had an otherworldly feel to it.

About midmorning, Erica told the others she was going to ride nearer the coast and headed off. She stopped for a time on top of a hill to watch the breeze scatter whitecaps over the broad blue surface of the Pacific. As Erica turned inland, the strong wind buffeted her, and she was glad of her visor to keep the sand out of her eyes. She roared down into a gully and was about to head up the other side when she heard a motor rev. Suddenly, an ATV roared out from a side hill, heading straight for her.

Erica turned sharply but was unable to avoid a collision as the other ATV hit her broadside, sending Erica and her ATV rolling. When it stopped, the ATV was on its side. Erica unbuckled her belt and fell onto the sand. Moving slowly, Erica sat up, trying to get her bearings.

"Are you okay?" Carrie ran over, lifting her visor. "I'm sorry, I didn't see you. I was coming out of that wash, and there you were, right in front of me."

"I'm fine." Erica looked around wildly. "Where's Chad? I thought he was riding with you."

"He's with Trent and Courtney."

Relief flooded her. A crash like that could have caused serious injuries. "Thank goodness." When Erica took off her helmet, the gusty wind blew her auburn hair in all directions. She and Carrie righted her ATV, the sand shifting under their feet as they pushed.

"Whew, glad it didn't cause any major damage," Carrie said, looking over the ATV.

"To us or the ATV?" Erica grinned then leaned against the machine. "So, how are things going for your new business?"

"Great! I'm looking at places to rent, but now that I've won Trent over to the idea, we might just do it as a sideline at Sun Coast."

"It certainly seems like a good fit—I mean, Sun Coast already does rentals."

Carrie seemed surprised at Erica's approval. "I think it would be great for both of us. But I have to talk Shaun into it. Maybe he and Trent can talk about it tonight. I guess you know they're having some kind of meeting?"

Looking out to the ocean, Carrie threw out her hand to indicate a boat towing a person attached to a brilliant red, white, and blue parachute. "Look at that! People are already getting into parasailing here. And Grandma thought I was nuts. She was so old-fashioned—couldn't see that people would love it and that it would benefit Sun Coast. I told Grandma I would refer customers to them if they would refer customers to me. It was a win-win proposal, but she shot it down."

"But now you can move forward with your plans." Erica squinted as she looked out over the ocean. "You're going to see your dream come true and get what you've always wanted because of Grandma."

There was an abrupt change in Carrie. A shutter dropped over her eyes, turning them dark and unreadable. "I'm not sure what you mean." Her words were clipped. "I'm very grateful to Grandma. I'm thankful for the money she left us and sorry she isn't here to see this dream come true for me and Trent. And, just so you know, I'd rather have Grandma here than open my own business." Turning, Carrie said, "I'll try the engine and make sure it works."

Their little tête-à-tête was over. Almost. "Before you do, could I ask where you and Trent were late yesterday afternoon?"

Carrie gave her a searching look Erica couldn't interpret. Over the years, Erica had become adept at interpreting people's expressions, but she knew that with Carrie Coleman, she would only be able to glimpse as much as Carrie would permit.

"Why do you want to know?" There was a steely edge to her voice. Carrie's claws were beginning to show.

Diplomatically—and in as few words as possible—Erica explained her visit to Lake Oswego and Bryant Woods.

Without replying, Carrie threw her a cold look and put on her helmet. She tried the engine, which started immediately. Carrie raised her voice above the rumble.

"You've made it plain you suspect Trent and me of murdering Grandma, and now you think we went to Lake Oswego to kill you?" Over the arid landscape, a seagull circled, its shrill cry floating eerily on the wind. "For your information, Trent worked late, and I went out shopping."

Carrie flipped her visor down. "No one in the family appreciates you suspecting us of murder. If we weren't capable of it before, you're pushing us to it now, so let me give you some advice—*back off.*" With that, Carrie hopped on her ATV and roared off.

* * *

That evening, Erica was going down the stairs when she heard footfalls behind her and turned. It was Shaun, carrying a thick folder.

"Ready?" Erica asked as they went down the steps together.

"As ready as I'll ever be," Shaun said, a mixture of determination and resignation on his face.

The doorbell rang as they reached the foyer. Walter was on the porch, tall and lean in a black suit. When he entered, Erica shut the door, opened it, then shut it again.

"Erica has to make sure the door is shut," Shaun explained to Walter with a wink at Erica.

"Ah, yes, I'm familiar with that one," Walter said.

They went into the family room, where Trent was already waiting. After a shaking of hands that was so civil it was almost frightening, Erica sat next to Walter on the couch. Shaun took the chair by the gas fireplace, where orange and yellow flames flickered above ceramic logs.

With a belligerent look, Trent asked, "What did you want to talk to me about?"

Shaun went right to the heart of the matter. "I've become aware that you've been engaging in some unethical business practices, such as lowering prices in an attempt to force our competitors out of business, paying for confidential information, and coercing employees to spy."

"Is that what this is about? Yes, I lowered prices, but that was only to stay competitive." Trent's voice was full of scorn. "One of the cornerstones of business is to try to sell products cheaper than anyone else." He sounded as if he were explaining things to a child.

"But it's unfair to sell goods at or below cost, forcing your competitors out of business, then raising the prices to what they were before or higher. And you asked at least one employee to spy by getting competitors' customer lists, data, and marketing plans."

A sick feeling welled up in Erica's stomach as Shaun went on. "Worst of all, when this employee refused to do what you asked, you threatened to fire him. He and his wife had just had a baby, and since he couldn't afford to lose his job, he did what you asked."

Trent was swift in his rebuttal. "So Marty came complaining to you, did he? There's nothing wrong with finding out about the competition. All I did was ask Marty to help. He seemed agreeable. I didn't do anything illegal."

"Those practices may not be illegal, but they *are* unethical and I find them disturbing." Walter's tone held a note of distaste. "Lawrence and Blanche always ran an honorable business."

"Maybe this is what was bothering Grandma," Erica said. "If she knew about this or suspected what was going on, it might explain why she changed her will."

"Grandma wouldn't have changed her will if Shaun hadn't talked her into it." Trent fixed Shaun with a challenging look.

"I didn't talk Mom into anything," Shaun said. "But that's not the issue. What I'm talking about is your unethical actions."

Trent was red-faced. "What you label unethical, I call trying to keep the family business solvent and viable in a fluctuating market." Trent spoke furiously to Shaun. "This isn't about me, it's about you. You've been on the sidelines until a short time ago, and now you want to throw your weight around and show how important you are. The power's gone to your head."

The antagonism in the room was a tangible entity. It ebbed and flowed like the dancing flames in the fireplace. Trent went on. "You're at the top now, but you don't seem to realize what everyone else knows—you didn't get there because of any real ability or talent. I'm the one who's been in charge of directing and guiding Sun Coast since my father passed away."

Shaun neither flinched nor paled, but Erica could see the tautness of his jaw. "You're not in charge anymore. I am, and Sun Coast is going to be run ethically." Shaun's voice was not as steady as it had been. Standing up to such a formidable man as Trent seemed to be taking a toll.

"All I've been doing is ensuring the company's growth," Trent said in a reasonable tone.

"By buying confidential information and coercing employees to spy?" Shaun was incredulous.

Walter gave Trent a steely stare. "Lowering prices unfairly to drive other companies out of business is a serious charge."

"Again, there's nothing illegal about any of that!" Trent's face was thunderous. "As for lowering prices—what do you call it when one gas station drops its price? Gasoline stations aren't the only ones to lower prices; everyone in the world does it! You have to in order to stay competitive!" He stabbed a forefinger at Shaun. "Besides, you can't prove I was trying to force our competitors out of business."

Shaun tapped his folder. "I have reports and comparisons of Sun Coast's prices over the past three years, along with written statements from a number of people that prove otherwise."

Trent seemed both surprised and angered at the way Shaun was standing up to him. Erica caught Shaun's eye and gave him a look of encouragement.

When Shaun spoke again, his voice was steady. "To make sure these practices don't continue, I've drafted a few guidelines that will be added to the company's bylaws." He pulled papers out of his folder. "I've already run them past Carlos, and when the board meets in three weeks, I'm sure they'll be ratified." Shaun straightened, and Erica swore he grew several inches. He looked at Trent. "Also, because of the seriousness of these charges, I'm going to change your position. Effective immediately, you'll be executive vice president. Your salary will remain the same, but your duties and responsibilities will change."

"You're putting *me* in your old position?" Trent jumped to his feet, his face dark with anger. "What will people think? I'll be a laughing stock if I'm demoted to executive vice president."

Shaun's face grew hard. "I held that position for three years."

"You can't demote me without approval from the board." Trent's eyes were hard, black marbles. "Who gave you the authority to make a change like that?"

Walter spoke up. "Blanche Coleman did when she named him chairman of the board."

"That was the biggest mistake she ever made," Trent spluttered at Shaun. "I'm the one that's been involved in every major decision while you've been on the outside, afraid of your own shadow."

"In case you haven't noticed," Erica said, "Shaun is no longer on the fringes."

Shaun looked at Trent. "I know you've worked hard for the company. If, after a year, your conduct has been in compliance with the new guidelines, I'll appoint you CEO."

That *was* a surprise. Erica's eyes opened wide. "That's a generous offer, Trent."

Trent scowled at her. "You're the one who started all this. You had no right to butt into things that were none of your business."

"Problems at Sun Coast *do* concern me," Erica said sharply. "Have you forgotten Grandma asked me to investigate the company?"

Walter drew his bushy eyebrows together. "In my opinion, Shaun is being quite lenient as well as charitable. You would be wise to graciously accept this reprimand, knowing it is not a permanent one and is actually quite deserved."

It was apparent the lawyer's words had struck home when Trent's shoulders drooped. He remained quiet for a time then turned to Walter and Erica. "If you don't mind, I'd like to talk with Shaun privately."

Walter stood. "Erica, will you and Shaun walk me to the door?" Once they were there, he turned to Shaun. "Would you prefer that I stay?"

Indecision played across Shaun's face for a moment. Then he said, "No, I'll be fine."

"There's something I want to tell you." Walter's voice was low but penetrating. "When Blanche asked to change her will and put you as chairman and CEO, I tried to talk her out of it. However, since her passing, you have managed to change my mind." He paused, looking thoughtful. "I think now that Blanche—as always—knew best. She had a remarkable head for business and was an uncanny judge of people. I believe Blanche chose you to lead Sun Coast because she knew you had the moral courage and convictions to run Sun Coast in an honest manner."

The approbation in Walter's voice was clear as he went on. "Shaun, you've developed into a real leader. Before your mother died, I don't think you would have stood up to anyone like you just did to Trent. You're doing the right thing. Stand firm." Walter shook Shaun's hand formally and left.

Trent's eyebrows went up when Erica walked in with Shaun. "I hope you don't mind," she said, "but I'd like to stay." With that, Erica sat on the couch, and Shaun took the chair beside her. Trent had turned off the gas fireplace, and it seemed portentous that before, where there had been bright flames, now there was only a cold darkness.

Trent seemed to have recovered and was now utterly calm. "When two sides disagree, it's important to negotiate. This whole matter can be taken care of, Shaun, if you and I both compromise. For my part, I admit I went a little overboard." Trent spoke lightly, as if it were a simple thing. "I only wanted to do what was best for Sun Coast, but since you disagree, I'll abide by the decision you've made." Erica couldn't help but notice that Trent's smile did not reach his eyes. She'd never seen Trent in action in the business world, but seeing the cool, calculating person in front of her, Erica understood how Trent had become so successful at Sun Coast.

Shaun wanted to be clear. "There will be no more spying, coercion, and unfair pricing?"

"Correct. Go ahead and present your guidelines to the board. All I ask is that you don't mention anything we've discussed tonight. Just say you want to make sure Sun Coast is run ethically. There's no need to say more than that."

"I can go along with that," Shaun said. "I don't want to embarrass you."

"I appreciate that. Now, I know we both want to do what is best for the company. One thing that will help is for me to go back to my old position as CEO. You have your hands full enough being chairman of the board."

Erica could hardly believe it. After all Trent had done, he still thought he should be CEO?

"Grandma is the one who put me in as acting CEO," Trent reminded Shaun, who sat very still. "I'll follow your guidelines about ethics to the letter." Trent's tone grew more velvety, showing how sensible he was. "I'll do everything you ask and take a lot of pressure off you." A telltale gleam of sweat appeared on Trent's brow. "Plus, you might want to think how this could affect Kristen."

"Kristen? What does this have to do with Kristen?" Shaun asked.

"I've noticed how well you and Kristen are getting along, but I doubt she'll think highly of you after I explain how you worked on Grandma until she agreed to demote me and put you in as CEO. Once I explain things thoroughly, Kristen is going to see you in a new light." There was something cold and deadly in Trent's voice. "Plus, morale at the company will fall apart when employees find out about the methods you used to reach your current position."

Erica broke in. "And the employees will know this because you'll explain it to them so well?"

"What other choice will I have?" Trent said, as if he could do nothing else.

"I told you what I was willing to do." Shaun's words came heavy and slow, as if he could only get the words out if he spoke in measured tones. "You don't seem to understand how lenient I'm being. I could fire you, and no one on the board would ever question it once I explained what you did."

Trent dropped his eyes briefly. "Perhaps I am asking too much. What if we compromise and you let me stay as CMO? I can help you a lot in that position—I know it inside out."

It occurred to Erica that it had been Trent's plan all along to persuade Shaun to let him stay as CMO. He had to know how ludicrous it was to ask Shaun to appoint him CEO. Trent probably assumed that once Shaun said no, he'd be more likely to accede to Trent's request to stay in his current position. Erica had to practically stuff her fist in her mouth to stop from jumping into the fray. It was difficult to stay silent when inwardly she was seething.

Trent went on, "You don't want me explaining to Kristen how you've been undermining me for years, filling Grandma's head with misconceptions, and twisting facts so she finally turned against me."

This was blackmail of the darkest kind. Kristen and Shaun's feelings were still so new that the thread that bound them was just that—a thread. Anything could snap it. It was clear from the stunned look on Shaun's face that Trent's missiles had struck home. Erica felt sick. Shaun knew, as she did, how close Trent and Kristen were and how she always spoke of Trent in glowing terms. Kristen trusted him implicitly.

Trent's voice was silky and persuasive. "I'll give in on everything you ask—if you'll just leave me where I am. And Kristen will hear nothing but good things about you."

"And you'll be totally supportive when I bring up my guidelines with the board?" Shaun sounded like a robot.

"You have my word."

In a way, this would be a victory for Shaun. The spying, the coercion, and the unfair price lowering would stop. He'd get his guidelines for ethical behavior passed with ease.

Shaun seemed to come to a decision. There was a visible stiffening that showed the edge of steel that had been newly forged the past weeks.

"I didn't meet with you tonight to compromise," he said. "You acted unethically and covered it up because you knew Blanche Coleman would never agree to or condone your actions. Nothing I've said is negotiable. New procedures will be written up, and you will become an executive vice president—for at least a year." Shaun paused. "You know as well as I do that if Mom had known of this, you would no longer be working for Sun

Coast. However, because you are family, I'll let you continue working at Sun Coast as long as I'm able to monitor you." Although he spoke quietly, it was clear Shaun meant every word.

Trent flushed as Shaun continued. "One other thing. If you continue trying to have me taken off as chairman, I'll have no choice but to explain to the board exactly what happened." Shaun didn't have to say what would happen next. Once the board knew what Trent had done, he would no longer be working at Sun Coast Sales and Rentals.

Shaun wasn't finished. "I also find it extremely offensive that you would use Kristen as a bargaining chip." His eyes burned as he glared at Trent. "If you want to retaliate in such a despicable way when I'm only trying to do what's best for the company, that's up to you. But I've got a responsibility to Sun Coast. And to my mother."

Trent stood, his face mottled with rage. "Then say good-bye to Kristen." He strode out, slamming the door shut behind him.

Chapter Eighteen

SHAUN WALKED INTO THE KITCHEN and laid his suit coat over the back of a chair. When he saw Erica helping herself to a bowl of shredded wheat, he was unable to suppress a grin.

"Breakfast for geriatrics," he teased as he poured his own cereal.

They said a blessing on the food, then Erica asked, "How are you feeling after last night?"

"Still angry. I didn't expect it to be pleasant, but I can't believe Trent brought Kristen into it."

"I'm surprised myself, but you handled things very well." There had been many times since Blanche's death when Shaun had bent like a reed in the wind, but last night he had found enough strength to hold firm and do what needed to be done. Erica was glad he had not given in to Trent's outrageous maneuvers. She had always liked Trent but didn't like this new side she had been shown last night. It was like eating a piece of bread and discovering a piece of mold on the edge. Trent needed to learn to control his temper.

They ate in companionable silence for a while, then Shaun asked, "Are you still going to dinner with Trent and Carrie tomorrow night?"

"It's still on as far as I know. We're going to the Sea Lion Cave first. Want to come along?"

"Yeah, right," Shaun scoffed. "Trent would get out his shotgun if I showed up. But I wouldn't be surprised if they disinvited you. It sounded like Carrie was pretty upset with you at the sand dunes, and Trent wasn't too happy last night."

"Oh, Trent will cool down—he always does. As for Carrie, I think she'd curl up and die if she couldn't be upset about something. I'm pretty sure they won't disinvite me. They're curious enough about the case to want to stay close and find out what's going on. And the feeling is mutual. I'm staying in close contact for a lot of the same reasons—and to get information."

"Aren't you going somewhere tomorrow?"

Erica touched a napkin to her mouth. "Yep, I'm going to Vancouver to see Bradley Quinn. He's the jeweler that looked over Martha's stuff."

"I hope that's the Vancouver near Portland and not the one in Canada."

"Definitely *not* Canada."

"Wait a minute," Shaun said, looking curious, "are you thinking Martha was killed because of the stuff she bought? I thought someone killed Martha to keep her quiet."

"Both are possibilities. I'll know more after talking with Mr. Quinn."

Shaun was putting away the milk when Kristen came in. She looked very pretty today with shining hair that curved just below her chin. Her dark red sweater complemented her fair complexion. But Erica was surprised to see her in jeans. The last few Sundays, Kristen had attended church with them. They didn't even need to ask; she simply went with them.

"Good morning," Erica welcomed her. "Come in and have a little brekkie."

"You're becoming very English. Apparently, I'm rubbing off on you." The words were cheerful enough, but Kristen's usual bright smile was missing as she stood stiffly by the table. "I'm not feeling the best this morning," she told Shaun and Erica, "so I won't be going to your church today."

There was something fragile about Kristen today, something different in her expression, as if she were fighting to stay in control. Shaun looked puzzled as Kristen avoided eye contact and made a detour around him to get to the fridge.

Kristen pulled out a yogurt. "I'm just going to take this to my room."

In a flash, Erica knew what had happened. "Kristen, did Trent call you this morning?"

The girl's eyes flew to Shaun, who stood very still by the table. Kristen's eyes were bright. Much too bright. "He did." Kristen's voice was small as she yanked open a drawer and grabbed a spoon.

So, Trent had already done what he'd threatened—poison Kristen's mind against Shaun. Erica hadn't believed he would actually go through with it. Seeing Shaun's hurt, dazed expression and Kristen's upset one, Erica wanted nothing more than to grab a rolling pin and hunt down Trent.

"Ah, Kristen—could I talk with you before you go?" Shaun took a step toward her. What happened next was a tableau frozen in time.

Kristen actually flinched before taking a step backward. Erica could have wept—not only for Kristen moving away but because of the way Shaun had spoken. He'd reverted back to the hesitant, timid way he used to talk—nothing like the self-assured man he'd been recently. Kristen's withdrawal had wrung all the confidence out of him.

"I can't right now," Kristen gulped. "Please understand. I need some time to think." She whirled and was gone.

* * *

After the block of meetings, Erica got on Skype and talked to David, who was still worried about her. She assured him she was fine and that she would take extra precautions from now on. Erica happily visited with the children one by one. She missed them but felt reassured she would soon be with them. The investigation was moving steadily forward, and Erica knew it was only a matter of time before all would be revealed.

* * *

Gold and maroon leaves were dropping in earnest from the oaks and maples in the backyard, and when Erica saw Nathan raking early Monday morning, she opened the French doors and gave him a cheery wave. Then she went to the garage, and after a quick wipe down, she was off.

It was a lovely day for a drive. Russet, garnet, and deep ruby were interspersed with strands of yellow poplar, whose leaves fluttered like gold coins in the light of the sunny new day. Erica stayed on the interstate until she passed Portland then crossed the Columbia River to reach Vancouver.

When she walked into the jewelry store, a small, elderly gentleman with a high domed forehead and white hair looked up from a glass case filled with glittering wedding sets. Erica went over and held out her hand.

"Mr. Quinn? I'm Erica Coleman. Thank you for meeting with me."

The store owner eyed her warily from behind horn-rimmed glasses. He nodded to his assistant then led Erica to the back workroom. Erica looked around admiringly. The floors were swept, and filing cabinets and cupboards lined three walls. The fourth had large plastic storage boxes, neatly labeled and stacked six high. In the middle of the room was a long work table with six chairs.

"I understand Martha Bessinger sent you jewelry to be appraised."

"Tell me again how you're related to her and why you want to know." Mr. Quinn's manner was stiff, but Erica was prepared for this coolness, having heard it in the jeweler's voice when she'd called. Erica explained at length.

"It was my understanding that Martha had very little to do with her family." Mr. Quinn's lips were pressed thin.

"That's true," Erica admitted. "Martha didn't like to leave her house, so we didn't see much of her. In fact, I had never met her until she came to Florence for my grandmother's funeral."

"Since you met Martha, you know a little about her, ah, rather unique personality." He watched her carefully.

"Very friendly and honest, with a charm all her own. I liked her very much." Erica's smile was tender. "Martha was quite a character."

Mr. Quinn's face relaxed. "Yes, she was. I had a sister who was remarkably like Martha. So earnest, open, and warmhearted."

There was a surprising depth in his voice. Apparently he had fond memories of her. Erica asked, "How long have you known Martha?"

"Why don't we sit down?" Mr. Quinn suggested, pulling out a chair for Erica at the work table. "I met Martha when she and Phillip married. At that time, Phillip and I were working at a jewelry store in Portland. After they divorced, I kept in touch. Martha's always held a special place in my heart. She may have been a bit simple, but she was always happy. I was glad when Gail went back to live with her."

"Went back?"

"After the divorce, Phillip stayed in Lake Oswego, even after he remarried. I gather there were some conflicts between Gail, who was a teenager at the time, and her stepmother. Eventually, Gail went to live with Martha. At least until Gail went and eloped with that sleazy fellow."

This was news. "So she eloped, just like Martha?"

"Phillip tried to stop it, of course. I think he saw a little too much of himself in the fellow." Mr. Quinn permitted himself a slight smile. "You see, Phillip had been pretty wild growing up—he liked to steal cars. After spending some time in jail, he turned himself around, but naturally

Phillip didn't want his daughter marrying someone with a record." He sighed. "But Gail was headstrong and wild. When she wanted something, Gail would find a way to get it, and she wouldn't listen to her father."

Erica did her best to look sympathetic. Thus encouraged, Mr. Quinn went on. "From what Phillip told me, Gail soon found herself wishing she'd paid attention to her father. Apparently, her husband had the same penchant for stealing cars that Phillip had in his younger days. I also believe he was abusive. Gail seemed afraid of him."

"I see." What an awful situation for Gail to be in. It was good she had Martha to turn to.

Mr. Quinn caught himself. "I didn't mean to get into all of that." His cheeks pinked up a little. "Anyway, when Martha started buying jewelry, she asked me for help."

"Gail told me about that. It was kind of you to take so much time with her."

Mr. Quinn appeared embarrassed by the praise. "It didn't take long, and it meant so much to her. At first, Martha sent me everything she bought, but it was all costume jewelry, so I told her to just send me a letter describing the jewelry. That's when Martha started sending me what she called her 'reports.' I received them like clockwork every Friday."

"I've seen her journals," Erica said. "She kept track of everything."

"Although Martha was a bit slow in some ways, she was quite methodical about her record keeping, even if they were in spiral-bound notebooks." Mr. Quinn permitted himself a small smile.

"How could you tell if a piece of jewelry was valuable by her description?"

"Usually, I couldn't. It's much better to see the piece in person. But I told her what to look for, and she did a fairly decent job. I also suggested Martha get a camera and take pictures." He smiled. "I'm not sure Gail has ever forgiven me for that. You see, Gail was the one who had to teach Martha how to use it—quite a laborious process, I'm sure. Since Martha couldn't manage a computer, Gail got a color printer and taught her how to print pictures. It helped a great deal."

"I suppose that old cliché is true—a picture is worth a thousand words?"

"Exactly. Once in a while, I asked her to send something to me, so I could check it out. I can usually tell just by looking if a piece is valuable or not."

"Did Martha send you anything of value the past few months?"

He thought back. "Not that I recall—it was all the same old stuff."

"Do you mind if I look at the last few reports she sent?"

Mr. Quinn sat very straight. "I don't think so. Those were Martha's personal reports. She asked me very specifically never to show them to anyone."

Rats. And things had been going so well. Rising, Erica walked over to an open cabinet, admiring the rows of square baskets with their labels. She called over her shoulder, "It's amazing how organized you keep things." There was genuine admiration in her voice.

He came over. "Sometimes my employees complain, but I tell them putting things back where they belong saves time in the long run. Then you don't have to go searching for anything."

"My thoughts exactly. A place for everything, and everything in its place."

"It pays to be neat and tidy."

When Erica nodded reverently, a gleam came into Mr. Quinn's eye. He went to a closed wooden cabinet and flung open the doors. Inside were innumerable small bins, holding a variety of clasps, chains, wires, seed pearls, charms, and other assorted materials, all neatly labeled.

Erica exclaimed with pleasure, hands clasped tightly. "Oh! This is amazing!" It was as if she were seeing the Eiffel Tower for the first time. If she ran a business, it would be just like this.

Encouraged, Mr. Quinn flung open another cabinet, which was filled with row after row of black binders, each one labeled and neatly lined up. The corners of the jeweler's mouth turned up as Erica ran her hands over the binders with exclamations of delight.

Mr. Quinn wore a pleased expression. "I do think it's important to be organized."

"I couldn't agree more," Erica declared emphatically. How nice it was to find a kindred spirit! Someone who really understood and felt the importance of having things orderly—of having a logical system in place.

Mr. Quinn opened one of the tall file cabinets, and Erica tiptoed closer. "They're alphabetized, *and* color coded!" She gazed in wonder. "You're really an expert organizer. Why, you ought to teach classes—at the college or even community classes."

"Ah, well, I'm not sure about that."

"Oh, you should! You *need* to. People could learn so much from you."

Mr. Quinn seemed to swell visibly. He went to another smaller cabinet and pulled out a binder labeled *June-July-August-September— Martha Bessinger.* He handed it to Erica. "These are the latest reports I have from Martha."

Cradling it carefully, Erica wanted to be clear. "It's all right if I look it over?"

"As long as you don't mess up the order."

Erica's green eyes sparkled. "Believe me—I've never messed up the order of anything in my life."

"All right, I'll leave you to it. I'll be out front if you have any questions."

Erica took the binder to the table. She recognized Martha's large, loopy handwriting. It was easy to see what Mr. Quinn meant by Martha being organized. They were similar to her journals at home. She had meticulously recorded the type of jewelry, the date purchased, the price paid, and a description.

Each item was numbered. Stapled to the page were pictures with numbers on the back that corresponded to each item in the report. It was apparent Martha sometimes wrote while eating since some of the lined pages had splotches on them. Occasionally, a page had been torn and Scotch-taped back together. When Erica was done, she kept one file out and replaced the binder in the cabinet.

Out front, Mr. Quinn was working at a desk in the corner. "Did you find something of interest?" he asked, glancing at the folder she carried.

"I think so. Would you let me keep this file for a little while? There's something interesting here that I don't quite understand. If I have more time, I might be able to figure it out." When Mr. Quinn hesitated, Erica assured him, "I promise I'll bring it back and return it to the right spot."

His shoulders relaxed. "All right."

"Did Martha ever find anything valuable?" She always liked to double-check, and Mr. Quinn wouldn't know Leslie had already told her about the ring and necklace.

"One time she found a good ring. Another time, Martha found quite a nice necklace that she'd bought at an estate sale. I gave her several hundred dollars for it, as I recall."

"Leslie, the woman who went with Martha to garage sales, said Martha found some nice things a while ago. One was a bracelet that had a crisscross pattern and looked like it had diamonds on it."

"I don't recall seeing anything like that, but Martha sometimes kept jewelry she liked." Mr. Quinn gave her a quizzical look. "Do you think Martha was killed because she bought costume jewelry?"

"The killer might not have known it was costume jewelry."

"Ah." Mr. Quinn's brow furrowed. "I should tell you that Martha was always worried that someone might steal her jewelry. I tried to reassure her that burglars did not want costume jewelry, but Martha thought everything she had was valuable. To ease her mind, I told her I would keep all of her reports. That way, if someone did break in and steal something, I'd be able to provide the police with a written description and a picture so jewelers and pawn shops could watch for stolen goods. That made Martha feel much better. But in the end, it really didn't do her much good, did it?"

Chapter Nineteen

FALL WEATHER COULD CHANGE QUICKLY, and the following afternoon was chilly and gray. The air was thick with sea mist when Trent pulled his Cadillac Escalade into the parking lot. Pamela had been persuaded to come, and Courtney and Chad were so excited that Carrie had to remind them sharply to hold hands with an adult as they crossed the road to reach the Sea Lion Cave.

"A lot of seals are in the cave today," the cashier told them when Trent paid for their tickets in the gift shop. "The seals usually enter in late September and winter there." A TV monitor behind the cashier had a live feed to the cave, and the children stared at the sea lions lounging on the rocks.

At the back of the gift shop, Trent helped Pamela down the stairs, which had been built into the side of the hill. The group stopped to take pictures at the statue of the two Steller sea lions with their pup. Then the children raced down the trail to the lookout with Carrie and Trent in hot pursuit. Although the path was paved with a white wooden railing on one side, it was steep and unmanageable for Pamela, even with her cane. She tried—without success—to convince Erica to go with the others.

"I'd rather stay here," Erica insisted, and they sat on a bench facing the Pacific.

"I hear there was a real brouhaha Saturday night," Pamela said.

The air was thick with the scent of saltwater, and Erica examined the ocean, hoping to catch a glimpse of a whale. "Did you hear it or just hear *about* it?"

"Both. Trent's voice does carry when he's upset. I talked with Trent and Shaun about it." She glanced at Erica. "I know you try to shield me

from what's going on at Sun Coast, but I know more than you think.
Anyway, I told Trent to forget about contesting the will. With everything
Shaun's found out, there's no way any judge is going to overturn the
will." Her voice turned sad. "Tell me, do you think what Trent did had
anything to do with Blanche's death?"

"I'm not sure. I've still got a few things I'm looking into, and there
are other things that are confusing." Erica shook her head slowly. "Like
eyebrows . . . I can think of one reason to explain the reason behind that,
but it would mean—" Sighting something out on the ocean, Erica broke
off and nudged Pamela.

"Look out there at that black spot." She gazed through the
binoculars then cried, "It *is* a whale!" She handed them over, and Pamela
watched in rapture as a black shape rose from the water, bulged up, and
sank down again. The whale was nearly a mile offshore, huffing breaths
over the flat, heaving plain of the ocean.

When the others returned, they each had a turn looking at the
whale. Then Carrie led the way to the elevator that went down to the
cave. Though the children had been many times, they were still excited.

Chad told Erica, "This is the biggest sea lion cave in the world."

"Who says?" Courtney broke in. She was at the age where she would
challenge her own shadow.

"*The Guinness Book of World Records.*" Chad stuck out his tongue and
ran out as the elevator doors opened.

At the railing, they looked down into the huge cave, where the rocks
were lined with sea lions. Incoming waves sloshed in rocky crevices, and
the lions kept up a steady barking. Near the opening to the ocean, the
wind-roiled surf churned against the shoreline rocks, sending up geysers
of white spray as the sea lions swam in and out of the cave. One seal
silently broke the surface of the water. From where Erica was standing,
she could see its eyes and its stubby snout with nostrils flaring as it took
in air. The seal rested for a moment then dove underwater again.

Pamela and Trent went with the children to watch a video about the
history of the cave, and Carrie and Erica meandered to the north end of
the observation area. A large, window-like opening gave an unrestricted
view of the ragged shoreline, where sea lions and cormorants spread
themselves on the rocks. The cliffs were almost sheer. Large boulders
lined the ocean, looking as if they had been cast in bronze in the late
afternoon light.

While seagulls cawed overhead, Carrie spoke quietly. "Trent told me you were there when Shaun talked to him the other night." There was a steady slap and hiss as the waves darkened the lowest fringe of rocks with shining dampness.

"Yes, I was."

Carrie walked around the floor-mounted binoculars where visitors could pay to view the seals. She still had the slender, youthful figure of a girl, and her long hair was shiny and straight. "I don't mean to be rude, but that wouldn't have happened if it wasn't for you. Why are you trying to cause trouble? Trent told me that you asked Shaun and Walter to dig up dirt at the company."

That wasn't quite the way Erica would have explained it. She wondered how Trent had found out. The ocean boiled and chapped against the shore's rocky barrier, sending its spray high as Erica replied, "I told everyone I was going to investigate Sun Coast. And it's not logical for you to blame me for Trent's actions."

But logic had nothing to do with Carrie's feelings.

"I don't know what you mean by that," Carrie hissed. "I can understand you investigating Grandma's murder, but you have no business butting into things at Sun Coast. All you're doing is making everyone all upset and getting involved with things that have nothing to do with you."

It was beginning to dawn on Erica that Trent hadn't told his wife everything. As she considered how to reply, Erica looked off in the distance where the Haceta Head Lighthouse stood on a green cliff overlooking the ocean. Closer, several long-necked cormorants rose screaming from their nearby ledges. The great birds circled once then flapped away as Erica reached for her pendant.

"It's very possible that whatever's going on at Sun Coast had something to do with Grandma's death."

Carrie's rose-and-cream complexion paled. "You don't think Trent had anything to do with . . . with Grandma's death?" It was a definite possibility, but right now, Erica had no answers.

"I'm not pointing any fingers."

"Then I will," Carrie said emphatically. "Take a good, long look at Shaun. You have no idea how much trouble he's caused at Sun Coast since Grandma died." Then Carrie stalked off.

With a heavy sigh, Erica shook her head and looked through the rock window. In the ocean, a couple of sea lions had positioned themselves to ride a wave up onto the rocks. At first glance, the steep rocky wall seemed impossible to scale, but the sea lions managed by waiting for a large wave which propelled them up and into a crevice. From there, they waddled up farther to join the others.

When the children finished watching the video, they clamored to go to the gift shop. Everyone rode the elevator up. While Pamela looked at books, Trent joined Erica, who was examining the stuffed sea lions.

With a furtive look around to make sure they were alone, Trent said in a low voice, "Carrie said she'd talked with you." His face reddened slightly. "I guess you found out I didn't tell her everything."

When Erica nodded, he hurried on. "She knows most of it, and I'm going to tell her the rest, but I want to go slowly. Carrie can get a little emotional at times. Probably learned it from me." Trent smiled in a self-depreciating manner. "But people who don't understand Carrie might take her the wrong way."

Wait a minute. There was another way?

"Basically, she's insecure," Trent added.

"Are we talking about Carrie?"

"She puts on a good show, but Carrie's not as secure as she looks. It's the way she was raised." Trent glanced around again to make sure his wife was still engrossed in the handbags. "Her folks were very poor, and Carrie hangs onto what she has with both fists. Plus, Carrie's always felt she had to live up to an image. When she was growing up, her mother made her feel that appearance was everything. She was never allowed to be herself, and so, even now, Carrie feels she has to put on an act."

"I guess everyone has something in their childhood they have to overcome."

Rats. Did this mean she couldn't dislike Carrie anymore?

Trent grimaced. "It hit me hard when Shaun took over my job at Sun Coast, but it crushed Carrie. I've never seen her so upset." Trent's glance flickered toward his wife again. "I don't know if Shaun told you, but he and I talked this morning."

"No, he didn't. How did that go?"

"Fairly well. We got some things ironed out." When she looked curious, Trent added, "I'm accepting his deal—since I don't really have a choice. And Carrie and I aren't going to contest the will either."

There was the sound of running footsteps, and Chad came running up with a rubber snake, with Courtney close behind, carrying a jewelry box. "Dad, can I have this?" they cried in tandem.

In the end, they all left carrying something. Pamela had her book; Carrie, a bag; the children, their treasures. Trent bought a box of fudge, and Erica had a plush Steller sea lion.

* * *

They drove straight to Trent and Carrie's home, where Erica had left a casserole on timed bake, so it would be ready to eat when they returned. Erica headed for the large kitchen and put a loaf of foil-wrapped garlic bread in the oven to heat.

Trent told Erica, "It's awfully nice of you to bring dinner. Is there anything I can do?"

"If you would get a couple of cutting boards, you and Pamela can cut up the tomatoes and cucumbers for the salad."

Pamela went to the sink to rinse off the tomatoes and cucumbers.

Carrie walked in sniffing the luscious aroma wafting from the oven. "Sorry, it was hard getting the kids settled down enough to start on their homework." She turned on the oven light to peer inside. "Whatever it is, it smells great."

"It's called Summer Garden Casserole,[8] and you'll love it."

"And you made it?"

Erica smiled to herself. Apparently, it was hard for Carrie to believe food could come from any place other than restaurants or delis. "Pamela helped me this morning."

Carrie took out a plastic container from the fridge. "I bought cheesecake for dessert," she said, as if to prove she could be useful as well. As Trent and Pamela cut up the tomatoes, Carrie picked up a cucumber. "Want me to slice this?"

"That would be great. Chop it, but don't dice," Erica said.

"What difference does it make?"

Erica's eyebrows drew together. "That's like asking if there's a difference between margarine and butter, or fresh lemon juice and bottled." When Carrie was unable to comprehend those examples, Erica put it in language she could understand. "It's like the difference between diamonds and rocks. Then she added, "Chopping leaves the food in bigger pieces, while dicing is smaller."

"Boy, everything has to be perfect for you, doesn't it?"

---

8   See the appendix for this recipe.

"If at all possible," Erica said then smiled.

When they sat down to eat, Chad and Courtney weren't too sure about the casserole, but once they tasted it, they ate enough to satisfy their parents. After dessert, everyone helped clear the table.

Setting aside her cane, Pamela carried out some glasses. "That was a great dinner."

"It certainly was," Carrie told Erica. "You ought to be a cook instead of a private eye."

Trying to be helpful, Chad carried Pamela's cane into the kitchen. "You left this by the table. Don't you need it to walk?"

"I certainly do. Thank you." As Pamela rinsed dishes, she asked Erica, "How's Gail doing?"

"Good, but she's worried about her job. Her boss is probably going to close down the floral shop. Oh, and remember those kittens Gail has? They're nearly old enough to go to new homes."

"Kittens? What kittens?" Chad asked. After Erica explained, Courtney squealed and turned to her father, "Daddy? Can we have one?"

Carrie, who had been putting food in the fridge, turned a murderous eye on Erica. "Thanks, Erica." Then to her daughter, "Courtney, we'll talk about the kittens later."

"But why can't we have one, Mom?" Courtney cried. "All my friends have pets."

"Time for you two to go finish your homework," Trent commanded.

Chad began to whine, sounding remarkably like his mother. "I don't get my math problems."

"I'll be glad to help," Pamela volunteered. She wiped her hands and went off with the children.

When the dishwasher started running, Trent asked Erica, "Do you mind if we go outside and talk?" Carrie came out with them to the long, curved patio, where they sat in thick cushioned chairs around a gas fire pit. The night had grown cool, and Trent turned on the fire, holding his hands out to the yellow and orange flames. They sat for a time in silence, watching the cracking flames.

"I want to apologize for getting so upset Saturday night. I let my temper run away with me."

Erica appreciated his apology, especially since it sounded sincere. And she was even gladder that he'd talked with Shaun. She knew Trent was smart enough to realize that with all the documentation Shaun had, Trent would be facing a losing battle if he tried to contest things.

"I was only trying to help Sun Coast, but I guess I went a bit too far," Trent said listlessly.

You could say that again. In his determination to grow the business, he had crossed the line. Erica was glad that her grandmother hadn't known of this, although Blanche certainly had suspicions.

"You were just trying to do what you thought was best for the company," Carrie said. They sat for several minutes, each thinking their own thoughts.

Then Trent spoke. "It seems strange not to have Grandma around. I keep expecting to see her or have her call. I miss not having her around at the office, even if we didn't always see eye to eye."

Once again, Carrie tried to console him. "Blanche had her ideas, and you had yours."

"Grandma could be very forceful—she liked to get her way," Erica mused, thinking of Shaun.

Trent winced. "She did, but I wish I'd backed off more often."

For a second, Erica was taken back. But of course Shaun wouldn't have been the only one who argued with Blanche. Grandma was a dynamic person, used to having people bow to her wishes. Erica remembered how vehemently Shaun had denied arguing with her. Perhaps he had been telling the truth. Erica decided to take a chance and see if a bluff would pay off.

"What were you two arguing about the day before Grandma died?"

"How did you know about that?" Trent asked, looking at her sharply. She remained quiet, trying to smoke him out. A muscle in Trent's jaw jumped, and his hands tightened on the armrests. "It wasn't a big deal."

"What was it about?"

"I wanted to stop renting sandrails because ATVs are safer and more reliable. Grandma disagreed—we've been renting sandrails forever, and she wanted to stick with them. That's it."

So, Shaun *had* been telling the truth. Vicki had said she'd heard Shaun, but apparently, it had been Trent. But then, Shaun and Trent were cousins, and their voices were very similar.

"The police think Shaun argued with her that day," Erica said. "They need to know about this."

Trent's square face registered alarmed. "Do you have to tell the police? I mean, it wasn't a big argument."

"It doesn't sound important, but I do have to share any new information with them." She hoped he would understand.

Carrie flashed Erica an angry look. "Why are you always trying to cause trouble?"

Reaching out, Trent put a hand on his wife's arm. "It's all right Carrie. The argument wasn't important; I have nothing to worry about."

* * *

The next morning was a busy one. Erica went to see Detective McGuire then made a number of phone calls. That afternoon, Erica was eager to go for her walk and stretch her legs. Bandit began dancing around her legs the minute she opened the drawer in the foyer where his leash was kept.

It was a perfect day, with a clear blue sky and mellow golden light. Trees dressed in autumn colors poured great lakes of shadows onto the road as they walked along at a brisk pace. Virginia creeper—in gorgeous red and maroon—lay in garlands over the fences.

When Erica heard the revving of an engine, her first thought was that it seemed out of place. It was usually quiet along Rhododendron Drive in the early afternoon. When the noise grew louder, she glanced over her shoulder. It only took a few seconds for Erica to realize an SUV was headed straight for her. There was no time to think—only to act. Erica flung herself off the side of the road. The incline was steep, and as she rolled, she let go of the leash. Then Erica collided with a tree and lay motionless.

Chapter Twenty

CAUGHT UP IN A SINKING blackness, Erica struggled to breathe. There were sounds—but she was unable to place them. Swimming closer to consciousness, Erica opened her eyes and blinked. A woman with worried brown eyes was kneeling over her, speaking in a soothing voice, but Erica couldn't quite make out the words. With a groan, Erica eased herself away from the tree with the woman's help.

It was hard to think. Memory of a big black dog came back, and terrified, Erica called out, "Bandit!" The lab sprang to Erica's side and began licking her face.

"No!" Erica tried to push him away, despite the sharp pain in her side. "Ack! Dog germs!" Erica dug into her pocket for her wipes, ripped one out and scrubbed her face.

A fair-haired young man wearing tight bike-riding gear came running down the embankment. "Is she okay?"

"I think she hit her head," the woman replied, her voice concerned. "She's upset about the dog."

The world spun as Erica tried to focus long enough to explain. "Dog germs. He licked my face." Surely they could understand that. She was breathless, else she'd try to explain more.

"She must be in shock." The man pulled out his cell phone. "I'll call 911."

"No. Don't call. Hate dog germs." It was difficult to get the words out and impossible to string them into a cohesive sentence.

The man and woman looked at each other. Then the biker dropped to his knees and looked into Erica's eyes. "What state are you in?"

"Oregon."

"What city?"

"Florence." Tiring of the game, Erice cried, "Some fool nearly ran me over. Did he stop?"

"No, he kept going." This was from the woman.

"Crazy idiot," the bicyclist said. "I saw the SUV pull out of Siano Loop right after you went by. It looked like he was heading straight for you."

"Did you get the make or model?"

The biker shook his head. "It was silver. Midsized. That's all I know."

"I didn't catch it either," the woman said.

When Erica began to tremble, the bicyclist said, "She's going into shock."

Erica started to shake her head then stopped because it made her dizzy. "I'm all right. Just help me up."

The woman took Bandit's leash as the man helped Erica stand. She was surprised by a stabbing pain in her chest and was unable to stand upright.

"You're hurt." The woman's voice was matter-of-fact. "I can either drive you to the hospital or we can call an ambulance. Which do you want?"

The man held onto an unsteady Erica. As the world spun around, she got out two words: "Drive me."

The woman turned to the biker. "I live across the street. I'll get my car while you help her up to the road." She told Erica, "I'll put your dog in my backyard. It's fenced." As the woman hurried up the incline, Bandit bounded alongside her through the brush, happy to be playing a fun, new game.

* * *

At the emergency room, Erica called Pamela before her mind cleared enough to remember her mother-in-law didn't drive. Pamela reassured Erica she'd call someone, and to Erica's surprise, it was Trent who rushed into the treatment room, tie askew and looking anxious. It was embarrassing, yet touching, how Trent grilled the nurses about every procedure and the amount of time everything took. He was worse than David would have been.

"If I ran a business like this," Trent fumed, "Sun Coast would be out of business in a week."

It would always be about the family business to him, Erica thought.

The doctor told Erica she had two cracked ribs, a lot of bruising, and minor scratches. Trent plied the doctor with questions about x-rays, pain medication, and what activities Erica could or couldn't do. Finally, a nurse wheeled her to the door. When Erica hesitated to get inside then fished a wipe out of her purse to wipe down her seat, Trent took it with a groan and did it for her. After helping her into the car, he seemed subdued as he drove along.

Finally, Trent remarked, "I never thought someone would try to hurt you over your investigating."

Erica was surprised he'd been thinking the same thing she had. Still, there were other possibilities. "It could have been an accident," she offered limply.

"You don't really believe that, do you?" Trent shot a glance at her, and she was surprised at the look on his face. It was almost as if he was angry. "You've got a lot of courage, but it's obvious you're dealing with a dangerous person." He hit the steering wheel. "But who? Shaun? Walter?" He gave her a sideways glance. "Maybe you think it was me." He paused. "But it has to be one of us, doesn't it?"

She didn't want to answer, but inside, that's exactly what Erica thought. Trent turned up the long driveway and stopped by the front door instead of pulling into the garage.

"I can walk, you know," Erica told him.

"I hear you roll pretty good too."

She started to laugh then winced. "I can tell I'm going to have to cut out laughing for a while."

Trent helped her up the steps even though Erica insisted she was fine. After they went in, he closed the front door, opened it, then closed it again. "There," Trent said. "Just following your ritual so you'll feel better."

Erica smiled.

There was a *tap, tap, tap* of a cane as Pamela approached. Her eyes were enormous and her face haunted as she gave Erica a careful hug.

"How are you?" Without waiting for a response, Pamela hurried on. "We've got to get you lying down. Trent, help Erica into the family room. I've already put a sheet on the couch."

Once Erica was settled, Pamela hovered nearby, giving more orders, as though the accident had damaged Erica's vocal cords. "Trent, take Erica's shoes off; she'll be more comfortable that way. Would you get a pillow from upstairs to go under her knees? And bring down any books Erica has in her bedroom."

Then Pamela turned to her patient. "I've already cleared off the coffee table so you'll have room for your books and things. There's an afghan on the floor in case you get cold. I'll go get you some water."

Trent caught Erica's eyes then rolled his to the ceiling. "You survived the cracked ribs—let's see if you can survive your mother-in-law."

When he returned with books and a pillow, Pamela had brought not only water but a small box from David. Erica opened it and found it full of chocolates.

"As usual, David has impeccable timing," Erica said with a purr of contentment as she rifled through the box, picking out a Toblerone bar. She then held the box out to Trent, who helped himself to a Snicker's bar.

"Can I get you anything else?" Pamela asked. "Are you hungry? Of course you are. Let me get you something to eat." Pamela was halfway to the door before she paused and looked back. "Trent, do you want anything?"

"Do I have to break my leg first?" Then he grinned. "No thanks. I have a dinner meeting." He glanced at his watch. "In fact, I need to get home and get cleaned up. I still can't believe how long it took at the hospital." He looked down at Erica. "Now remember, the doctor said to take it easy."

"Okay, okay. I'll put off reroofing the house until tomorrow." With a groan, Erica repositioned the pillow. "Can I ask you something before you go?"

A wary look crossed his face. "You can ask. Whether or not I answer remains to be seen."

"When we talked in your office, you insinuated Shaun might have poisoned Grandma. Do you have any reasons for that?"

"You haven't been listening to me, Erica. I've gone over all of this. Grandma told me *I* was next in line to be CEO. Why would she suddenly change her mind? It can only be because Shaun went behind my back, misrepresented the facts, and brainwashed her into changing her mind."

The words were there, but the force that was so much a part of Trent's nature was not. It was all rote, which told Erica that, deep down, Trent didn't really believe it. He had let his temper speak for him, and now that the embers had cooled, he kept the same old story so he didn't have to admit he'd gotten carried away. Trent was intelligent, and he knew his cousin well enough to know Shaun would not scheme and maneuver to take Trent's place as CEO.

Then Erica spoke out loud. "Let me ask you this—have you *ever* been able to talk Grandma into changing her mind—*about anything?*"

Trent thought a moment then laughed. The sound was like a cannon firing in the room. "Touché."

"One other question: what did you tell Kristen?"

Trent's expression changed—hardened. "That's my business."

"I think you ought to talk to Kristen and get things straightened out between her and Shaun."

"Look, Erica, I feel very sorry for you right now, but don't push it."

Irritation bit her. "Well, I'm going to. You need to talk to Kristen, and you need to do it soon." The forcefulness of her words caused her to grimace in pain.

Trent looked down at her, concerned. "Take it easy."

"I can't take it easy when Kristen and Shaun are hurting so much." It was such a disadvantage lying down—there was no way she could deck Trent. Erica started to rise. "Now, are you going to talk to them or not?"

"Lay down, Erica. Geez. I already told you I talked to Shaun." He hesitated. "And yes, I'll talk to Kristen."

* * *

Erica had called her husband from the hospital, but after Trent left, she pulled out her cell phone and dialed David's number. It took a very long time to reassure him she was fine and that there was no need for him to come to Florence as he was insisting.

"I just rolled down an embankment," she said, putting all kinds of amusement in her voice. "It's kind of funny to think about it."

"You'll notice I'm not laughing." David's voice was tight with worry. "I want to come out and be with you, Erica. I'm worried sick about you."

"But I'm fine, really, and it *could* have just been one of those things. But just in case, I'm going to be extra careful from now on. No more walks, and I'll take all kinds of precautions whenever I leave the house and even while here. Besides, there's nothing you can do. I'm going to do just what the doctor said—take it easy. And your mom is making sure I do. I hope the kids aren't worried."

"They were at first, but I explained you were okay and you'd talk to them tonight. Right now I'm at Ryan's soccer game. Aby is at your mom's house, and Kenzie is at your brother's house, playing with her cousins." He paused. "I wish you'd gotten a better look at the car."

"Yeah, well, I was busy trying not to become roadkill."

It was the wrong thing to say. Erica smacked her forehead when David started in again. "That's why you need to come home! And don't tell me Grandma wants you to find her killer. She'd much rather have you alive and well."

"I'll be all right. Don't worry. I'm going to watch my back from now on. And I've taken my revolver out of the lock box so it's ready in case I need it."

"Good idea. And don't trust anyone. Hear me? *No one,*" David warned.

"Do you want me to send you a few Dilbert comic books?"

"That would be great. The only other thing I need is chocolate, and I got your lovely box today. Thanks, honey."

"How are you feeling? You sounded like you were in a lot of pain earlier."

"I took a pain pill, and I'm fine. The doctor said the pain would gradually decrease and the ribs will be healed in about three weeks."

"I'm worried about you. This is getting too dangerous."

"We don't even know it was intentional. You're in cop mode right now, suspecting the worst, but maybe it was just a distracted driver. He could have been reaching for a french fry."

"Erica, be straight with me. I've always trusted your instinct—what do you think? Was this an accident or not?"

She sighed. Sometimes honesty was overrated. "Okay, my gut tells me it was intentional. Most drivers would have stopped, unless they were dirtbags or too drunk to see me jump out of the way."

"You're scaring someone, and they're trying to stop you from investigating."

"Could be. But just so you know, when you talk to your mom or anyone else here, I'm not going to tell anyone that I think it was intentional—except for Detective McGuire."

"That's probably a good idea—so you don't put whoever did it on guard."

"Because then he or she would only be more devious—"

"—and more dangerous," David added tersely, finishing her sentence. "I don't like this one bit."

"I know, but I can't give up now—I'm too close."

"Promise me you'll be super careful. Remember, 'Courage is a virtue only so far as it is directed by prudence.' Francois Fenelon."

"How did you remember that name?"

He laughed. "Because it's hanging on the wall in the dispatcher's office."

"You know, I think now that I've been on the wrong track—jumping to conclusions and making assumptions the killer wanted me to make. I've been viewing this case from within when I think the answer will come from without. But things are starting to come together. I should be able to get a few more answers when I go to Lake Oswego." Erica had a few things in mind.

"What? Are you still planning on that? You can't drive up there by yourself."

"Darling, don't worry. I'm going to wait a day or so. I want to talk to that boy who supposedly saw Martha walking in the woods after she was killed."

"Kid," David said. "I don't know if you'll get much there."

"Maybe, maybe not. I'm going to stop and see Gail too. I have a few more questions about Martha that I'd like answered."

Chapter Twenty-One

KRISTEN STOOD BEFORE HER, A vase of mixed flowers in hand. "You look like you've had a punch-up with some bloke." Then she looked at the small box on the table.

"David sent me some chocolate," Erica said.

Kristen looked confused. "How did he know?"

"Lucky guess," Erica joked. "Have some, the ones in the little box are from Mrs. Cavanaugh's, in Bountiful. Try one. They're sinfully good."

"Don't mind if I do." Kristen set the flowers on the far end of the coffee table and, sitting on the other end, took a chocolate. "How are you feeling?"

"In a moment, I'll be perfect." Erica took a chocolate haystack, peeled back the brown pleated paper, and took a bite. Her eyes closed in bliss. "Chocolate isn't a food," she murmured. "It's a medicine. They could sell these things as antidepressants."

"How are the ribs?"

"If I could dip them in chocolate, they'd be fine. Actually, they'd be better if you'd move David's box a little closer so I don't have to reach. I'm lazy as well as injured." Erica picked up the book she'd been reading. "A good book in one hand and chocolate in the other. I must be in heaven."

Kristen smiled then asked, "Are your ribs cracked or broken? And which side?"

"Right side, and they're just cracked."

"Did they tape you up like a mummy or just put on elastoplasts?"

"What are elastoplasts? Sounds like something in a science fiction book."

"They're bandages." Kristen laughed. "I keep forgetting you can't speak the King's English."

"No elasto-thingies and no taping. The doctor said they can't do much except let them heal. They used to tape cracked ribs but not anymore. I'm thankful it wasn't any worse."

"Can I get you anything?"

"I'm good. Carrie and Courtney stopped by—brought me a Happy Meal for dinner, but Pamela had already fed me. Now, what about you? How are *you* doing?"

"I'm fine."

"I wish you'd talk with Shaun."

"I will soon, I promise. Now, I'm going out with friends tonight, so I'd better get going."

She hadn't gotten far when Shaun walked in. He stopped abruptly when he saw Kristen.

"Hello, Shaun." Her voice went flat, all the liveliness gone. "I was just leaving."

Shaun's face seemed suddenly empty, as if all the life had drained out. "You don't have to leave on my account."

There was something like despair in the look on Kristen's face. "I wasn't—it's just that I have to meet some friends." As she slid by, Shaun reached out a hand, but she was gone. He turned and stood a few moments looking after her. When Shaun came over, Erica saw that his eyes had the glazed look of an animal in pain. How long could things go on like this? Shaun looked wretched, and he ate next to nothing. This rift with Kristen was like a festering sore.

Shaun pulled a chair over to the couch. "Heard you were playing a game of chicken and you were the first one to flinch."

Erica laughed then winced. "Don't *do* that! No jokes!"

"Sorry. How are you feeling?"

"I'm fine."

"Right. This bottle of pain meds sitting here says something else. Tell me about it."

When she went over everything, Shaun's eyes were dark with worry. "Pamela told me it was an accident. She may have bought your story, but I'm not so sure. *Was* it an accident?"

How could she weasel her way out of this without lying? "It could have been," Erica said carefully.

"And it could be that someone is out to get you. I don't like this, Erica. Forget about the investigation. Go home—where you're safe."

She looked into Shaun's kindly brown eyes. "Can't do that. But I will ask you for a favor."

"What's that?"

"Go up to my room and bring down my gun. I'd like to have it handy, and right now, I'm in no shape to be running upstairs to get it."

Shaun's mouth had a straight, grim look to it. "You *are* worried."

"Just cautious." She flicked a hand at him. "Go. Top middle drawer in the dresser, under my jeans. It's in my belt holster—just bring the whole thing."

When Shaun returned, Erica sat up with an effort, put the Glock in the drawer of the coffee table, then leaned forward and slipped a pillow behind her back. Getting comfy, she asked, "So, how are things going at Sun Coast?"

"Actually, they're going pretty well." His face registered surprise. "I've got a lot to learn, but Carlos has been a great help and I'm finally getting to know what I'm supposed to do and how to do it." There was a confidence in Shaun's manner that had not been there before.

"I'm so glad."

"Carlos isn't the only one that's helped me—Heavenly Father has too." He gave a slight smile. "I think my knees have calluses." His voice became quieter. "And I swear I've felt Mom every once in a while. I can just *feel* her sometimes, you know?"

"Oh, Shaun. I'm sure she's been here for you." Tears stung Erica's eyes. "She loved you very much, and though she knew this would be hard, she also knew you could do it." Erica shifted to get more comfortable. "David told me a little about your life growing up. You overcame a lot of problems. That shows a lot of character."

"Ha! I didn't dare get into trouble or Mom would tan my hide." There was a smile in his eyes.

"From what I hear, you *did* get into trouble but turned your life around. You're not giving yourself enough credit." He didn't reply, and Erica pushed the box of chocolates over to him. "Have a few—chocolate helps anything." After Shaun popped one in his mouth, she said, "You and Kristen really need to talk."

He scoffed. "What am I supposed to do? Hog-tie her? You saw how she is. Kristen tells me she needs time, but how much time am

I supposed to give her?" His expression hardened. "I've never known someone as stubborn and hardheaded as she is."

"Oh no? What about Trent? And Grandma? And Grandpa Lawrence was legendary. I think it runs in the family."

Shaun was not amused. "If Kristen is determined to believe the worst and won't talk things through, it's a good thing I found out now."

So, that was the way of it. Had Trent succeeded? Although Erica had seen the love in Kristen and Shaun's eyes when they were together, they had not spoken of it openly—at least not to her. Yet his comment revealed how much he had envisioned Kristen as part of his future. And now he was having doubts. Did Kristen and Shaun still have a future? Erica wasn't sure.

"I talked with Trent today," Erica said.

"Does he still want me drawn and quartered?"

"Come on. He told me you two had talked. He didn't say much about it, but I was hoping you two had worked things out like gentlemen."

"Right. Pistols at twenty paces." He tugged at his ear. "Actually, we did have a good talk. Trent even came close to apologizing."

Erica thought, not for the first time, how amazing it was that men could get over major arguments as easily as they could shrug their shoulders.

"I asked Trent to talk to Kristen," Erica said.

"Great—all Kristen needs is another one of his pep talks. If she talks with Trent again, she'll probably key my car. By the way, when I talked to Trent, I told him what I thought of him for bringing Kristen into this." Shaun's voice was rigid, but it held a tinge of surprise as he added, "He took it amazingly well."

That sounded good. "Kristen told me she'd talk to you soon."

Shaun scoffed. "That's what she tells me too—but I'm tired of waiting. Kristen says she needs time to work things out, but how are we going to do that if she won't talk?" Shaun shook his head. "If Kristen can turn against me because Trent spouts off a pack of lies, then I'm better off without her." Agitated, he rose. "But thanks for trying, Erica." Then he was gone.

* * *

The next time Pamela came in, she carried the cordless phone. "Dearheart, I'm fielding a lot of calls, so I'm going to leave this with you." She handed Erica the phone. "It's Walter."

"Erica! Trent called and told me what happened. He said you were all right, but I wanted to hear it from you."

"I'm fine. I'm just lying here, pondering the meaning of life."

"I see." The old lawyer's voice was as somber as an undertaker's. "And what have you come up with?"

"All evidence to date suggests it's chocolate." He laughed, and she went on. "Don't worry about me—I'm being spoiled rotten. Pamela is waiting on me hand and foot. I'm surprised she can get around and do as much as she can, with her back the way it is."

"I've heard a person can perform extraordinary feats during times of stress," Walter remarked in his slow, dry voice. "Pamela's worried about you. She asked me to talk you out of going to Lake Oswego."

"I'm really not an invalid. Besides, I'm trying to find Aunt Martha's killer too. I have a feeling the two are connected."

"How are things coming along there?"

"I'm getting close. It's like the answer is right in front of me, staring me in the face, just waiting for me to connect the dots. I'm hoping to get some more answers by talking to a boy who said he saw Martha walking in the woods after she died."

"Is that so?" Walter sounded surprised.

"I also have an idea I want to check out. If I'm right, it might be the dot that connects everything." Then she said, "I wanted to ask you something. Gail told me Martha didn't have a will. Is that right?"

"Blanche tried for years to get Martha to draw one up. In fact, this summer I was all set to drive up there and get it done, but Martha said she'd talked with Gail and since she didn't have anything of value and the house was in Blanche's name, there was no need for one."

"That's interesting. I think I know why Martha said that."

"Am I missing something?"

"No, but you just gave me one more dot."

* * *

The doorbell rang. Erica wanted to answer it but knew Pamela would have had a fit if she got up. It was probably Detective McGuire. When they'd talked earlier, he'd said he'd stop by. In a minute, Pamela escorted the detective into the family room. Tall and lean in his blue uniform, Detective Vince McGuire sat in the chair Shaun had pulled over.

"How are you feeling after your tumble?"

"Blessed."

"Hmm, that's unusual from someone who almost got flattened."

"The operative word is *almost*."

"Well, you look good, but I know how painful that kind of injury can be. I wasn't too worried when you said someone followed you in the woods, but this is different, Erica—you could have been killed. The murderer must be worried." When Erica didn't respond immediately, Detective McGuire went on. "I'm glad you had the presence of mind to get the names and phone numbers of those two witnesses. I guess it's your training. Once a cop, always a cop."

"Did they have any information?"

"Nothing more than what you told me. Neither one could tell if it was a man or a woman driving. They didn't notice any passengers or get a license number. But I'm glad you got the first two letters of the license—I still can't believe you remembered that. It narrows things down."

"The SUV also had a damaged right front bumper."

Detective McGuire stroked his black goatee. "I don't know how you saw that when the witnesses didn't."

"I'm the only one that saw the SUV from the front. By the way, I haven't told anyone about that part or that I remembered the first letters of the license plate."

"Good. Don't want the killer feeling that we're closing in—he or she might get desperate. I've got my men and the highway patrol looking for the vehicle. Hopefully we'll get a line on it soon. Now, who knew you took Bandit for a walk every afternoon?"

"I think everyone, but I did go a little earlier today than usual."

"I'll check on people's whereabouts." Detective McGuire gave her a somber look. "Erica, I've got to say this. You've been a great help in the investigation. I appreciate your persistence and logical mind, but I think it's time you backed off. You might be putting yourself at risk. If the killer has tried once or twice to stop you and not succeeded, he's going to try again."

"If you're trying to scare me, it's not working. I have a black belt and Little Suzie." She leaned over and opened the drawer in the coffee table to reveal her Glock 19 in its holster. "But don't worry—I haven't taken it outside the house. I know Oregon doesn't recognize Utah's concealed weapons permits."

Detective McGuire grimaced. "If you were a resident of a contiguous state, we could go to the country sheriff and explain that you have a legitimate need and get the residency requirement waived. But that's not going to fly since you're from Utah. And there's no getting around the requirement on taking a class on Oregon's gun safety laws."

Erica already knew all about Oregon's laws and didn't argue. "There's one other thing I need to tell you, even though it probably isn't important." She filled him in on Trent's argument with Blanche.

The detective stroked his goatee again. "I've always been interested in Trent, ever since you told me he was the only one that didn't want an autopsy. Still, it sounds like Shaun also did his share of arguing with Blanche. Anyway, thanks for letting me know. It doesn't mean much by itself, but it does build a picture."

Detective McGuire's eyes lit on the chocolates, and Erica told him to help himself. As he picked one out, he said, "I talked to Detective Pocharski yesterday. He now thinks the motive for Martha's murder lies with the jewelry Martha was buying. I'm not so sure, since you said 99 percent of the stuff she had was junk."

"Still, if someone heard Martha was buying jewelry and didn't know it was junk, he might have thought it would be easy pickings," Erica said. "That would explain the burglary, but it wouldn't explain the murder. However, the biggest hole in that theory is the fact that the burglar didn't take any of the boxes of jewelry in Martha's closet."

"Yeah." Detective McGuire looked glum. "Did you get anything from your visit to Mr. Quinn?"

"I believe so. There's a file on Martha I'm trying to figure out."

"I got a call from Captain Stanbridge today."

Could any good thing come from Lake Oswego?

"The captain was going over some accident reports and came across a name that sounded familiar. He double-checked and found that a member of your family was in Lake Oswego the same afternoon Martha was killed. The person was involved in a minor traffic accident." Detective

McGuire raised an eyebrow. "You said you'd checked with everyone as to their whereabouts."

A chill went through Erica. "I did. No one said anything about being there. Who was it?"

"Kristen Edwards."

Chapter Twenty-Two

"Kristen, hold up." Erica tried to hurry down the stairs the next morning, but the pain forced her to go slower than she wanted. She had to catch Kristen now, before she left for work.

When Erica reached the foyer, Kristen had her hand on the doorknob. "Are you okay?"

"I think everything stiffened up in the night. Maybe my joints need some WD-40."

Kristen tried to smile. "I have to get to work early today. What's up?"

"We didn't have much time yesterday to talk about Shaun. Or better still, I wish you'd talk with Shaun and hear *his* side of the story."

"I will. It's just that I've been in such a stroppy mood I thought I ought to wait."

Erica looked into Kristen's troubled gray eyes. How could she tell Kristen that silence was only making things worse? And was it only the trouble with Shaun that was bothering Kristen, or was there something more?

"Wouldn't it be better to sit down and talk this through with Shaun?"

"It would, and usually I'm the last one to put things off, but I've been so mad and upset that I don't know what to do. I'm angry at Trent, yet I feel guilty about it." Kristen was close to tears. "I've always trusted him— up to now, that is." She rubbed her temple. "Believe me, I know I should talk with Shaun, but I've been so upset I figured I'd just make things worse. I thought I ought to take some time and think things through so I didn't make a clanger."

"Translation, please."

"A big mistake."

"But you're making a clanger by not talking to Shaun."

"I want to talk, but I have to figure things out first." Kristen's eyes were bright. "I know I'm hurting Shaun, and I feel terrible about it. I will talk to him—soon."

"There is one other thing I wanted to ask you."

Kristen looked at her expectantly.

"Why didn't you tell anyone you were in Lake Oswego the afternoon Martha was killed?"

"Who told you I was in Lake Oswego?" Kristen's words were short and staccato.

"The police."

For a second, Kristen closed her eyes. She leaned against the front door and said in a flat voice. "They told you about the accident."

"Why did I have to hear about it from someone else?"

Color surged into Kristen's face. "Oh, it was all so stupid. I was embarrassed, and I was afraid of what people might think."

"Why *did* you go to Lake Oswego?"

"Not to kill Martha, if that's what you think," Kristen shot out. "The truth is I felt sorry for her. No one ever visited her, so I decided I would. But I never even saw her. No one was home, so I decided to go shopping and check back later." She grimaced. "That was a mistake."

"What happened?"

"When I backed out of a parking lot, I wasn't watching and hit a car. There wasn't much damage, but the lady was pretty angry and called the guards. For a while, I thought I was going to get nicked, and it scared me. I don't know how your jails work here. Anyway, they gave me a ticket, and I was so upset I just came home." Kristen's hands twisted around each other.

If Kristen's remorse was an act, it was a fine one. "You might as well know that Detective McGuire wants to talk with you."

Kristen made a face. "I knew it. Now I'm a murder suspect, and why? Because I went to visit an old woman."

* * *

"Walter?"

"Hello, Erica! Nice to hear from you." Then worry invaded his voice. "Are you all right? Nothing else has happened, has it?"

"Were you expecting something else?" There was a trace of amusement in her voice.

"I suppose I'm a little nervous about you. How are those ribs?"

"Right now, they're resting comfortably. Pamela insisted I lie down and rest this afternoon, so I lay on the couch and watched an old movie. I have to admit, it felt pretty good to do that."

"Cracked ribs can take a while to heal, from what I've heard. I just called Carlos, and he told me Trent is backing off. Is that true?"

"Hard to believe, I know—but true. Trent is giving in as gracefully as he can."

"Good," Walter said. "I thought that, given time, Trent would see reason. The last thing Blanche wanted was to divide the family when she put Shaun in as CEO."

"So far, it sounds like Trent and Shaun have been able to work things out. I suppose miracles never cease."

"I suppose not," Walter acknowledged, "and that's certainly been true with Shaun. I've been amazed to see the changes in him. Well, as the old saying goes, 'the cream will rise to the top,' and he certainly has."

"People seem to live up to what you expect from them."

"That's true," Walter said. "I'm glad you've been here to support Shaun."

"I've just tried to get him to believe in himself. And I've done a lot of praying."

"Apparently, your prayers have been answered. I feel sure Shaun will run Sun Coast the way Blanche would have wanted. And Trent will have to learn to cope with his fears."

Erica was confused. "Fears? You mean his fear of not being head honcho?"

"No—his fear of failure. You know that Trent's father, Randy, was a great businessman. He was so extraordinarily successful that Trent was always in his shadow—at least until Randy passed away. I've sensed for many years that Trent wanted to show everyone that he's just as good a businessman. I suspect that's what led Trent to do what he did," Walter said shrewdly. "I think it was very important to him to prove to others that he's just as capable as his father."

* * *

Pamela had gone to bed early, and Erica and Shaun were watching TV in the game room when Kristen came in. Erica hit the pause button. "You weren't kidding when you said you had to work late. Are you hungry?"

"Not really. I had a late lunch." Kristen stood awkwardly by the door.

"We're watching an old movie—though I had to talk Shaun into it—*Roman Holiday*. I love Audrey Hepburn. Do you want to watch it with us?"

"Oh, no, you go ahead. I don't want to interrupt."

"It's okay," Erica assured her then glanced at Shaun, who was focusing on the TV screen as if it was the most fascinating thing in the world. Something had to be done. And fortunately, she had just the thing. Feeling a need to calm herself and think, Erica had done some baking earlier. By the time Pamela discovered her in the kitchen, the brownies were in the oven, so Erica didn't feel too bad about being ignominiously banished to the family room.

"Hey, let's go into the kitchen and have some Texas Brownies."[9] Erica tried to ignore the pain as she rose but still moved as if she had arthritis. "Come on, Shaun, they're rich and chocolaty."

At first Shaun looked interested, then he caught himself. "Sounds good, but I think I'll go to bed."

As he approached the doorway, Kristen made no move to let him by. "Don't go, Shaun."

Erica threaded her arm through Shaun's. "Come on. Let's have a treat. You'll love them." He went with some reluctance and sat stiffly at the table while Erica brought over the brownies she'd cut into even, two-inch squares. She'd frozen two plates to take with her to Lake Oswego on Friday.

Kristen poured some milk, and when she set a glass by him, Shaun spoke without looking up. "You've been avoiding me for days. Why are you talking to me now?"

"A lot of reasons. Trent talked to me today; Erica asked me to talk to you; something important has come up, which I'll tell you about later; and most important, I've had time to think things through." Kristen continued in a low voice as she slid into a chair beside him. "I'm sorry to have taken so long. I know I've hurt you, and I'm sorry." She put a hand on his arm.

Shaun was unbending, though he did not move away. "You made it clear you didn't want anything to do with me."

---

9   See the appendix for this recipe.

"I needed time to process the things Trent told me. I'm not going to get into what he said, but I'm sure it's the same things he told you. It threw me, and I needed time to process it. You know how forceful and persuasive Trent can be. I think that man could sell chain saws to beavers."

There was a slight softening around Shaun's mouth. "Sometimes I think I don't understand a soul in this world—especially women."

"What makes you think you should?" Kristen replied pertly.

"Umm, I think I'll let you two talk alone." Erica sidled toward the doorway.

"It's all right," Kristen said, motioning her to stay. "You've been right in the middle of this." Kristen took a deep breath. "It's hard to go against someone you look up to as much as I've looked up to Trent. Ever since I started flying out here to visit, Trent has been like a brother to me. He helped me get a job and has always been the one I turned to for advice and counsel. Plus, Trent's never steered me wrong—until now."

Finally, Shaun raised his head, and Kristen looked into his eyes. "I'm so sorry I hurt you, Shaun. I just needed to have some time on my own to think without feeling pulled one way or the other. I couldn't talk to Trent either until a little bit ago." Kristen's voice turned firm. "We got a lot of things straightened out. Trent's a great guy, but he's a little too used to getting his own way, even if it means being a prat. I told Trent he had a lot of cheek butting into our relationship. Trent admitted he'd bodged it and said he'd apologize to you."

"I'll believe that when I hear it." Shaun looked at her. "I thought things were over between us." Misery showed on his face.

Kristen scooted her chair closer. "I know I should have talked to you sooner. But I'm not the only one who has trouble communicating. How many times have I asked you to tell me what was going on at Sun Coast? You wouldn't say a word."

"I didn't feel comfortable talking about what Trent had done. It was a sensitive matter."

"I didn't expect you to tell me everything—I know you have to keep some things confidential." Kristen eyed him. "All I wanted is some general information. When you wouldn't share anything, I felt like you didn't trust me and began to wonder how things stood between us. Besides, I also asked about how *you* were doing in your new position, but there again, you barely said a word."

"I guess I can understand that," Shaun acknowledged. "It's just that I was struggling and didn't want to complain. Plus, you were always gone early in the morning and coming home late at night."

"Shaun, Shaun, Shaun." Kristen shook her head ruefully. "You did the same thing. You're not the only one putting in a lot of hours, trying to get a grip on a new job. Although, I'll admit that lately I've been working longer than I needed just to keep busy, but a lot of times when I did come home, you were still working."

"If you knew the stress I've been under—"

"Right. I wouldn't have a clue about the stress that comes from being in a new job and trying to figure things out." She smiled. "Shaun, I really am sorry for hurting you. I made a real bodge of things. I was miserable and was just trying to work matters out in my mind. I've always trusted Trent, and this was the first time I've ever gone against him. I didn't know what to think. I also worried because I thought we were getting close but you didn't trust me enough to really talk to me." She spoke sternly. "You've got to be more open with me."

"I will. I promise. I didn't mean to hurt you," Shaun said.

"You may not have *meant* to, but you did."

"All right. I'm sorry."

"And I'm sorry too, for not talking to you sooner. That was wrong."

Shaun looked at Kristen as if he'd been blind from birth and had suddenly been given his sight. As he reached for her hand, Kristen gave it without hesitation, flashing Shaun a smile. A current as ancient as time seemed to spring between them.

"I'm glad you're going to be more open with me in the future," Kristen said.

"So, there *is* going to be a future?" Shaun's voice was full of tenderness and hope.

Erica's eyes became misty as Kristen looked at Shaun thoughtfully. "I was going to wait until tomorrow, but maybe now is a good time to tell you now. Remember I said something important had come up? Well, there's something I've been meaning to tell you."

A goofy look came over Shaun's face, and he glanced at Erica. "She's going to tell me that she loves me."

"That's not it," Kristen told Shaun.

"You don't love me?"

Kristen sighed. "Shaun, of course I love you, but this is about something else."

"Tell away." Shaun's grin was lopsided.

"Do you remember when I told you that I'd found Tammy, your mother? Well, we've been talking, by e-mail. And, well . . . I bought her a plane ticket. Tammy is here in Florence, and I've arranged for you to meet her tomorrow."

Chapter Twenty-Three

"*YOU DID WHAT?*" SHAUN'S EYES were close to popping out of his head. "How could you do something like this without talking to me first?"

"You've been feeling hurt and abandoned your whole life. You're not going to heal until you can talk with Tammy and face it."

Shaun was incensed. "Don't even try to give me that psychogol— psychologic—" He gave up. "Don't give me that stuff."

"Until you clear up your past, you can never get on with your life." Kristen was pleading.

Shaun's face had hardened. "Thank you, Dr. Freud. It's nice that you know what's best for me and even more enlightening to know that I haven't been 'getting on with my life.'"

"I didn't mean it that way." Kristen looked stricken. "Oh, now I've gone and bodged things up again. I just thought it might help to talk with your mother about why she left. There's more to the story than you know."

"Don't—call—her—my—mother."

Tears sprang to Kristen's eyes. "All right. I just thought you might be able to feel more at peace with your past if you were able to talk with, ah, Tammy." Her voice was a small thing.

Shaun remained still, and in the silence was something unnerving, as if he was holding some rush of shattering emotion in check. Finally, Shaun said flatly, "Kristen, I think we ought to end this conversation before I say something I'll regret."

Gray eyes brimming with tears, Kristen rushed out.

"Kristen's always been set on me meeting Tammy," Shaun said, his voice harsh, "but I never thought she'd set something up without discussing it with me."

Erica hadn't either. She patted Shaun's arm. "Try to put it out of your mind and get some sleep."

When Erica went to her room, Kristen was sitting on the bed, mopping up tears. Erica was too exhausted to be tactful. "How could you bring Tammy here without asking Shaun first?"

"And what would he have said, huh?" Kristen's voice overflowed with intensity. "Of course he'd say no. But Shaun's never gotten over being abandoned, and he'll never get over it until he faces Tammy. I thought the benefits outweighed the risks."

"It wasn't your call to make. To use your words, you were being a little cheeky."

"But Erica, I thought there had to be some reason Tammy left the way she did, and there was!" Kristen said urgently. She chewed her bottom lip. "Shaun just *has* to meet Tammy. Maybe I should go talk to him again."

"I think Shaun could use a little space right now," Erica advised.

* * *

The next morning when Erica walked into the little alcove by the kitchen, Kristen was there dressed for work in a slim navy-blue suit. Erica noticed the table had been set for four people—obviously, Kristen expected Shaun to sit down to a nice breakfast with her, Pamela, and Erica.

Kristen, Kristen—always the optimist.

Then Erica asked, "Is anyone else up?"

"Not yet. I made French toast and put it in the microwave. I hoped to talk with Shaun this morning before work. Go ahead and sit down, Erica—I'll bring some over. " Kristen stepped over to the microwave, heated a few slices, then sat.

They were just finishing when Shaun walked in, his tie neatly knotted. Kristen had been pouring juice and overshot her glass when she saw him.

The look he shot Kristen would have reduced a less confident woman to a puddle, but Kristen took it in stride as she wiped up the spill. "Good morning, Shaun. I made some French toast. Do you want me to warm some up for you?"

Shaun faced her and said coolly, "Despite being damaged beyond repair by my past, I can still operate a microwave."

Oh boy. Apparently, sleeping on it had only made Shaun more aggravated. When he turned away, Erica mouthed sotto voce to Kristen, "Let him eat first."

Kristen nodded. "I've got to get some papers from my room. I'll be right back."

Shaun was rinsing off his plate when Kristen returned. She took a deep breath and squared her shoulders. "Can I talk with you, Shaun, before we go to work?" When he looked pointedly at his watch, she added, "It's important."

His eyes narrowed, but Shaun assented. As Kristen shut the door, she glanced back, and Erica gave her a discreet thumbs-up. Curiosity kept Erica in the kitchen area, where there were plenty of windows to witness the tableau unfolding outside and to see if blood was being spilled.

Erica's heart went out to both of them. Each had valid viewpoints. Shaun *had* admitted being troubled his whole life by Tammy's abandonment, and Kristen clearly wanted what was best for him and thought talking to Tammy would help. Yet Shaun was also right that it should have been his decision. Regardless, Shaun faced a choice today that could have long-lasting consequences. Could he find the strength to face Tammy and his past?

Bandit trailed after Kristen and Shaun as they walked around the lawn. At times they stopped to face one another, talking animatedly, with much waving of hands. At one time Shaun threw up his arms in what looked like indignation. Another time, he must have spoken harshly, for Bandit turned and slunk away with his head down. Finally, Shaun shook his head and stalked toward the gazebo. Kristen followed with determined steps. While Erica wiped the table, the couple sat on the bench. Occasionally, Kristen swiped at her cheeks as if wiping away tears.

"What are you looking at?" Pamela asked, making Erica jump and turn around guiltily.

"Oh! I was just seeing how Kristen was getting on with Shaun." Erica explained the drama unfolding outside.

"Come sit with me?" Pamela asked after heating her French toast. They sat at the table, and by leaning to the left, Erica could see perfectly. Shaun was speaking now—in earnest. After a time, Kristen put a hand on his leg as if in supplication. Pamela finished as Erica's cell phone rang. It was David, and as they talked, Erica wandered into the sitting room for a time then returned to the kitchen. Pamela had left. When Erica peeked out the window, her heart leapt. Kristen and Shaun were walking back to the house, and they were holding hands.

The moment they came through the doors, Kristen burst out, "He's forgiven me! Isn't he great? And we *are* going to meet with his moth— Tammy. For lunch. And we want you to come."

"Oh no," Erica said decisively. "It would be better if you two went alone."

"We need you to come—to run interference," Kristen explained frankly. "You have a wonderful way with people, Erica, and we figured you're just the person to come with us and break the ice. It could be a little awkward in the beginning."

A *little* awkward? How about off-the-charts and shooting-into-outer-space awkward? Erica looked at Shaun. "Do *you* want me to go?" It was only fair to give him some say in the matter—he'd had precious little so far.

Shaun raised his eyebrows in surprise. "What? You're asking *me* what *I* would like? How thoughtful and *unusual* for someone to consider *my* feelings. Then again, maybe you ought to ask Kristen. She's the expert at knowing what's best for everyone else." Fortunately, his tone of voice took most of the sting out of his words. Yet, there were quite a lot of feelings still there. Erica wondered if Kristen might have been stretching things by saying Shaun had forgiven her.

"Please come, Erica," Kristen begged.

Erica looked at Shaun. "I'll come, if you want me to."

"I do." Then he added, "Oh wait, you did say you were buying, right?"

* * *

Walter called that morning to invite her to lunch.

"I'd love to, but I'm already spoken for." Erica explained what was going on.

"Tammy is here? In Florence?" The staid, calm lawyer sounded genuinely upset.

"That's right. Why, is something wrong?"

"This is *quite* unexpected."

"I'll say. I can't believe Kristen didn't tell Shaun she was setting this up."

"Kristen had no business getting involved. No business at all. Who knows what Tammy will say—" Walter broke off, anxiety in his voice.

"Kristen wants Tammy to explain why she abandoned Shaun."

"That's exactly what I'm afraid of." Erica listened in amazement as Walter Hancock, the dignified lawyer, mumbled to himself, "What to do? I have to think."

"Walter, what's going on?"

"You don't happen to have Tammy's phone number, do you? No, well—just a thought. I'll call Kristen and get it. Good-bye."

It was unusual for Walter to be so abrupt. What was wrong with him?

Erica wondered even more an hour later when Walter texted her— *Talked with Tammy. Will come over tonight.*

What was going on?

* * *

Shaun rode shotgun, with Erica in the back, as Kristen drove through Old Town Florence. She was able to park on the street near the popular ICM Seafood Restaurant with its blue slate roof, on the banks of the Siuslaw River. A short, plump hostess welcomed them then escorted them past log-plank tables and outside, where the sun was shining, making the blue water sparkle. It was a glorious fall day—the air crisp and cool. At one of the picnic-style tables near the wooden railing, a thin older woman sat facing the long dock with its line of white fishing boats. Across the river, a few picturesque houses were tucked among the towering green pines on the rolling hillside.

Hearing their footsteps, the woman turned her deeply lined face toward them expectantly. The breeze rippled her shoulder-length brown hair, which was liberally streaked with gray.

Taking a firm hold of Shaun's hand, Kristen inquired, "Tammy Coleman?"

The woman nodded, her eyes big and uneasy.

"I'm Kristen Edwards. This is Erica Coleman, and this is Shaun."

Tammy's eyes were fastened on the handsome young man, as she smiled uncertainly, hands twined in her lap. Self-consciously, they all turned their attention to their menus and then gave their order.

Erica and Kristen made small talk as the wind ruffled the fringe on the orange umbrella over their table and rattled the lines against nearby masts. For the most part, Tammy seemed content to listen, watching them with sad eyes that kept returning to Shaun, who had little to say.

He kept darting glances at Tammy, his eyes flying away if she happened to glance in his direction. When Tammy picked up her glass of water, her hand trembled, and she took only a single sip before setting the glass down. Her hands returned to their hiding place.

Erica was so involved in coming up with small talk that it took some time before she noticed that the sugar packets in the small metal box on the table were in disarray. "Will you look at that," she said, pulling it closer. "They're all uneven." She spent a productive few minutes straightening the packets while Tammy looked on with a small, bemused smile.

Some of the tension was released when the waitress brought their food. Tammy began talking more, taking miniscule spoonfuls of clam chowder—the only thing she'd ordered. Kristen worked hard to carry the conversation, she and Erica doing their best to find common ground with weather, airports, and traffic. Kristen chatted brightly, and her smile was so wide and continuous, her mouth must have hurt.

Whenever Shaun made a comment, Tammy watched and listened as intently as if he was about to explain the origins of the universe. Lulls in the conversation were filled with the sound of water lapping against the pilings, cries of seagulls overhead, and the warble of a radio on a passing boat.

They declined dessert, and Kristen suggested they go for a walk. They passed a number of tiny shops before turning left into a small park-like area that held the Old Town Gazebo, which gave them an unimpeded view of the river and the historic Siuslaw Bridge with its unique art deco–style obelisks and concrete arches. The spot was originally a ferry landing, then a public fishing dock, before becoming a viewing platform.

"I used to bring you here, Shaun, when you were little," Tammy confided, looking over the railing. "You loved to watch the birds." Shaun seemed to be struggling to remember as he gazed out at the decayed pilings in the water that now served as perches for cormorants, kingfishers, ospreys, and other birds.

"You know what?" Kristen said. "I just remembered that a frame I'd ordered at the Old Time Photo Studio is ready. Erica, would you come with me to get it?" An alarmed look flashed across Shaun's face, but Kristen assured him, "We'll be back in a couple of minutes."

Kristen tugged at Erica's arm, and they were off like horses out of the starting gate. Once they'd rounded the corner, Erica complained, "You're going too fast."

Contrite, Kristen slowed. "Sorry. I forgot about your ribs." She looked around. "There's a bench in front of Wizards of Odds; we can sit there."

"Well, that was real subtle," Erica said once they were seated.

Kristen grimaced. "I warned Tammy I planned to leave her and Shaun alone after we ate and that she had to be ready to talk—really talk—to Shaun."

"You are *such* a meddler. Shaun's going to be furious with you—again."

"He'll be fine," Kristen said heartlessly, glancing at her watch. "But I need to keep track of the time. I want to give them enough to reconnect but not so much that Shaun wants to strangle me."

"You took a big risk having Tammy come out."

Kristen's gray eyes were thoughtful. "She took a bigger one coming here, knowing how Shaun felt about her."

"Well, Tammy's the one that abandoned him."

Kristen looked at her. "You don't know the whole story. It took a long time, but eventually Tammy told me. But I'd better not go into that. I'll let Tammy or Shaun tell you."

"Since when do you have a problem talking about things that are none of your business?"

"Since Shaun gave me a good talking to this morning. I'm going to mend my ways."

They talked idly about Erica driving to Lake Oswego the next day, then Kristen decided it was time to get back. When they turned into the small park, their steps slowed. Shaun and Tammy were sitting close in the gazebo, deep in conversation. Tammy glanced up as they approached and gave them a watery smile. Although there were tear tracks on her cheeks and a number of balled-up tissues in her lap, Tammy looked more relaxed, and her eyes were a little less haunted. Shaun's face had also changed—softened. Erica took it as a good sign when Shaun made no mention of how long they'd been gone.

"So, it went all right?" Kristen asked softly.

Tammy looked tentatively at Shaun, who nodded. They walked slowly back to the street and down to Shaun's SUV.

"If you don't mind waiting here," Shaun said to Kristen and Erica, "I'll walk Tammy to her car."

Kristen unlocked the SUV and, after getting in, peered at Shaun and Tammy, who were talking by the side of Tammy's car. "It looks like things went all right, don't you think?"

"Seems so," Erica agreed. She only had body language to go on at this distance, but she figured that every minute the two spent together was a plus.

Ten minutes went by, then twenty, with Shaun listening to what seemed to be a flood of words. When Kristen and Erica spoke, they kept their comments short and one eye down the road. Occasionally, Tammy wiped her face. Then, Tammy hugged Shaun as if she was never going to let him go, and Erica smiled, full of hope. A hug was certainly a good end to this visit and the first step toward healing past hurts.

When Shaun returned, his eyes were bright, but it wasn't until they were back on Highway 101 that he spoke. "Tammy told me Walter called her today. He's going to come by the house tonight. Oh, I also invited Tammy to come over for dinner. I'll order a couple of pizzas."

"Pizza? For someone you haven't seen since you were a toddler?" Kristen was appalled.

"What's wrong with that?" Shaun looked genuinely puzzled.

Erica and Kristen looked at each other in disbelief then set about making plans.

"Let's have something simple," Erica said. "What about soup and a salad?"

"Sounds good," Kristen said. "I'll stop at the Krab Kettle on my way home and pick up some soup."

"I'll make some breadsticks and a dessert," Erica said. "And we have stuff in the fridge for a green salad."

"I still don't see what's wrong with pizza," Shaun grumbled.

Chapter Twenty-Four

"ARE YOU SURE YOU WON'T come for dinner?" Erica had called Walter when she got back to the house. "It'll just be Shaun, Pamela, Kristen, and me. Oh, and Tammy."

"Thanks, Erica, but I'll come later."

"We'll expect you for dessert, then. I'm making scrumptious Chocolate Dream Dessert."[10]

"If you're making it, I'm sure it'll be wonderful." Walter was always chivalrous.

"Everyone raves about it, but the secret is using freshly beaten whipped cream—none of that glue-paste-in-a-tub you find in the frozen food section." Then she asked, "Do you want to explain what's going on with you and Tammy?"

"It'll keep until tonight."

That evening Pamela and Tammy became reacquainted during dinner. Although Tammy was still pale, her face had lost its strained expression. Kristen kept them amused with her energetic brightness, and Shaun looked relaxed. Earlier, Erica had asked Shaun how things went with Tammy, hoping he'd volunteer information, but he only said they'd talk later.

"Since Walter will be here any minute, let's go ahead and dish up dessert," Pamela suggested.

"Good idea," Kristen said. She carried the glass pan to the table while Erica got saucers from the cupboard.

"This one is chipped." Erica headed for the garbage can.

---

10   See the appendix for this recipe.

"Let me see that." Pamela stopped her and examined the saucer. "Dear-heart, you can barely see the chip. There's no need to throw it away."

"It's ruined," Erica objected, tossing it in the garbage can. "No one would want to eat from something like that."

Shaun pulled out the saucer and looked it over. "This is still good."

"Not when it's been in the garbage, for goodness sake," Erica cried. "It was already unusable, but now it's contaminated too."

"Maybe for you, but not for me," Shaun said. "I'll use it."

Erica was horrified. "You can't do that!"

"Watch me."

"At least let me wash it good to sanitize it."

"Get a grip, Erica," Shaun replied. "There was nothing disgusting in the garbage can."

A mask of calm fell over Erica's features. "All right. Have it your way, but at least let me wash it." Shaun handed the plate over. Erica started toward the sink, stopped short, and dropped the saucer, which shattered on the tile floor.

"Oops! Clumsy me," Erica said in a singsong voice. "Guess you'll have to use an uncontaminated saucer now."

Kristen burst out laughing, and even Tammy smiled.

When the doorbell rang, Kristen returned with Walter, who, for once, was wearing tan pants and a sports shirt. He nodded gravely to everyone, but his gaze lingered on Tammy.

"Hello, it's nice to see you again." His words were polite, but the tone was stilted. He and Tammy shook hands formally.

"You're right on time," Erica said. "Let's go into the formal dining room."

They carried in their saucers, and after a few bites, Walter said, "This is terrific, Erica. My daughter loves to cook. Could I get the recipe?"

She grinned. "I charge $20."

"I consider that a bargain."

When her mother-in-law refused to let Erica help clear the table, Shaun snickered. "Because Pamela doesn't want to lose any more saucers."

They went into the family room. Bandit followed, surprising them all by lying down by Tammy, who sat on the end of the couch next to Shaun. She stroked Bandit's head as Pamela turned on the fireplace. Flames began to pulse and leap as they talked idly. Then it was time to talk about the elephant in the room.

"I—I talked a little with Shaun today," Tammy began, sounding shy and uncertain. "But I feel like I ought to explain things to the rest of you. That is, if it's all right with Mr. Hancock." She gave him a beseeching look.

What did she mean, if it was all right with Walter? Erica gazed at the old lawyer. What part did he play in this? Yet, from the comments Walter had made earlier, it was clear he was involved somehow.

"Tammy, you don't have to explain," Pamela said.

"I know, but I want to." Tammy licked her lips nervously. "Kristen and I have been emailing a bit, and she told me that sometimes, in order to progress, you have to heal from your past. I think she's right. I want this to be a new beginning, and it can't be unless I explain what happened."

Walter's eyes were grave as he spoke up. "I've done a lot of thinking since Erica told me you were in town, Tammy, and although I wasn't sure about it at first, I think it's time matters were brought into the light."

Erica looked at Tammy, then Walter. "It seems you two know something the rest of us don't."

The lawyer glanced at Tammy from under his bushy eyebrows, noticing how she clasped her hands together so tightly her knuckles were white. "It's all right," he reassured Tammy. "Blanche and Lawrence are both gone now, and you're not bound to the agreement anymore."

Tammy swallowed hard. Shaun took her hand in a warm, encouraging clasp. "Just tell them what you told me."

"You really don't have to explain anything," Pamela repeated, her eyes large with sympathy.

"I know," Tammy said, her voice a little unsteady. "But I want the family to know. For years I've wanted to explain, and now, finally, I can."

She took a deep breath. "I'm going to make it short, but I have to go back to when Wayne died in Vietnam. I was kind of a wild child when I met him. Wayne knew I took drugs once in a while, but after we were engaged, I promised him I wouldn't take them anymore. And I didn't, not until he was killed. I was young and lonely and started using again—heavily this time—and I got hooked. I knew I was neglecting Shaun, but I couldn't help myself. When Blanche and Lawrence found out, they had me and Shaun move in with them. I tried to stop using but couldn't." Tammy bit her lip.

"Did your parents help you at all?" Erica asked.

"My father took off when I was ten. I never heard from him again. My mother was an addict herself and died from an overdose when I was fourteen." She brushed her hair back. "Lawrence and Blanche stepped in—they hired a nanny to take care of Shaun, paid for me to see a counselor, and a couple of times sent me to a treatment center. Each time I got out, I started using again. Lawrence was angry and stopped giving me a monthly allowance. That's when I started selling drugs to pay for my own. Then I got arrested. That scared me, but when I got out, I started using again."

Tammy's shoulders were stooped, and tears ran down her face. "When I got arrested the third time, Lawrence was fed up. He said I was an unfit mother—which was true. He told me that if I got arrested again, he wasn't going to bail me out and that I would have to leave his house. I tried to go straight, but I couldn't make it. I started selling again and got arrested." Tammy's voice faltered and died. Shaun handed her a box of tissues, which she plucked at and wiped her eyes. Her face looked empty.

"Do you want me to tell the rest?" Walter asked. Tammy nodded. "At this point, I became involved," Walter explained, "because Lawrence asked me to write up a contract."

Erica stared into eyes that had faded to a silver blue. "A contract?"

"That's correct. Lawrence made a deal with Tammy. He said he'd bail her out of jail one last time and pay for a top-notch attorney—which she needed because of her record. Lawrence also said he'd pay for Tammy to go to another rehabilitation center. If she finished the treatment, Lawrence would pay for her to attend college, including room and board. I wrote up the contract, and Tammy signed it."

Something in the stilted way Walter was speaking made Erica uneasy. She knew a little of Lawrence Coleman—how tough and harsh he could be. This contract seemed exceedingly generous. Surely there was something Lawrence required in return.

"That was generous," Pamela began, but her words faded when she saw Tammy's face.

"Generous?" Shaun practically spit the word out. "Tell them about the rest of the contract, Walter."

The lawyer sighed. "In order for Tammy to receive all of those benefits, she had to agree to six conditions." Obviously, Walter knew them by heart, and he began to reel them off. "One, Tammy had to finish the treatment center's program. Two, she had to stay off drugs and out of jail. Three, she had to get a part-time job while she was in school. Four, she had to sign adoption papers so Lawrence and Blanche could formally adopt Shaun. Five, Tammy could have no contact with Shaun unless Blanche and Lawrence initiated it, until both of them had passed away, or unless Shaun was eighteen or over and contacted her first."

Erica felt her heart turn over. "Oh my," she gasped, glancing at Tammy, who was studying her lap.

"It may seem harsh," Walter declared, "but you have to remember Lawrence and Blanche tried for two full years to help Tammy, but there had been no change in her lifestyle."

Tammy swallowed hard. "Lawrence said he and Blanche could provide Shaun with a loving, stable home and give him an expensive education, music lessons, private tutors, sports trainers—everything a child could want. He told me I'd damaged Shaun enough and that if I truly loved my son, I'd do what was best for him and let them adopt him."

Erica felt a sinking in her stomach. Had Pamela known about this? She glanced at her mother-in-law. Pamela's pained expression face told Erica she hadn't.

"And all this time, I thought you'd just decided to leave," Pamela said to Tammy.

"It wasn't much of a choice, was it?" Kristen burst out angrily. "Either go to jail or give up your son. Lawrence backed you into a corner."

"That's what I thought, for a long time." Tammy sighed. "But the counselors at the rehabilitation center told us we had to stop blaming other people and face up to the consequences of our own actions. All my life, I'd blamed others. I blamed my mother for being an addict and my father for not hanging around. I blamed my addictions on Wayne's death then blamed Lawrence for forcing me to give up my child and walk out of his life. But the truth is that I was responsible for myself. I always had choices—I just made the wrong ones. It took a long time to see that it wasn't Lawrence's fault I lost my son—it was my own."

She went on. "Although I hated to admit it, Lawrence was right—I *was* a negligent mother. All I cared about was my next fix. Lawrence and Blanche were the ones who took Shaun to the park, fixed his meals, sat up with him when he was sick. Blanche even potty trained him. I was too stoned."

There was silence. Erica thought of the ravages of drugs and addiction—of lives torn apart. Thank goodness Blanche and Lawrence had been there for Shaun. Then Erica said, "Wait a minute, Walter. Didn't you say there were six conditions? You only listed five."

Walter looked tired. "The sixth one is that Tammy was never to discuss this contract with Blanche."

There was a quick intake of air from Pamela. "Blanche didn't know about it?"

"Not all of it, no. Lawrence only told her that Tammy wanted them to adopt Shaun and that he was going to pay for another stint in a rehabilitation center and that if she completed it, he'd pay for her to go to college. He also told Blanche that Tammy felt it would be best if she stayed out of Shaun's life."

"I didn't think Tammy wanted me—she'd never written or called—so I never asked Mom or Dad about contacting her." Shaun's voice was full of anger and remorse.

"Lawrence was tough, but I knew he would tell you how to find me if you asked," Tammy told Shaun. "And since you never did, I knew you didn't want any contact with me."

"There is one other thing you all ought to know," Walter said with a quiet, melancholy look. "Blanche *did* find out about the contract."

"When?" Kristen asked.

"About a year ago, Blanche came to my office to look over some files. I wasn't in. When my assistant called me to ask what files to pull for Blanche, I didn't answer my cell because I was in a meeting. So Blanche, in her usual determined way, demanded my assistant hand over a stack of files, most of which had nothing to do with what she needed. Inadvertently, the file with the contract between Lawrence and Tammy was included."

"How did Grandma take it?" Erica wanted to know. It was hard to know how she would react to such information.

"At first she was angry, but with time, she realized Lawrence had done what he thought was best. Still, Blanche was upset and felt Shaun had been cheated out of a relationship with Tammy."

Walter looked at Erica. "When you asked me why Blanche changed her will and I told you she'd been influenced by a particular piece of information, I was talking about this contract. Blanche felt an injustice had been done and wanted to correct it. That's why she changed her will and gave half of her estate to Shaun."

The color ebbed from Shaun's face. "Is that why she made me CEO and chairman of the board—to make it up to me?"

Erica held her breath and waited for the lawyer to speak.

"No, it was not." Walter's voice was deliberate. "Although I don't know for certain, I think Blanche was suspicious of Trent. Even though she wasn't sure exactly what Trent was doing, she knew it wasn't right and decided she wanted Shaun to run the company."

Kristen squeezed Shaun's hands. "See, it's what I've been telling you all along. Grandma picked you because she knew you could handle being CEO and chairman. She trusted you."

Pamela turned to Tammy. "What happened after you graduated college?"

"I started teaching school. Later, I got married and had three children. I stayed off drugs, and my life was very ordinary—at least until Kristen contacted me." Tammy's eyes were bright as she looked at Shaun. "I was afraid to come—scared I might find out you hated me. But Kristen talked me into trying."

Shaun put his arms around her, and Tammy laid her head on his shoulder and wept.

Chapter Twenty-Five

GAIL WAS WALKING TOWARD THE shed, carrying a shovel, as Erica pulled into the driveway. Gail turned, and Erica thought how haggard and worried she looked.

Picking up a plate of brownies, Erica hurried over. "Doing a little gardening?"

"No, burying a cat."

Erica inhaled sharply. "Not the mother cat—"

"She came streaking across the road when I came home. I swerved but hit her anyway." Erica felt her throat tighten as Gail went on. "I didn't think she'd live."

"You mean she was still—alive?"

"I had to finish her off."

Wordlessly, Erica went to the shed, setting the brownies on a crate and going to where three little furry bundles pressed themselves against the back of their box. There was a clank as Gail put the shovel in the corner. Moving gingerly, Erica pulled on her gloves, leaned over, and picked up one of the wide-eyed kittens.

"What's the matter? You look like you're hurting."

"I am, as a matter of fact," Erica explained as she held the kitten.

Gail was horrified. "That's terrible! Did the police find out who did it?"

"They're looking, but I don't know if they'll find them."

"I'm surprised you still drove up here."

"The pain's not too bad, and I'm learning to be very careful how I move. Plus, Tylenol helps." Erica put the kitten back and picked up another, stroking it tenderly. "Poor baby. I bet you miss your mommy." The kittens lost their initial fear and meandered around the box, their tiny spiked tails held high. "I'm glad they're eating well. They're nearly old enough to go to new homes."

"I don't have time to take care of a bunch of kittens. Now that the mom's gone, I thought I'd take them to the animal shelter."

"Oh, don't do that!" Erica was aghast. "They already have automatic feeders. I'll refill them before I go. Just spend a little time with them to get them more socialized."

"I'm too busy for that."

Holding the kitten cupped in the palm of her hand, Erica raised it to eye level. The kitten stared back, bright-eyed, then meowed. Erica put it with the others, suppressing a groan of pain as she leaned over. "I'll take the kittens with me. I can feed and socialize them, and I'll find them good homes."

"Are you sure you want to take all of that on? Especially after your accident? Surely you're not well enough to do that."

"I'll be fine, and since the mother is gone, it probably would be best if I took them today."

"I'm not sure about this." Gail sounded worried. When Erica went to pick up the brownies, Gail said, "Let me carry that for you."

"They're Texas brownies," Erica explained as they walked to the house. "You're going to love them. And each one is two inches square."

Nutmeg and Cocoa were waiting by the front door, watching with golden eyes. When Gail opened the door, the cats walked in, their tails swishing back and forth regally.

"They think I'm their personal doorman," Gail remarked, "as well as their cook and maid."

They went into the front room, and Gail uncovered the brownies. "I can't resist." She took a bite. "Umm, these *are* good!" She sat back. "Say, did you go see Bradley Quinn?"

"I did. Have you ever been in his store? His back room is amazing! It's awesome how he's organized everything—not one thing was out of place." Erica spoke in reverent tones. "And his files! Perfectly organized *and* color coded." She went on. "Mr. Quinn seemed a little suspicious of me at first, but he finally let me see Martha's reports."

"You mean he kept all of her old reports?" Gail looked taken back.

"Mr. Quinn said you showed Martha what to look for in jewelry."

"Well, yes. I didn't want anyone taking advantage of her. People could tell right off that Martha was—you know—a little simple, and I didn't want anyone to cheat her."

"So you know a lot about jewelry?"

"A little. To know for sure if something is valuable, you really need to have a jeweler look at it, but my father taught me some basic things to look for.

Erica was interested. "Like what?"

"For one thing, gold-tone jewelry is brassy and shiny. Real gold doesn't glitter in the sun. Also, look for sharp ridges or edges, which are common with costume jewelry. If the metal is very smooth, it's probably real gold. And look at the corners and edges where it might be worn. If you see a change in color, the jewelry is just gold plated." Gail warmed to her subject. "To tell if stones are real, look at how they are set. If they're set with prongs, the stone is probably real, but if it's glued, it's junk. You can also look at the fastener. If it has more than one closure, it's probably genuine."

"What about the bracelet you showed me when I was here before—you thought the chips were rhinestones."

"Yes, because they were glued. I also did a breath test. You breathe on the stones until they get misty and then watch them. A real diamond will turn clear almost immediately, but a fake one will stay cloudy for ten or fifteen seconds. Sometimes when I went with Martha, I'd take a small mirror with me. Diamonds are harder than glass and will scratch a mirror."

"Did you ever find anything at a garage sale that was worth a lot?"

"Never." Gail looked regretful. "Personally, I like auctions and estate sales better—they usually have higher-quality items. But I never found anything of real value."

Erica looked at her watch. "Detective Pocharski ought to be here soon. We're going to go talk to Travis Staheli. He lives a couple of houses down, doesn't he?"

"I heard about the rumor Travis started." Gail's face flushed. "I think it's terrible—talking about Martha like that. Kids can be cruel."

Changing the subject, Erica said, "Afterwards, I'll go to a pet store and get a few supplies for the kittens. Is it okay if I come back here after and pick them up?"

"Sure. I go to work at two, but I'll give you a key to the house. Just lock up and leave the key with the neighbor like you did before."

* * *

Waiting on the front porch, Erica thought about Kristen and her visit to Lake Oswego, which she'd kept secret. Kristen had always seemed so open, but apparently, she could be secretive. Had Kristen really come to Lake Oswego just to visit Martha? Erica hated suspecting Kristen—but she hated suspecting anyone in the family. But if she and Detective McGuire were correct, the same person had killed both Blanche and Martha. What motive did Kristen have for killing Blanche? Kristen's inheritance was good sized but not a fortune. And would she really kill Martha just to keep her quiet?

A police cruiser pulled up in front of the Staheli house, and Erica picked up the two plates of brownies she'd already gotten out of her car. One was for Simon, and the other was for Travis—a ploy to win the boy's heart and loosen his tongue.

"Hello, Simon! I brought you some brownies."

"Gee, thanks." Simon reached out and took both plates, a happy smile on his face. His brow furrowed as he glanced toward the house. "I don't think I ought to eat them in front of the Stahelis."

"Um, maybe you could give them one of the plates."

"Oh, yeah. Good idea." He hesitated, looking at the brownies. "I'll hold this one while you put your plate in your car."

When Simon rejoined her, they headed for the white brick rambler, which had an amazing assortment of skateboards and bikes scattered on the lawn and front porch.

As they walked past a small flower bed with daisies and straggly chrysanthemums, the detective said, "Captain Stanbridge told me what happened." He looked at her sympathetically. "How are the ribs?"

"A bit sore," Erica admitted, pressing the doorbell.

"I don't understand why you want to talk with Travis." Detective Pocharski was puzzled. "You don't believe his story, do you?"

Before she could answer, Mrs. Staheli, a pleasant-faced woman in her late thirties, came to the door. She shook their hands, her blue eyes a bit worried. "Travis is out back. Follow me, and watch your step." Mrs. Staheli led them through the obstacle course, avoiding Legos, a baseball mitt, a purple unicorn, and assorted cars and trucks. The patio overlooked a large backyard where a number of children were playing on a wooden swing set. The lawn ended at Bryant Woods, which was alive with yellow, maroon, and bronze trees.

Travis, a bright-eyed boy with rosy cheeks, arrived out of breath when summoned by his mother. He stared in open-mouthed awe at

Simon, who sat up a little straighter and moved his arm so the boy could have a better look at both the badge and the holstered Glock 21 he wore on his belt.

"Hi, Travis," Erica began. "I'm Erica Coleman, and this is Detective Pocharski." She handed him the plate. "I brought you some brownies. Is it all right if I ask you a few questions?"

The boy nodded and handed the plate to his mother. His gaze returned to Simon—more specifically, to his badge. Simon told Travis, "You can touch it if you want."

Wide-eyed, Travis put out a careful finger and touched the badge as Simon looked on proudly.

Wearing a little smile, Erica asked Travis, "Do you like to go walking in the woods?" The boy nodded solemnly. "Martha liked to walk there too. Did you ever see her?"

"Lots of times."

"There was a rumor that you saw Martha's ghost in the woods after she died."

Travis's eyes darted toward his mother, who blurted, "That was just a misunderstanding. You see, what happened was—"

"If you don't mind, Mrs. Staheli, I'd like to hear it from Travis." Erica turned to the boy. "Did you see Martha's ghost after she died?"

"No." Travis looked scornful. "My brother made that up." The boy frowned. "When I told my brother I saw Martha in the woods, he wanted to scare his friends and told them I saw Martha's ghost. But I didn't see a ghost. It was her."

"How can you be so sure?" Simon was curious.

"You can see through ghosts." Travis's voice was a touch disdainful, as if he'd been asked what color a bluebird was. "And they float above the ground."

"And Martha wasn't doing that?" Simon asked.

"No, and I saw her *before* she died—on Monday."

Erica's voice was gentle. "But Martha was in Florence that day—she was at her mother's funeral. You couldn't have seen her."

Travis's chin came up. "I did. I saw her."

His mother jumped in, her voice apologetic. "Travis, honey—we talked about this. You have baseball practice on Mondays. You didn't have time to go to the woods that day."

"I went to the woods, and she was there," Travis insisted with a scowl.

Simon tried to comfort the boy. "You probably got the days mixed up. It happens all the time." He puffed out his chest a little. "Of course, not to police officers."

"Did you see anyone else in the woods that day beside Martha?" Erica asked.

"There was an old couple. The man had a cane. There were some kids too—older than me." He thought. "And there was a woman with a little boy. He kept falling down."

"I think that's about all," Erica said, getting to her feet. She shook hands with Mrs. Staheli and Travis. "Thanks for talking with us."

Simon also shook hands then told Travis, "If you want to touch the badge again, you can."

Reverently, Travis reached out and touched the shiny metal. Simon smiled.

"Travis, hurry and change into your uniform." Mrs. Staheli sounded stressed. "You have practice this afternoon."

The boy looked puzzled. "But Ryan told me the coach cancelled it."

"His assistant is going to take over today." As Travis ran off, Mrs. Staheli said, "It's a busy life, trying to keep track of all of the children's practices and games." She showed them out.

After Simon drove off, Erica stood there for some time, thinking. Then she went back to the house and rang the bell.

When Mrs. Staheli opened the door, she blinked in surprise. "Did you forget something?"

"Yes, I did. I wanted to look at your calendar, if that's all right."

Ten minutes later, Erica came out wearing a Mona Lisa smile.

* * *

At the pet store, Erica bought a collapsible exercise pen, a crate, litter, and a litter box. She took two more Tylenol then stopped at the Lake Oswego Theater House. After gassing up the car, Erica drove to Gail's house. She got a drink of water and, on her way out, paused to pet Nutmeg, who was curled up on the couch. Then Erica noticed some magazines on the bookshelf were protruding slightly, but when she tried to push them back, she couldn't because something was behind them. Erica pulled out the magazines, stared at the wall curiously, then brought out her Leatherman. It was some time before Erica finally put the magazines back and took the key to the neighbor.

As she left the house, Erica remembered she'd left a sack of scraps for the chickens in the car. Grabbing the sack, Erica went to the chicken pen and found Gail had put the large garbage can in the spot where Erica usually fed the chickens. *Ugh.* She couldn't go *there.* Instead, she went to the far side to be as far away from the can as possible. Leaning against the fence, Erica contentedly watched the chickens snap up the bits she'd thrown in. Then she looked closer and frowned. The board that held the chicken's feeder and water was lopsided. She wondered why she hadn't noticed it before. It must have been like that for quite a while and was just more visible from this angle. Erica tried to ignore it, but her gaze kept returning. It bothered her that the board was higher on one end. The longer she stayed, the harder it was to resist the urge to go inside and straighten it.

Finally, Erica gave up and went to get a shovel. She opened the gate and went inside to level the board but ran into an unforeseen dilemma. It was late by the time Erica finished, put the kittens in the crate on the backseat, and headed for Florence.

It was a relief to turn down the curving driveway and push the button to open the garage door. Her trip had been a success, and a nebulous idea, formed during the past days of forced inactivity, had taken shape then become clear. At first it had seemed too fantastic to be possible, but now it was the only solution that made sense. All that was left were minor details to iron out. While still in the garage, Erica called Detective McGuire to share her ideas and enlist his help.

Later that evening, Erica called and talked to her children. Then David got on the phone. She purposely avoided using Skype, knowing she looked tired.

"How are you feeling?" David asked, sounding worried. "You overdid it by going to Lake Oswego, didn't you?"

"Yep." Erica admitted it freely as she sat on the floor in the middle of the exercise pen she'd put up. The kittens were exploring, holding out tiny paws to tentatively touch the fence and ready to jump back should it attack. "But I'm home now, and the pain pills have kicked in. I didn't dare take them earlier when I was driving."

"What did that boy—Travis, is it—have to say? Wait a minute, what's that sound? Are you in the house?"

"I'm in the alcove next to the kitchen, and there's someone here that wants to say hello. Hold on a sec." Erica scooped up one of the orange marmalade kittens, with its hard little potbelly and slanted green eyes. When it started meowing, Erica held the cell phone to its pink mouth. Then she asked her husband, "Did you get that?"

"Very funny."

"But I didn't hear you answer. Didn't you understand the question? The kitten asked, 'Can I come live at your house?'"

This was met by a moment of silence. Then David bellowed, "Erica!"

"It's only one tiny kitten. Actually, there are three. Maybe I should bring them all home. After all, we have plenty of mice in the barn." It was an evil plan, but one that usually worked. David would get so worked up about three kittens that only one would look good in comparison. Unfortunately, she had used this ploy before, and David wasn't taking the bait.

"Our cats take care of the mice just fine."

"But they'd love having three new friends to pal around with."

"Erica, you've got to stop doing this!"

"Doing what? Giving little orphan kitties a good home?" She explained about the mother then caved. "Okay, I'll try and find homes for them here."

"Try very, *very* hard."

"I will. I promise."

Bandit came through his doggie door and padded over to investigate. Terrorized, the kittens arched their backs and stood frozen, their spiky tails quivering as they hissed and spat at the black Lab, even though they probably didn't weigh as much as Bandit's nose. Erica ordered the dog outside, and he slunk back through the doggie door.

"Sorry about that." Erica shifted, trying to get more comfortable, but nothing helped. "I talked with Detective McGuire tonight. He said they found the SUV. It had been abandoned behind a warehouse."

"Stolen?"

"Yep. And it had lots of prints. Unfortunately, all of them were the owner's, except for a couple on the gas cap. They're running them now. But it doesn't matter anyway."

"What do you mean it doesn't matter? Wait, you mean you've figured it out?"

"Yep. So I'll be home soon. Being hurt and laid up gave me time to do a lot of thinking. And I got some questions answered today. It seems like I've been apart from you and the kids forever, but I guess it's only been a little over two weeks."

"Too long for me."

Erica stroked one of the kittens as it curled up in her lap and dozed off—a boneless ball of sleep. "There's just a couple of things to check, and Detective McGuire said he'd take care of that."

Chapter Twenty-Six

FOR HER LAST PHONE CALL of the night, Erica called Walter Hancock. "I apologize for calling so late, Walter, but it's important. Do you remember when I asked you to wait on giving out Grandma's Lalique Crystal and Armani figurines?"

"Yes. I never understood why."

"Because I thought it might provide a good opportunity to get everyone together. And the time has come. Would you be able to take care of that at the house tomorrow night?"

"Tomorrow? That's not much notice, but I can do it if everyone else is available. I've had the paperwork done for some time." He paused. "Is there more to this than giving out those items?"

"Umm, yes."

"Do you know who poisoned Blanche and killed Martha?"

"I believe so."

"Have the police arrested the person?"

"Not yet. Detective McGuire needs to check on a few things tomorrow. Plus, he'd like to get a confession, so the killer will be put away for good. I suggested we talk to everyone at a family gathering."

"Are you sure this is a good idea?" There was a lot of hesitation in Walter's voice.

"I am. So, will you call everyone and tell them that as executor of the estate, you want to give out Grandma's bequests? That way, everyone will be sure to come."

"Are you up to this physically?"

"Cracked ribs will never stop *me* from talking—"

"All right," he replied. "I'll start calling right away."

* * *

It was a restless night of tossing and turning, and Erica felt nearly as tired when she got up as she had before going to bed. She ate breakfast while watching the kittens play and was rinsing out her cereal bowl when Pamela came in.

"Walter called and said he wanted to meet with the family tonight and give out the Lalique crystal and the Armani figurines. I was beginning to wonder if he was ever going to get around to that—usually he's so prompt." Pamela stopped short, and her eyes narrowed as she looked at Erica.

Averting her gaze, Erica dangled a crumpled-up piece of paper she'd tied with string over the fence for the kittens to bat.

"Did Walter talk to you about the meeting?" Pamela's voice was direct and questioning.

"I talked to Walter last night, and he mentioned it."

"Is there anything I should know?" There was a smidgen of anxiety in her tone.

"I don't think so." Erica kept her eyes on the cavorting kittens.

"Are you sure? I always worry when you won't look at me, dear-heart. You told me once that avoiding direct eye contact is a 'tell'—something that lets you know when someone isn't telling the truth."

Sighing, Erica looked at Pamela, who then sat heavily into a chair.

"Oh dear. I knew it," Pamela sounded ill. "Perhaps it would be better if you didn't tell me a thing."

"That probably *would* be best."

* * *

Walter called the next morning. "I contacted everyone. The only person who can't come is Vicki. She's in Portland with her daughter, who just had a baby." He sighed. "Ah, Erica. I hope you know what you're doing. No one is expecting anything else other than Lalique Crystal and Armani. It's going to be a shock."

"Especially to the killer."

* * *

"I guess Walter called you about meeting tonight to disburse the crystal and Armani figurines," Shaun said that evening when he got home from work. He set his briefcase on the table, startling the kittens, who fled to the safety of their box.

"I talked with him." Erica sat on a chair, keeping a careful eye on Bandit as he lay on the floor, his black nose pressed against the fence, watching the kittens.

Shaun came over to stand by the fence. "What are you going to do with the little beasts?"

"Bandit's grown quite fond of them. I thought you'd want to keep at least one." To her surprise, he didn't argue.

"I like that one in the corner. The one with a lot of white on its face."

Erica got a packet of kitty treats and held one of the moist treats through the fence. "Here, kitty, kitty, kitty!" Two of the kittens came over. The third, waking from a nap, opened its green eyes and yawned widely, unfurling its little pink tongue.

Shaun leaned over and, picking up a kitten, fed it a treat. "You said they were half-wild, but they seem tame to me." He stroked the kitten, which began to purr.

"Music may have charms to soothe the savage beast, but tasty treats do it in half the time."

* * *

"Is everything all set?" David asked when he called early that evening.

Erica was relaxing in the recliner. "Yep. Detective McGuire is coming too."

"That'll raise a few eyebrows. Did he get the results back on the fingerprints from the SUV?"

"He did."

"So you know who tried to run you down?"

"I do." Erica sounded complacent.

"Well, who was it?" There was a bit of impatience in his voice.

"Oh, come on. You know I don't tell until the fat lady sings."

"I know—and I'm used to it by now—I only want to make sure you're safe."

"I'm fine." Erica's voice was firm. "Now that I know who did it, there's no need to worry. And I want to thank you, darling, for getting me that Leatherman tool for my birthday a few years ago. It was really invaluable."

"Aha. I take that to mean it helped you with the case?"

"It did indeed. I used it to find something that had been hidden."

"Well, I'm glad you've got things figured out."

"With Detective McGuire's help. And Simon. Anyway, we all did it together. I have to admit a lot of clues were there at the beginning, but I

didn't catch them. Like a fake cold. A tissue. An out-of-place comment.
A savage beating. But the real turning point was the broken statue. Then
again, eyebrows were also important."

"You lost me."

"And tulips," Erica said dreamily. "Don't forget the tulips."

"I wouldn't, if you'd tell me why they're important."

"Soon, darling."

* * *

Everyone gathered in the sitting room that night. Erica talked first to
Gail, who sat by the piano, then went over to Pamela, who was in her
favorite recliner, looking pale.

"Did you take something for anxiety?" Erica whispered.

Her mother-in-law nodded but clutched at Erica's hand. "Dear-
heart, are you sure you know what you're doing?"

"Absolutely." Erica's voice was confident as she nodded a welcome to
Walter, who came in wearing his usual suit and went to sit in a straight-
backed chair. "This is what I've worked for—what Grandma would have
wanted."

"You're a very determined young woman," Pamela said weakly. Erica
then went to Kristen, who seemed nervous as she perched on the couch.

"Is it just me, or is everyone on edge?" Kristen asked.

"I don't know about everyone, but you sure look like you're sitting
on coiled springs."

Shaun came into the room with a quick resolute step. *If only
Grandma could see him now,* Erica thought proudly. The hesitation and
uncertainty had all but disappeared, and although he had an air of
apprehension, his bearing was straight as he came over to sit by Kristen.
Detective McGuire leaned over to talk to Shaun. His uniformed presence had caused a stir, and anxiety hummed in the air as Trent and
Carrie darted glances at the detective from across the room.

As Erica walked by, Carrie reached out and stopped her. "What is he
doing here?" she asked, looking at the policeman.

"I'll explain in a minute." Erica stood with her back to the grand
piano and addressed the group. "First off, I need to tell you that while
Walter plans on distributing Grandma's crystal and Armani, that isn't the
main reason for this meeting." There were murmurs all around.

"I knew it. I just *knew* it," Carrie said, clutching a sweater around
her narrow shoulders and giving Erica a sour look.

Trent spoke up. "Since Detective McGuire is here, I assume you've found out who poisoned Grandma."

Erica nodded. "And who killed Aunt Martha."

Chapter Twenty-Seven

AN UNEASY TREMOR SEEMED TO pass through everyone as they stared at Erica. Being together in an enclosed room was an indication they were in a trap—a trap that had closed.

"In the beginning," Erica began, "none of us, except for Martha, suspected Grandma had been murdered. And no one, except Walter, took Martha's ramblings as anything other than deranged statements from an eccentric old woman."

Walter shifted uncomfortably. "I felt a certain amount of anxiety because Martha had always had a propensity for blurting out unwelcome truths. It seemed that no matter how outrageous her statements, Martha was always right."

"It turned out Martha was this time as well," Detective McGuire said. "When Martha was murdered, we considered it possible that she had been killed to keep her quiet—that the killer didn't want her saying Blanche Coleman had been murdered."

"Martha thought Grandma had been killed either because of problems at Sun Coast or because she'd decided to change the will," Erica said. "I started investigating the company and turned up a number of problems there." Out of the corner of her eye, Erica saw Trent run a finger around the inside of his collar. "But they were red herrings and had nothing to do with Grandma's death. I then wondered if Grandma was murdered because of her decision to change—or change back— her will. Again, I was on the wrong track. It took a long time before I realized Grandma was killed for one reason, and one reason only—*to provide a cover for the murder of Martha Bessinger.*"

A commotion ensued as buzzing whispers filled the room.

Trent scoffed openly. "But Martha hadn't been killed when Mom was poisoned."

"No, but plans for Martha's murder had been made long before Grandma died," Erica said. "Let me go back. From the beginning, there were discrepancies that bothered me. For instance, Martha said Grandma told her she was going to change the will and that there were problems at Sun Coast." Erica frowned as she leaned against the piano. "But it seemed out of character for Grandma to trust Martha with such delicate information. Martha lived an isolated life. Why tell Martha when she was so detached and uninterested in the family and Sun Coast? Plus, I doubt Grandma would disclose such sensitive, volatile information when she knew Martha was prone to blurting out unpleasant truths and might tell other family members."

Shaun's leg was bouncing spasmodically. "Are you saying Martha lied about that?"

"In a way." Erica glanced around. Shaun wasn't the only one who seemed anxious. Carrie was biting her lip, Gail clutching her purse, and Kristen leaning forward, her hands clasped tightly. "I want each of you to think back. Not counting the funeral, when was the last time you saw Aunt Martha?" Erica looked at Walter. "How about you?"

"I suppose it was after she and Phillip divorced. I went to Lake Oswego to have Martha sign some papers. That would be about thirty years ago."

Erica turned to Pamela, who responded, "After I hurt my back, I couldn't ride in a car for very long, so it's been about thirty years for me as well."

"Carrie and I have never met Martha," Erica said. "And Shaun, David, and Trent hadn't seen her since they were children."

"Why does all this matter?" Carrie was impatient. "What's your point, Erica?"

"The point is that people change over the years, and if you haven't seen someone in a long time, you might not recognize them."

"Okay, so what about it?" Trent said, a touch of annoyance in his voice.

"What if the person who came to Grandma's funeral wasn't Martha?" Everyone stared at Erica.

"What are you talking about?" Pamela spluttered. "We all talked with her."

"Martha hadn't left Lake Oswego for thirty years. She didn't come back for either of her brothers' funerals or for her father's. Why then, did she come to Florence for her mother's funeral?"

"Anybody would want to attend their mother's funeral," Kristen said, gripping Shaun's hand.

Erica rested her arm on the piano. "When Martha came, Pamela—the only one besides Grandma who talked with her occasionally on the phone—said her voice sounded different."

"That's because she had a cold," Pamela blurted. "You knew that. She was always asking for a tissue."

"Yet when Martha asked for a garbage can and threw away her tissue, it fluttered in and lay flat. It had not been used. Martha was only pretending to have a cold."

"Why would she do that?" Trent burst out.

"Because Martha—or rather the person who was impersonating Martha—needed a reason to explain why her voice sounded different."

"You think someone was impersonating Martha?" Walter was incredulous. "Because of a tissue thrown in the garbage?"

"There were a few other things," Erica said. "During the family dinner we had a few days after the funeral, Trent asked Shaun why he didn't take Martha home that day. Right after, Martha suddenly announced that she always walks through the woods every afternoon."

"I remember that," Carrie said. "It was kind of weird because it came from out of nowhere, but since it was Martha—"

"Since Martha was eccentric, you accepted her out-of-place comment. But actually, that was a carefully prepared statement. It was important that the family know Martha walked in the woods because the impersonator wanted the police to think that someone in the family killed Martha.

Vince McGuire spoke up. "And that's what happened. After Erica told me what Martha had said, it seemed not only possible but very likely that one of you went to Lake Oswego and killed Martha before she could say anything else that might incriminate him or her."

"I still don't understand why someone would want to impersonate Martha," Pamela said.

"To plant the idea that Grandma had been murdered by someone in the family and to draw attention away from a planned, second murder—that of Martha Bessinger."

Silence was a living entity in the room.

Then Trent spoke up. "I'll say one thing for you, Erica. You've got quite an imagination."

"The first thing we do after a homicide is look for a motive," Detective McGuire began, "and in this case, everyone in the family had a motive—money."

"Shaun had the biggest motive of all," Carrie shot out.

Ignoring her, Erica asked, "Detective McGuire, when a person is murdered, who do the police usually suspect first?"

"If the person is married, we take a long, hard look at the husband or wife. If they're not married, we look at the boy- or girlfriend or whoever is living with the victim."

"So when Martha Bessinger was murdered, you'd normally suspect her roommate, Gail Oakeson."

"That's correct," Detective McGuire said.

"Which is why Gail played an elaborate game of charades with us," Erica said.

All eyes turned to Gail, whose eyes widened as she sat with her hands folded over her purse.

Pamela was the first to speak. Gaping at the woman sitting next to her, Pamela asked, "What do you mean, Erica?"

"Some time ago, Gail decided to kill Martha. However, Gail knew that she would be the number-one suspect. To divert attention away from herself, Gail came up with an elaborate plot that would make it look like the same person who murdered Blanche Coleman was responsible for killing Martha."

Erica looked at Gail, who was set faced and rigid. "I'm not sure when you first got the idea of impersonating Martha, but I suspect it was the last time Grandma went to Lake Oswego. You overhead her telling Martha about the birthday party and decided that would be the perfect time to put your plan in action."

"But how could Gail pretend to be Martha?" Shaun frowned.

"It's easy to impersonate a woman no one knows," Erica said then turned to Gail. "Leslie told me about your plucked eyebrows. I puzzled over that because penciled-in brows are so outdated. Leslie also mentioned your spray-on tan. Those two things alone can alter a person's appearance a great deal. I knew they had to be recent changes or Leslie wouldn't have mentioned them."

Erica told the others, "I found out Gail had a flair for acting and enjoyed being in plays. Later, Gail's boss, Chaleh Henderson, said Gail was a talented actress—and boy, was she right. The last time I went up there, I stopped by the Lake Oswego Theatre House and talked with some of the people there."

Gail's face was deathly white as Erica looked at her. "Everyone told me what a natural actress you are, Gail. They said you played a man, Dr. Craven, in the current play, *The Secret Garden*. They showed me around backstage and let me look at the dressing rooms. I was especially interested in the extra padding you wore for your part. You took latex to construct a replica of Martha's nose, wore plumpers in your mouth, and got contact lenses to change your light-brown eyes to Martha's darker ones. Getting a wig was easy—you simply took one from Martha's closet. When you put on Martha's clothes, your own mother wouldn't have recognized you. And, having lived with Martha for so long, it was easy to mimic her mannerisms and way of speaking."

For the first time, Gail found her voice. "I don't know why you're saying all these terrible things. It's all nonsense."

"Is it? Impersonating Martha wasn't as risky as someone might think. You were comfortable attempting this charade because you knew that no one, other than Blanche or Randy, had seen you or Martha for years. And since they were both dead, you were certain you could pull it off."

Erica continued to talk directly to Gail. "You already knew about Martha's childhood and the house where she grew up—and you questioned Martha further until you knew more than enough to take her place at the funeral. You learned the layout of the house and repeated some of the anecdotes Martha had told you, which was enough to fool Pamela and Walter completely. You had to be careful though. Since we would all meet you as Gail later on, you couldn't take the chance that someone might recognize you—even without the padding, nose, wig, and plumpers—hence the plucked eyebrows and spray-on tan."

Gail defended herself. "The only reason I plucked my brows and got a tan was because of the play."

Erica wore a look of amusement. "Since when do men have penciled-in eyebrows?"

"Your impersonating Martha also explains why the real Martha was beaten so savagely," Detective McGuire said. "Martha's face had to be disfigured enough so the family would opt for a closed casket. That way, no one would recognize that the woman in the casket was not the same person who came to Florence for Blanche Coleman's funeral."

"This is unbelievable," Shaun said, looking astonished.

"I should have seen it sooner." Erica's voice was regretful. "There were things I didn't pick up on right away. Gail told me Grandma visited in January, but Grandma only went once a year. She told me that the last time she went, Martha's tulips had been beautiful. So the visit had to have been in the spring. I didn't remember Grandma's remark until I went to the floral shop and saw a bucket of tulips."

"I just misspoke and got the month wrong," Gail said shakily.

"It was a little slip, but a significant one," Erica said, "because it let me know you were not a truthful person. A Frenchman once said, 'Liars need good memories,' and yours wasn't so good. You slipped because you were intent on embellishing the story to make it sound like it had really happened. Later, you made another mistake. When I asked to see the bracelet Leslie mentioned, I watched as you went upstairs. You went into your own bedroom—not Martha's—to get it."

Turning to the family, Erica said, "Another thing that bothered me was that Gail never told me that Martha wrote down everything she bought and that she sent weekly reports to a jeweler. I had to learn about that from Leslie. That seemed like a significant omission."

"All of these things are just coincidences," Gail choked out. "I never impersonated Martha."

"Your biggest mistake happened at your house," Erica said, eying Gail. I saw a ceramic statue of a girl and a kitten, and you said it was a twin to the one Blanche had in her sitting room."

Erica asked Kristen in an easy, conversational manner, "Do you remember the statue that used to be on the coffee table?"

"Yes. It was a statue of a boy with a puppy. I accidentally broke it." Kristen looked guilty.

"Gail, when did you see Blanche's statue?"

Gail blinked. Her face was white except for hectic red splotches on her cheekbones. "Why, when I came here for Martha's funeral."

"But Kristen had broken it nearly two weeks before—the day after Grandma's funeral. The only way you could have seen it was when you were here impersonating Martha."

There were gasps and murmurs from around the room.

Walter's long face looked disturbed. "But if Gail killed Martha, then who killed Blanche?"

"Gail did that too."

"But she wasn't even here," Kristen pointed out. "She couldn't have poisoned the berries."

"Oh, Gail was in Florence, all right," Erica said, "dressed as Dr. Craven. She's the one who paid those two boys to deliver the strawberries."

Gail started like a nervous horse then grabbed her purse as it started to fall off her lap. "This is crazy. You can't prove any of it."

"A nice lady at the Lake Oswego Theatre House was kind enough to show me a picture she had of the cast in costume, including you dressed as Dr. Craven. I borrowed it and gave it to Detective McGuire."

"Today, I showed the picture to the boys who delivered the berries," Detective McGuire said. "They identified the person in the picture as the same one who paid them to deliver the strawberries."

Then Shaun asked, "But why did Gail want to kill Martha?"

Going to the piano, Erica picked up a padded box. "To get this. I wondered if Martha was murdered because of the jewelry she bought, but from all reports, most of what she bought was junk. Until she hit the jackpot, that is, and found this."

Opening the box, Erica went around the room, holding it so everyone could see the necklace with its sparkling blue stones. "Beautiful, isn't it? And yes, those are real sapphires."

"Where did you get that?" Gail snapped, looking as though she wanted to snatch it away.

"When I stopped to pick up the kittens, I went in the house and noticed that some of the magazines on the bookshelf were poking out half an inch. I couldn't push them back because something was behind them. When I pulled them out, I saw that the wall behind it had a piece of plasterboard that had been cut. I used my Leatherman tool to pry out the plasterboard and found this."

Erica addressed the main group again. "I called Leslie after finding the box. She remembered it and said Martha had bought a box of jumbled up jewelry at an estate sale. Leslie thought it was all costume jewelry, but as soon as Gail saw the necklace, she knew it was worth a fortune. Gail needed that necklace. Martha's health was uncertain, and it was only a matter of time before she died, leaving Gail homeless. Also, Gail was about to lose her job. The floral shop where she works is closing, and the only trade Gail knows is being a floral designer." Erica took the necklace out and held it up. "Gail knew the money she could get from this would solve all of her problems."

As if hypnotized, Gail stared at the necklace as Erica went on. "Gail had always dreamed of owning her own shop, and when Chaleh offered to sell her the shop at a discounted price, Gail was ecstatic. But when she went to the bank, they wouldn't give her a loan."

Detective McGuire said, "Detective Pocharski checked out the local banks today and found out you'd applied for a loan at three different banks. Each one turned you down."

Setting the necklace back in its box, Erica nudged the chain until it was in a perfect curve. "Gail, you told me once that you'd always been one to take care of yourself. You planned to continue taking care of yourself—even if it meant committing murder. To quote Benjamin Disraeli, 'Desperation is sometimes as powerful an inspirer as genius.' Your desperation led you to murder."

Erica touched the necklace again. "When Martha came home with this, her fate was sealed. The necklace would provide you with the money you needed so badly."

Gail licked her dry lips. "You have no proof."

"The police do. Isn't that right, Detective?"

"One of the setbacks we faced was not being able to find the murder weapon," Detective McGuire declared. "The police searched the woods but came up empty. Then we had a stroke of luck. On Erica's last visit, she said that when she went to give the chickens some scraps, there was a garbage can in front of the pen, so she had to go around to the side. That's when she noticed that the board in the corner was tilted."

"Well, I couldn't very well leave it like that," Erica said, "so I got a shovel and went into the pen to level it out. When I moved the board, the dirt underneath was soft, like it had recently been disturbed. Now why would anyone want to dig underneath a board in a chicken coop?"

Not a muscle moved in Gail's face as she watched Erica.

"There could be only one reason, so I called Detective Pocharski, who came right out. After a bit of digging, he found a tire iron."

Detective McGuire spoke up. "Detective Pocharski sent it to the lab for testing. The tire iron had traces of Martha Bessinger's blood and hair."

"It's all over," Erica told Gail.

Coldness passed like a mask over Gail's face, blotting out all expression. "Not quite," she said, looking at Erica with strange, glittering eyes. She pulled her hand out of her purse, and Erica saw the gleam of a revolver. In one smooth motion, Gail raised the gun and pointed it at Erica.

Chapter Twenty-Eight

A SHOCKED SILENCE RIPPLED AROUND the room, like the ripples of a rock when tossed in the middle of a pond. Gail rose and motioned Erica over to where she could keep the gun on her. Gail stood and positioned herself with her back to the piano, facing the others. Erica's mouth was dry, and a deep fear welled up against her ribs.

"Trent, Carrie, move over by Walter," Gail commanded. As they obeyed, Detective McGuire's hand reached for his pistol, but Gail caught the movement and told him, "I can shoot Erica a lot faster than you can pull your revolver out. Toss it to me."

Detective McGuire's mouth was in a hard line when he removed his Glock and caught Erica's eye. Neither one of them had expected this.

Keeping a wary eye on the others, Gail went to the telephone and yanked the cord out of the wall, stuffing it in her pocket. "I want everyone's cell phones. Give them to Erica, and don't try hiding them. And detective, your radio."

Erica's knees felt weak as she collected one from everyone but Kristen, whose gray eyes were wide and frightened. "I don't have mine. It's in the kitchen, charging."

"Come here," Gail ordered. Kristen glanced at Shaun, who made a motion to rise, but Gail swung her revolver toward him. "Don't be a hero."

Gail stuck the nose of the gun into Kristen's back and patted her down. "Okay, go sit down."

Although her heart was pounding, Erica willed herself to stay calm. "Gail, you're never going to get away with this."

"That's where you're wrong. As you know, I'm great at disguises. I also learned a few things from my ex-husband about hiding out. All I need is a head start. That's where you come in, Erica. You're coming with me."

Pamela gasped, and Detective McGuire started to rise, saying, "No, you don't."

Then Shaun blurted out, "If you want a hostage, take me."

"Both of you stay where you are," Gail said. "If it wasn't for Erica, I wouldn't be in this mess."

"Please don't take her," Pamela cried.

Ignoring Gail's orders, Shaun rose in slow motion. "You're not going to take Erica."

"Sit down." Gail's eyes were like flint and her voice harder still. "I'm warning you."

"Shaun, please sit down," Erica begged.

Several things happened at once: Shaun took a step forward. Kristen grabbed Shaun's arm to pull him back. A shot rang out.

There were several screams as Shaun clutched his arm. Blood seeped between his fingers and dripped onto the beige carpet. Erica was barely breathing when Detective McGuire leapt to his feet.

Gail pointed her gun at the detective. "Sit down!" Kristen grabbed Shaun, who sank back onto the couch as Detective McGuire slowly took his seat. Gail picked up the boxed necklace and snapped the lid shut before motioning Erica toward the doors.

When they went through the double doors, Gail told Erica, "Close the doors and lock them."

"I'll have to get the key from the kitchen."

After warning the others to stay put, Gail went with Erica to get the key. Once the doors were locked, they went into the dark night to Gail's car. A gusty wind blew.

"You're driving, so get in," Gail directed. Erica opened the door and froze. "Get in!" Gail's voice had a dangerous edge to it. The look in Gail's eyes wasn't quite sane.

With an effort, Erica thrust her upper body forward, but her feet remained planted. She asked Gail beseechingly, "Could I just wipe the seat off? I've got some wipes in my pocket—"

She started fumbling at her pocket but stopped when Gail screamed, "*Get in the car! Now!*"

Erica started forward again then stopped. "I—I just can't." Her voice was soft and regretful.

Gail shot a look at the house. "Okay, okay. Get your blasted wipes. You have two seconds."

In a flash, Erica wiped the seat. As Gail got in, she added, "I could do yours—"

"If you don't sit down and shut up, you'll be wiping up your own blood."

Erica started the car.

As they pulled out, Gail told her, "Go up to Highway 101 and turn left. And don't try anything stupid like running a stop light to get a cop to pull you over. Not if you want to see your family again." Goosebumps rose on Erica's arms.

The car went in and out of halos formed by streetlamps. "I haven't got much time before they're through those doors, even if they are security ones," Gail mused. "That means I need another car and fast."

As they approached Fred Meyer, Gail peered around Erica to get a good look at the parking lot. "There's always someone who doesn't lock their car. Turn left on the next road."

"Don't you want me to pull into the parking lot?"

Gail's expression turned malevolent. "You must think I'm stupid. What good would it do for me to steal a car and leave mine in the same lot? The police would put that together in two seconds." As they traveled west, Gail instructed, "Turn left on that road." And a few moments later, "Turn in here, and park behind that warehouse."

Erica's heart sank as she saw the deserted buildings. No one would notice Gail's car here.

"I'm going to walk back to the store and get a car," Gail said.

"You know how to hotwire a car?"

"It's another skill I can thank my ex for. I got a beauty of an SUV last Wednesday." Gail smiled—a rather twisted smile. "I couldn't believe you managed to jump out of the way." There was a cold malignity about Gail's words that froze Erica to the marrow. "Move over to the passenger seat. I have to make sure you stay put." When Erica slid over, Gail went to the driver's side, pushed the button, and lowered the window a few inches.

"Put your hands through and keep them there. I'm going to roll the window up enough to pin them."

Erica tried and failed to stifle a groan as she raised her arms. Gail took the phone cord out of her pocket and tied Erica's feet together then reached in the back for a cloth grocery sack.

"This will stop you from calling for help." Erica twisted her head away, but Gail was able to force part of the bag in her mouth. Then the door shut, and Erica was alone. She tried but was unable to spit the bag out.

Although her legs were tied, Erica thought she could swing them up to honk the horn, but she'd underestimated Gail, who'd thought to tie the cord around the lever under the seat. Wiggling to loosen the cord only served to make it press cruelly into her ankles. It was no use. Finally, Erica held still, resting her aching wrists as she looked around to see if anybody happened to be nearby. The wind was still blowing. Clouds scudded across a large gibbous moon that gave off a shifting light.

Quicker than Erica thought possible, Gail pulled up in a Honda Accord, whose owner would soon regret leaving it unlocked. She released Erica, who rubbed her wrists and ankles.

"Let's go," Gail said, picking up the jewelry box and using the gun to motion Erica over to the Honda.

Erica opened the driver's side door and stopped, looking at Gail in mute appeal.

"You've *got* to be kidding—get in the car!"

Erica made a valiant effort but could not get her body inside.

"I ought to—" Pulling her gun back as if to strike Erica, Gail thought better of it and lowered her arm. She glanced around to see if anyone was in sight, then breathing hard, ground out, "Okay, hurry up with your stupid wipes."

Chapter Twenty-Nine

As Erica drove north on Highway 101, blood resumed flowing in her arms, causing them to tingle with a thousand pinpricks. At times the clouds parted, allowing moonlight to show the dark blue line that marked the beginning of the Pacific Ocean and the silver water.

It was only when Erica's hands started aching that she realized she'd been gripping the wheel in a death-like vise. Feeling like she was trapped in a tight cage of terror, Erica tried to hide her fear, knowing instinctively that to show courage was the safest way to act.

Forcing her voice to stay steady, Erica broke the silence. "A lot of things fell into place for you, didn't they?" When Gail didn't respond, Erica went on. "You must have been happy when Shaun and Pamela decided to have an autopsy."

Gail eyed her speculatively and admitted, "That *was* a great stroke of luck. I thought everyone would assume Blanche died of old age and that it would be hard to raise suspicion."

"When Grandma visited Martha, she didn't say anything about Sun Coast, did she?"

"Martha didn't pick up on it, but I could tell Blanche was worried about something. I asked a few general questions about the company, and although Blanche never answered directly, she said enough that I knew something was wrong there. It worked out very nicely when you and others thought Blanche might have been murdered because of problems at Sun Coast."

"Did Grandma say anything to you or Martha about the will?"

"Of course not. Why should the great Blanche Coleman tell me anything?" There was a great deal of bitterness in Gail's voice. "After all, I'm a nobody. I threw in the part about the will because I heard Carrie say something about it. I was pretty sure the money grubbers in your family would pounce on that, and they did. Rich people make me sick."

Erica darted a look at Gail's face, which was tight with anger. "Blanche always looked down on me. She was so patronizing. Whenever something in the house needed repairing and I asked for money to fix it, she acted like I was trying to rip her off. Blanche would give me or Martha the third degree, and Martha backed down every time—saying that maybe we didn't need this or that fixed after all. Martha always made me look like a fool with Blanche."

"Maybe Grandma was just asking to find out what was wrong."

Gail scoffed. "No, Blanche Coleman wanted me to know who held the purse strings. She was always high-handed and never appreciated all the things I did for Martha. As rich as she was, Blanche still had to be in control and put me in my place. She made me feel like a freeloader."

"But you said you'd worked out the rent with Grandma."

"I did, but she still put me down every time she came to visit. One time, Blanche had the nerve to tell me to take control of my life, get a place of my own, and stop sponging off Martha. It's all right for the high and mighty to tell others how to live." Gail shook her head, incensed. "Not everyone can afford a house of their own, but that's not something the great Blanche Coleman would understand. She was exactly like my father—he was a controlling person too. I couldn't take a breath without his say-so. That's why I ran off and got married. Unfortunately, he turned out to be a loser."

So, it wasn't just the present circumstances that had led Gail to her acts of desperation. Gail truly *was* a consummate actress—adept at hiding her true thoughts and feelings. She only showed others what she wanted them to see. Gail fell silent and stared stonily ahead as the car's headlights bored through the darkness.

Thoughts of David and her children made Erica's eyes mist until she had to blink to see the road. Would it do any good to beg Gail to let her go? Erica didn't think so. Tonight, Gail had been revealed as a murderer, and now she was desperate and on the run.

As the miles passed, Erica fought moments of panic. It was a continual fight to stay in control. Gail had already killed two people. In her present circumstances, she wouldn't think twice about killing a third. Erica prayed silently, asking for protection and a way out of her predicament.

Occasionally, her thoughts drifted to her grandmother, and once, it was almost like Erica could hear her voice: *All you can do is keep going, no matter how dark things look.*

"I'll try, Grandma," Erica said, moving her lips and speaking without sound. "I'll try."

The highway was nearly deserted. Only rarely did they meet another car. Ordinarily, Erica would have thought it a beautiful night. Clouds kept racing across the moon like smoke from a fire, but tonight, terror was a constant, and it was difficult to remain outwardly calm. Whenever they passed an exit, the car was briefly illuminated by the tall lights. Glancing over, Erica could scarcely see Gail's face. There was only the gleam of her eyes or the sheen of the gun she held.

Finally, Erica had to break the silence or go crazy. "Leslie said Martha was thinking about moving back to Florence."

"When Blanche found out Martha's health was going downhill, she kept pushing Martha to move back home—said she'd hire a nurse to take care of her. Martha didn't want to move but was thrilled at the idea of having her own private nurse, and she'd about decided to do what Blanche wanted."

"And you were desperate—knowing that once Martha left, you wouldn't have a home anymore."

"I lived each day in dread knowing that soon I'd lose my job and be homeless."

"Then Martha came home with that necklace."

"I couldn't believe it," Gail admitted. "I was so excited that it was hard to look gloomy and tell Martha everything in the box was junk. She didn't have a clue that necklace was worth a fortune."

"Was it really worth enough for you to buy the floral shop?"

"And the house." Her words were clipped. "It would have solved all my problems, but you had to butt into things."

Gail opened a bottle of water and ventured a question of her own. "You must have known for a while. Why didn't you say something sooner?"

"I was suspicious but needed proof." Erica thought how surreal it seemed to be talking about the case so dispassionately. "I'm really thirsty. Do you have another bottle?"

Gail held up her bottle, which still contained a few inches of water. "You can have the rest of this, but only if you don't wipe off the top."

"Um, never mind."

"I'm curious," Gail said. "I thought I had everyone fooled. What made you suspicious?"

"Well, besides the things I already mentioned, Leslie told me Martha had lost a ring on the Fourth of July. Since Martha was so careful about her jewelry, I wondered about that. I asked Detective Pocharski to check your bank account to see if there had been any unusual deposits. He found a large one in August that didn't match your salary, and we wondered if you had pawned Martha's ring."

Gail's voice was frosty. "You're too clever for your own good, Erica. Martha wanted to call the police, but I convinced her she'd just lost the ring."

"I suppose you couldn't keep stealing Martha's jewelry and telling her she'd lost things, or she'd eventually catch onto you."

There was a grim set to Gail's mouth, but she made no reply. Off the coast in the dark Pacific came lights from great ships. Erica felt like she was in some kind of twilight zone where nothing was real. Because of that disconnect, Erica continued to ask questions. Gail was free with her answers, though from time to time, Gail stared at her with unblinking eyes, making Erica almost lightheaded with fear. It was her eyes that scared Erica the most—not Gail's gun, but those ruthless eyes.

Falling silent, Erica tried to think of a way to overpower Gail. But whenever she looked over, Gail was awake and alert—her gun pointed toward Erica, who felt a growing sense of despair.

From time to time, Erica wondered why she kept driving. Gail was surely planning on killing her at some future point. She was only going to her own death. Maybe she should just careen off the side of the road and take her chances in a crash.

Erica passed another exit. As the lone freeway light flickered in the darkness, illuminating the car for a brief moment, a small voice inside whispered, "Just keep going, no matter how dark things look." For just an instant, a feeling of peace wrapped itself around her. She clung to it, but the feeling faded as the miles continued to fall away.

Erica began rubbing her eyes. The clock said it was just past midnight, but it felt like she'd been driving for days. Once in a while, she had to shake her head to come fully awake.

Gail noticed. "I think we ought to stop and get a couple hours of sleep. We'll pull off at the next campground."

It was thirty minutes before Erica saw a sign with the brown symbol of a tepee. "This one will do," Gail said.

The gravel road gleamed ghostly white as Erica pulled alongside the self-service pay box. Up ahead, a sign indicated a trailhead. The twin beams of the car's headlights tracked into a thick tangle of trees and vegetation, and on either side, shadows lay thick and black. Farther off to the right, a couple of lights shone like pinpricks in the thick, velvet darkness—other campers. The whole world was black and silver, like a photographic negative.

"Pull up by that sign," Gail said. "I don't want to go near the campsites in case you decide to call for help. We'll sleep an hour or two then go on."

As Gail came around and opened Erica's door, the moon broke through the clouds and illuminated the clearing with a luminous silvery brightness. It felt good to stand up. The cold wind slapped at her face, waking her and sharpening her senses.

"Go around to the passenger side," Gail told her. "I'll tie you up there."

There was a quiver in the pit of Erica's stomach as Gail got the telephone cord from the backseat. Then she looked out into the inky darkness of the black, silent woods. Erica shuddered as long ago fears washed over her in shallow waves. She fought against childhood memories, thankful that her initial feelings of panic were mitigated by the moonlight, the brightness of the headlights, and the fact that she was with another person—even if that person happened to be holding a gun. For an instant, all Erica wanted was to return to the car, but she didn't like giving into her fears of the dark, and besides, her muscles demanded action.

"Can I walk a little? We've been in the car for hours." When Gail hesitated, Erica pleaded, "Just to that information box and back." At least it was lit by the glare of the headlights.

"I'll come with you." Their shoes crunched on the gravel, and the moon, which was washed over with thin clouds, bathed the clearing in a hazy radiance. The breeze, smelling of pine and salt, stirred Erica's long hair as she walked to the post, which had a metal box on top. Four or five pamphlets lay scattered on the ground.

Such a travesty. Erica bent to pick them up, feeling a sharp pain from her ribs as she did.

"What are you doing?" Gail hissed. "Leave them alone."

Erica paused painfully in midcrouch, looking up at Gail, whose face gleamed white in the moonlight. "But they're on the ground. I can't just leave them here."

"Why not?"

Erica didn't answer. "You know, I bet kids did this," she said, picking up two more. "What were they thinking? Where were their parents?"

"Come on," Gail said roughly.

"Just a couple more." Carefully, Erica reached out, mumbling, "I don't know what this world is coming to."

Then, she saw her chance.

Chapter Thirty

THERE, NEXT TO THE LAST two pamphlets on the ground, lay a fist-size rock. It only took a split second for Erica to decide. Surely this was the chance she had been praying for. Erica could not wait for another opportunity because another might not come. No time to glance back to see if Gail had seen the rock or to think about the pain that would come from her ribs.

In one smooth motion, Erica grabbed the rock, twisted round, and threw it as hard as possible at Gail before rolling to the side. There was a thud and a split second later, a gunshot.

After checking herself for holes, Erica launched herself at Gail, who was bent over and clutching her chest. They toppled over, and Erica fought to wrest the gun away, but somehow, Gail managed to free her arm.

She struck so quickly Erica had no time to dodge. It was an awkward blow, but the revolver still hit Erica's forehead with enough force to leave her stunned. She rolled off the older woman, and her head hit the ground, leaving her further dazed. Gail landed another wicked smash, and hot blood ran down Erica's face. Then, hands scrabbled at her throat as Gail climbed onto Erica. The heaviness felt like sandbags on her chest and stomach, and pain ricocheted through her body. As Gail's fingers tightened, Erica fought even as she struggled to draw a breath.

The moon was hidden behind clouds, and the night was a black entity, pressing on them. Frantic now, Erica alternated between prying at Gail's fingers and swinging wildly. Although she connected several times, it seemed to have no effect on Gail's stranglehold. Erica thrashed her legs to dislodge Gail but began to grow lightheaded. Gail leaned closer, and Erica managed to claw Gail's face. The hands around her throat loosened, and Erica drew new breath.

Yanking Gail's hair, Erica pulled the howling woman to the side, and they rolled. Finding herself free, Erica staggered on all fours, searching for the gun. The clouds shifted, and moonlight showed a crouched Gail beginning to rise. There wasn't time to stand. Erica plowed forward and sent Gail tumbling backward. As they wrestled, it was clear Gail remembered Erica's cracked ribs, for she seemed to aim for Erica's rib cage. Each connecting blow filled Erica's body with agonizing flashes of fire. Then, Gail reached out and picked up something off the ground.

The gun.

Scrambling in the dirt, Erica struggled to keep Gail's arm outstretched while trying to grab the revolver with her other hand. Gail shrieked like a madwoman, and for a moment, Erica wondered if she could outlast the woman. Erica's own breath was high and shallow in her throat when she noticed Gail seemed to be tiring.

Another minute of struggle, and Erica's hand snaked out to Gail's wrist. They rolled over, then back, and the gun was pointed toward the sky when it went off—a shattering sound in the dark night. One final stretch and Erica's hand reached the revolver and snatched it away. She thrust herself away from Gail, rose to her knees, then stood unsteadily.

It was over.

Thin clouds raced across the moon as Erica wavered on legs that were shockingly weak. Her fingers trembled as she pushed back the curtain of hair from her face. Gail was slumped on the dirt looking up at the gun Erica held pointed at her.

A flashlight tunneled through the darkness. "What's going on?" a male voice called.

Blood was still thundering in Erica's ears as she yelled, "Help, please!"

Erica's skin was pearled with perspiration, and her breath came in trembling gasps as the beam of a flashlight came closer. When the light went to the side and shone on Gail, Erica saw a silhouette of a large man. As Erica began to explain what had happened, Gail cut in and, in a hysterical-sounding voice, refuted Erica's account.

"Just shut up, Gail," Erica said tiredly.

There were sounds in the darkness, indicating others were standing back, listening. The man with the flashlight flicked his light over Erica's face.

"You're bleeding, lady." He turned and yelled at one of the others, "Someone get some rope and a first aid kit."

"I need someone to call the police."

"There isn't any cell phone service here. I guess I could drive up the road until I can get a call through." The man sounded a little hesitant.

"You can trust me, really," Erica said. "What's your name?"

"Brian." He didn't volunteer his last name.

"Okay, Brian, when you get a hold of the police, ask them to contact Detective McGuire in Florence. Tell him you talked with Erica Coleman, and he'll corroborate everything I've said."

Her words seemed to make him decide. "Detective McGuire. Got it."

A woman inched nearer. When Brian saw her, he motioned her closer. "Rebecca, this is Erica, she's a private investigator and was taken hostage." Brian inclined his head toward Gail, who was still sitting on the ground, looking weary and dazed. "That one is a murderer who kidnapped Erica. I've got to go call the police, but you stay with this lady. She's hurt."

Before he left, Brian gave instructions to one of the men who had brought rope. Once Gail was tied, Erica put the gun aside, pulled the wipes out of her pocket, and scrubbed at her hands. Other campers gathered to whisper among themselves and gape at Gail and Erica.

Sooner than expected, officers arrived in a roar of flashing lights and sirens. Rebecca had taken Erica to sit on a nearby log, and Erica shielded her eyes as the lights of arriving police cars cut through the darkness. An officer handcuffed Gail and put her into the back of a squad car.

One of the young officers came over to Erica and handed her his radio. "Detective McGuire wants to speak with you."

The detective got right to the point. "I talked with Officer Grant, who went over everything with me. He also said you need medical attention but refused an ambulance. I told him to check you over. If Officer Grant determines an ambulance is needed, he has my permission to handcuff you until one arrives."

Erica gave a ragged little laugh, and Detective McGuire went on. "So you and Gail got into a brawl. I don't know how you managed that with your ribs. Officer Grant said you have a big knot on your head, can hardly walk, and are bleeding from a cut on your forehead. So, tell me the truth, how do you feel?"

"Awful."

His mouth quirked. "Don't sugarcoat it—give it to me straight." Then he asked, "Are you sure you don't want an ambulance?"

"I'm positive. It's just that the adrenaline has worn off, and now my ribs are complaining."

Detective McGuire was sympathetic. "I bet they are." He went on in a gruff voice. "It gave me a bad turn when Gail took you as a hostage."

"Me too." Erica's voice was higher than normal as she took shallow breaths to ease the pain.

"Next time you want to have a sit-down and point out the killer, I'm going to say no. Either that, or have people go through a metal detector at the door."

It was impossible not to laugh, but when Erica groaned in pain, a passing policeman paused to look at her. "Who says there's going to be a next time? I'm getting out of town as soon as possible."

"I understand this is the second murder you've solved. You'll have to let me know how your next case goes. I'm sure it'll be a doozy."

"At least this case is now closed, and you've got the murderer."

"Thanks to you. We needed a confession to convict Gail, and we've got that now. Even though we had the murder weapon, there were no prints, and much of the evidence was circumstantial. A good defense attorney might have gotten her off, but there's no way that'll happen now. Oh, one other thing—that glass you took from Gail's house? We compared those fingerprints with the one on the gas cap of the SUV that tried to run you down, and they match." He chuckled. "Good thing the vehicle Gail stole was nearly out of gas. Now, hand the radio back to Officer Grant. I'll have him drive you to the closest hospital to get checked out. Then he'll take you to Florence."

"Only if he'll use the siren. I've kind of missed that since leaving the force."

Detective McGuire chuckled. "You got it."

Erica listened as the detective gave Officer Grant final instructions. She couldn't help but smile when she heard Detective McGuire say, "Oh, be sure to wipe down the seats of your cruiser first or you'll never get Erica on the road."

After answering a few more questions, Erica was free to go. She climbed into the cruiser, which was equipped with a laptop computer and had a mike in front of the center console. When Officer Grant started the motor, the engine roared with a ferocity that made Erica's Camry sound like a golf cart.

Oh, the memories that brought back. "Boy, I've missed that," Erica said. Then she confided, "I used to be a police officer."

"It's why I became one," the officer replied with a grin.

As they went along Highway 101, she looked over at the officer. "I'm *so* glad someone else is driving."

Ragged clouds raced across the dark October sky. Occasionally, a touch of moonlight broke through the patches of gray. It seemed like the night had lasted forever. She laid her head back, thankful that the nightmare was over.

As soon as service was available, Erica used the officer's cell phone to call a frantic David, who had been on the phone intermittently with Trent and Pamela. After reassuring her husband half a dozen times that she was all right, she finally handed the phone to Officer Grant.

"Will you please tell my husband I'm all right?"

"Sir? Mrs. Coleman is fine. The kidnapper is in custody, and I'm driving her to the hospital."

In vain, Erica made a wild grab for the phone before the fatal word *hospital* was spoken, but it was too late. Officer Grant tried to hand the phone back to Erica as David's voice boomed in the background, but she refused.

"You're the one that had to mention the hospital. *You* settle him down, *then* I'll talk." However, after a minute, Erica relented and took the phone.

"David, haven't you got anything better to do than harass this young man?"

"I'm worried about you."

"I know, honey, but I really am all right. It's all over, and I'm on my way to Florence." After David gave a heavy sigh, Erica went on. "You don't have to say it—I know I totally underestimated Gail—I never thought she'd bring a gun to the house." Erica's mind was still in overdrive, and she thought of a quote that seemed appropriate for the occasion. "Gail 'wasn't about to go gently into that good night,'" she quoted, "and forgive me, Dylan Thomas for warping the meaning of that quote, but it seemed to fit."

David didn't give any lectures. As they talked, he was remarkably understanding and even came up with a quote of his own. "'The best laid plans of mice and men often go awry.' Robert Burns." Then he said, "I've been wondering—how come none of the neighbors saw Martha when Gail was in Florence pretending to be Martha?"

"Because Gail frightened Martha into staying inside the house. Martha was scared of Gail's violent ex-husband, so Gail told Martha that her ex had found out where she was living so she had to leave for a few days. She told Martha not to answer the door or the telephone and to stay in the house, because if the neighbors saw her, they'd tell Gail's ex that Martha was home."

Erica went on, "At the time, I wondered why Gail had Shaun drop her off at the floral shop when he drove her home after the funeral. But it was probably because Martha was so unpredictable. Gail was probably afraid Martha might forget her instructions and come out of the house if Shaun dropped her off."

"But Martha didn't stay in the house. She went out for a walk, anyway. That must have been when Travis saw her."

"Yep. I guess Martha thought that if she slipped out the back door, it would be all right. When Detective Pocharski and I talked to Travis, he was so positive he'd seen Martha that I started to wonder if he really had. He seemed like a sensible kid, and he knew Martha. The only thing that would explain him seeing her would be if the person who came for the funeral was *not* Martha. After Simon and I left the house, I thought about it and went back to ask Travis's mom if I could look at her calendar. On the day Travis said he saw Martha, there was a line through baseball practice. When I asked Mrs. Staheli about it, she suddenly remembered that practice had been cancelled that day. She was really embarrassed."

"As she should have been," David said sternly. "Maybe it wouldn't have come to this if she'd remembered a little sooner." Then his voice brightened. "Now you'll be able to come home."

"Call my brother, and have him set me up on standby for the first available flight home."

"Will do." David was quiet a few moments. Then he said, "Well, Erica, you did what you set out to do—find Grandma's killer. She'd be very proud of you."

A warm place bloomed in her heart as Erica fondly touched the pendant Blanche had given her. A smile touched her lips. "I hope so."

Chapter Thirty-One

AN EARLY MORNING FOG WREATHED the house in vapor as Officer Grant pulled into the driveway. Light from the windows cut through the mist, welcoming Erica home. Officer Grant escorted her up the steps, and she thanked him for driving her to Florence and for staying with her at the emergency room while a doctor stitched her forehead.

She had alerted her mother-in-law when they were near, and Pamela, teary and leaning on her cane, flung open the front door at their arrival. Erica limped in, her long auburn hair tangled and clothes dirty and disheveled. Standing under the brilliant light of the chandelier, Walter looked stricken. His white shirt was rumpled and his brow furrowed with concern. Carrie's blue eyes widened, and her mouth formed a large O as she gaped at the bandage on Erica's forehead.

Swearing under his breath, Trent hurried over and offered Erica his arm. "Let me help you. Do you want to go to your bedroom or the family room?"

"Family room." As they went in, Erica said, "Everyone, please check your weapons at the door."

"That is *so* not funny," Carrie said.

Everyone surrounded Erica, bearing her up like wings as Trent led her to the couch and gave her a pillow to put behind her back. "I'll look a lot better once I've changed clothes and showered," she assured them, but there was grave doubt on Walter's face.

Everyone looked exhausted, even though Pamela explained, "When we heard you were okay and that the police had Gail, we tried to sleep a few hours until you got here."

Carrie perched on the coffee table, looking a bit glassy-eyed from lack of sleep. "Trent wanted to go to the hospital, but we knew by the time he got there, you'd have been discharged."

Touched, Erica gave Trent a warm smile, then she asked, "Where is Shaun? David told me he was all right, but I've been so worried."

"Shaun's in bed. He was exhausted when he got home from the hospital," Pamela replied. "Kristen's sitting with him." She turned to Carrie. "Would you go tell them Erica's back?"

When Erica demurred, Carrie said, "They insisted on knowing the minute you got back." She hurried off.

"How are you feeling now?" Trent asked. "David called us after you left the hospital."

"I'm doing okay. A little sore but all right. But how is Shaun?"

"He's going to be fine," Pamela said. "He bled quite a bit, but Trent tore up his shirt and wrapped it around Shaun's arm to stop the bleeding until Detective McGuire and Trent could get the doors open."

Being very gentle, Pamela brushed Erica's hair back from her face, carefully avoiding the bandage above her left eye. "I'm—I'm just so glad you're okay." Tears flooded her eyes. "I don't think I stopped praying the whole time you were gone." When Pamela began to weep in earnest, Erica patted her hand. Pamela's bones felt like a bird's, light and fragile.

"I'm okay," Erica said reassuringly. "Really. I'm fine."

Finally, Trent said, "Pamela, it's nearly 5:00 a.m., and you're exhausted. Now that you know Erica's fine, you need to get some sleep. Let me help you to your room."

Walter took Pamela's place. "I still don't know how you caught onto Gail's little charade."

"A lot of luck," Erica said with a tired smile. "There were so many small, baffling pieces that it was hard to know which ones were important and which weren't."

"Well, the police were certainly stumped," Walter declared. "If it wasn't for you, they still wouldn't have a clue."

"They'd have figured it out in time."

"Perhaps, but you seem to have an uncanny ability to notice what others miss," Walter said. "I suppose that's because of your OCD. Without that, you'd be like any other private investigator."

Trent returned and sat on the couch, and Carrie came in just after. "I woke Shaun," Carrie said, "but he's so groggy, there's no way he'd make it down the stairs. I told him to stay put and that when you came up, you'd stop and see him."

"I've been thinking about Martha's jewelry, and there's one thing I don't understand," Trent said. "If that necklace was so valuable, why didn't the jeweler ask Martha to send it to him when he got her report? Couldn't he tell from Martha's report that it was worth a lot?"

"Mr. Quinn never got the full report," Erica said. "Gail made sure of that. She knew Martha sent her report every Wednesday, and she intercepted it. She took the picture, cut off the part that told about the necklace, then put the report back in the envelope, and mailed it."

"You'd think the jeweler would notice if part of the letter was missing." Carrie was incredulous.

"With a normal letter, yes, but Martha's reports were often messy. It wasn't unusual for them to be creased and stained with food. Mr. Quinn probably never even noticed that the top of the paper had been cut off."

Trent said, "But because of your OCD, you did."

"I'm not sure that had anything to do with it," Erica demurred. "But I did notice that one page was shorter than the other. When I looked closer, I noticed #7 was at the bottom of the first page, but that the top of the next page started with #9. That's when I checked the pictures and saw that picture #8 was missing."

"If I ever need a private investigator, I'll know who to call," Carrie said as she stood and stretched. "Trent, I think it's time we went home."

"I'd like to talk with Shaun first," Trent said. "I didn't have a chance when he got back from the hospital."

"Well, I'm so tired that I'm about to pass out. I'll just lie down here until you're ready to go." Trent stood and laid an afghan over Carrie as she curled up on the couch.

Walter spoke up. "I'm curious about one more thing, Erica. A while back, you told me that Martha's lack of a will was a clue to her death. What did you mean by that?"

"That was conjecture on my part, but I think Gail was already thinking about killing Martha when Grandma first began talking to Martha about making a will. I bet that when they discussed it, Martha planned to leave everything to Gail—which meant that Gail *had* to talk Martha out of making a will."

"Why is that?" Trent asked.

"Gail was smart enough to realize that if Martha left everything to Gail, the police would be highly suspicious of her."

"I see." The light dawned in Walter's eyes. "One more thing Gail did to throw the police off the track." He rose stiffly and, with a roguish attempt at humor, said, "I'd better get home. I believe it's past my bedtime."

"What a night," Trent said after Walter left. "When you first started talking tonight, Erica, I thought you suspected me or Carrie."

It was probably best not to admit that she had suspected both of them. "There was a lot of information to sort through. I learned long ago to believe nothing I hear and only half of what I see."

"I think I read that once in a fortune cookie."

Their laughter helped dissolve some of the tension they'd been living with for so long. Gone was the suspicion that had hung over them. Knowing that no one in the family was a killer was a tremendous relief. It was as though a tangled string had snapped, setting them all free.

Trent's dark eyes were thoughtful. "Why didn't Gail just stage a fake burglary and take the necklace? She didn't need to kill Martha."

"Oh, but Gail *did* stage a burglary. She broke a window and made it look like it'd been forced open. She also put on a pair of old boots, stomped in the mud, then climbed in the window to provide the police with footprints on the carpet. She didn't dare just take the necklace because she'd already taken a ring and convinced Martha she'd lost it. Gail was afraid that if she took another piece of jewelry, Martha would call either Mr. Quinn or the police. They would then notify pawn shops and jewelers, making it difficult or impossible for Gail to sell the necklace." Erica made an effort to rise. "My eyelids are getting heavy. I'd better go up and see Shaun."

"I'll come with you," Trent said, helping her up. He stayed close to Erica as they climbed the stairs, as if worried she might not be able to manage.

When they went into Shaun's room, Kristen, who was sitting in a chair, put a hand to her heart. "Erica, you look awful! That must have been some punch-up." Then she jumped up from her chair beside the bed. "Sit here."

Erica was too tired to argue and sank into it gratefully.

Bandit was curled up on the floor next to Shaun, who had been sitting with his back against the headboard, eyes closed. There were dark circles under his eyes, and his arm was in a blue and white sling. When he heard voices, Shaun roused himself and surveyed her. "I hope Gail looks worse than you."

Erica smiled. "How are you?"

"A lot better after David called and said you were okay." There was a looseness in Shaun's speech that indicated his pain medication was working. But the change in his master's voice must have been worrisome to Bandit, because he rose and thrust his nose under Shaun's hand. Shaun stroked the dog absentmindedly.

"So, tell us what happened," Kristen said, sitting on the end of the bed while Trent pulled up a second chair.

"That will have to wait," Trent objected. "Erica's been up all night."

"Just give us the *Reader's Digest* version," Shaun said. "I've been thinking the worst."

Erica made it brief.

At the conclusion, Kristen gave a little shiver. "Wow! I can't believe how brave you were."

"Not really. I was scared most of the time," Erica admitted. Then she stood. "I think it's time we all got some sleep."

Rising, Trent went over to the bed. "Before I go, I want to say something. I've put it off too long." He looked at Shaun. "I want to apologize. I've been under a lot of strain lately, but that's no excuse for—for—"

"Being a jerk?" Kristen suggested.

Trent frowned. "That's not quite the word I was looking for."

"Fits though, doesn't it?" she replied.

"You're not making this any easier." Trent straightened his shoulders. "I should have said this before when we talked, but I didn't. First of all, Shaun, I'm sorry for suggesting you manipulated Grandma, and it was unforgiveable to suggest you might have poisoned her. I'm also sorry about being out for blood when you took over my job. Grandma is the one who changed things, and since I couldn't get angry at her, I took it out on you."

"And—" Kristen prompted.

"I'm getting to it," Trent snapped at her then returned to Shaun. "And I never should have tried to use your relationship with Kristen against you. I'm sorry."

"Apology accepted."

Chapter Thirty-Two

PAMELA PEERED INTO THE SMALL, soft-sided crate Erica held on her lap. Shaun was in the front passenger seat, talking to Kristen as she drove to the airport. "The kitten is so quiet," Pamela said worriedly. "Are you sure she's okay?"

Erica peeked in. "I'm sure. She's just sleeping. The vet said the sedative was mild but effective. Besides, it's only a short flight from Eugene to Salt Lake City."

"And they'll let her fly inside the plane?" Pamela wanted to make sure.

"As long as she has a health certificate and stays in the carrier, she's good. I'll just slip her under the seat. And you're all right with Kristen bringing the last kitten with her?" Kristen was going to move in with Pamela that weekend. Erica was glad that her mother-in-law would have someone with her.

"I told Pamela I'd take good care of it," Kristen called from the front seat.

Erica sighed with satisfaction. The kittens all had good homes. Even Trent had taken one.

Pamela smiled. "The kitten will be company for me while Kristen's at work."

"So, Kristen, are you still house hunting?" Erica asked slyly.

"She's put that off," Shaun informed Erica, who already knew all about it.

"So, what are your plans for the rest of the day?" Erica asked.

"It's Tammy's last day in Florence, so I'm taking the day off," Shaun replied. "Kristen and I are taking her to the Haceta Head Lighthouse and the Sea Lion Cave. Tonight, we'll have dinner with Pamela, Trent, and Carrie."

"Then I'll be moving in with Pamela on Saturday," Kristen said.

Leaning over, Pamela said in a low voice to Erica, "The way things are going, I don't think Kristen will be with me very long."

"I heard that," Kristen said as she pulled up at the curb at the airport.

Using one hand, Shaun tried to help Kristen unload the bags, even though she kept slapping his hand away. Finally, Pamela engaged a Sky Cap.

Once her baggage was carted away, Erica said, "Looks like I'm set." She gave Shaun a careful hug.

"Thanks for believing in me." His voice was full of emotion.

"I always have," she assured him.

Kristen came and hugged Erica. "I'm going to miss you," she said, her eyes shining. "I liked having a sister around."

"Come and see me in Utah; it's not that far. And David and I will be out next spring—or sooner if necessary." Erica cut her eyes toward Shaun. "Be sure to keep me updated."

Smiling broadly, Kristen looked at Shaun, her eyes overflowing with tenderness. "He's a keeper, isn't he?"

"I'll say."

Shaun put his arm around Kristen's waist and grinned. "Even though I'm addicted to being stupid?"

"You're never going to let me forget that, are you?" Kristen groaned. "But you know what? I'm addicted too—to you."

"Ah, how sweet," Erica said. "Shaun, if you don't kiss her right now, you're crazy."

Shaun obliged, causing more than one passerby to stare at the handsome couple.

Pamela was the last to give Erica a long hug. "Be sure and call when you get home."

"I will."

When she reached the sidewalk, Erica looked back, aware of a buoyant lightness as Pamela, Shaun, and Kristen smiled and waved. Then she turned, and the glass doors slid apart with a whoosh as Erica walked into the terminal.

Appendix: Recipes

Kimmi's Chicken Enchiladas..............................298

Melanie's Zucchini Bread.................................299

Tiffany's Breakfast Casserole.............................300

Monica's Texas Brownies.................................301

Easy Chicken Rolls.......................................302

Crab Dip..303

Carolyn's Chocolate Dream Dessert......................304

Karen's Summer Garden Casserole.......................305

Classic Carrot Raisin Salad...............................306

Tana's Beef Chowder....................................307

Kimmi's Chicken Enchiladas
Kimmi Abbott

¼ C. vegetable oil
¼ C. flour
½ C. chili powder
4 C. water
½ C. tomato sauce
1 Tbsp. garlic powder (or to taste)
1 Tbsp. cumin (or to taste)
1½ tsp. salt
3–4 chicken breast halves

1 small can diced green chiles
Tortillas
Shredded Mexican-style cheese
Diced tomatoes (optional)
Guacamole or avocado (optional)
Sour cream (optional)
Olives (optional)
Lettuce (optional)

Directions

1. In a large saucepan, or dutch oven, heat oil. Mix in flour and cook for 1 minute. Add chili powder and cook for another minute.
2. Using a whisk, slowly add the water and bring to a boil. Add tomato sauce, garlic powder, cumin, and salt, and cook for 15 minutes.
3. Add chicken and can of chilies. Cook on low heat for 7 hours or on high for 4 hours. Stir 2 to 3 times while cooking.
4. Preheat oven to 350 degrees.
5. Remove chicken and place in a large mixing bowl. Add about 3 cups of enchilada sauce, and shred the chicken using 2 forks.
6. Cover the bottom of a 9 x 13–inch casserole dish with sauce from the pan. Fill corn or flour tortillas with the shredded chicken and cheese. Roll and place seam side down in casserole dish. Pour remaining sauce over the top and sprinkle with cheese. Cover with foil and bake for 25 minutes.
7. Remove foil and bake an additional 5 minutes. Serve with sour cream, guacamole, lettuce, olives, and tomatoes.

Melanie's Zucchini Bread
Melanie St. Onge

3 eggs, beaten until foamy
1 C. vegetable oil
3 tsp. vanilla
2 C. dark brown sugar, packed
2 C. grated zucchini
3 C. flour
1 tsp. salt

1 tsp. baking soda
¼ tsp. baking powder
3 tsp. cinnamon
1 C. chopped walnuts
½ C. raisins or dried cranberries
1 C. chocolate chips (optional)

Directions

1. Mix wet ingredients in one bowl, in the order given.
2. Mix dry ingredients in another bowl.
3. Mix all ingredients together well, and pour into 2 greased loaf pans.
4. Bake at 325 degrees for 65 minutes or until the sides begin to pull away from the pan. Check for doneness by lightly pressing the top of the loaf. If it's done, it will spring right back.

Tiffany's Breakfast Casserole
Tiffany Jones

1–2 lbs. sausage
1 pkg. (30 oz.) hash browns
¼ C. butter
3 C. shredded cheese

6 eggs
1½ C. milk
Salt and pepper to taste

Directions

1. The night before, brown 1–2 lbs. of sausage and cook hash browns in butter. Refrigerate.
2. In the morning, spray 9 x 13 pan with cooking spray and layer hash browns, sausage, and cheese.
3. Beat together eggs, milk, salt, and pepper, and pour over casserole.
4. Bake uncovered at 350 degrees for 40 minutes or until egg is set. Serve warm.

Monica's Texas Brownies
Monica Miles

Brownies:
2 C. flour
2 C. sugar
½ C. butter or margarine
½ C. shortening
1 C. hot water
⅓ C. cocoa
½ C. buttermilk
2 eggs
1 tsp. baking soda

1 tsp. vanilla
1 tsp. salt

Frosting:
½ C. butter or margarine
2 Tbsp. cocoa
¼ C. milk
3½ C. powdered sugar
1 tsp. vanilla

Directions

1. Combine flour and sugar.
2. In saucepan, combine butter, shortening, water, and cocoa. Heat until boiling.
3. Pour boiling mixture over flour and sugar. Stir, then add buttermilk, eggs, baking soda, vanilla, and salt. Mix well.
4. Pour into 11 x 17½ greased pan, and bake at 400 degrees for 20 minutes.
5. To make frosting, combine butter, cocoa, and milk in a saucepan, and heat until boiling.
6. Remove from heat; stir in powered sugar and vanilla, and beat until frosting is smooth.
7. Frost while brownies are still warm.

Easy Chicken Rolls

3 chicken breasts, diced
½ tsp. poultry seasoning
½ C. chopped onion
1 pkg. (8 oz.) softened cream cheese (can use light)
1 Tbsp. dried parsley
3 pkgs. refrigerated crescent rolls

Butter and bread crumbs (optional)

Sauce
1 can cream of chicken soup
Milk, just enough to thin soup to gravy-like consistency

Directions

1. Sprinkle chicken lightly with poultry seasoning and sauté with onion.
2. Add cream cheese and parsley. Stir well, and set aside.
3. Pinch together 2 rolls, put on greased cookie sheet, and add a spoonful of chicken mixture. Seal edges.
4. Brush outside of each filled roll with melted butter, and roll in seasoned bread crumbs.
5. Bake at 350 degrees for 20 minutes.
6. For sauce, heat cream of chicken soup with enough milk to make a gravy-like consistency. Pour over each roll just before serving.

Crab Dip

1 pkg. (8 oz.) sour cream or mayonnaise
1 pkg. (8 oz.) cream cheese, softened
1 Tbsp. lemon juice

¼ C. minced onion
½ C. finely chopped celery
¼ tsp. salt
1 lb. imitation crabmeat, flaked

Directions

1. Mix sour cream or mayonnaise, cream cheese, and lemon juice.
2. Add onion, celery, salt, and crabmeat.
3. Chill 2 hours, and serve with crackers.

Carolyn's Chocolate Dream Dessert
Carolyn Justice

Crust
2 C. flour
2 cubes margarine or butter, softened
½ C. chopped nuts
1 pt. whipping cream
1 tsp. vanilla
⅓ C. sugar

1 pkg. (8 oz.) cream cheese, softened
Milk
1 large pkg. (5 oz.) chocolate pudding, cooked or instant
1 large pkg. (5 oz.) vanilla pudding, cooked or instant
½ C. chopped nuts

Directions

1. To make crust, mix flour, margarine or butter, and ½ cup nuts. Press into ungreased 9 x 13 pan.
2. Bake at 325 degrees for 15 minutes, and let cool.
3. Beat whipping cream with vanilla and sugar until stiff. Divide in half.
4. For first layer, mix half of the whipped cream with cream cheese. Add enough milk to thin mixture to spread over crust.
5. Make puddings according to directions. If using cooked pudding, allow to cool.
6. For second layer, spread chocolate pudding on top of whipped cream and cream cheese layer.
7. For third layer, spread vanilla pudding on top of chocolate pudding layer.
8. Top with remaining whipped cream, and sprinkle with nuts.
9. Chill at least one hour or, preferably, overnight before serving.

Karen's Summer Garden Casserole
Karen Luthy

6 C. diced summer squash
1 C. (2–3) grated carrots
1 small onion, diced
1 Tbsp. butter
1 can cream of chicken soup

1 C. sour cream
1 stick butter or margarine, softened
1 pkg. seasoned bread crumbs

Directions

1. Sauté squash, carrots, and onion with butter until barely tender.
2. Mix soup, sour cream, and ½ stick butter or margarine, and put in 9 x 13 pan.
3. Add vegetables and stir.
4. Mix bread crumbs with ½ stick butter, and top vegetables with bread crumbs.
5. Bake at 350 degrees for 20 minutes.

Classic Carrot Raisin Salad

⅓ C. mayonnaise
1 Tbsp. lemon juice
¼ tsp. salt
1 Tbsp. sugar

1 C. drained crushed pineapple
⅔ C. white raisins
2 C. grated carrots

Directions

1. Mix mayonnaise, juice, salt, and sugar.
2. Add pineapple, raisins, and carrots. Toss.

Tana's Beef Chowder
Tana Sullivan

1½ lbs. ground beef
½ C. diced onion
2 (16 oz.) cans tomatoes
1 (17 oz.) can kernel corn
2 cans cream of celery soup
2 C. water
⅓ C. diced green pepper

½ C. sliced celery
3 medium potatoes, diced
2 tsp. salt
¼ tsp. pepper
¼ C. parsley
1 bay leaf (optional)

Directions

1. Fry ground beef and onion, and blot off grease.
2. Mix all ingredients, and simmer until potatoes and green pepper are tender.

Author Biography

MARLENE HAS BEEN PUBLISHED EXTENSIVELY in magazines and newspapers and has written seven nonfiction books. Her first novel, a mystery/romance, is the best-selling *Light on Fire Island.* For all of her novels, Marlene travels to the area to do research for the setting. For *A Death in the Family,* Marlene traveled to Florence and Lake Oswego, Oregon, studying the area in order to ensure accuracy for the setting.

Marlene Bateman was born in Salt Lake City, Utah, and grew up in Sandy, Utah. She graduated from the University of Utah with a bachelor's degree in English. Marlene is married to Kelly R. Sullivan and lives in North Salt Lake. Her hobbies are gardening, camping, and reading.